Untried Origins

Ka Lee

CONTENT WARNING

While these are not all the focus of this book, please be aware that this book contains scenes of: Knife play, abuse, abduction, allusion to rape, familial abuse, emotional abuse, mental health, gore/blood, torture.

Untried Origins
Book 1 of the Till Our Ends Meet Series

Story Copyright © 2023 Ka Lee
THE PEOPLE THAT MADE THIS BOOK POSSIBLE
Cover Design by Molly McDonald
Editing by Jennifer Donovan and The Fiction Fix
Formatting: Luna Laurier
Betas: Rikki Boetticher & Brittany Bishop
Financial and Moral Support: My Husband Tycer
Motivation by: Luna Laurier, Jordan Day, Kristen M. Long
My Lifeline: Baddie, PA

IDENTIFIERS
ISBN 979-8-89034-604-9 (Paperback)
ISBN 979-8-89034-603-2 (Hardcover)

All Rights Reserved. No part of this book may be reproduced, stored in, or introduced into a retrieval system, or transmitted in any form or by any means (electronic, mechanical, photocopying, recording, or otherwise), without the prior written permission. Any reproduction of this publication without prior consent from the publisher is an infringement of copyright law.

This is a work of fiction. Names, places, characters, and incidents are the product of the author's imagination. Any resemblance to actual persons, living or dead, events, or locales is solely coincidental.

First Edition: August 2023

*To all the indie authors that came before me and
taught me that this was possible.*

Area 8
The Vanta Pits

Area

River of Soul

Warantless

Area 6

Inferis

Prologue

The feeling of watching someone you love bleeding out and dying in front of you is something that can never be explained. It cannot be understood, until you are there with their blood coating your hands and nothing you do will stop it from pouring from their body.

The rage that fills me is never ending now, it oozes from every pore and opening of my body.

She did this, and I did not see it coming. I will not have him taken from me, I may have hidden in the shadows for the majority of my life, but that ends today.

I will no longer hide from who I am and what I am capable.

I reach for the fallen sword, the cold metal biting into my hand, a respective thought in my mind.

She will pay.
Even if it kills me.
She will pay.

Ka Lee

I glance back down at the only person that truly sees me and accepts all the dark and twisted bits of my soul. I press a kiss to his forehead, and whisper softly in his ear, "Hold on, stay alive. Stay alive for me."

His only response, a soft wince of pain, forces me to grind my teeth and tighten my grip on my borrowed sword.

I stand up, feeling taller and stronger than before.

For him, for them, I could do this. I could make this sacrifice.

I twist the sword around in my hand getting a better grip and feel for its weight, before charging forward. I scream a battle cry as loudly as I can. I want her full attention on me. Nothing, and no one else but me.

I feel my vocal cords stretching and tearing from the amount of fury falling from my throat.

She turns to me, her long hair blowing into her face hiding those sinister eyes. She snaps her fingers expecting it to hurt me as it had the others. It drags a wicked smile to my face, when her wings stretch out in frustration and the look of shock reaches her flawless face. The look on her face gives me the extra push to run a bit faster and scream even louder, because she had no idea till this moment that her magic would not be her escape this time.

I make it to her a moment later, leaping into the air to drive my borrowed sword down into her neck.

I do not know if I made contact. I do not know if I just hurt or saved my friends, and my love. All I know is sorrow and darkness. All I know is death.

Chapter 1
KAISERA

"Put the Fae down, Kai," I hear Madis say over my shoulder. I shrug and release my grip on his throat, throwing him straight over the edge of the open balcony and off the mountain cliff's edge. She is standing behind me, arms crossed and shaking her head at me in disapproval.

She is my only friend, due to the fact that we are the only females in my father's Demon court here in the underworld, known as Inferis. I am not completely sure if Madis would still be my friend if we had not been forced into friendship, but here we are now, closer than most.

Madis is one of the most stunning females the world of Inferis has ever seen, even as she stands there judging my actions in her Area Six uniform. She is well over six feet tall, with a warrior's body one can only achieve from years of training at the DWA, Demon Warrior Academy.

Ka Lee

I always thought they could have produced a better name, but it was founded over a thousand years ago, and I guess they had better things to worry about than naming an academy.

Madis is lean and built for speed and endurance. Long, straight, almost white hair tumbles down to her waist, with high cheekbones, slightly tilted crystal blue eyes, and dark olive skin that gives her an exotic look. Not to mention her stunning wings. Madis' wings are white with sparks of almost diamond-like spots throughout them and are a leathery, bat-like material, like most winged demons are.

She is my exact opposite, even in our styles of clothing. I am wearing a fitted V-neck T-shirt that has little holes in it from years of wear and tear, tight-fitted, high-waisted pants with a pair of boots I had specially made with a higher heel than normal. I am much shorter than Madis, by nearly a foot.

I am short compared to most people, though.

I am built more for power than endurance. I have always loved my thicker build. I am still muscular, but I have a little more to grab onto than Madis does. My jet-black hair down to my waist, I tend to always keep it pulled back in some sort of fashion, tonight being no exception. I have bright green eyes; not the green you normally see but a more electric color. Unlike Madis' olive skin, I only sport a slight tan. My wings, however, make me stand apart from everyone. My most treasured things about myself are my black-as-night wings, and the spectacular thing about my wings is that they are feathered. No one, including my father, knew what to make of them. Feathered wings are for Valkyrie, and I am extremely far from one of the guarding angels of Valkeria. To get to see the upper world Valkeria where all manner of God-like creatures live, such as a Pegasus horse and angels with gold and white feathered wings, would be a true dream come true.

Madis raises her eyebrows and shrugs in a *are you going to tell me what that was about?* kind of way.

"What? He had it coming." I cross my arms and glare. "Plus, he could fly." I shrug and flip my long ponytail over my shoulder. "I think?"

I have never been the 'ask questions first' kind of girl.

Untried Origins

Madis turns to follow me back to the bar, sighing. "What did that poor Fae do to you, Kaisera?" She uses my full name in that motherly, disapproving tone of hers.

I roll my eyes back. "Poor Fae? When did you become so sympathetic towards them?"

The Fae, along with all other types of mortals from Erathina, are here in Inferis for a reason: to serve their sentences for the crimes committed in their world. They are not here for their great behavior.

Taking our seats back at the bar, I wave my hand to signal to the bartender that we will be needing drinks. The bartender must be new because I have never seen him before. He is a very handsome demon, with a half-shaved head showing off a tattoo on one side of his head and black, almost purple, hair swept back on the other side.

"What will it be ladies?" he says from across the bar.

Madis starts to speak, but I yell over her before she could tell him nothing for her. "Two Flashers, please."

Madis rolls her eyes at me but does not protest.

As the bartender turns to grab our Flashers, the Demon whiskey you light on fire before drinking, I turn back to Madis, waiting for her answer.

"I am not sympathetic towards the Fae. I am simply curious as to why he needed to be dropped off a cliff," Madis states so matter-of-factly.

I huff a breath. "If you must know, that Fae scum thought it would be a great idea to come up behind me and run his fingers over one of my wings without my permission, and when I asked him to stop he replied," I clear my throat and say in my best impression of a male's voice, "Come on baby girl, I bet you enjoy it," before I continue in my own voice, "hence the dropping him off the cliff." I finish with a who-gives-a-shit shrug.

Because I know I do not give a shit, and I'm no one's baby girl.

I am, and never will be, anyone is anything.

I own me.

Madis smiles. "Well then, in that case, I hope his wings got clipped on the way down."

You do not touch another creature's wings without full permission; actually, you do not touch anyone anywhere without their permission.

It is plain rude.

We may be demons, but I still expect a bit of common courtesy.

The bartender walks over with our Flashers, and as he leans over the bar, I spot the lip ring, a hoop through the lower left side of his lip. He catches my staring and flashes me a quick smile.

"See something you might like?" He places his elbows down on the bar and leans further in towards me.

"Maybe. Do you?" I smile, wiggling my eyebrows, leaning over just a bit to tease him the same way he is attempting to tease me, a dare in my eyes.

I jolt backwards when a little blue and black dragon appears directly in front of my face.

Nija, Madis' familiar, tilts his head to the side and lets his tongue lop out the side of his mouth. I slide back onto my seat, shaking my head in disapproval at the little dragon.

"What in the Eight Areas of Inferis, Nija?" The miniature dragon stands on his hind legs and tilts his head to the side, the look on his face saying he has no idea what I mean.

The miniature dragon who can shift between sizes has been with Madis since I met her.

He is no bigger than a small lap dog, but I know if Madis commanded, he could be as large as a building.

Sitting back fully into my seat, I reach out and pet the dragon's head, smiling. He purrs his approval in response. I could never stay mad at the little guy.

The bartender had already left to return to his bartending duties. I stare over at him while he assists the other customers in the tavern. If I play my cards right later, I'll get to see what he likes to do with that lip ring.

Untried Origins

I turn back to Madis. "So, what took you so long to get up here?" Here being our favorite tavern, Warrantless, at the very top of Mount Warrant.

Now that is a clever name.

Warrantless Tavern overlooks the Areas of Inferis, which is why it is one of my favorite places. One of our jobs as demons here in Inferis is to bring to light the sins the mortals of the middle world already have in them, but not to break their free will.

Erathina is the world between worlds. I have never been able to see the true punishment in making souls serve time here. Inferis is not bad, unless you were truly terrible and ended up in Area Eight, the Vanta Pits. A chill runs down my whole body even thinking of such a place.

As noble demons, we can easily travel to Erathina, if we are willing to give up just a small blood sacrifice to the well of Vanta. The well leads to The Vanta Pits, where the king of the worst sorts of demons will grant you access to the mortal world. Erathina residents, however, cannot just travel here. Not that any Fae or mortal would want to travel to the underworld – they believe we are the purest forms of evil. No one from either Inferis or Erathina can travel to Valkeria. Only the truest of pure hearts and souls are allowed through its gates. Or so it is said, I know of no one who has done this.

Not that King Braxton, my father, would ever allow myself or Madis to go anywhere outside of Area Six. Even if it was within our power to do so.

Warrantless, our favorite hangout spot, is not much to look at, from its unmatched wooden chairs and tabletops to its always slightly dirty floors that your boots kind of stick to. But you cannot beat the view here. The open balcony with absolutely no railing allows you to see all the way to where the oceans of Area Three meet my land of Area Six.

"Our fathers are planning something. I was trying to eavesdrop and see what," Madis said a little too quietly, fiddling with the drink in front of her. Madis has always been the quieter of the two of us. She keeps to herself, always disappearing for huge chunks of time. I never question what she does during her free time.

"Did you catch any of what they were saying?"

My father, King Shiva Braxton, the Demon King of Area Six, is not one to let others hear things that are not meant to be heard, especially conversations he is having with his righthand, Commander Pike, Madis' father.

Commander Pike has always been the stern uncle I wisely chose to keep my distance from. He was our instructor for all our combat training, and he is a brute of a man.

Not that he could ever do anything to me; I am the princess after all. I never let him forget that fact, either.

Madis shakes her head, her long, blonde hair swaying slightly. "No, but I believe it has something to do with our betrothals."

I can hear the sadness in her voice. Clearly so can Nija because he crawls into Madis' lap. Madis lets him and starts to rub under the small dragon's neck, getting a soft purr out of him.

"We have known for years that this would come, Madis," I say, placing a hand on her shoulder.

She has always been more against the idea of marrying than I have. I will marry one of the kings, yes, but I have no intention of settling down. I enjoy life too much to be tied to one stuffy, asshole king.

Madis, on the other hand? I think she wants to see all the worlds, to see what other places have to offer her. I also believe Madis thinks she can marry for love and not to gain more power and influence. I would wish the same, but I am the future Queen of the Sixth Area of Inferis. I know better than to wish on dead stars.

There are eight areas of Inferis, each one ruled by a king of their own species. The Areas are broken down by species and divided into eight regions: dealing demons, shifters, water creatures, mystic creatures, witches, vampires, creatures of the darkness, and us, the demons of sins.

Untried Origins

Daughters are extremely rare in royal bloodlines. So, my father will pick the king who will offer Area Six the most power and influence, allowing our Areas to merge and gain strength and wealth.

This has only ever been attempted twice, but the marriages did not last, and the areas split again. The kings would never allow a queen to rule alone. Therefore, the queens were exiled to the Vanta Pits. The two queens have never been seen or heard from again, and no one speaks of them or their stories. The goal is to breed the most powerful of the Demons, in order to only have one ruler over all species and one Area. Only the most powerful of two bloodlines could rule over such a place. There is a prophecy that says, "The Areas will only see peace when two are left to rule all." We would never see that in our long lifetimes, though. We are centuries or more away from that kind of kingdom.

My father will have it no other way for me, so my fate is sealed.

We have always said that when I become a queen, I will release Madis from whoever she is wed off to, but I know that may not be possible when it comes down to it, even if I am not willing to admit it aloud.

"I know, but I thought we would have more time," Madis says while continuously petting Nija.

"We might still. You know our fathers; these plans you tried to hear may be a century away from now." I am not sure if I am convincing myself or her. I am nowhere ready to be bred by a king, even though I know it is inevitable. Hybrid demons make the strongest demons, even though demons do not like to do so, if only for the pride of believing each species is superior to the other.

Of course, winged demons, such as myself, are the superior ones.

With that lovely thought in my head, I raise my glass of lite Flasher to Madis. We clink the glasses together. "Till our ends meet," I say and Madis replies, "May they be Epic ends."

We throw the shots back before slamming them back down onto the bar.

"I have to get going," Madis says.

Madis has been disappearing more than usual as of recently.

"But why? We can go dancing, or just get drunk here," I whine. I really did not want to be left to drink alone. Again. It makes me look a little too desperate.

"My father is expecting me," Madis says, and I see her shoulders tense up just a bit, as they always do when it comes to her father.

"So, ditch him," I try.

A flash of something crosses her face, but it is gone as quickly as it came. It is as if that thought terrified her. I must be mistaken, though, because that makes zero sense. Madis is an insane warrior, a true badass. Nothing scares her.

"I cannot. He will already be pissed if he finds out I am drinking and not training." Madis responds.

I shrug and wave to the bartender to bring just one shot this time. He nods at me and smiles back. "Alright, suit yourself. I think the bartender will keep me better company anyways."

Madis gives me a kind smile goodbye, and then walks over to the balcony and dives down and away.

Chapter 2
KAISERA

Hours later, I slip out of tangled bed sheets, slightly out of breath from the fun times I was having with the bartender, Blade. At least, that is what I think he said. Remembering names has never been my strong suit.

I finally figured out what he liked to use that lip ring for, and I greatly enjoyed the feel of it all over me for the past few hours.

"Where do you think you are going?" Blade tries to grab for my wrist, but I spin out of his reach, yanking all the covers with me and revealing him in all his glory. Blade leans back, with both arms going behind his head. I had already learned last night that he did not have a shy or modest bone in his body.

His bones are quite nice... I have to bite my lip to keep from laughing at my own corny joke.

Burning demons, he is spectacular, but I absolutely must get going. My father called for me with his telekinesis hours ago, and he is already going to be pissed at my delay.

"Duties call. I will have to leave you to take care of that," I say, pointing my chin toward his morning wood, "all by yourself, Blade?" I say it as more of a question than a statement.

He rolls his eyes at my attempt to remember his name. "It's Max."

"Yikes, sorry."

"You could make it up to me by coming back to bed," Max says, with a sly grin, as he flexes his pecks to try and persuade me.

I groan. It is tempting. "I really cannot. Sorry."

He pokes out his bottom lip with that sexy lip ring. "No, you are not."

I shrug, snap my fingers once, and all my clothes are back on. My hair is still a complete mess, but I can blame that on the flight I am about to take. I bow into a curtsy, snap my fingers again, and blink out. It's a skillset that is so rare, I am the only known creature to possess the ability. I smile at myself, as I am sure I just left poor Max with his mouth hanging open.

I have two powers, which is pretty rare. I can manipulate objects, with a specialty in metals and stones, and I can jump through space. Not far, only a couple of feet at a time. All of this I can do by simply snapping my fingers.

I would like to think I could visit him again, but I can't. A man is not going to stick around for a woman they know will be promised to another. It would be for the best to never see him again. He does work at my favorite Tavern, though, so I will.

And that is why you do not sleep with the bartender at your favorite spot, Kai.

I roll my neck and stretch out my wings to prepare them for flight. I shoot up into the early morning sky with a quick, hard flap of my large, feathered black wings. I need to hurry, but the breeze is just the perfect balance of warm and frigid air, without a hint of the humidity that this Area sometimes puts off. All the Areas of Inferis have different, extreme weathers, to accommodate the creatures that live in each of them. This Area, Area Six, has a dry, desert climate, red mountains as far as the eye can see, edged by Area Three's large, sprawling ocean.

Untried Origins

I take in the sights of the red clay city and the Demons and souls that work the Area. The demons have the easier jobs, as they are born here. The mortal souls have the hardest, most grueling jobs that they are forced to do while serving their sentence in Inferis.

My morning flight is ruined by my father's demanding voice in my head. "Kaisera, I do hope for your health and safety that you are about to walk into this throne room." I cringe just a bit at my father's stern tone, as I always do.

"Yes, Father. I am walking through those doors in five, four, three, three and half…"

"Kaisera, you are not funny. Not in the slightest," my father says into my head.

"Two, one!" I say back into his head but walk straight through the throne room doors, before saying out loud for everyone to hear "Now come, Father, you know I am your favorite jokester."

My father is a stern man, but fair. I cannot say he is the most loving man in the world. The only thing my father has ever said about my mother is that I look like her, and that she is dead. He refused to even tell me how she died, just that she is, in fact, dead.

My father gives me a look only a father can give that says it would be best for me to keep my mouth shut for the time being. As I walk into the room, I take in the scene around me. The large, open room is built in the same clay as the rest of our Area. You would think it would be dirty or sandy, but the clay is so old that it is more like stone now.

Madis and her father, Commander Pike, stand to the right, just behind my father's throne. Commander Pike is wearing his Commander's uniform. Unlike Madis' uniform, it is all for show. His uniform consists of black dress pants and a coat decorated with all his shiny awards and ribbons. I shoot Madis a questioning look that she shoots right back at me.

Great, a secret meeting that neither of us is prepared for.

No one else is in the throne room, which is odd. No staff. No guards. *No ears.*

Ka Lee

This cannot be good.

This is going to be one of those super-duper secret meetings.

"Kaisera, come take your seat," my father says in his gruff, annoyed voice.

At least he is not wearing his formal robes, so this cannot be a royal decree or something of that nature. He is instead wearing brown riding pants, matching boots, a buttoned-up shirt, and a thin coat fitted to his medium height and build. Also absent on top of his jet-black hair, which has started to get specks of white in it over the past decade, is Area Six's crown.

My father looks younger than he is because it takes Demons longer to show signs of aging, but he still looks older than most. Demons do not keep up with age, since we can live for centuries or more.

Taking a very deep breath and holding onto it, I take the few long strides to my throne next to my father's and sit before releasing a slow breath out.

My father says, "Commander Pike Malias and Lady Madis Malias, come stand before us."

What the actual shit is going on?

I can feel my pulse picking up in anticipation of what this could possibly be about.

My father continues looking at Madis. "Commander Pike Malias and I have been considering that it is time for you to take on your role as Princess Kaisera's Protector fully by swearing the Blood Binding to her."

I gasp in a sharp breath. That is not part of the plan.

Where is this coming from?

If Madis takes a Blood Binding to me, she will be sworn to me forever.

No one takes Blood Binding oaths anymore. Commander Pike was not required to take one for my father. It has not been done in decades. She would not be leaving to get married. She could possibly have lovers, but she could never marry. She would be sworn to me and me alone. She would never be able to leave or travel on her own. She would give up everything to serve me and be always by my side.

Not much is known of the binding anymore, but it is rumored that bindings cannot go more than a few miles from their Binded without it causing them both severe pain. The only way to be free of a Blood Binding is death of one or both parties.

If I am being honest with myself, I do not want anyone by my side that much. I do not want to be bound to any soul, ever. I do not like the idea of being forced into anything, especially eternity attached to someone else, even if that person is my closest friend.

"No!" "Yes." We both answer at once.

"What?" Again, we say it at the same time. Both of us seem to be in utter shock of the other. I look at Madis with a bit of fury in my eyes and she gives it right back to me.

Why is she mad? I am saving us.

"Ahhh, well." Commander Pike speaks and claps his hands loudly together. "You both must agree for this to work," He turns to face my father. "My King, maybe we should give them some time to discuss this." Before he turns back to give Madis a stern look, passing on some kind of silent demand, she nods her head.

Madis and I stay staring each other down, fire burning in our eyes, Madis quite literally. The element of fire has been in her control since she was a young child, from what I have heard. So now, a century older, she could fully control the element and bend it to her ever will. She could even breathe fire with the help of Nija's dragon power. Not that Madis would ever let herself lose control.

My father says, "Kaisera, this should thrill you. Madis is your friend and happens to be at the top of the Demon Warrior Academy. She will make for a fine second and a perfect Blood

Bond." He stands and walks toward Madis and Commander Pike. He places a hand on Madis's shoulder. "Please speak some of your sense into my daughter's thick skull." Then, he and Commander Pike give a quick nod to Madis then to me, and they both walk out, leaving Madis and I to our staring contest.

Chapter 3
MADIS

    I already know how stubborn the princess can be, and that she does not always think things through before opening that charming mouth of hers. However, I never would have guessed in a thousand years she would think me incapable of serving her or Area Six.

    I can feel my fire burning brighter as King Braxton and my father walk out of the throne room. I learned the hard way, a long time ago, how to keep it under control, so I do as I always do and tamp it down.

    "What are you thinking?" Kai says from where she still sits on her throne. She is still in her clothes from last night, which means she did go off with that demon bartender after drinks. I have to make sure she is still taking her supplements. The king would not only murder the Demon who impregnated his beloved daughter, but me too for not stopping it. It is my duty to make sure those types of things never happen. My father has always made it clear that it is my duty to keep the princess out of trouble, since her father thinks it okay for her to do as she wishes. I never know my father's true intentions, but I know they do not always fall in line with the king's.

It has never bothered me that my dark-humored, short-tempered friend will be queen and I will always remain under her rule. At this moment, however, I want to be eye to eye with her, so I take the two small steps up to the throne. I am so much taller than her that I still have two steps before the top of the dais.

"What were you thinking? Our king asked this of us." I want to fume and yell that she should listen to the king and my father. She does not understand what not following their orders can lead to. "Am I not up to your standards for guards? Perhaps one of the men would better suit your needs?"

A look of shock goes across Kai's face. I do not normally question her, but I am willing to do so on this. If this is our fathers' wish, it will happen one way or another. I hate fighting with her. Kai stands, now towering over me, as I am still two steps below her. Kai could be someone to fear if only she took the time to learn how to wield her gifts rather than use them as parlor tricks.

"You may be my friend and the top of your Academy, Lady Madis Malias, but I am still your future queen. You will do well to remember that." Kai turns her back to me and storms toward the doors leading out of the throne room, a true sign that she does believe herself more powerful and that this conversation is over.

I wait till the princess is out of the throne room completely before letting just a little bit of my power slip, just a small band of flames wrapping their way around my fingers. As I let my power go, I get the slightest relief. I let the flames slither there for a brief moment before letting them fade to smoke on the wind.

Back in my room, I unstrap my blades from my thigh holsters and slump into my favorite comfortable chair. Nothing about the uniform I am made to wear every day is comfortable, but it is better than the gowns my mother prefers me to wear. My chair, however, is comfortable. It is a dark emerald green and has tears in the arm rest from being slept in on countless nights. I positioned it in the corner of my room so that I could see the entirety of my room and have full coverage of my back. It keeps anyone from sneaking up behind me.

Now, I can try and think through what just took place in the throne room. I know my father and the king are up to something. Something big. This is just the start. My father and the king have been taking private audiences with all sorts of odd characters.

My father more so than the king.

My father tends to set plans into motion and convince the King they were his own ideas. My father has always been a great puppet master.

I wish I knew more, but I cannot risk my father's wrath by trying to question him.

I look around my sitting room at the stacks of books lining the floors and walls – books I did not genuinely enjoy but books that I am told to read, nonetheless. Books on battle strategies, sword and hand-to-hand combat, and interrogation methods. All the books a warrior or soldier needs to have and know to protect everyone else.

When will someone protect me?

I laugh to myself. What a silly thought.

You are the protector.

Other than my books being scattered around, my room seems bare. As a trained warrior, I do not "need" things. I have the essentials: a bed, a single nightstand, a wardrobe, and a desk to work. My bathing room is the same: a single standing shower and sink. We have staff who can clean our rooms, which Kai takes full use of, but my father has always said that no one cleans things better than you do yourself. He sent the housekeepers and staff away ages ago, saying I needed to learn to tend to myself.

I sigh.

Ok, Madis. Stop thinking of the past and focus on the issue at hand.

Ka Lee

I was shocked with the "Blood Binding" but also thrilled. This way, I will not be forced into a loveless marriage. I can take my time, and maybe one day find a mate, a real mate.

Finding mates is rare, but not unheard of. One person always knows before the other, but both have to be willing to accept each other in order for the bond to form. There is a time limit, though; if one person takes too long to accept the bond, it can be destroyed beyond repair. I will not be allowed to marry, but I can live with just being in my mate's life.

Right?

I know Kaisera will never force me to marry someone I do not love. It is my duty to protect her already, this will just make it more official. Not that I will be given a choice, if this was my father's idea, it will happen.

I cannot wrap my brain around why she would not want me to take this Binding. I wasn't fully serious about my comment about her wanting a male warrior instead, but maybe I am not far off base. Kaisera is the closest thing I have to a real family. Until tonight, I had believed she felt the same.

Nija hurried after me when we left the throne room, and I can tell the little guy is concerned for me. He plops his head onto my lap and huffs out a small ball of fire. Luckily, I had the seamstress, Ellie, change all my clothing to fire resistant after I accepted the light blue and black miniature dragon as my familiar. I throw the little fireball across the room, and Nija yips like a puppy and takes off after it.

Chapter 4
KAISERA

    I made it back to my room in record time. My massive bed, with way too many red and black pillows, sits to the right of the huge balcony doors that overlook the desert city. I consider taking a nap on one of the large black couches that sits in the middle of my sparkling clean room, thanks to the staff.

    I am exhausted from my late-night activities, but I will not be able to sleep with all these thoughts in my head. I start to pace in front of the open balcony doors, the heat of this Area leaking through on a breeze and blowing the sheer black curtains around.

    I had turned my back on Madis, something I never do. What was I thinking, throwing my future queen bullshit at her? She did not deserve that.

    Even if it was true.

    Madis is the first person to ever stick by my side; everyone else in my life has always pushed me away or abandoned me.

    I had meant to protect us both from the Blood Binding by declining it, but I could have handled it better.

Ka Lee

Or maybe. Just maybe she could think of herself for once in her life and not let her father choose for her.

Madis is as close as family, but it drives me insane that she always follows the rules and never pushes back. Rules are meant to be bent and broken, or else there would be no joy in life.

I decide we should talk, and not with me sitting on a throne. Sitting on a throne does things to your ego that sometimes I do not even understand, even if I do greatly enjoy the way it feels up there. It does lead one to feel overly powerful.

I walk through my open balcony doors, lift my wings, and in one, swift flap, I am on the balcony directly next to mine, Madis' room.

Madis's balcony doors are closed, but I can see her playing fireball fetch with Nija. It makes me think I should accept a familiar. Then, Nija can have a friend.

She sits in the only crappy old chair she has in her room. Her room is the exact same size and shape as mine, but for unknown reason to me, she has chosen not to have it furnished, leaving her room to look bare. Leaving it to look as if it was put together with scraps.

I knock softly on Madis' balcony window, and she seems to be ignoring me at first. But then, Madis and Nija both stop their playing and turn to me. Madis seems reluctant to come to the balcony to let me in. Maybe she needs more time to cool down.

Her flames were intense in the throne room.

Madis hides her strength and power well. I do not think anyone else would have noticed she wanted to lose control, but I know her better than anyone. I am not sure why she keeps her power tampered down. I asked her once, and she claimed it is "just necessary."

She opens the door and bows in an overexaggerated, mockery of a curtsy. "My future queen, how can I be of service?"

Okay, I deserve that. I still cross my arms and roll my eyes at her dramatics. "I should not have pulled rank on you, but you have to see that this is not a great idea."

Madis stands from her curtsy, sighing. "Fine. Then explain to me why you do not want me as your Blood Bonded." There is a look of hurt in Madis' eyes.

Untried Origins

"Explain to me why you would want to be?" I say.

She relaxes a bit, letting out a long breath. "Kaisera, this is an honor to me, a great privilege. You know I do not wish to marry unless it is for true love or a true mate. This gives me more time unless you also intend to marry me off?" She bows her head at that last bit.

Now I am hurt. Did she honestly believe I would not accept her? That I would so easily send her away? This is our fathers' fault for throwing this at us so suddenly, without explanation, an explanation I already knew they would not give even if we asked. My father's word is law. No one, not even his only daughter, can question him.

I put my hands on each of her shoulders, and then pull her into a tight hug.

"I will never be rid of you, Madis. It would be a great honor to be Blood Bound to you as well. It is just you didn't want to be tied down or forced into anything. This would force you to go and be where I am." Madis huffs a laugh and squeezes me tighter.

"I already am everywhere you are." Madis says.

We both laugh and pull apart to be eye to eye again. "We are already close; what harm could a little Blood Binding cause?"

Madis just nods her head in agreement. "Exactly. This would just make us closer." The look on Madis' face almost looks desperate for just that.

"I am sorry," we say at the same time, then giggle softly at each other.

"Do you know everything that comes with Blood Binding? I do not. It is so rarely done now."

Madis shakes her head no. "I know that Blood Bindings in the past have been unstoppable, and that sometimes, the bonded pair inherit a bit of each other's powers, or so I have heard."

"Throwing fireballs sounds like a ton of fun to me," I say with a bit of humor in my voice.

Madis sighs. "Yes, well, being able to snap my fingers and have all objects bend to my will would be nice too."

I giggle and snap my fingers, disappearing for a few seconds and then reappearing with two shot glasses full of a clear liquid and a lemon.

"We cannot be drinking this early," Madis says.

I roll my eyes at her and snap my fingers, disappearing again. This time, I replace it with a cream-filled pastry replacing the shot glasses.

Madis squeaks with excitement, then narrows her eyes at me. "You know, if Samantha sees these missing from the breakfast trays, she will know it was you."

Shoving one into my mouth and handing the other to Madis, I talk around a mouth full of pastry. "And?" I chew a bit more. "Samantha does not scare me."

Samantha is the bakery chef for the royals. She is a small demon who weighs a whopping eighty pounds.

"But Samantha will tell Chives." Both of our eyes go big, and a small shiver goes down my back. Chives, on the other hand, is the main chef of the castle, and he is a four-hundred-pound mountain of a demon I swear is half troll.

I look at Madis, all the joking aside. "Are you sure you want to do this, Madis?"

I can do this one thing her way. If it means that much to her, I should put my fears of being permanently bound to someone else aside.

"Yes. Yes, Kaisera, this is exactly what I want, although I am curious what our fathers are gaining from this. We both know they do not do anything without reason." Madis turns to pick up Nija, and I reach over and pet the little demon familiar on his horned head.

"But if this makes us even stronger, our fathers might even run scared from us one day," Madis continues, with something that looks a little like hope in her eyes.

A twisted smile spreads across my face, and when Madis sees it, she smiles back at me. "Are we good?"

Madis reaches over and gives me a tight hug. "Yes, we are good."

"Great. I have to go to bed now."

Madis releases me and steps back. "Long night with the bartender?"

I grin devilishly. "It was a very long and very nice night." I wiggle my brows a bit.

Madis shoves me lightly on the shoulder. "Do you always have to be so dirty?"

I fake a shocked expression. "I am never. That is your mind that just went into the gutter, Madis."

"Mmmhmm," Madis says as she shifts her weight from one leg to the other. "So?" Madis continues.

"So what?" I am a bit confused about what she is getting at until I remember I came over here for something important.

She seems almost nervous to ask, but then she does. "So, we are going to do this?"

I nod my head up and down slowly. "Yes, if this is truly what you want, Madis. We will do this. Together"

Now that I have heard her side and seen how much this would mean to her, I am not sure I could deny my only friend.

She smiles sweetly at me and opens her arms, waiting for me to walk into them for another hug. I walk into her and hug her closely. "Together." She repeats.

Chapter 5

MADIS

  Feeling better after our conversation this morning, I start my long trek down to the DWA. I could use a good fight right about now. The only problem is, there really is not anyone in the academy now who presents an actual challenge to me, which is why I am walking to the Academy rather than flying. I mean, what is the rush? It also gives me a bit longer to think.

  Our conversation went well. She had explained in detail how she was only protecting me from myself. By the end, I had convinced her, and I think this is the right thing to do for the both of us, even if it does bind me to this realm and Area forever. That is my duty, what I am meant to do. I still have this sinking feeling that our fathers are doing this for their own benefit, rather than for ours. I really do not know a whole lot about this Binding, and from my understanding, nobody ever knows exactly how it will affect the parties involved. We will be telling our fathers later tonight that we will accept each other and do the Binding.

Untried Origins

Nija jumps up and down by my feet as we walk, pawing at me to get permission to hop on my shoulder.

I sigh, something I realized I have done way too much today. "Come on up, Nija." My familiar flaps his light blue wings until he is airborne, and then he perches on my left shoulder.

Nija has been with me since I was a teenager, which was young to accept a familiar. Most do not accept familiars until well into their second century. Nija found me one night, cradling a broken arm after a sparring match. A match that I had been forced into by my father, with a Fae warrior twice my size. He had crawled straight into my lap and breathed his healing magic into me, and I instantly accepted the familiar bond.

The familiar bond is simple: it allows us to know how the other feels, physically and emotionally, and how to best help the other, but not by verbal communication. It is a feeling. I can also access a little of his power, which allows me to breathe fire, and he follows my commands. A familiar bond is vastly different from how I believe the Blood Binding will go. I do not know if Kaisera and I will be able to access each other's emotions or powers.

Nija sits on my shoulder as we make our way through the crowded streets of Area Six. The Area is packed with demons of all kinds prowling through the streets. This part of Area Six is clustered with larger buildings. The homes on these crowded streets are also made with the same, hard stone, all small spaces sealed to the elements as best as possible. Area Six is one of the poorer levels, but not the poorest. People here still must work for everything they have. Even the castle nobles know what a hard day's work looks like.

Well, nobles in the sense that they are higher demons. We are demons so there really isn't anything very noble about us, even if I believe there should be. Although we are not evil, we do not shy away from sins the same way creatures of the mortal realm do.

The lowest level demons, known as Hollows, haunt the shadows of this world and cannot travel between worlds. They were bound to this world thousands of years ago after they nearly destroyed all worlds. Now, they lurk in the shadows, too weak to do much else.

Hollows were given their name because they are hollow inside; they have no soul at all. Hollows were always searching for souls to take. Luckily for us, they tended to only crave mortal souls, not the souls of demons born to this realm, so we never really see them.

Middle level demons are here to help escort the souls to their rightful Areas. In order to do that, they must search the soul in its entirety to see its true depths of sin. Some souls are easy and move on swiftly to be servants until the debt of their sins from Erathina is repaid. Once their sins are atoned for, they can cross over to Valkeria and rest in peace. Other souls, like those in Area Eight, are tortured in all manner of ways and will never leave, unless all the kings of Inferis wished for it. That has never happened in all of our existence.

To my right, a blur of flesh, blood, and fist catches my attention and steals me from my thoughts. People are pushing and shoving, trying to get out of the way of the males fighting. One of the males shoves the other one back a few feet, as if he is no more than a bag of flour, knocking over an unbelievably cute coffee table and matching chair set at a café, destroying both. I glance at Nija, who is gearing up for a fight, shifting from paw to paw on my shoulder.

Oh, this is just the fight I was looking for! A small smile forms on my lips from the excitement.

I pull one of the smaller throwing knives out of my thigh holster and hurl it toward the closest male, directly into the demon's right shoulder. All at once, everyone stops and looks at me.

The male with my dagger sticking out of his back drops to the ground when the other male surprises him with a sudden fist to the jaw right below the ear, the perfect spot to hit to end a fight.

"Boys, boys, boys! If you are going to kill each other... take it..." My breath catches a little as the male who just delivered that perfect punch meets my eyes.

Chapter 6
KAISERA

Glad to have cleared things up with Madis, I hop back over to my room with a quick flap of my wings. I look to my bed, desperate to get under its comfortable silk sheets. I did not sleep last night due to that bartender.

I must bathe first, since I am still wearing my clothes from last night. I strip off my shirt and chunk it over to a nearby chair.

I pass by my bed, kicking off my boots as I make my way into my bathing room. My bathing room has a large, black clawfoot tub with a large window that faces the same direction as my balcony, so that I can look out at my city while I bathe. I see my lady's maid has already laid out everything I will need for a nice, toasty bath: lavender bath salts, foaming bath mixture, and my favorite dirty romance novel about a girl who falls in love with her stalker, lies on the black stool next to the tub.

Yes, this is just what I need.

Something about a hot bath has always soothed my soul. I crank the water to a scorching temperature and settle in.

Ka Lee

I soak for longer than necessary, trying to finish my novel. I have to stop and calm my racing heart when the main character is being fingerbanged by her stalker in a movie theater where they could get caught. Something about a man willing to stalk you until you love him back makes my heart sing.

I might have mental problems.

After stepping out of my bath, I snap my fingers to make a towel appear in my hands. I shake out my large wings until they feel fully dried, and I snap my fingers again to make my lavender silk night slip and matching shorts appear on me. I know others think I should work on and grow my powers, but I have never felt the need to do more. Snapping my fingers to get what I want is all I have ever needed. Of course, I was trained in combat, and I am right there next to Madis in strength and speed, but that's only because I was required by my father to keep up my training. I just never felt the need to dig deeper to see if I could do more.

What would be the point? Especially now that Madis will be my Blood Bound, I will never really need to. She has enough strength and power for both of us.

I slip deep into my sheets and close my eyes, not letting any of tomorrow's problems enter my mind.

I fall into a deep, dreamless sleep.

Chapter 7
MADIS

I am utterly stunned. I am not sure if I am still breathing. I have a vague idea that Nija has disappeared to wherever Nija disappears to.

This male is stunning.

He stands a good foot taller than me, which is a feat. He has light brown, almost blonde hair that is cut short on the sides, but still long enough on the top to be combed straight back with a part cut into it. He does not have a single hair out of place, even after the scuffle he has just been in. He has a perfect jawline that ends in a perfect chin. Just the right amount of stubble is perfectly trimmed on his face.

But his eyes are what I can't look away from. They are a darker blue than the deepest parts of the sea. Even though we are several feet apart, I can still see those eyes. I believe I will be seeing those eyes in my dreams. He is still just staring at me, and that is when I realize I am still staring at him.

He tilts his head a bit and then shakes it, as if trying to come out of a trance, something I wish I could have the sense to do. He is on me in seconds, and before I know it, I am pinned to a stone wall with this stunning male standing over me. *Towering* over me. I guess he is more than a foot taller than me. Now that we are this close, it is easy to see. I can also see that his deep-sea blue eyes actually have a perfect ring of light gray around each of them that fades harshly into the blue. They are spectacular.

"You smell amazing." Even his voice is pure deep male.

At that very moment, as if his words have broken through the haze in my mind, I realize that I am allowing a male to dominate me, and that just will not do. So, with a quick foot behind his ankle, I use his own off-balance body weight to flip him around so that he is the one against the stone wall. With another quick movement, I have a dagger at his throat, and a second one at what I'm sure is probably his favorite body part.

"I am sorry, what did you just say to me?" I say, pushing my dagger just a little harder into his throat to make sure I get my point across. It's not hard enough to draw blood, but enough to grasp my intent if he breathes wrong.

He laughs, sending an unwanted tingling to my core.

What in the underworld is wrong with me?

"I said, you smell good. Wait, no, I think my exact word was 'amazing,'" he says firmly and flirtatiously, a small smile playing on his lips.

"I am not food, so stop sniffing me." The male is leaning over my blade, trying to catch my scent.

I try to take a deep breath in to see what he is talking about, but I only smell his own scent of forest and spices. I do catch a hint of lavender on myself from being around Kaisera earlier, though.

"What are you, some kind of cannibal demon?" I press my dagger in a bit more, drawing the smallest droplet of blood. It doesn't seem to faze him.

He shakes his head, then leans his head back against the stone and closes his eyes. He takes another deep breath and seems to relax, despite the knife still at his throat.

He is an extremely strange male.

Untried Origins

I take a moment to look closer at him, this time not just focusing on his stunningly perfect eyes. He has tipped ears. He is Fae.

When he brings his bottom lip between his teeth, I see just a glisten of one slightly pointed fang. "No, I am not a cannibal; however, you do smell good enough to eat, or at the very least, lick." He takes another sniff. "What is that? Sugar pastries and a hint of lavender?"

Who in the Inferis does this Fae think he is? I dig my blade in even further, drawing more blood. Finally, this catches his attention. He gives me a half smile and puts his hands up in surrender.

"Alright, I give. Can we start over?"

I just stare at him, and I even let out a little bit of a growl.

"Please?" he adds.

I lower my daggers but do not holster them; I keep them ready. There is something about him. I cannot place this feeling in my middle, like I know I need to know him. I take another step back and gesture for him to continue.

"Thank you. My name is Tribax, but my friends call me Bax." He holds his hand out to me. I raise my eyebrows, standing up out of my fighting stance and crossing my arms, still holding onto my daggers.

"We are not friends."

"I trust that we will be, though," he says, but he lowers his hand to cross his arms over his broad chest, propping a foot up on the stone wall. The muscles bulging from his arms and pecs are impossible to miss. This is the perfect picture of a true alpha male in his element.

"I would never trust anyone named cunning," I say in my driest tone.

"You know the old language?" he says in surprise.

I drop my arms and turn to leave without giving him an answer. Before I make it more than a step, a large, warm hand wraps around my wrist. In a split second, I have him back against the wall, my daggers ready to meet blood. The small cut I gave him a minute ago is already nothing but a drying bloodstain.

He is an extremely powerful Fae.

"Okay, okay. No touching. I just was not ready for you to leave. I need your name." He still has a grip on my wrist.

Dropping my dagger away from his throat again, I try to back away, but he still has a firm grip on my wrist. I nod my head down and stare at where his hand is still wrapped around me. It is not a tight hold, but firm enough that I know it's there.

"Let me go." I use my power to heat my skin to an uncomfortable level for him. I know the moment he feels it: his eyes go a bit wide, and he quickly releases my hand.

"I have always had a thing for hot women," Tribax says as he shakes his quickly-healing burnt hand.

If that is his attempt at a joke, it's terrible.

"I am not a hot woman," I say, taking a few steps back to give myself space.

He laughs softly. "Then what do you call that?"

I feel my eyes scrunch together. "Defending myself."

Something shifts in him; I can't tell what it is, though. I spread my wings wide.

"Wait." He reaches out for me, but I shoot into the sky before his skin can make contact.

Chapter 8
KAISERA

After a wonderful day of rest, my lady's maid, Ellie, assists me with my dress. I admire myself in the mirror. I have a dark gray color on my eyelids with a hint of red on my lips. My dress for this evening is long and made of the darkest reds. It is floor-length, with several slits up to my thighs, topped with a few gauzy, see-through layers. The top of the dress is a snug, off-the-shoulder corset with small white beads all over.

I have always loved getting dressed up, just as much as I love my cotton pants and oversized shirts. As always, Ellie, who is also the best seamstress in the Inferis, has outdone herself. I can always manipulate the fabric into my own designs, but I do not have the eye for it the way she does. My father will not be pleased to see me in this unacceptable court attire with its overly chesty top, but I feel hot, so I do not care.

Madis and I both need our fathers happy with us for tonight's conversation. However, I'm not willing to give up my fashion sense for it.

Madis and I might have agreed to do the Blood Binding, but we still have no idea when they expect it to happen. Why are our parents just now telling us they want it done?

It's a question I intend to ask them tonight.

Ellie finishes the last knot on my corset, and I look over my shoulder to thank her for her always perfect work. She curtsies in her light long blue and white maid's dress and asks, "Is there anything else for the night, Princess?" It is not totally unusual for her to hurry off, but it's also not common.

"Going anywhere special tonight, Ellie? And for the thousand and tenth time, call me Kai, or at least Kaisera."

Ellie bows her head as she always does and says, as she always does, "As you command it, Kaisera."

I know we will have this same conversation tomorrow, as we have for close to a century now. "So, Miss Ellie, where are you running off to tonight?"

Ellie's cheeks turn a bright red as she bows her head, trying to hide the blush while twiddling with her fingers. "One of the Demon Guards, Mica, has asked me to a formal dinner."

I squeal in excitement and run to hug her tightly, restraining her arms to her sides. "Where is he taking you? What will you wear? Is he the one with the super sexy bulging arms and messy brown hair?" I pull back to look at her, but she seems to be in utter shock at my questions and excitement.

"Well, ma'am, I plan to wear a dress similar to this one. I am not sure where we are going, and I do believe we are talking about the same male." She continues to stand with her head bowed, her fingers now playing with her apron's strings.

It is not a very flattering gown, and I refuse to let her go on her date in it or anything like it. "Ellie, how would you feel about wearing one of your own designs tonight?" She looks up, shock in her eyes.

"I would not have the time or the fabrics to put something together," Ellie says.

"No, silly duckling, wear one of my dresses that you have already made. They are as much yours as they are mine. Pick one out and I will shape it to you." I put my hand on her shoulder and spin her around to face the full body mirror on my wall. "On second thought, I will pick it out. Stay right here. I will be right back."

I run to my wardrobe and pull out my one and only truly feminine-looking dress. I look carefully at it. I wore it only once to one of my father's ridiculous court balls he uses to make me attend. It has long, sheer sleeves in the lightest pink material. The bustier is fitted and dips just low enough to show cleavage but without being too scandalous. I am chestier than Ellie, but I can adjust it to her with my magic. The dress swooshes out at the waistline and ends just above the ankles; the length should be perfect for her. She would need shoes, too. Searching through my rooms, I find sparkly white shoes with a pointed toe and the slightest bit of a heel. Cute but not too hard to walk in. "Perfect!"

I run back and hand the dress and shoes over to Ellie, her eyes lighting up. "Oh, Princ…" I stop her with a clearing of my throat. I will get her to stop the princess crap one of these days.

"Right," she says. "Kaisera, are you sure I can borrow this?"

"No." Her eyes drop. So, I smile and continue. "Keep it. You made it. Plus, pink has never really been my color. You, on the other hand, will look flawless in it." Her eyes snap back up to me and she smiles brightly when I smile back. "Go put it on so I can shape it for you."

She nods then runs off to my bathing chamber to change.

I wait patiently for her to change, admiring myself in my dress again. It does not take long before she emerges in the slightly oversized dress.

I wave her back over to the mirror and she hurries to me. I get to work snapping my fingers while focusing on the bust to bring the material in closer to her body, getting rid of the excess material. I snap them again to stretch the shoes to fit her more comfortably. Ellie watches herself in the mirror, smiling wider and wider.

"Hmmm, one last touch." I add a long strip of black down the side of the dress to give it more dimension and just a little touch of me.

There is a *tap, tap, tap* on the door, and I know that's my cue to head down to dinner.

I smile at Ellie one last time. "Use my rooms to finish getting ready. And Ellie, I will not be needing you in the morning, so do stay up very, very late with Mica. I hear the caverns under Warrantless Tavern are quite the place to stay up late."

I do not see her face as I walk out the door, but I know that blush has returned, and I can't help but laugh at her innocence. This is the underworld; late nights with hot demon guards are the least sinister thing to happen around here.

"What are you smiling about? You do remember we are going to dinner with our parents, right?" Madis joins me in the hallway so that we can go to dinner as a united front.

Madis is dressed in battle armor, consisting of black metal chest plates form-fitted to her body and shoulder pads made of the same black metal, molded to look as if a dragon is laying across her shoulder and halfway down her arm. Long black sleeves run down her arms, ending in leather wrist cuffs that assist with keeping a bow's string from popping you when you release an arrow. As always, her black leather pants and her deadly crystal throwing knives cover her muscular thighs. When my eyes snag on something strange. I notice there is a blade missing from its holster.

"Umm, did you forget something?"

Madis goes a little stiff. "What?"

"Madis, one of your throwing knives isn't where it belongs," I say.

Madis looks down at the holster. "Umm yes, I lost one. Just forgot to replace it."

I know there must be a story there. Madis never just forgets or loses a crystal knife. She is all edges herself, she *is* a knife. Something must have happened after we went our separate ways this morning. Now that I am paying attention, I can tell something is up with her, something different. I just cannot place it. Whatever this strange new thing with Madis is, it will have to wait.

Now is not the time to worry about things like this. Now is the time to prepare myself mentally to deal with our parents. If it is something important, Madis would tell me.

Untried Origins

 I focus on what I have in front of me as we make our way down the red stone and clay hallways to the dinner that will change our futures forever.

Chapter 9

ELLIE

I must admit, I am excited for the first time in a long time. I stand in front of Princess Kaisera's mirror in her bathing chambers, looking at my freshly touched up self. I have kept to myself over the years, listening and watching as this world around me changes. I have secrets that are not ready to be told. The prophecy is not finished, and we are not ready for it, but it is coming.

The world changing can wait for one night, though, because I have a date. I have seen Mica in the hallways of this castle thousands of times by now, but he never noticed me. I have made it a point to not be noticed. Last week, though, I was lost in a trance when I slammed into a hard body. That hard body belonged to Mica, and this time, he noticed me. His boyish smile and messy hair had me hooked. I swear, I can still feel the warmth from the blush he left on me, when the only words he said as I walked away were "See me again?"

Simple enough words, but I did want to see him again. So, I did, increasingly. I made it a point to walk past his stations. We only exchanged small smiles and waves as we went about our days until he stopped me again to ask, "Go to dinner with me?" and in response I nodded and said "Tonight, eight o'clock."

Now here I am, at seven fifty-eight, standing in this beautiful dress with a hint of soft makeup, giddy as a schoolgirl.

I make my way to the door and when I open it, there is a bright-eyed guard looking down at me with the most perfect smile I have ever seen.

My heart knew from that very moment, I wanted to see that smile for the rest of my days. My stupid heart forgets I am not a normal demon. If I want this male, I will have to tell him things I have never spoken since my parents' deaths. I will have to trust him with things that others could never know. My smile falls as I think of all the things to come.

Mica turns sideways and holds out his elbow for me to take, and I notice a large blood stain on his shoulder.

"Oh, you are hurt!" I speak.

He looks over his shoulder at the red stained material of his shirt. He chuckles. "I will be fine. I will tell you all about it." He offers his arm to me again. "I would like to see if I am capable of keeping that hidden smile on your face all night tonight" Mica says playfully.

I take his arm, smile returning. "I would like that."

I take a deep breath in and decide that just for tonight, I can let myself forget tomorrow's problems.

Chapter 10
KAISERA

As we enter the dining hall, both Commander Pike Malias and Viscountess Mesa Malias sit on one side of my father at the large, rectangular stone table. My father, as king, sits at the head of the table, leaving myself and Madis to sit on the other side of him.

Our dining hall is simple. Low hanging chandeliers lit with hundreds of candles, even though we have long since had electricity, hang perfectly placed throughout the room. Small black flowers line the table, along with tall, thin black candles. Our parents watch our every step, as if we will jump onto the table and start dancing with our hands in the air.

As I sit, I say, "Good evening, everyone. You can all release the breath that you are holding. I believe you will all be happy with our decision." Finally, everyone takes the bricks off their chests, and the tension in the room dissipates.

"You have decided to be adults for a change, how refreshing. Although, Kaisera, you know I am not a fan of all those flashy gowns you choose to wear" This comes from my father.

Untried Origins

With my finest bright smile and fighting the urge to roll my eyes, I reply, "Yes, Father. After we put our childish toys away, we asked the magic crystal what we should do."

I know I shouldn't have this attitude toward my father, but he has been so uptight these past few years. I miss the father who taught me how to coax humans into their sins, like picking their nose in public or eating that extra piece of cake when they thought no one was looking. Silly sins, I know, but a young demon must learn somehow.

"Kaisera, enough! If you cannot take these matters seriously and act your age, then you are excused from this table." He cuts those fatherly eyes at me that say he is not in any way joking.

"Yes, Father. I am sorry. Madis and I have spoken seriously about this matter." I hate that my father's stare has me bowing my head even in the slightest, but at least I can still hold my shoulders back.

Commander Pike chimes in, "Well, Madis, let's hear of this serious discussion."

"My King, my husband, could we at the very least receive our drinks, maybe even the first course before talking shop?" This comes from Viscountess Mesa Malias.

Madis and her mother are nearly twins in every way. The signs of aging and Mesa's short, bobbed hair holds them apart, of course, but the real difference between them is that Madis' mom does not have wings or much power. Commander Pike met her after a battle in Erathina, when demons helped mortals destroy an evil that had started to take over their lands.

She is half human and half demon. Commander Pike always says that the moment he saw her in that half-destroyed pub, trying to clean up, that he would never spend another day apart from her. He did not. She had felt the same way when they met and chose to give up her soul to come here with him. It is rare for mortals to give up their time in Erathina, but it is not unheard of.

My father was not happy at first, but he learned to like her as time passed, at least enough to deal with her in small portions.

Father replies to everyone. "As you wish, Mesa." Mesa might be half demon, half human with truly little power, but she is still not someone you want to upset. That woman can hold a grudge, and when demons hold grudges, other demons pay the price for an exceedingly long time. It would mean a very unpleasant evening for everyone for the foreseeable future.

My father gestures to the servants. Our wine is poured, and the salads are brought out.

"Now that we have food and wine in front of us, may we speak of the important things?" my father asks condescendingly.

Mesa bows her head toward my father. "Of course. Madis, please tell us all what we are so eager to hear."

There is silence. I look over to see Madis staring at her salad like it is a map she must find her way across.

What is going on with her?

I elbow her in the stomach, a little harder than necessary, forcing a sharp breath out of her. I had expected her to catch my arm. She always stops my blows before they hit.

I will absolutely be talking to her after this dinner!

Madis clears her throat and looks up from her salad. "I am sorry, what was the question? My mind was on a training lesson from this afternoon."

Oh, it's on something from this afternoon, but I highly doubt it was a training lesson.

Mesa looks at her daughter with concern, or annoyance. With Mesa, it is always hard to tell. "We all would like to hear your and Princess Kaisera's decision about the Blood Binding," her mother says in a polite and proper tone.

"Of course, Mother. The princess and I came to a conclusion this afternoon," Madis says, finally getting her head back in the game.

"Oh, for Valkeria's sake! Ladies, tell us at once what you have chosen." He looks as if his head is going to pop, it is turning so red. Lucky for all of us, his power is telekinesis and not fire, or we all might be set it alight with the look he is giving us. He has never been the most patient of men.

I grin just a bit, happy to get under his skin for a change. "We have decided that we will accept each other in the Blood

Bond." All at once, all the tension in the room seems to fade away, as if even the dining hall has been waiting anxiously for that answer.

My father says, "Ah, I am so glad you both gained some sense. This is the right decision; you will see." He claps his hands together loudly with the largest grin I have ever seen from him.

This Blond Binding is a little too important to him.

Could it be that he just genuinely wanted to keep me safe?

"King Braxton?" Madis asks. "Why is this so important to everyone suddenly? Blood Binding, from what I understand, is rarely done anymore."

Both he and the commander look at each other. I can tell they're having one of my father's telepathic conversations.

I slam my hands down on the table. "What are you keeping from us?" My temper is getting the best of me. Not an uncommon thing for me, but damn it, I do not like being excluded from my own life.

My father drops a death glare at me, a reprimand on his tongue.

It is Mesa who speaks first, though. "Nothing serious, my lady. Your fathers just want you both fully protected, and you will be stronger if you can share in each other's strengths." Her smile is a bit too sinister for my liking.

That cannot be it. My father loves me in his own way, sure, but he is the king of Inferis, the underworld. The rulers here are not known for their kind heartedness. He would not be so adamant about us doing this if it did not help him in some way. I just know something else is going on.

"We do have questions. Will I be able to use Madis' fire gifts?" I am both excited and terrified by that thought.

My father responds, "We have no way of knowing exactly what the Binding will do to you both, but at the very least, you will be better attuned to each other."

Madis and I glance at each other. I can see questions racing through her mind just as my own mind begins to race. Better attuned with each other? Power sharing?

"I think Madis, and I would like more information, Father," I say before turning to Madis. She nods her head in agreement with me.

My father speaks up again. "We shall all find out very soon. Tomorrow night."

Tomorrow night?

"But Father, what is this rush for? I do not see…"

I am cut off. "This is not up for debate any longer, Kaisera. You both have agreed, and you will be completing the Blood Binding tomorrow night."

"But—"

"Kaisera Allison Braxton, I am your father and the King of Area Six. You will remember your place, and you will obey by me without question."

Oh, so this is what Madis felt like when I pulled rank on her.

I bow my head fully and sag my shoulders. These are not merely words; they are said with a hint of my father's powers, meaning this is his will and this *will* happen.

"Yes, sir."

I want so desperately to defy him, to fight him on this subject. I do not like going into this agreement with such little information. Madis places her hand over mine under the table. I glance in her direction; she shakes her head no.

I absolutely hate being told what to do.

Madis is right, though. This is a battle I do not see us winning.

Chapter 11
MADIS

As soon as the last course is done, I excuse myself from the table, claiming to be worn from the afternoon of training at the DWA. I receive a side eye from Kai that says, 'something is up with you, and I am going to find out what.'

I am not sure I will be able to answer her when she comes searching for me later. My mind keeps going back to that damned Fae male, Tribax.

What are you thinking? You do not have the time to be thinking of some Fae male.

I must admit, even just to myself, it felt good to have someone's full attention on me, but it really doesn't matter what I admit or feel. My fate is sealed; I will be Bound to Kaisera tomorrow.

Had he stolen my dagger? There is no way. I would have noticed. That's when I remembered I must have left it embedded in the other demon's shoulder at the cafe. Very uncharacteristic of me to simply forget.

Ka Lee

No one ever gets the drop on me, except Kai at dinner tonight, with that quick blow to my stomach. I am distracted, thinking of the way Tribax sniffed me, and how it seemed to have taken all his focus to break whatever trance he was in.

"AHHHHH!" I screeched loudly at a sharp pinch to my ass. I flip around quickly, ready to pummel whoever had the nerve to touch me.

Standing there in her revealing red dress is Kai, with her arms crossed, tapping her heeled foot against the ground.

So, this conversation is happening.

"So...what has you so distracted that you allowed me to get the drop on you, not once, but twice now? And I am in six-inch heels! Even the merfolk of Area Three could have heard me coming. From underwater," she deadpans at me.

I do not even know where to begin on this one. This guy should mean absolutely nothing to me, but he has grabbed my attention.

"I.... I don't know, Kai." I cannot even seem to get my words out properly.

"Madis, we are about to be *Blood Bonded* to each other. I don't know a lot about this thing we are doing, but I am sure we should not be going into it with secrets. Plus, you are practically my sister, and we've never kept things from each other before. Why start now?"

This isn't true. Kai never keeps anything from me. I keep everything from everyone. Some things, you just need to bear on your own. I guess this encounter did not really warrant a secret.

With my usual huff and sigh, I say, "I am not trying to hide things from you, Kai. It's just, this Fae male today... he got into my head somehow..." I turn and start down the hall to my room.

Kai, who is standing there looking extremely confused by my words, finally starts jogging loudly in her heels to catch up with me.

Damn, I must have truly lost my senses if I let her get the drop on me in those things.

Untried Origins

Kai loops her arm through mine, and we continue the walk back to our rooms. Kai is peeking glances up at me every few moments.

"What?" I finally return her glance.

She lets out her breath. "When you say you let a guy get in your head... do you mean he fucked you senseless?" Kai says it quietly, but I can tell the idea of it excites her.

Laughing, I say, "I actually had a dagger to his throat."

"Hmmm, spicy. I like it. Hey doll, you know I would never kink shame. You could have told me that."

Laughing even louder now, I also shake my head. While I know what she said about not caring is true, I'm not as frivolous as Kai, and my "spicy" side isn't that spicy. Sure, I have had my fun in the sheets, but it's always very much vanilla and never with anyone I care for. It's always more to pass the time or to take my mind off the things going on around me.

We make it back to our rooms and Kai unhooks our arms, waiting for me to speak.

A new thought comes into my mind. A nice girls' night might help. "Hey, want to call for a couple Flashers and some of that Fae wine? We can have a sleepover like old times," I ask Kai.

My father should not be calling for me again tonight, and if he does, I just have to hope I can hide the alcohol from him. The Fae may not be my favorite, but they know how to make wine. The deep purple drink that swirls around as if the galaxies lay within it can have you giggling and dancing until your legs give out. We are told that if mortals consume it, they will dance until they literally die. I cannot confirm or deny this, since I've never been to their realm or met a human in the underworld worth asking.

"I would love that, but we are going to be having it in my room. Your rooms are always so drab," she says, pausing before a thought seems to pop into her head. "Oh! But I told Ellie not to come back tonight. Hmmmm, hold on." Then, Kai blinks out. Not ten seconds later, she blinks back, arms now full of a bottle of Demon whiskey and two bottles of Fae wine. That is a neat little trick I would not mind gaining from the Binding.

She squeals with glee, "Ok, we are set! Let's go!" And with that, we walk one door over to Kai's room.

Hours later, as the sun begins to rise, Kai pours the last of the Fae wine into our glasses. We were up all night laughing and reminiscing on old memories of when we used to play tricks on the humans that ended up in this Area of the underworld. Kai does not bring up the event with Tribax again. We laugh at all the trouble Kaisera had gotten into in her youth, at how red her father's face gets every time she is caught.

We have not shared a night like this in a long time. I'm always so tied up at the DWA, either training the new recruits or working on being the best. Kai has taken a different route, the route of partying and enjoying sharing beds. We are complete opposites, but somehow, we have always fit.

Kai gets serious. "Okay, tell me about this Fae. I must know more, and do not leave out the juicy details." She bites her lower lip and gives me a goofy, seductive look.

I knew I could not go the entire night without this coming up.

I will try to explain. "There was a fight in a cafe outside of the DWA. When I went to break it up… or join in…" I give Kai an evil smile. "There he was. I don't know what this feeling was, but I was in – I don't know – a trance of some sort."

"Like he was using magic on you?"

"No, not like that! I could not stop staring at his eyes. Kai, they were amazing. But it doesn't matter anyways," I say.

It really does not matter; it can't matter right now. I do not even want to think of the things my father would do to me or any male I am with who is not of his choosing. One day, I will be able to make a choice of mates. At least, I hope to be able to, but that day cannot come until Kaisera is queen or my father dies.

It is why I added "May they be epic ends" to our motto, because I have to believe that one day, our lives may be more than our fathers' choices.

Untried Origins

"So, what part of this is messing with your head?" Kai asks.

"Like I said, I don't know. I know he managed to throw me so off track that I forgot one of my daggers at the cafe. I know I want to see him again."

Well, I did not know that last part until I said it.

"Ok."

"Ok? What do you mean ok? I tell you I met a male, held a dagger to said male's throat, and now my world is shifting... and you say 'Ok'?"

Damns, I am learning all kinds of things about myself tonight. Goddess-damned Fae wine.

"Yes, ok. We can find him. We *will* find him and find out why he is so, as you put it, 'world changing'." She looks mischievous. "And if he changed your world after just a small dagger to the throat, can you imagine what being in bed with him would be like?" Her smile gets even bigger at her own statement.

My jaw drops, and I throw a pillow at her.

The heat fills me to my core at the quick image of what it might be like with a male that matters. I could not see what he looked like under his simple riding pants, boots, and cream-colored shirt, but I know what I felt under those clothes when we were pressed up against that wall. What I felt was nothing but unforgiving muscles and pure male dominance.

I know my cheeks must be turning all the different shades of red right now. As much as I want to see him again, I know it's for the best that I don't. Nothing good can come from him, and it would not matter anyways.

Kai laughs at my red cheeks, and I have to join in with her.

Kai yawns. "Okay, we both have to get some rest. Since we are to be Bound to each other for all eternity after tomorrow, I do not wish to share my bed with you tonight."

Taking the hint, I start to stand.

"Madis."

"Yes, Kaisera?"

She tosses back the last of her wine. "Are you ready for what comes tonight? Are you one hundred percent sure this is what you want? I could convince my—"

Ka Lee

I cut her off. "Kai, this is my duty. I want to do this."
She sighs. "See you tonight, then."
"See you tonight."

Chapter 12
KAISERA

After Madis leaves, I flop straight onto my bed. The sun is fully up now, but I need my rest. I still have no idea what the Blood Binding ceremony will entail tonight, but I am sure I will need my energy.

I have to smile at myself after the fun girls' night spent with my friend.

Madis with a Fae male.

I do not know what to make of that news. I'm not going to worry too much about it. Madis is duty bound. She will never let anything get between her and her duties to the kingdom. Plus, I'm hoping we will find this male so she can get her brains banged out, and that will be that. Then, we can move on. It is not like she would settle down with him. Well, more like she cannot. She has made it extremely clear she wants this Binding to happen, and she knows that our laws say she can never settle down once we are Bound.

That has my thoughts turning to my own future, and with whom I will be forced to settle. I have met all the Area Kings throughout the years. I am most acquainted with the King of Area Seven. None of us could agree completely on the best of days, and none of them were my type. It has been decades since I have last seen any of them, though.

One day, I will rule, and things will change. I will make them change. Ruling is my birthright, and I plan to claim it.

After seeing the way my father and Commander Pike acted at dinner, I know something big is coming. I am starting to feel it in my bones. I'm too tired to think too hard on that now. After all, I am immortal, and these things can be figured out tomorrow. No reason to drag tomorrow's issues into today.

I can feel the Fae wine starting to really take effect on me. The dizzying haze of the alcohol is filling my brain and sending that warm, fuzzy feeling all over my body.

It isn't long before the alcohol drags me under into another peaceful slumber.

Chapter 13
MADIS

    I want a little fresh air, so I go out on Kai's balcony and spread my wings to make the short hop over to my balcony. As soon as I land, I notice an incredibly happy Nija napping on the railing's edge, basking in the early morning sun.
    "Where, oh, where have you been?"
    Nija opens a single eye, peeking a look at me. A small smile seems to form on his face before he closes his one cracked eye and rolls over onto his back, begging for a belly rub. I swear, this miniature dragon is more of a puppy than a demon spawn dragon.
    I start toward him until I catch a scent floating around in the area. I glance at my balcony door – the doors are slightly ajar.
    I grab one of my throwing knives and spin it around in my hand. I stop it so it's held in a close combat position. If anyone is stupid enough to break into my rooms, they will not be getting the quick death a throw from one of my knives can offer. No, it will be slow and satisfying in the sweetest of ways.

Ka Lee

I slowly open the door and creep into my room from the balcony. I smell something familiar; I am just having a tough time placing it. At least, until I catch a stronger whiff of it. The forest and spices. My heart is racing faster than ever, hard enough I can feel my blood pulsing through my body. My body starts to heat, and I can feel my powers wanting to break free.

Before I can even start to place where the smell is coming from, I find myself with my back against the floor and a muscular male pressed against my front, a male with the deepest of blue eyes, a ring of gray around them. I find those eyes staring straight back into my own.

Every inch of him is in contact with every inch of me, except our mouths. A mouth that I foolishly take a quick glance at. It looks so perfect with its little bow-shaped top and full bottom. I watch that mouth turn into a full smile.

He had thrown me to the ground but had kept me from landing too harshly. Even with all his care, the air is still knocked from my lungs. He lays there on top of me, just breathing and smiling down at me. He looks at me in a way that causes chills to run down my spine.

"One inch closer, and your kidney will be on the floor," I say.

"You are such a vicious thing. I enjoy that about you." His voice is deep and rugged, and it only adds to his attractiveness.

I cannot stop myself from taking a glance at his lips again. On my second inspection, I noticed a tiny scar on the top left side. It is very faint; it would be easy to miss if you were not looking closely. I find myself desperately wanting to run my finger across it, wanting to find out what caused it.

I have to stop this.

Demons, being able to manipulate people into their sins, have a higher sense of their own wants, and I want this male. However, something within me is saying he is not mine to have, but that same strange part of me is saying he is meant to be a part of me. It is like no other feeling I have ever felt.

I dig my blade in a little deeper. "You have no clue just how vicious I can be."

Untried Origins

I feel his hand move, but somehow, I let him past my defenses yet again. I feel the hard, cold metal against my neck and curse myself. I am so distracted with my thoughts; I did not even notice him removing my own blade from one of its holsters.

What is it about you?

"Darling, if you cut me, I will be forced to cut you. Then, there will be all this blood, and it will make our kissing very messy. But if that is how you enjoy it, I will oblige." The smile that spreads across his face pulls at the tiny scar, and his toothy grin is so wide, I can see the tips of his Fae canines, shorter than vampires but longer than normal.

This cocky prick. He just thinks he can walk into my room and start talking about kissing me!

On the other hand, maybe I should let him; I do not know what tonight's Binding will hold.

Gritting my teeth, I say "How did you know where to find me?"

How is that my only response? I wish desperately I had Kai's quick wit and confidence right now.

He rolls, dragging me with him so I am now straddling him, a knee on each side of him. His whole body is lined up perfectly with mine. I can feel his erection in just the right spot, and it makes me gasp. I am completely bothered within a split second.

"I followed that amazing smell of yours. I did tell you how amazing you smell." He still holds that grin, with his perfect white teeth and the hint of those canines that are starting to look very appealing.

I sniff the air, but all I can smell is the Fae wine and the lingering of Kaisera's lavender scent on me. "It is a little creepy that you just walked around sniffing the air for me."

"So creepy that you are still enjoying being on top of me?" He grinds his hips up just a bit, sending another wave of heat through to my core.

I lean over a bit, pressing my dagger deeper into his side. The blade he is still holding to my throat bites a bit, the pain nothing compared to things of my past. We are so close, our noses grace each other's.

"Why?" It's all I get out before Tribax lifts his head and crashes his mouth to mine, and we instantly drop our daggers. They clatter to the ground, and I let him consume me. I could easily stop this from happening, but I do not want to stop. It feels too good, even if it still feels off in a deep part of myself. It feels so great to be wanted by this male.

His tongue rushes in to find mine as if he is searching for something he lost.

There is a nagging feeling in the back of my mind that I am not what he is searching for. I push that thought aside for later.

I soak up every part of him touching me, wrapping my hands behind his head and sinking into him, wishing and wanting to feel closer to someone.

Tribax sits us both up without breaking our connection. I am sitting, still straddling his lap, my knees bracketing his hips, hands tangled in his hair. He wraps his arms fully around me, and I am swallowed by his large, masculine arms. I am not a tiny female, so the fact that he can completely consume me in his arms is a testament to just how big of a male he is. I can feel every bit of him, the tightening of each muscle as he moves his arms up and down my back before finally settling them on my hips.

I finally pull back and gasp for air. I look into those eyes that I will forever dream about, and I just stare at him. He stares back, now looking hungry and intrigued.

"Who and what are you?" I ask in between shallow breaths.

He is breathing just as heavily as I am, and his grip on me is so firm, I know he is not going to let me go easily.

"I already told you, my name. Did you forget me that easily?" He is looking into my eyes as if the answer to his question is there in them. There is a bit of confusion in his eyes, the same confusion I am positive reflects in mine.

"I am the one who is still waiting on a name," he continues. When I do not immediately respond, he leans in to nip at my lip, getting a small moan out of me. "Hmmm, I like that sound."

I giggle a small feminine sound, one that does not sound like me.

Untried Origins

He moans this time. "That is another sound I think I am going to like."

My body goes completely still. "Wait. Going to like? Tell me who you truly are and why you are here! Now!"

He pulls me tighter, something I did not think possible.

Well, with our clothes on, at least.

I silently curse myself for even thinking that. This cannot happen. I have too much on my plate right now. *And if my father were to find out...* I have to stop that thought. I start to reach for another dagger. He shakes his head at me, tsking me. I narrow my eyes at him.

"You must not truly know who I am to tsk me." The strict, commanding tone is back in my voice.

He sighs and leans back onto his hands. I am still sitting firmly in his lap, and we're still on my floor.

"Should I know who you are? A princess perhaps?" Tribax asks.

My laugh is humorless. "I am definitely not a princess."

"Tell me your name and who you are. Then, I will tell you everything you wish to hear." He sits back up, close enough to brush the back of his hand over my cheek, and then tucks a piece of my hair behind my ear, as if he has done this to me a thousand times.

"Fine. My name is Madis Malias. I am the General Commander of Area Six and Personal Guard to the royal family and its princess," I say with a slight growl as I stare him down. I already want to feel his lips back on mine, to know what those lips feel like as they roam all over me. I need information first. I have to remember, even in this male's distracting presence, that duty and honor have to come first.

"Well, Madis Malias, I am Tribax Xanadriel, due to start as the new Captain of the Royal Army of Area Six."

I cock an eyebrow at him. "A Fae Commander in the demon army?"

"Who said I am only Fae?"

I narrow my eyes at him and start to stand. He grabs both sides of my hips to keep me in place.

Ka Lee

I look back into his eyes waiting to see if he will give me more information. He bows his head ever so slightly, a very stern expression on his face. A smile stretches across his face before he says, "I believe we could be mates."

Chapter 14
KAISERA

Ellie dresses me in a simple, thin-strapped, black silk gown that has a very risqué neckline. I am in love with it; it's simple, elegant, with just a hint of danger. I am having a hard time believing this is the dress my father instructed me to wear tonight. I have to hand it to myself: the long nap and the power of makeup has done absolute wonders for me.

Ellie, on the other hand, looks thoroughly exhausted. The hint of a blush still on her cheeks gives me the impression she had an exceptionally good night with the shaggy-haired Demon Guard.

"So, Ellie… How was your night?"

The lady's maid becomes an even darker shade of red somehow. "It was lovely, Princess."

I roll my eyes and let out an 'ugggghhhh' sound. *The princess shit is never going away with this one.* I try again. "Was Mica any good?"

That gets Ellie's full attention as she looks at my eyes in the reflection of the full body mirror we are currently standing in front of.

"He was a perfect gentleman," she says with a stern nod.

I can tell she does not want to give me any more information, but I am not going to settle for that answer. We are both demons, for fuck's sake; there is no such thing as a 'perfect gentleman' down here. So, I take a stab in the dark. "Oh, so he was lame in bed?"

Ellie's mouth pops open, jaw halfway to the ground as she stares darkly back at me. "No!"

"Okay, so he was good?" I am going to get it out of her.

"Kaisera, I would never make love and then stand around and gossip about it." She says it oh-so ladylike and proper.

"Mm, made love, huh? So, is he the one?" I cannot stop my grin from widening. I turn a bit, as if to walk away. "Shall I go grab him and let him know the spectacular news of your pending nuptials?"

Ellie's eyes turn from their doe brown to a bright baby blue, clouds of black swirling throughout them. Power radiates from her in a way I have never seen before. I do not cower or turn away as I should. It overly fascinates me. Her whole body seems to darken, and the shadows in the room seem to be reaching for her. Her lips start to pull back over her teeth slowly.

Abruptly, Madis walks in. "Leave the poor girl alone," Madis says to me with a stern look on her face. Her arms are crossed lightly over her chest as she leans against the door frame to my room. Madis is dressed in a white gown that is the exact same cut as mine. They are identical in every way but color.

Madis' voice must have been all the distraction Ellie needed, because from one second to the next, she is back. Her eyes lighten back to their soft brown, and there is no longer any power in the air.

"What was that?" I am eye-to-eye with Ellie now, curiosity filling me up, searching for the power I had witnessed.

She bows her head, looking ashamed for her outburst. "I am sorry, Princess. I do not know what came over me."

Untried Origins

Madis walks over. "Yes, you do. Her royal Princess Pain in the Ass was baiting you." She puts a hand on Ellie's shoulder and pokes me in the sternum with her other hand.

"Umm, ouch," I say, stepping back from the pressure of her finger hitting the tender center of my sternum.

Madis rolls her eyes. "Yeah, that didn't hurt, and we have to get going. Your father has never put up with tardiness, and I doubt tonight will be any exception."

I have a full body chill. "This is absolutely true. I do not know what we are walking into, and it has my nerves rattled. So, the quicker we get there and get this over with, the quicker I can get a drink."

I turn to look back into the full-length mirror. My hair is down for a change. My long black hair is curled softly and all over to the right side of my head. The left side is tightly braided back. My makeup is done to perfection, thick black liner coating my bright green eyes, and my lips are topped with a deep shade of red lipstick.

Madis steps up to my side and tucks my arm into hers. "You ready?"

I take a few moments to look her over, too. Her makeup is just as stunning; all nude colors, which shine brightly against her darker skin tone.

Fear creeps into my head. The fear of the unknown. The fear that rumors of the Blood Binding are true, that it can rip your soul apart only to be pieced back together in new ways. I cannot help this sinking feeling that has been growing since the moment we agreed to this, that something is off. Something is not right. My father could have tamed these fears if he had only been willing to answer our questions or explain. Everything is happening too quickly.

I look to Madis, hoping her calm nature will leak into me. "I hope this Binding does not change who we are or what we mean to each other."

Madis seems to think it over. She sighs. "If it does, we will remind each other each and every day of who we are. No matter what happens tonight, we will remind each other. We are and always will be stronger together."

Ka Lee

My nerves have never been this bad. I am not an anxious person. I need Madis' reassurance in this. I turn to face her head on. "Madis, swear to me you will always remain my rock."

Madis' eyes soften, and she gives me the softest of smiles. "Kaisera Allison Braxton, I promise to always be your rock."

"Let's get this done then." I still have the sinking feeling of stones settling into my stomach, but with Madis's surety, I feel a bit more stable.

Madis leans in for a hug, and with her closeness, I catch the most intoxicating scent I have ever smelt in my entire existence. Madis pulls away and gives me an odd look. She shakes her head at something she sees in my eyes.

Madis grabs my hand, and I blink us out. My father had sent word that he wanted this to happen in complete secrecy. Something about not wanting any extra eyes and making Madis and me more comfortable.

That last part is complete and utter bullshit.

We appear outside of my father's study. I take a deep breath, release Madis's hand and open the large stone door. My Father's study is dark and set with comfy-looking furniture that is both inviting and yet not. The curtains, made of thick, purple, silk-like material, are drawn closed to keep any light from getting in, even though it is the dead of night. The only light in this room comes from dimly lit candles.

Again, we have electricity.

My father has always been stuck in the old ways, and I believe he enjoys making the servants light the candles and then go behind him to put all of them out. There are books on the shelves that look as if they are millennia old, the backs ripped and torn in their leatherbound covers. I hear a soft humming coming from one of the shelves, and when I turn to look, I see nothing, but feel my body wanting to move toward it.

My father steps in front of me, blocking my movement and drawing my full attention. He is in his formal, black, and red royal robes. He has his crown on, and in this lighting, the red and black crown looks as if it is on fire and slowly melting on his head.

My future crown.

Untried Origins

My father's jaw looks like it is clenched tight enough to break, the muscles twitching constantly beneath his skin. I cannot for the life of me place where his frustration could be coming from. We did everything he wished of us.

With no attitude, I might add.

Commander Pike and Viscountess Mesa aren't here. I was sure they would want to be present, if this *is* such an honorable thing. At the very least, they should want to wish their daughter the best of luck. Madis, on the other hand, does not seem to be shocked or worried at her parents' absence.

"Father," I say in greeting.

"King Braxton," Madis says right after me, lowering her head in respect.

My father just nods. I catch movement behind him. Madis and I both take a sharp breath and take a step back as an old crone steps forward.

The old woman, if you can call her a woman or even a person, stands around four feet tall. However, she hunches over a wooden cane enough to make her look closer to three. She has stringy gray hair that hangs out from under a thick, dark green hood with a long cape. Her clothing underneath looks tattered and worn. Luckily, she is standing far enough away that I can't smell her. From the looks of her, I can only guess it is not a very pleasant smell. Her eyes are black, the kind of black that peers through one's soul and strips it away. Her skin is ancient, greyish, and dried like leather on a hot summer's day. Her long, skinny fingers end with black, razor-sharp nails that grip onto her cane tightly as she steps forward.

"Good evening, Lady Madis and Princess Kaisera." Her voice is raspy, and as dry as her cracking skin. The old crone hobbles a few steps to stand next to my father. The crone is from the Witch Area, Area Five. Witches hate to travel out of their Area and hate doing services for other Areas even more. They believe they are the superior race and tend to demand things from others, rather than assist anyone with anything. My father must have paid a fortune to get one all the way here. No one had mentioned a crone being used in the Binding.

"Kaisera," my father says. "A crone must be present and conduct the spell in order for the Blood Binding to be completed."

"But I thought all we would have to do is swear loyalty to each other and you would seal those binds with your magic," I say. That was just my assumption, though, because no one was willing to tell us more. I reach over to Madis and grab her hand. I need her to ground me right now. I have never been the kind of girl to back down from a fight, but something about this feels so very wrong. The witches' magic is hardly ever used for good, especially witches from Inferis.

Madis grips my hand back. "Sir, is this necessary? I will swear a Binding oath to always protect Princess Kaisera at all costs, no matter what." She sounds way more stable than I feel. She sounds like none of this is affecting her at all. Madis is never affected by anything and I am envious of that right now.

My father shakes his head. "No, this is what must be done." I am confused by the way he says this, though, almost as if he is convincing himself. He straightens and rolls his shoulders back before continuing. "Now, listen to every word the crone says, and do only as she commands. Do you both understand me?"

We do not verbally respond to him, but we shake our heads up and down in agreement to his demands.

The crone gets to work. She pulls out more candles from a satchel on her hip and two twin crystal daggers. I squeeze Madis' hand just a bit tighter and look to her, hoping she can read my expression, before I mouth, 'What are those for?'

Madis squeezes back and glances down at me with a slight tilt of her mouth. *I am with you.*

I send up a silent prayer to Valkeria. *Please, for the love of the seven sins of Inferis, let us survive this.*

On the plus side, we might be able to hear each other's thoughts after this. Madis and I tell each other everything when we are in private, but it would be nice to be able to speak to each other when we are not supposed to be speaking. Like right now, I can take a guess at what she is trying to relay to me, but I cannot hear her, and I can only see gaining that ability as an advantage.

"Come, come. You both need to join me in the center of the room. King, you are done here. Leave."

Untried Origins

My father shoots daggers out of his eyes at the crone for demanding anything of him, let alone being told to leave his own study, but he walks toward the door anyway. I am shocked he's listening to her commands.

"Kaisera, do know I—" he starts, but he doesn't finish his comment. He clears his throat. "You will be fine. See you shortly." With that, he walks out of the study.

That is strange. My father looked almost disturbed, but that is not possible. This Binding is his idea, after all. My entire body is demanding that I get out of this room as quickly as possible, but I cannot, and I just stand there with Madis' hand clutching mine.

The crone ushers Madis and me to the very center of the room. She has placed black, red, and white candles everywhere around the room. The floor shelves and tabletops are scattered with them. There are so many, the room starts to heat from the flames.

How did she fit all of those into that small satchel? Focus, Kai. That is not something you need to be wondering about at this moment.

The crone hands each of us a crystal dagger. I hold it up to my face; it is spectacular. The blade itself is black and has small specks of white in it that remind me of the night sky in the Fae world of Erathina. I have never seen it in real life, but the paintings in books that I have seen were stunning. The handle is almost solid white, with not a single imperfection. The only part of the dagger that isn't white or black is in the hilt of the blade, where there is a small, bloodred stone.

I look over to Madis' blade. As usual, our blades are the exact opposite. Hers is white with black specks, resembling hard granite. The handle of her dagger is the darkest black of shadows. Their only similarity is the bloodred stone in the hilt. I wonder how the crone came to own such blades when her clothing indicates she has nothing. Witches are strange creatures.

The crone speaks. "You will each slice your wrist with the dagger I have given you. Then, you will drink from the other's wrist."

Madis and I stare at the crone as if waiting for her to grow a second head or spit fire. We both turn to look at each other, each as confused as the other.

Madis speaks first. "So, we drink each other's blood and then it's done?"

The crone cackles a hideous laugh that sends disturbing chills through to my bones. She sounds more like she is choking. She reaches back into her bag and removes a few tiny vials and a chalice. The crone begins to mix in vial after vial before she speaks to us again.

"No, you imbecile."

I turn, ready to knock the shit out of the crone. Madis grabs my wrist and shakes her head. As much as I would love to take this old hag down right now, I know it will not end well if I start a fight with this witch. So, I do not fight against Madis' hold on me.

The crone might look old and decrepit, but I know how evil witches can be, and you don't want to piss one off. Especially a Crone as old as this one appears to be. Witches in Inferis grow their powers by draining the souls that land themselves in their Area. They do not keep the souls to be workers or pay off their debts. No, if a soul ends up in the witches' area, they will be kept there and fed off until there is nothing left of them. It means the older the witch, the longer she has been draining souls for power. In short, the older the witch, the stronger the witch.

It has also been said that every now and then, a witch will get ahold of a sterling witch, or a purely good witch, and drain their souls to make themselves even more powerful. Draining a purely good soul from a creature will give anyone from Inferis a heck of a power rush, but it doesn't last forever. Taking that kind of life form will tarnish you; it's how Hollows are made. Demons of all species who take too much power from souls end up soulless and hollow.

Madis tries to speak to the crone again. "What will happen after we drink each other's blood?"

The crone now seems irate that we are not doing as she asked. "You will first drink from this chalice. It will grant you the ability to move within your own consciousness. You will both fall

Untried Origins

into a dream state after you drink from the other. I cannot tell you what you will face there. I cannot tell you how to make it out. Now, your father paid me to see this done. I will force you both to listen, or you will do it willingly. Choose wisely." The crone smiles in a way that says, *"I dare you to try it the hard way."* She only has two teeth in her whole mouth, and those two teeth look damn near ready to fall out as well, so it was more of twist of lips than a smile.

I reach for the chalice and snatch it out of the crone's hand. She hisses angrily at me, and I have the strongest urge to stick my tongue out at her but choose to just sneer.

The crone chants something in an unfamiliar language. I lift the chalice to my nose and take a sniff. It is a nasty green color but smells of lemons and something stronger that burns my nose.

"Here goes everything." I raise the glass a bit in Madis' direction before I hold my breath and take a quick swig.

Not the worst thing I have ever had.

I hand the glass over to Madis, and she quickly downs the last of it before handing the chalice back to the crone. She wipes her mouth with the back of her hand and inhales deeply.

Madis raises her left arm up and brings the dagger to it, ready to make the cut. The look of reassurance in her eyes and the firm nod of her head gives me what I need to do this. I follow her lead.

I have always followed her lead, and I always will. Madis is my sister, if not by blood, then by a deeper bond. This is the right call; I tell myself repeatedly. We will be connected deeper now, hopefully able to help lead each other through whatever comes next. I say the one thing that we always say to steady each other, the motto we made so many long years ago. "Till our ends meet."

I slice the dagger over my wrist. Blood drips down my arm and onto the rug-covered floor. The candles sizzle and flicker as small drops of my deep red blood hit the flames surrounding us.

Madis does the same and responds, "Then may they be epic ends."

Blood now trickles out of both our wrists onto the floor. Madis offers her wrist to me, and I offer mine to her and we place our lips to each other's wrist. We both take hard pulls from the other. The metal tang taste of it is not terrible, but for a moment, I still wonder how the vampires want to taste this every day.

The crone continues to chant something in the background, but it starts to sound muffled. Within seconds, I could no longer hear her. I can no longer hear anything. I cannot move. I try to release my mouth from Madis' wrist, but my body will not obey. I shift my eyes over to Madis', her mouth still firmly pressed to my wrist. Her eyes are solid white, no pupils, no color.

That is the last thing I see: Madis' milky colorless eyes staring deep into me.

Chapter 15
MADIS

    My heart races as my vision starts to blur. The image of Kaisera's lips on my wrist and the urge to pull more and more of her blood into me is strong. I try to latch onto reality for a bit longer. Kai's eyes have gone completely white, and she isn't drinking from me any longer, her body turned to a statue, a blank, unseeing stare on her face. The only reassurance I have is that I can still feel her pulse from her wrist that I have firmly latched to my mouth, the blood still flowing steadily into me.

    The crone's cackling laughter leaks into my ears, and I know then we have made a huge mistake. I walked into this room thinking our lives would be changed for the better, even when every instinct in me was telling me to run, telling me to get Kaisera out of here. I should have done more. I should have tried harder to uncover my father's plans. I knew from the moment I saw the king's face this had not been his intention. No, this situation screams of my father.

    Now, it is too late. Now, we will have to fight whatever comes next. I will protect her; it is my duty and honor to do so. I try to shake myself from this trance again, but it is impossible. I continue to be dragged under this spell.

"Strong one, I see," I hear the crone say.

"You cannot fight this, girly; it is too late. The only way out is through." With those last words, the crone vanishes. Her form fades away like ashes and embers on a cold winter's breeze.

I slam my eyes shut and try to breathe. I feel the second I lose all control. We release each other's wrist as our bodies drop like stones to the floor. I feel my head hit the ground and then I feel nothing at all. All I have left is the hollow darkness stretching out before me.

Chapter 16

ELLIE

I knew when I dressed the Princess and Lady Madis what would happen tonight. I know it will hurt them. I know it will be life changing for them both. I hate sitting by and waiting for what is to come.

"Are you ok? You are getting that lost look in your eyes." Mica's voice breaks though my thoughts.

I put on a fake smile. "Of course."

Mica and I had only been on one date. We have been with each other for only twenty-four hours. Yet, here I lay, in his arms, in his bed, feeling as if I have spent an eternity here.

"You are not being honest with me," Mica responds as he sits up, releasing me from his arms so he can turn to face me fully.

"Oh, you know me so well already?" I say teasingly.

Mica looks boyish, but he speaks with all the surety in the world. "Yes."

I feel my cheeks heat. Mica had admitted to me within the first hour of being together that he was ready to accept our mating bond. It had caught me off guard, his confidence and blatantness.

After releasing the breath, I had not known I had been holding, I leapt into his arms and crushed my mouth to his.

I have so many doubts and questions in my life; of course, the goddesses above would send me a mate that made me question nothing.

He leans in, placing a soft kiss on my nose before leaning back. "You can tell me. You can trust in me."

I believe him. For the first time since my parents' deaths, I am going to share with someone the whole truth. Now that I have chosen to tell him, I can feel a bit of weight fall from my shoulders. Not a whole brick, but at least I can feel a few crumbles starting to break off and fall.

"Let me carry some of this burden," my sweet mate of less than a day responds, already understanding my needs and wants.

I take a deep breath in and lean over to place a peck on his lips, and that kiss leads to a deeper kiss. Before I even realize what, I am doing, I crawl on to Mica's lap to straddle his hips, and he gladly latches back onto me. His hands roaming from my shoulders to my butt calms my soul, his kiss growing more enthusiastic by every touch of his tongue against mine. I pull away to fill my lungs with air. I lean my forehead to his, breathing in deep gulps of air.

"Ok," I say quietly.

I spend the next few days tangled in the sheets with my mate, telling him everything.

Six Years Later

Chapter 17
ALLISON

My eyes pop open, heart beating hard in my chest, sweating through the thin material of my nightshirt. I slow my breathing and heart rate when I realize it was just a nightmare, the same exact nightmare I have had for the past six years: the night that changed everything for me, while also changing nothing at all.

My head starts to pound, and I let out a low, painful moan. I start to get up, but I am being held down by something heavy. I look down and see a large, muscular leg slung over my side. I throw my head back down onto my pillow. I drank myself into a stupor last night, like I do most nights.

I try to recall what all occurred last night. I went to the brothel, where my friend Katie works as a bartender. Really, she is more of an acquaintance.

But tomato, pickle. Same thing, right?

I close my eyes and recall the night.

Untried Origins

I was sitting at the bar, drinking my usual drink, when a man approached me. He had a scraggly kind of beard, and I could smell the smoke and alcohol coming from his crusted lips. He was thin and had little muscle to his figure, and he was stumbling slightly. He leaned on the bar and turned to get a better look at me.

"Hey there, baby doll," the drunk man got out between hiccups. His fowl breath hit me like a slap to the face.

I rolled my eyes. "Get lost."

He hiccups again. "Oh, come on, baby." He reaches over to try and grab or touch my arm, but I snap out and grab his hand before he makes contact with me.

I grip his wrist tightly before bending his hand back, to the point just before it snaps. "Do not touch me."

He yelps, and I release his hand in a quick motion, hoping that was the only motivation he would need to leave me alone. He laughs and hiccups at the same time. "You know you want my fingers in your wet puss."

I snapped. I reached down and grabbed the blade that I always keep in my boot. I slammed the blade down into the man's knee and back out before he even realized what was happening.

"Oops, was that your kneecap?"

I could feel the blade between the tissue and the actual patella of his knee. It was completely severed from his tendons. I had to smirk a little bit at my perfect blow.

His mouth falls open and a screech comes out. "You cu-"

I pulled the blade back. "Finish that sentence, and I will take the other one."

He stumbled away murmuring something under his breath.

I turned back to my drink, chugging the last of my whiskey with my blade still in my hand. I raised my glass up to show Katie I needed another.

"Now that was impressive," a male voice says.

I downed another shot before I responded. "He deserved it." I did not even bother to turn and see who the voice came from, because I did not care.

Katie slides another shot my way. I saluted her before throwing that one back just as quickly.

I try to remember anything past that, but it gets fuzzy after the fourth or fifth shot Katie gave me. I turn my head to the side to see who is attached to the leg wrapped around me.

Please don't be ugly. Please don't be ugly.

I relax a bit when I recognize the man. He is a local blacksmith, a few shops down from my little apartment that I now call home in the mortal realm of Erathina.

I believe his name is Dale or Drake... something along those lines. It starts with a D.

Apparently, it ended with a D for me, I thought to myself, laughing just a little.

Dale / Drake stirs a little at my quiet laughter. I freeze, not wishing to wake him up, at least not until I get my head a little clearer.

He is a decent looking guy: burly, with a shaggy, short black beard and lean muscles from working in the heat, bending metal daily.

I move his leg over gently, pulling the covers off myself and standing. I glance down at myself. This is not my nightshirt.

I strip out of the oversized shirt and walk over to my dresser. I hear Drake moving around. Yeah, Drake sounds right to me. I take a quick glance over my shoulder.

He is propped up on his elbow with one leg bent upright, blanket covering most of the family jewels but allowing me to see the rest of him.

"Well, that is quite an amazing sight to wake up to," he says.

I bet. I am standing here completely naked.

I turn back around and reach into the top drawer of my dresser to grab a pair of cotton pants and a thin strapped top. I close that drawer and reach into the second drawer to pull out a white matching set of undergarments. I quickly and quietly dress. I have stopped relying on my magic a lot since I got to Erathina. I also found a way to conceal my wings. They bring too much attention to me.

When I am done, I make my way back over to bed.

"Look, Drake, last night was last night. No need to repeat, unless called upon, and no reason to hang around this morning."

Untried Origins

Better to get this conversation out of the way so I can have my bed back.

He laughs deeply, and it makes all the muscles in his abdomen flex. He is an attractive male, but he is a *human* male, something I want nothing to do with other than a quick romp in the sheets.

"Well, Allison, my name is Alex, to start." He grins and huffs at the same time.

I laugh mockingly at that. "Okay, I apologize for not knowing the name of the man I bumped into at the local brothel."

I was at the brothel simply because I wanted the cheap booze I get from Katie. She is the friend I party and drink with to keep reality away in this little town. I roll my eyes at him. Alex tugs at my arm to sit back down. He is a human, though, so the tug feels like a child's tug to me.

I turn back to him.

"What? I do have things to get done, and I am sure you have things of your own."

He lets go of my arm. "I was not at the brothel looking to pay for a whore. Okay?"

I narrow my eyes. "First off, do not call them that. Some of them have no choice. Second off, I do not care. This," I point my fingers between me and him, "is literally nothing more than a one-time drunken night." I do not do more than that; I never will again.

I bend down, snatch his clothes off the floor, and throw the shirt and pants to him.

"You seem like a nice enough male; you will find a nice female. It just will not be me." I cross my arms over my chest, staring at him, waiting.

He huffs again, throwing the little amount of the blanket still on him off, puts his clothes on, then heads for the door. He gives me one last look, and I give him a shrug of my shoulder in a "What did you expect?" kind of look. He rolls his eyes, turns the doorknob, and is out of my room.

This time, I am the one huffing.

I relax a little, having my room to myself again. If you can really call these rooms. It is a small apartment with a bed, one nightstand, and a single dresser with a mirror. The bathing room is a sink, a standing shower that has a perpetual ring of dirt around it, and a toilet. Since I had grown up with maids everywhere and don't really know the first thing about how to clean things properly, it stays pretty messy in here.

Clothes are thrown over every surface, and empty food containers that I really need to take out are piled up in a small waste bin by the door.

This has been my home for the past four years. It sits on top of a small bakery, so it smells heavenly throughout the day. That is the reason I selected it in the first place. I walk over to the mirror attached to my singular dresser and survey the damage of last night's partying.

My eyes have smudged kohl all around them, and the dark circles under them make me look half dead. I do not sleep much these days, and the circles have become normal to me. At least my lips are not smeared terribly with leftover lip coloring. My long black hair is in a messy ponytail slung over my shoulder, parts of it sticking out in every way imaginable. I already know it is going to take me half the morning to brush all the knots out of it.

My eyes travel down to where my thinly strapped shirt hangs slightly over my left shoulder, showing a small portion of the tiny blade tattoo a crone gifted me with, a gift I had not asked for. The tattoo is my constant reminder of that terrible night so many years ago. It sits right underneath my collarbone and runs the length of it. It is a small, solid black blade with a handle holding a small red stone.

I try my best to hide it. I hate to look at it. I hate any reminder of that horrible night, when my best friend betrayed me so deeply that I left with nothing but the dress I had on and that stupid matching blade tattoo. I keep the blade on me still to this day, though. It calls to me. I tried to rid myself of the stupid thing many times, but I never can. I can never face her again after that night, not knowing what I know now.

Not knowing I was never going to reach the expectations of everyone around me. It was easier to leave, it was easier to give them what they wanted. Sometimes, I think of returning, but I shut those thoughts down, because I am not ready to face the truth.

    I gained nothing that night. Not an ounce more of power, not a bonded best friend, nothing. I lost everything. She gained everything. My kingdom. My father's respect. She gained everything that was my damn birthright. She took it all with a smile on her face, and I hate her more every single day for it. She is the one they so desperately wanted.

Chapter 18

MADIS

I sit up straight with my shoulders back, trying with everything in me to look like the perfect image of royalty while listening to Commander Amos talk. He is one of those men who takes a lifetime to get to the point of anything. My father, Commander Pike, finally chimes in, and I try not to show my relief.

"Commander, what exactly are you trying to tell us?"

Commander Amos sucks in a breath after his long-winded speech and finally says, "Hollows from Area One and Area Seven have been found getting through the veil into Erathina. There have also been reports of them attacking other Demons courts within this realm unprovoked."

The entire room gets a little more tense. Hollows cannot get through the veil; they were tethered to this realm long ago. The Hollows do not have souls of their own, so the veil should rip their forms to shreds. You cannot be present in the mortal realm without a soul. The Hollows would wreak havoc throughout the mortal realm if they gained access. That many souls ripe for the picking would lead to a blood bath, and our worlds would be jolted out of balance. It would cause an all-out war between worlds. Hollows take souls to claim as their own, unlike demons, who claim them to forever be damned here in Inferis.

King Braxton is at the head of the table to my left, my now mentor of sorts, and speaks up. "That is not possible. Hollows cannot cross the veil."

The king is looking worn down these days. His hair is completely gray and falling out in patches all over his head. He has never been the same since that night, something shifted in him. His magic has been fading swiftly.

Although I agree with the king that Hollows cannot easily cross the veil, I will still be looking into this. I do not dismiss things so quickly. Plus, I have been hearing whispers of this for a while now.

Commander Amos starts to speak again. "Your Highness, I have reports..."

The king lifts his hand into the air, and the Commander shuts his mouth.

"I am tired of this. We can continue at the next council meeting."

Commander Amos goes to speak again. "But sir-"

"Silence," King Braxton screams so loudly, I cannot help the little wince from his voice jolting my eardrums.

He slams his hands on the table as he stands, vibrating everything on top of it that wasn't already shaking from the power of his voice. "Everyone out."

Everyone, including myself, stands, gives a swift bow, and starts for the door.

The king grabs my wrist and states very firmly, "Not you. Sit." The grip on my wrist is not painful, but also not completely comfortable.

It is not a request; it is a command. Not that anyone ever gives me a request. For anything. *Ever.* Everything in my world is a demand or an order that must be followed. I will never know how Kaisera ever stood up to this man.

She was always the brave one.

"Yes, your Majesty," I say and curtsy the best I can without having both of my hands.

The king waits for everyone to exit the room before he releases my hand and gestures for me to sit before sitting back down himself.

"Madis, you seem less than pleased today. Is it this issue with the Hollows? Because I can assure you, it is a lie." He says this like he wants me to believe he is telling the truth, even though something in his face tells me he is not so sure himself. He looks so defeated all the time; it is hard to tell what his true thoughts are.

"No, your Highness. Training kept me up late; I am just a little tired. A little rest, and I will be fine." The lie slides off my tongue like I have said it a thousand times, because I have. My training is not tiresome. The training I do nowadays consists of studying histories and laws along with political strategies.

That is not why I'm always exhausted. No, my nights are usually spent looking for Kaisera. I have not gotten even a glimpse of where she might be or what might have happened to her. Most believe her to be dead, but I know in my very being she is not. Kai could not be killed so easily.

After that terrible night with that horrible crone, Kaisera vanished. We had awakened after the Blood Binding, and she had looked at me like I had ripped out a vital organ. She had snapped her fingers and vanished. She left me here to deal with the mess.

Left me alone. Again.

The king, on the other hand, took it as a sign she had given up her throne and named me the new heir within a week of her disappearance. I did not want it then, nor do I enjoy playing this role now. Not even after six years of playing it.

The king searches my face, then stands abruptly from the head of the table. "Fine. I will be leaving tomorrow night to visit the other Areas to ensure they have not fallen for this blatant lie of Hollows accessing Erathina through the veil. I will also be seeing which of the other Areas kings might be a suitable match for you."

If the Hollows gained access to Erathina, Inferis would be blamed for it, and that could result in a war. A war we could maybe win if it was just against Erathina, but if Valkeria got involved to save their innocents, it is a war we would lose.

He begins to walk away, then pauses, although he doesn't turn around. He speaks to me through my thoughts. "I know you do not love how you got to be my heir, but you are now. You will be the queen, and you will marry a king. I demand you take your duty as heir more seriously and stop searching for her. I know your father will see to it that this demand is met."

My only response aloud is, "Yes, your Highness."

The king knows exactly how my father would see that his orders are met.

He huffs like that is not the correct answer. With the king, I am not sure there ever is a correct answer. He turns around this time to say, "You will be overseeing everything in my absence for the next few days. Think of this time as a trial run."

No, my father will be overseeing, I will be doing his bidding, which is not much different from when I will be married off and forced to rule under my husband.

I guess it is a trial run, then.

"Yes, your Highness."

He turns and starts for the door again, leaving me with my head bowed, twiddling my thumbs.

He speaks to me through his gift as he walks out of the meeting room. "Stop looking for her, Madis. I mean it. She is long gone." Then, he slams the door behind him.

I let out a long, slow breath and count to five. I hate these meetings. I hate politics. I am a warrior, built for battles, not a damn bargaining chip. I command armies, not a kingdom.

I look around the stale room. A large, stone, rectangular table sits in the dead center of the room, with large, wooden, highbacked chairs around it. It has no windows and no decorations. It is a room for conversations with the council and advisors, and that is it. This room has only one way in or out, and it is always guarded by two guards when in use.

I turn to the doors where the guards stand. Major Tribax stands in his black uniform, holding his spear out at arms; one arm behind his back and one arm stretched out with a long, sharp spear out away from his body. He keeps his eyes straight and refuses to look my way.

I ran into Tribax on the training field the day after everything happened. I was a confused wreck, and he comforted me that entire night. He even helped devise a plan to look for Kaisera, whom he had never gotten a chance to meet. I never got the chance to tell Kaisera more about him. She did not even get the chance to learn his name.

It did not matter in the end, though. The pull we seemed to have toward each other when we first met was gone the day after the failed Blood Binding. I still wanted him close; I still wanted a friend, but just a friend.

Everything changed after the king named me the heir. I would never be allowed to be with a captain in the royal army. Even though Tribax had been promoted to major three years ago, he was still forbidden. It is now my duty and honor to do what is best for the kingdom, and being with anyone other than the man the king selects will not happen. My heart has no place in this kingdom or this world.

This part is non-negotiable, and I will do the one thing I never wanted to do: marry for anything other than true love. Tribax hates me for this. He feels I did not even try to fight for myself.

I remember the night I told him.

"I must marry to benefit the Kingdoms of Inferis," I had told him.

I could have sworn I saw his features shift and his teeth lengthen just a bit in his anger. Then he said, "You aren't willing to fight for yourself, not even with all the strength you hold?"

I had responded with what I still felt to be the truth. "I do not have a choice."

"We always have a choice, Madis," Tribax responded.

"Why do you care so much? I know you can feel our connection has been broken." I wanted to yell, I wanted to scream. I had just lost my best friend, and my world was changing too quickly for me to grasp everything that was happening.

"Even if the connection is broken, I still believe you have to stand up for yourself. Can you not feel the power you hold?"

Untried Origins

"You do not understand," I tried, but Tribax would not have it.

"I cannot fight for someone not willing to fight for themselves," he said before walking away.

His words should have hurt me more than they did, but in the end, I felt only the hurt from Kaisera's disappearance. He had walked away from me, and I had turned away from him.

The connections and bond Kaisera and I had formed over years of friendship seem shattered. I still feel the need to protect her. I still worry for her, and I have this gut feeling that the whole world has been off kilter since that night. I know Inferis needs her back. I need her back.

I walk toward the door. As I approach the guards, they lift their weapons back into the ready position to show their respect.

I lean over toward Tribax and whisper, "Can you at least look at me, Tribax?"

"Only if it is a command, Princess." He says this while also grinding down roughly on his teeth. He hates that I allowed my father and the king to change so much of me. Gone is the girl in her battle gear. Now, in her place, is a princess in tulle gowns and jewels. It isn't the jewels or pretty dresses that get under his skin. It is that he believes I am not being true to myself, but Tribax knowns nothing of what I must do. The pretty things I am forced to wear are the least of the things demanded of me.

I sigh lightly and softly. "I would never command you."

He grits his teeth, as if that is not the answer he wanted. "Then I will have to decline, Princess."

I glance at him one more time, his strong jaw clenched, his knuckles white on the spear as he holds it tight to his body. His rugged masculine features make him stunningly handsome. I turn back to the door and walk out, Nija appears on my shoulder, snuggling into my neck.

"Hello there, my dear friend," I say in greeting.

My only friend.

He lets out a little whimper.

"I know, I hate that you can't be with me in the meeting as well. You know the king isn't a fan of familiars hanging around during meetings; he says you are too distracting." I tuck my fingers under his horned head and give him a little scratch. He purrs with approval in his adorable little dragon way.

I wish Nija could have gotten the chance to meet Tribax's familiar. I believe they would have been dear friends. I have only met the little red fox one time, after the Blood Binding, and I was such a mess that I barely got a good look at him. I've seen the little fox running around the training yard next to Tribax since then. He trains right beside him, as if they were of the same mind. They are incredible to watch as they work as one to take down each opponent.

It is not like Nija. He can sense my distress and give assistance, of course, but he does not know my exact thoughts and wants. The way Tribax and his familiar move is like they know each other's next move.

As I make the long walk back to my room, I place my fingers on the black dagger with the red stone tattooed just below my right collarbone. It has become my comfort to feel that tattoo just slightly raised above my skin. I do not know how, but I know some way or another, it connects me to Kai. That's one thing I will not listen to the king on: I will not stop searching for her. The entirety of Inferis searched for her daily in the beginning. Now, I only trust a few people to look for her, and I've sent them to Erathina to continue the search, demons I know will not return without Kaisera. We are just not looking in the right places.

Yet.

I know we will find her, and I know it will be soon.

Chapter 19
ALLISON

After the night I had with Drake—wait, I mean Alex—I want to jump back in bed and fall into a deep sleep, but I have a job. I left with nothing but that damn dress that night, and it had only gotten me a few coins in my pocket, which were used to buy clothes I could actually walk around in. I have to pay for my rooms, food, and alcohol somehow. Of course, I missed being pampered, but that's not enough to make me want to return to Inferis.

I straighten out my hair, wipe the kohl from around my eyes, and brush my teeth. Then, I hurry down the stairs into the bakery. The sweet old man who runs the shop, Mr. Si, always leaves me something tasty. Sometimes, it is buttery biscuits, spiced bread if the season allows, or even a slice of sweet strawberry cake. He tells me he finds the little treats not suitable for sale, but I know he just finds me adorable. I see my loaf sitting on the counter, a nice warm chocolate chip bread roll. I swipe the mouthwatering treat and run back toward the front door.

"Slow down, Alli. That is to be enjoyed," Si calls.

I bite off a mouthful of it, dramatically rolling my eyes to the back of my head and chewing overly slowly. It really is delicious, but the dramatics are for his benefit.

He shakes his head and laughs at me before shooing me off with his hands, turning around to head back into the kitchen.

I turn fully, walk out the door, and head to the jewelry shop where I work. I walk down the busy streets, pulling off pieces of bread and eating it slowly.

The streets in the Mortal Realm differ so much from Inferis. No human souls suffering, no pranks being played. There are fights every now and then, though they are nothing like the bloodthirsty fights in my beloved home. I cannot lie and say I have not used my demon abilities here to cause a few of those fights to happen. What can I say, it helps me miss my old home a little less. I defiantly miss how much more open they are about sex in Inferis. However, I have not used my powers for that. Mortals frown greatly upon open acts of affection here in Erathina.

I know that sounds insane, but I am a demon, and we like to act on our impulses and explore the greater sins. That bitch never enjoyed what our home had to offer.

I do not know how I ever felt so close to her. I stop that train of thought as quickly as it comes. I refuse to ruin my day by thinking of her.

Out of habit, my hand moves to touch the left side of my collarbone where that blasted dagger tattoo lays.

I put those thoughts away and continue to take in everything on my way to Elena's jewelry shop, where I have been working for three years now.

People on the streets are polite and use their best manners as I pass by them, always giving a head nod or a simple "good day." The grass is green, and the flowers are blooming everywhere. It smells wonderful here, and I enjoy the changing of the seasons. It is late spring now, starting to turn warmer from the summer heat. I love the heat. My first winter here was the absolute worst, and I quickly learned I could not go any farther north than where I started. I have been traveling farther south throughout Erathina ever since, trying to stay away from any areas where there is a chance of snow.

Shocking, I know. A desert demon does not like the snow.

The jewelry shop is only a few shops down from the bakery, so I make it there fairly quickly. My ability to bend objects to my will makes me perfect for this job. Customers can explain or show me an image of the way they want things to look on all types of jewelry, and I simply will the metal and stones into their image. Humans in this realm know little about demons and my world, but they do know we exist. I doubt any here has even guessed what or who I am. My wings had stirred too many conversations and raised too many questions. Very few creatures of this realm have wings, so it was a blessing from the goddess that I was able to hide them so easily.

I walk through the front door to find Elena, already helping a customer. Elena has become my closest friend, and the reason I have stayed in this particular town for so long. If Katie is my escape from reality, Elena is who brings me back to it.

She stands with her freckle-covered arms on the counter, a bright smile on her face, showing the customer a long gold necklace with small pink gems spaced down it. Her short, strawberry red hair frames the sides of her face on one side and is tucked behind her pointed Fae ear on the other. Elena's face is covered in freckles, and on top of the freckles she has tribal-like tattoos along her cheekbones, forehead, and down her nose. The tattoos are just a few shades darker than her freckles, causing her dark blue eyes to really pop.

Elena is dressed in a green, fitted, long-sleeved dress with a chestnut brown corset top, paired with brown riding boots. She looks more like the princess of the tiny sprites that live in the forests here than an incredibly powerful Fae.

She peers up from the piece she is showing them. "You are late. Again."

I laugh. "I am late every day. You might as well change my hours."

She replies quickly, "Then you would show up even later. It's a good thing you are good at this. Otherwise, I would be forced to let you go."

I laugh even louder as I make my way over to the counter. "Yeah right. You like seeing my pretty little ass and talking to my pretty little face too much."

I reach over and place a quick soft kiss on her cheek.

She shows me a toothy grin, a hint of one of her elongated canines showing. "You aren't wrong." she rolls her eyes. "There is a list on the table in the back. Get started."

"Right away, ma'am," I say with the fakest of sincerity.

Elena flips me off. I wiggle my fingers in a little wave and head towards the back workshop to get started.

My day has gone by in a blur of bending items and dealing with customers. Elena and I are opening a bottle of Fae Wine and chatting about a mouthy customer we had dealt with early that day when the chime of the door pulls our attention.

I start to stand, hoping whoever is at the door does not keep me from my plans of drinking and relaxing tonight.

Elena stands and says, "I got this one. I will let them know the shop isn't taking any more orders until tomorrow."

I shrug my shoulders and put my feet up on the desk. I am not going to beg to work more. I had found out in my time here that if humans drink the Fae wine, they will quite literally dance until their legs give out. I look at the drink in my hand and giggle a little at the memory of seeing those humans and how much they enjoyed it, even though chances where they could not walk for weeks after. I start to sip my wine, then almost spit it out when I hear a voice that sparks my interest.

"Oh, I am sorry, ma'am. I saw the lights on, and we assumed you were still open," the familiar female voice says. Elena must have told them to come back later. That voice gives me a sense of nostalgia. I just cannot place it completely.

Untried Origins

Elena responds, "You both are more than welcome to come back tomorrow."

"Absolutely. We heard you have the best ring maker in all the realms!" the small feminine voice speaks.

I almost drop my wine glass. I set it on the table and sprint from the backroom of the jewelry shop. I yell, louder than necessary seeing we are in a small shop showroom. "Wait!"

The small-framed female turns around, and my heart almost stops. I know my jaw is close to reaching the ground. She looks just as shocked as I am.

"Ellie?" I whisper as a tear starts to form in my eye. My lady's maid and seamstress from Inferis. A friend from my life I had left behind long ago.

"Princess!" Ellie screeches.

She looks just the same as the last time I saw her, just as adorable, in a light blue sunflower dress and adorable ballerina flats. Her mousy brown hair is tied back, with pieces loosely falling around her sweet face, her rosy, red cheeks bring out the red tint in her brown eyes. She is still the most un-demon-looking demon I have ever seen.

Elena repeats, confused. "Princess?" I turn to look at her. There is an unreadable look on her face, a mix between confusion and maybe fear. I've never told her much about my past. She knows I am a demon, but not why I have chosen to stay here in Erathina.

I will have to explain this all to her, but for now, I want to hug someone of my own kind. Someone from a past life.

I turn back to Ellie and take off at a jog, reaching for her, but a hulking male, steps in front of her and bares his teeth just a bit. I stop short and look up at the male, with his shaggy brown hair and boyish face, even with the deep scowl on it.

"Umm, excuse me. Can you please move over? I would like to see my friend," I say with as much attitude as I can muster, which, for me, is a fuck ton.

He stands there, with his bulking mass, staring at me and not budging one bit. I realize this male was a guard from the castle. *Mica*. I take him in fully. He is in tight-fitted dark pants, black boots, and a navy blue, loose collared shirt, and he has an angry look on his face.

I give him the same glare right back.

Ellie's small hand reaches around and grabs his massive bicep, pushing him softly to the side. "Mica, it's fine. I know her. She was a friend."

I caught the "was" part, but I did not comment.

He lets loose a low growl. "We do not know why she fled, or if she has been plotting with the other Areas. I will not have her run at my mate."

"Mate! Oh! Congratulations, Ellie!"

Mates are so rare with our kind, because your souls must be perfectly aligned in every way. Literally soul mates, you also must be open to the merging of your souls as one.

So, that would always be a no for me.

I go to pass Mica again, but he stiffens. I look back up at him. "Either you move, or I make you." I'm already starting to reach for the dagger in my boot.

Mica looks back at Ellie and she nods her head. He begrudgingly steps aside, and I not so subtly smirk at him.

I fling my arms around Ellie in a tight hold. "Oh, how I have missed you, my sweet friend."

She hugs me back just as tightly. "I have missed you as well, Princess."

When we pull out of the hug, Ellie looks at me in confusion. "Excuse me, your Majesty, I do not mean to pry, but where are your wings?"

I toss my head back in a laugh, adjusting my shoulders and readying myself for the weight of my wings. I have gotten used to hiding them in my time here in Erathina.

I visualize two small holes near my shoulder blades and snap my fingers to cut a hole in my shirt so that my wings do not rip it open completely when I let them loose. I take a step back to give myself room and let out my night black wings, stretching them as far as I can in the little showroom. I let out an audible groan of relief as their familiar weight settles into me.

I hear Elena gasp over my shoulder, but Ellie's smile grows. My wings are too recognizable here in the mortal realm, and to be honest, the mortal realm's furniture is never very accommodating for them. When my wings are contracted into my back, you can hardly see them. To mortal eyes, they would believe I had a fading wing tattoo down the entire length of my back. To a more powerful creature such as a demon or Fae, they look like an iridescent outline of my exact wings, and you can see the power radiating from them.

I've occasionally gone out at night to fly when the urge has hit me. I still loved to fly but keeping them in my back has been a convenience I hadn't known I needed.

"Leave it to you, Princess, to find a way to cheat. You always have," Ellie says with a smirk.

I give her the most devilish smirk back. No sense in denying it.

Elena clears her throat loudly. "Um, not that this isn't touching, but are you sure you have the right girl? Cause Allison here doesn't exactly scream royalty, although the wings are quite the surprise." Elena is throwing and waving her hands in the air dramatically. "Actually, the wings are making me question *everything!*" Her gaze moves away from my wings and lands firmly on my face. She looks hurt, but at the same time, there is an expression there that I have never seen before. *Understanding or maybe guilt?*

I can't be sure. Elena has always been overly dramatic with her features, and she is very good at talking with her body and hands.

"I think you have some major explaining to do, Alli," Elena says as she crosses her arms over her chest and taps her foot comically on the ground.

I chuckle at Elena. I get a "hhmmff" noise out of her for that chuckle, plus a shake of her head no, indicating she is not going to allow me to get away with this tonight.

Ellie scrunches her eyebrows together. "Allison? Are you tired of your first name?"

I narrow my eyes and scrunch my lips together at Ellie, in hopes of keeping her from saying any more. She shrugs her shoulders upward and mouths "Sorry" silently. I turn back to look at Elena, preparing myself for this conversation.

Elena speaks again. "Alli, please fill me in on what's going on. Who are these people?"

I see Mica shift uncomfortably next to Ellie. *Ugh, overprotective males are the worst when they aren't protecting you.*

I turn all my attention to Elena. Well, damn, there goes my night of fun drinking and relaxing.

"Elena, you are going to want to go get that wine and a couple more chairs for my friends. Then, I will tell you all about the Demon Princess from Inferis."

Chapter 20
MADIS

I am startled awake by the sound of a siren blaring through the Area and a loud banging on my door. I jump up and reach for my daggers on the nightstand before remembering my mother made me move them to the armory. She made it clear that royalty had guards to protect them; they did not need weapons. I reach for my robe, throwing it around my shoulders quickly.

BANG! BANG! BANG! The knocking continues, but this time, it comes with a loud male voice yelling through the door. "Princess, you're needed immediately! There is an urgent matter!" I do not recognize the voice.

I throw the door open to find Tribax standing there next to another guard, one I don't recognize and whose voice I think I just heard. Tribax has a strange look on his face, one that might have possibly been a bit of joy.

I look to Tribax in worry. "What's going on?"

He turns his back to me and starts to walk. The other guard goes to usher me out the door and says hastily, "Please, your Majesty, just follow Major Xanadriel. He will explain everything when we get to a more secure location."

I sigh out a breath of laughter at that. *I highly doubt it.*

Tribax turns and pins me with a stare when I do not move.

I throw my hands up. "Fine, let me some of my weapons and—" I don't get a chance to finish my sentence before Tribax cuts me off.

"We do not have time for all of that. Here." He tosses me one of the swords strapped to his back. I catch it with ease, enjoying the feel of a blade in my hand.

The king has not been allowing me to train the way I like to, and he says carrying a large sword is not proper for royals. I am growing tired of his rules for royals, and I want to rule to the best of my ability. I can't fail my Area.

"There. Now you are armed. Let's go." They usher me away.

We walk at a swift pace, almost a full-blown jog. I realize we're running straight toward one of the councilors' rooms where we always have our meetings. When we get there, they throw open the doors and I walk in to see the council in the same state as I am; in night clothes, hair, and faces a mess from their rush to get here. Each one of the council members has a guard standing at their backs. *This cannot be good.*

The king is still on his tour of the Areas in search of my perfect match and trying to convince the other Areas that the Hollows are nothing to worry about, so I assume my role as leader and take the seat at the head of the table. As soon as I sit, the rest of the council follows.

Commander Amos, the talker that he is, speaks first. "Princess, what is the meaning of this?"

Tribax, who has taken the position directly to my right, says a little too proudly, "It is no longer Princess. It is Queen Madis Malias. The King is dead."

Chapter 21
KAISERA

    I spent the next hour explaining who I really am to Elena. I trust her. I've kept such a low profile here in Erathina to keep anyone from dragging me back, but Elena has become a close friend. She has her own secrets I hope she will share with me one day.

    Elena is a powerful Fae, too powerful to be just a jewelry shop owner. She has gifts of the tongue. When she speaks words with a touch of her power behind them, you must listen. It's close to the abilities of sirens, the difference being that she does not need to feed off your emotions. Elena can literally talk people into doing her bidding.

    I remember one time, a customer got out of control in the shop and threatened to take off the tips of Elena's Fae ears. She simply whispered into his ear that he wanted to do that exact same thing to himself. He did, except he was a human, so he took the whole top half of his ear off, and since Elena had charmed him into doing it, he thanked her for her kind words and left. There are still bloodstains we could not get out of the rug near the coin drawer from that day.

After telling Elena everything, I only have one thought running through my head. I do not want to go back to that place to watch Madis take everything that was mine, to that place where I got pushed aside. I still want what was my birthright to an extent, but I have no reason to return.

I'm not needed.

I catch myself rubbing at my tattoo as I tell the story of what happened the night of the Binding to Mica, Ellie, and Elena. I do not say the things that haunt my nightmares every night, just that I had known after that night that Madis would be taking my spot on the throne. The crone showed me the things that would come, and then she left me to my nightmares. She showed me what really lies within Madis's heart, and it was not a strong will to protect me.

Ellie lets out a big "Wow!" then says, "Princess, Madis sent us to look for you six years ago. We cannot return without you." She sounds sad about that last part.

Then it hits me: they must not be able to return because they do not possess the power in their blood to return, or the king of the Vanta Pits did not see fit to grant their request. They came here knowing they could not return without finding me, or at least another demon who could give up more of their power to help them return, and those are very rare.

"Ellie, why would you two do that?" I say, shaking my head. "I cannot and will not be returning. This is my home now."

Mica, who has been so quiet during everything, speaks up. "Your Highness."

I hold up my hand, "It is just Kai, you were just staring me down like you were willing to fight me. No need for manners now." I smirk just a little at him.

Mica continues, ignoring everything I just said. "Madis sent us because she has no idea you ran. She believes the crone did something to you that night. Shortly after your disappearance, the King did name her heir, but I do not believe it was Madis's plan."

Untried Origins

Even if I had known Madis would take my crown from me, it is still a challenging thing to digest, that it has truly happened.

What does that make me?

Mica keeps going. "She has guards from every Area looking for you. She even sent them to the Vanta Pits and to Area Five to hunt down the crone who cast the spell."

"But why? Madis got everything after that night." I question them both.

They look at each other. Then, Ellie shrugs. "You will have to ask her that yourself."

I can tell silent words have passed between them, and there is more than what is being said aloud. The room grows silent as everyone exchanges looks with each other.

I cannot face what I left behind. I cannot be unwanted again.

I am about to tell them that I am sorry, but that just is not going to happen, when we hear a piercing scream, a scream I know does not belong in this world. Everyone jumps up at once. Mica slides Ellie behind him, reaching to his side for the short sword resting there.

I look at Elena. "What is that about?"

She shrugs her shoulders then throws her hands up. "How am I supposed to know? I am sitting next to you. We know the same amount of information!" All of this is said while the yelling continues loud as banshee outside of the shop. I cannot help the eye roll I give Elena.

Another scream comes, this time with a slight tremor of the ground. I cannot just stand here and wait to hear about what is happening. I bolt for the door with Elena, Ellie, and Mica right behind me. Elena and I are out the door first, and I am having a tough time believing what I am seeing in front of me. Elena gasps, then turns back, running into the shop at a full sprint.

I guess she isn't going to stick around to help.

Hollows of all shapes and sizes are charging toward the town. In the evening light, the only parts of them that can be seen are their glowing red eyes and the red and orange glow that comes through the cracks in their skin. The Hollows are at the far end of the town, almost on the outskirts, and they seem pissed.

Letting out their loud screams, they sound like dying animals and people.

"Ellie, go back into that shop. Find somewhere sturdy and hide. I will come back for you," Mica says.

He places his hands on her face in the gentlest of ways. Ellie shakes her head up and down slowly. "Alright, I love you. Be safe."

Mica leans down and places a soft kiss on Ellie's mouth. He releases her and nods his head back toward the shop, "Go," and she runs back in.

"Mica, you have a couple extra of those short swords?" I ask with a little too much humor in my voice. After this night, I could use a good fight.

He grunts and reaches into his boot, pulling out a small crystal dagger. He tosses it over to me. "That is all I have. Would anyone in this town keep Hollow-killing weapons around?"

Elena runs back out the door, carrying a large wooden bow and a quiver of arrows. "What do you mean by 'Hollow killing?' Do regular swords not work?" Her blue eyes are the size of saucers.

My gaze is stuck on the bow in her hand for a second. It is beautifully carved, one that looks like it has been used for years. My questions about where it came from and why she has it have to wait.

I grin in excitement, which earns me a hard punch in the arm from her.

"Ouch! Damn, okay. No. We need crystal weapons. They do not have to be solid crystal like this one." I show her the dagger Mica has just handed me. "But they have to be at minimum crystal-infused and, luckily for you guys, I slept with the blacksmith last night!"

Elena rolls her eyes and puts her hands on her hips. "How does sex with a blacksmith help us?"

My smile grows so big, I can feel my eyes scrunching up. Not everyone in this realm knows what crystal weapons can do to a demon and would believe the crystal is for decoration, but a blacksmith would know their purpose. "Because I know where he keeps the high-end crystal weapons, and I can do this."

Untried Origins

I snap my fingers and I appear inside the blacksmith's shop to look for what I need. I spot two more swords and a quiver of crystal-tipped arrows. The people of this world might not know of Hollows, but the underworld has always been a place to fear. People who buy crystal weapons are superstitious and believe all demons will rise one day to claim this world. Most do not worry about such things, but most blacksmiths keep these kinds of weapons around for the right clientele. I knew Alex would have some, because the governor of this town has never been shy about his hatred for the underworld of Inferis' creatures. I snatch them up quickly and snap my fingers again, appearing back in front of the jewelry shop.

"Here," I toss the crystal arrows over to Elena. She snatches the quiver out of the air with more grace than I would have believed her to have. "Go to the roof. Aim center mass. It's always best if you do two to the chest and one to the head. Just to be sure." I say to Elena.

She starts to turn toward the door but stops. She grabs my hand and pulls me into a hug. I lean into it. Something about Elena always makes me feel a bit warmer.

"Don't die," she says. "Cause it's only fair that I get to kill you after you decided to hide so much from me." She winks.

I laugh and shake my head. "Okay. Deal."

Elena takes off back into the shop to head up to the roof. I look back at the outskirts of town. The Hollows have entered my tiny town and are starting to wreak havoc, shredding though this town and anyone they can reach. The screams of the creatures and the mortals echo off the buildings.

Mica and I take off in that direction. My arms and legs are pumping as fast as they can go. I am out of shape from drinking alcohol, eating bread, and pure lack of exercise, but muscle memory is an amazing thing, and my body knows exactly what it needs to do.

I run at the first demon in my sights, an ugly thing with a head shaped like horns, and eyes within those horns. Its mouth hangs wide open, showing off its numerous rows of sharp teeth. The thing has long arms, legs, and a craning neck, and its skin looks like the cracking bark of a pine tree.

Fuck, these things are ugly.

It runs at full force for me. I know it will try to go for my head, as Hollows like to look into your eyes while they suck out your soul. It goes high as I go low, sliding under it and across the ground, one leg stretched out in front of me and one bent, making it easier when I pop right back up and spin around before it even has time to realize I have done so.

I strike, my borrowed short sword driving just to the left of the spinal cord, striking right into where its heart should be. The Hollow screams ring out loudly. I can hear another one screaming to my left and notice Mica has taken one down in a similar way to me. I guess we would have similar fighting styles, seeing we both received our training at the DWA, even if I never really took mine seriously.

I barely have the chance to remove my dagger when another Hollow grabs my shoulder. I spin under its hold, coming around while thrusting my sword up into its head. Thick black and red blood leaks out around my sword. I rip out my sword, knowing that the suctioning sound will haunt my dreams for the next few nights at the very least.

The people of this town who are able to have started to try and fight back. The Governor can be heard screaming that we should have listened to him sooner. I spot the blacksmith Alex attempting to fight. He has skill with a blade, but his strength as a human is no match for the Hollow. I run for him to try and help, but the Hollow swipes out wide and sends Alex's body soaring through the air before it hits a tree, and he falls limp to the ground. He is not dead, just knocked out. I reach the Hollow before he can make a meal out of Alex. He is distracted by his prey, and my blade slices through his neck like butter.

I hear a woman screaming for help a couple buildings down from me. I turn to see what is going on and find that the Hollows have reached the brothel, sucking the soul out of a young girl. You can see the light of her soul being pulled from her body.

Oh, Inferis, no. They have suffered enough in this life.

I take off at a sprint again, realizing I am running out of energy quickly. I throw my shoulder into the Hollow attempting to take the young girl's life and soul from her. It throws him off-balance, and he falls over. It is too late; I am too late. The young girl, with her soft brunette curls and tiny figure, is lifeless, her brown eyes faded and looking into nothing.

Screams are ringing out from everywhere around me, and they are no longer just the screams of the Hollows.

The Hollow I knocked down recovers and grabs at me. He digs his claws deep into my shoulder. My lack of focus cost me. He spins me around, and I investigate his face. His all-black skin has dozens of small white eyes and all of them are looking at me, unblinking.

"Fuck you!" I spit in his face, both figuratively and literally.

He laughs at this. "You will be bowing to us in the end, Princess." His voice is gruff and terrifying.

I look at him in confusion. Since when did these assholes stop to have a conversation before taking a soul?

He must have seen the look on my face, because he tosses his head back, all his tiny eyes shifting to the sky as he laughs loudly at me. It sounds like not one person laughing, but multiple. It is eerie and disturbing.

When he swings his head back, it is to headbutt me squarely in my nose. Everything fades to black.

Chapter 22
MADIS

I might actually be having a heart attack. I cannot breathe. My lungs are caving in. I can hear the faded voices of people speaking, but I cannot make out what is being said.

I can see people moving about, but everything is in a blur.

My face and neck feel like they are heating. That makes my panic spike even more. I can't set this room on fire with this many people in it.

Breathe, Madis. Six counts in. Six counts out. Again.

I coach myself through this like I have done a hundred times without anyone noticing. It is something I taught myself at an incredibly young age; not out of want, but out of need. I cannot think about my childhood right now. That will only make me spiral down further.

Six counts in. Six counts out. One more time.

Now that I can breathe a little better, I need to ground myself.

Untried Origins

What can I feel around me? The chair. I can feel my arms resting on the arms of the chair.

I am here in the councilors' room. I was just told I am now the Queen of Area Six. Of course, I will not truly be queen until there is a coronation. The room is in chaos. People are screaming over the table in all directions.

I have to take control.

I calmly stand and speak. "Everyone, sit down and shut up." I say each word slowly and with authority, the authority I do not feel I have but must act as if I do. I catch a few of the members' attention, but others are still yelling at one another.

I let a little bit of my fire power flow through me, lighting my eyes and my hands.

"Silence!" Everyone stops and looks at me in either awe or fright. "Sit down, councilors, and we can discuss what has occurred."

Everyone still standing finally sits. Commander Amos goes to speak, but I hold up my hand, and his mouth snaps shut. I know that if he got started it would be impossible to get him to stop.

I feel Tribax step in closer to my side, and I gently push him away. Not because I do not want him close, but because if I am to be Queen now, I must be able to stand on my own. I also pray my father did not catch the movement, because he will take it for something it is not.

I try to calm my nerves enough to finally speak after what feels like hours of silence but is probably only a few seconds.

"We will hear what has happened to our king from Major Xanadriel first. Then, and only then, will we discuss what is to happen next."

I do not care so much that the king himself is dead. He had forced decisions on me the same as my father. He may not have been such a brute about it, but it does not change the fact he forced myself and Kaisera into the Blood Binding, or that he forced me to take on her role after she vanished.

He also knew what my father did to me and never tried to step in.

I take several calming breaths, the initial shock of everything slowly starting to simmer away. I look to my father to try and gauge how he is taking this information in. The expression on his face is deeply concerning to me. It is a mixture of rage and something that looks more calculating.

The goddess above herself would have a grim time determining the things that went on in my father's head.

"Major, please tell us what you know about this situation." I turn and look at Tribax directly in his painfully beautiful eyes. I may not feel the connection of any type of passion, but there is still this pull of a much-needed friendship. If he could only see things from my side, he may let that friendship grow. I fear that he believes me to be a part of the problem in this world, to be like my cruel father and my bitch of a mother. My family is well known for the brutal force they take towards everyone and everything.

I am not like them.

I want to shout that exact thing to him.

He turns his attention away from me without hesitation. I think he feels it too, the lack of that connection we once had. I am not sure why we collided so hard only to be pulled away. Is it possible that the blood binding could have broken my connection to everyone? Or was my draw to Tribax wishful thinking?

Tribax takes a small step forward, and I sit back down.

"Everyone in the king's guard and the king himself died," Tribax states. He turns and looks at me with a small tilt to his lips.

My eyes widen, and I hit him with a small death stare. This is not the time for him to be a smartass. Tribax never shared a love for our king, not after the events of the Binding. Something switched in him that night as well; if only he would speak to me so I could know what.

Tribax rolls his eyes and starts again. "The king was attacked by a hoard of Hollows near Area Seven. We received word from King Reign that he found the bodies and the remains of the king's escorts. That is everything we know currently." Tribax's voice is so deep, it is as if he is growling out the information, that little bit of a smile gone from his features.

My father places his hands on to the table, pushing himself up to speak. Everyone looks to me to tell him to sit back down, but

Untried Origins

I know what will happen to me if I disrespect my father in that way. I hold my chin high and nod at him to speak.

I may not want to disrespect my father, but I cannot and will not let the council see me as weak.

He speaks after my light nod. However, I did not miss the twitch of his eye at being given permission by me.

"We will go to Area Seven soon to see what has happened. Hollows do not just attack, and the king would have no problem fighting off a few lesser demons. Something else must have happened to our king." He stares each and every member of the council down, daring anyone to speak a word differently. His fire magic heats the room up a few degrees.

My father is a force to be reckoned with. When he is not punishing me for my attitude or my behavior, or my lack of attitude and behavior, he is punishing his men, anyone who dares to defy or cross him. There is a reason the king selected him to lead his army.

I am all too familiar with my father's punishments. I spent all of my childhood and teen years in my father's favorite room. The king and my mother were the only ones to know of my father's love of my screams. He spent a century training me to always follow his orders without question. The only purpose I serve my father is to see that his will and demands are met. I have shed more than enough blood and tears in his rooms to know not be the one to disappoint him.

I never spoke a word of this to Kaisera. She would not have been able to hold her hot-headed tongue, and my father would have set his sights on destroying her.

This is why I convinced her to do the Binding in the first place. I knew if my father wished it, it would happen, one way or another.

My father's favorite past time now is to remind me that now that she is gone, I truly have no one. I miss Kaisera more at this moment than I ever have. She would not have listened to my father or hers. Yes, King Braxton could put her in her place when needed, but he never lifted a finger to her, and I was glad of that.

Kai has no idea what our fathers put me through for all those years. They let me out of those rooms when they knew I was fully broken and would obey and do as they wish. I never disobeyed them again, for fear of returning to those rooms. I became their puppet to dangle from their strings.

And I hate myself more each day for it.

My father speaks. "Everyone, leave. I must speak to my daughter alone."

Everyone stands and starts for the door. Except Tribax – he stays by my side. My father's eyes leave mine and go over my shoulder to Tribax.

"You too, Major." My father's eyes return to me. He looks pissed, the raging fire in his eyes shining brighter with every second that passes. Even worse, he looks pissed at me. I have been doing everything he wished of me; I have followed his orders to a tee.

I say with my chin slightly lowered. "Tri…I mean Major. I am fine. Leave me."

Tribax turns to fully stand in front of me. "I can stay if you wish, Your Majesty. I am to be your personal guard from here on out."

I glance back at my father to see the rage and fumes boiling over his patience. I hold my chin high and push my shoulders back. With the most commanding tone I can muster and every bit of confidence in me, I look to Tribax. "I am safe with my father, Major. Leave us. Now."

He huffs and shakes his head but leaves me. I watch his every foot fall until the door closes behind him. I almost wish he would have fought to stay by my side, but who am I kidding? Why would he stay? I have given him no indications that I need or want him to stay.

Before my face is fully turned back to my father, a red-hot hand slams across it, knocking me to the ground.

I can already taste the blood leaking into my mouth from the hit.

My father stands towering over me. "How dare you nod to me in order to speak? You may be queen over this Area now that the king is dead, but I will always rule you, girl."

My father takes out a small burgundy pouch that I know too well. He starts to pour the contents into a small pile onto the ground in front of me. The tiny black pebbles look harmless, but I know from too much experience that they are far from it. The black pebbles glisten with infused crystals, crystals that cut easily through demon flesh.

He bends down and takes my face into his hands, just under my jaw, and squeezes my cheeks together, forcing my mouth to pucker.

"Kneel," he says, with a dark fire building in his eyes as he pulls me to the pile by just my face.

I move to do as he commands, knowing that refusing or fighting back will only make this worse for myself. I slowly kneel onto the sharp little pebbles, the sharp edges biting into my knees. I am in nothing but my nightshirt, shorts, and a thin robe. I did not have time to get properly dressed before I was dragged down here, so I have no barrier between my skin and the sharp rocks.

I do not let the pain show through my face. I cannot let him see the pain. He will only punish me more if I let the pain show. I bow my head and place my hands out in front of me, knowing this is how he will want to make me take my punishment.

He walks around me like a happy predator who knows he has his prey ready for slaughter. He takes out his short sword that hangs from his side. I hear the metal sliding out of its sleeve. I cringe, but only internally. He starts another pass before he smacks the flat side of the sword across my knuckles. He does not leave any cuts, just a burning pain.

He says, "Madis, why are you kneeling before me?"

I answer the way I know he wants. "Because this is my place. At your feet."

I hate the words that leave my mouth. I hate the degrading feeling of being down here on my knees. But, I have no choice in this matter. He is my father. I must follow him. He strikes my knuckles again.

"If that is correct, Madis, why would you function as if you are above me?" He starts to circle me again.

Every time he goes out of sight behind me, my nerves shoot up at the fear of not seeing the next attack coming. I can feel the blood starting to drip from my knees as the pebbles dig into my skin from the weight of myself and gravity pushing me down.

"I have no excuses, Father. I deserve this punishment." I try to say it as calmly as possible. The pain of the rocks and the burn of my knuckles are causing my breaths to come a little less evenly than I would like.

He makes another pass around me. *Smack.* Another rap to my already swelling knuckles. This one makes me wince, just slightly. I hear his light huff, and I know he has a smirk of enjoyment on his face from seeing that wince.

I feel my father's hand over my chin again and feel him pulling it up. I look into his black eyes, the ones with the same fire burning in them that I carry in me. The eyes that make it so hard to even look in a mirror.

"You will do well to remember your place, girl. Now, stand." He pulls at my chin to lift me up.

I stand, clasping my hands in front of me. My head bows, waiting for his next command.

I am a trained warrior, a commander of the demon army of Area Six. I know I can try and fight him; I have tried before. My father has an impressive amount of fire power. I am strong and fast, and have fire powers as well, but he has always overpowered me. Those beatings after my attempts to overtake him lasted days, weeks even. Long enough to understand that I should never try again.

He speaks more softly now. "Now, you will go with a group to Area Seven and you will prove that it was King Reign who started the fight and killed our king."

I look at him confused.

His eyes narrow. "You will not ask questions. Will you, Madis?"

I look back down at my hands clenching them together. "No, sir."

"Good. Now go back to your room and clean yourself up before anyone sees you like this. You look absolutely disgusting." The disgust in his voice sounds so genuine.

I bow low and turn to walk away to follow his commands.

I hear him over my shoulder. "Madis, if anyone tries to touch you again, they will die. You are not worthy of another until I command it so."

With that, I walk a little faster to my rooms.

Chapter 23
KAISERA

I feel sandpaper rubbing roughly along my face.
Is that wet sandpaper?
No wait, that can't be right.

I start to feel around to figure out my surroundings. There is not a soft bed under me. I think I can feel wet dirt under my palms. My head is pounding so hard, it is making everything more difficult to figure out. I can feel blood dripping from my healing nose.

I can feel heat coming from somewhere. Now that I can focus a little, I can hear roaring flames and the faint sound of people screaming in the distance.

My eyes pop open. The first thing I see is a small black kitten's face staring at me with bright green eyes. I jump up fast, throwing the kitten off me. My eyes adjust to take in my surroundings fully.

Ka Lee

Everyone is running away from where I am laying and yelling for everyone else to get back. I notice the building in front of me is on fire and slowly starting to collapse.

Without another thought, I snatch up the little black kitten and run as fast as I can away from the destruction, following the crowd of people already doing the same.

Remembering that the Hollows were here, I start to scan around me. I do not see any of them anywhere. I do not think we have taken them all down or stopped them from doing whatever it was they came here to do. So where are they now? The little kitten in my arms is squirming and screeching, not trying to get away but trying to get comfortable in my tight grip, not liking being jostled from my running.

When I am a safe distance away from the building, I stop and turn to look back, just as the building collapses. It is the brothel, the one I had friends in. The one I was trying to protect before the Hollow slammed his head into mine.

A "no" slips out of my mouth soft as a whisper.

My lack of training these past years cost me. No, it cost them. All I can hope is that some of the girls made it out.

This is not just my fault. How could Inferis have let the Hollows out into this world? It is the kings' job to keep these creatures in our world. How did they even get here? Someone would have had to help get them here.

The little kitten crawls up to my face and licks it again with a soft meow.

"At least I was able to save you, little one," I say to the little thing while petting its head. It lets out a soft purr in approval. It reminds me of Nija. I miss that little dragon.

I push the kitten out away from my chest and hold it in front of me to try and get a better look at it.

The little kitten is not just a kitten. It is solid black with bright green eyes and tall narrow ears with little tufts of fur sticking out of the tops of them. He or she? I hold it up to check; her it is. Along her shoulder blades are the tiniest of black, bat-like wings. I have never seen anything like her in my life.

"Hmmm, what are you, little girl?"

She tilts her head to the side and meows her answer to me. Of course, I do not speak winged kitten language, so I have no idea what she just said.

"Well, I believe you saved my life. The least I can do is get you a satisfying meal."

I look back at the building in disgust. I cannot let Inferis get away with this. They are responsible for the destruction of this innocent town. I had no reason to return to my old world, not until those Hollows gave me one. The years here have given me a better understanding of how the worlds work, of what is worth fighting for, and these people are worth fighting for. I have to return to Inferis, if only to see who has allowed this destruction to happen.

I turn from the collapsed building and head for Elena's shop. If the Hollows had a chance at all these souls, they would have taken it, but they had not. From the looks of it, they had simply vanished after doing the minimum damage to this town, which is still enough destruction for years of repairs.

Why had they left?

I push through the crowd and make my way back through the long narrow street to the shop. When I arrive, I see Mica stepping through the door. I take off into a sprint to catch up, or at least I try. My head pounds, and my body feels like it has taken a massive beating.

"Hey!" I holler at him.

He turns, sees it is me, and waits at the door for me to catch up.

I look around as I jog to him and see the ground covered in the remains of Hollows with crystals arrows jutting from their corpses. Elena managed to take out several of them.

"Oh, good. You did not die," he says with a small smile on his face, like he isn't surprised I have lived.

"Yep, I escaped with a new friend, too." I hold the little kitten out for him to inspect.

He jumps back in fear. "Get that thing away from me!"

The kitten lets out a small noise close to a hiss. I think she is offended by that.

"Ummm, you are like 6'6 and three hundred pounds...and scared of a four-pound kitten?" I pull the kitten back to my chest, cradling it.

"That is not a kitten. I am not sure how to describe it, but that thing feels as if Lilith herself came back from the black depths of Inferis and birthed it." He takes even more steps back from me and the kitten.

I laugh loudly and look down at the little thing in my arms. She looks up at me sweetly, relaxing as her big green eyes draw me in.

"I do not know, Mica." Scratching the tiny kitten under her chin, she purrs contently at me. I turn my eyes back to mica. "I am going to keep her and now that you say it, Lilith might be a great name for her!" If she is the spawn of Lilith, I might as well honor that. A large smile spreads across my face.

"Yep, you are with me from now on Lili." I say to her.

I walk through the doorway, and Mica gives me a huge berth to walk past him with the kitten.

"Oh, we are going to have lots of fun, aren't we, Lili?" I pet her little head. I swear I see her give me a little nod, as if she understands every word I say.

She crawls out of my arms when we make it fully into the shop and takes off to explore. Mica finally steps in behind me. Ellie comes out of the back in a sprint and jumps into Mica's arms, kissing him roughly.

I start to walk to the back, where the stairs lead to the roof, to give them a bit of privacy; not that they seem to care much. I hear moans and growling as I make my way to check on Elena. When I round the corner to go up the stairs, she is rounding them to come down. She crashes into me.

"Oh, thank Valkeria you are okay!" she says, holding me in a boa constrictor kind of hug.

I grunt out, "I am glad you are okay too." I hug her as tightly as I can right back.

She releases me and goes straight to pacing, waving her hands around in a panicked way. She nervously tucks her short, strawberry blonde hair behind her pointed freckled ears as her tribal marks move along with her overly exaggerated features.

Untried Origins

"What the Inferis, Alli? What was that? What were those things? I shot a couple like you told me. They bled strange black and burning red blood. They smelled terrible. Are those what demons look like? Of course not, because you are a demon." She finally takes a breath.

I cut in before she could keep going.

"Elena, calm down. Yes, those were demons. They are what we call Hollows, or lesser demons. They need souls, crave them, and yes, they smell of the burnt souls they have taken." I walk over and grab onto her shoulders to still her.

Lilith climbs up the back of my leg and back until she makes it to my shoulder. She is a curious little creature.

Elena's blue eyes dart over to Lilith where she is perched on my shoulder, and her eyes grow humorously wide.

"What in the actual fuck is that thing, Alli?" Elena says each word slowly, without moving more than her eyes. She is staying perfectly still, as though one slight movement will send the kitten into attack mode.

Why is everyone so scared of this adorable little thing?

"Oh, this is Lilith." I nod my head toward my little pet. "She saved my life, so she is mine now."

I let go of Elena's shoulder with one hand and scratch underneath Lilith's chin, causing her to purr loudly. I know I have her approval to keep her.

She isn't a familiar like Nija. We are not bonded like that. We are just attached to each other now. Plus, I do not believe she is a demon of any kind, even if Mica said otherwise.

"You went into battle and came out with a kitten?" Elena says, her eyes scrunching together at her brows in complete confusion.

"Umm, yea. I guess so." I just shrug; there's not much else to be said.

Now the tough part. "Look, Elena, I cannot be sure, but the brothel fell, and I don't believe anyone survived it."

Elena knew some of the girls there as well. She hangs her head and takes a deep, shaking breath. A single tear falls down her face. "I know. I saw it fall from the roof. I did not see anyone leaving the building."

We stare at each other in silence, knowing in our hearts that no one made it out of that building in time. Fury builds in me that this was my world's fault.

We hear glass shatter from the other room. Elena and I both run toward the front showroom where the noise came from to see what is happening.

Mica is pinned against a glass display case that is now broken, and Ellie is on her knees with Mica's cock in her mouth. Mica's head is thrown back through the shattered display case, not looking like he gives a shit about any damage to the case or his head.

"You know you will be paying to replace that," Elena says firmly, arms crossed over her chest.

Mica lifts his hand and shows her his middle finger, neither he nor Ellie missing a single beat or rhythm from their pleasure session.

I am kind of impressed by the display. I really would not have guessed Ellie had it in her to do that, especially not so publicly.

Mates will be mates.

I grab Elena's arm and pull her back to the workroom at the rear of the building.

"Wow, they just get it on like that? I mean, there is a window overlooking the street like right there. Anyone could just stop in for the show," Elena says, throwing her arm up and pointing in that direction.

I burst out laughing.

"They are from Inferis, as am I. Did you ever wonder why I was always so open about everything? Plus, they are demon mates. They do not care who sees how much they care for each other." I say between laughs.

"I just thought you were rebellious. I would never have thought it was a normal thing for people to do in public!" she replies.

"Well, in Inferis, no one cares. We indulge in our darkest and most basic desires." I wiggle my eyebrows at her.

"I am becoming more curious about this world you called home."

Untried Origins

I huff. "Well, I hope you never have to worry about those Hollows again. I think I should go back now to make sure those Hollows really are called back and dealt with. They do not belong in this world. They would destroy it."

As much as I hate to admit it, this world and its people have grown on me, and I do not wish to see them fall to the power of the Hollows. Clearly, the kings were not doing their part to stop it, so I will have to.

She looks at me with worry in her eyes, but she says nothing. We both turn when we hear Ellie and Mica entering the room.

Elena makes a very loud verbal "Humph" at them. "You guys done blowing each other in my lobby?"

Mica's eyes narrow, and Ellie turns the brightest shade of red.

Ellie starts, "I apologize. Sometimes the mating bond just takes over, and I..."

Mica walks up behind her and pulls her into him affectionately. He looks down at her so sweetly. "There is nothing to apologize for. They both know we were just showing our love for each other." He leans down and gives her a small, sweet kiss.

Ellie looks utterly at peace with everything. For a second, I start to envy them, but then quickly recover. It has never really been my dream to have a fairytale ending. I like my life and living it the way I want.

I thought I had my fairytale once upon a time, and when it was taken from me, I decided I would be better on my own anyways.

I take a deep breath before I look at Mica and Elli. I know now that I have no choice but to return. I cannot stand by and watch the Hollows consume this world. I know rejection and heartache wait for me back Inferis. I have this pull in my chest now saying it is time to face it. Ellie, Mica, and the Hollows all showing up on the same day cannot be a coincidence. The universe is telling me I have to return.

"Okay, I will take you all back. We can leave tomorrow night. I will need some time to say goodbyes and pay my landlord for a few months' rent," I say.

I like Si at the bakery; I do not want to leave him with nothing and no one to take over my tenancy. Plus, I know it is going to be hard to leave Elena. She has become my closest friend and my only constant, really the first person I have trusted since Madis nearly destroyed me.

I look at Elena and start to take a step toward her.

"No," Elena says under her breath, tears forming in her eyes.

"Look, Elena, I must go back. I can't let those Hollows just destroy this place." This is already hurting more than I thought. I have a deeper than friendship connection with Elena, as if we are cut from a similar cloth.

"Fine. I am going with you," Elena says firmly.

My jaw drops open. It is my turn to say. "No."

Elena looks at me up and down, crossing her arms over her chest. "I am pretty sure you have no choice in my decisions, Princess." She says the last word with more venom than I am used to receiving from her.

I narrow my eyes at her. "Yeah, actually, I do, and you are not meant for the Areas of Inferis. I have no way of knowing if you will be able to come back here to your realm if you come with us."

Souls come to the underworld for punishment. Mortals and Fae do not come willingly, and when they do, it is to stay.

"That is fine. If you are not here, then I have nothing and no one. You know I have no family and that I have been traveling, looking for a home. You have been that home for years now. So, if you go, I go." She seems to cement herself to the floor, as if that will finalize her words. "Plus, you will need help with these Hollows, and you have already seen that I am useful with a bow. I will not let my world fall while I do nothing." Elena said "my world" with such pride, I could not say no. It is the same pride I felt for the place I used to call mine.

I look back at Ellie curled up in Mica's arms. They look at each other, seeming to be having a silent conversation. They at once turn and give me a single nod.

I let out a heavy sigh. "I feel I may regret bringing you with me, but if I am honest, I may need you there at my side when I am forced to see Madis. I am not sure I will be able to hold myself back from killing her or be able to keep myself from breaking down. Either way, it will be nice to have a true friend at my side."

Lilith purrs from my shoulder and wraps her long tail around my neck, as if to say I am coming too. I leaned my head into hers, nuzzling the good girl. "Yeah, you are too."

Mica speaks in his deep voice, "Then it is settled. We leave tomorrow."

Ellie squeals and starts jumping up and down like a child given a piece of candy for the first time. I turn a sharp stare at her. She stops, pretending to fix her dress of wrinkles. "Sorry, Your Majesty."

I just roll my eyes.

My emotions rack up inside of me. I know I have to return to see why those Hollows are attacking Erathina, but I am nervous to see my father. I am terrified of what he will have to say to me. I can feel a spark of joy bubbling up at being back within the walls of the palace where I spent most of my life.

I might even get a chance to fly Elena up to Warrantless Tavern for a drink.

I smile at my friends. Yeah, maybe this will not be a bad thing, I try to tell myself. My heart and gut are telling me a different story.

Chapter 24

MADIS

Back in my room, I start to take care of my tender knees. The pebbles my father forced me to kneel on to remember my place are enchanted by the Witches of Area, laced with crystals that are spelled to tear through the thick skin of my kind. It will take my knees at least a week to heal from the damage the tiny stones have caused.

There is a soft knock on the door, and then a guard steps in to announce my mother's presence.

Oh, dear goddess of Valkeria, have I not suffered enough tonight?

My mother visits me sometimes after my father's disciplining to chastise me for disobeying him. I am sure there were times in my past when I needed discipline. However, I do not believe I have disobeyed my father for many years.

Once he finally let me be a part of the actual world and I was no longer confined to that room where the king and he trained me or taught me lessons, I did not disobey. I had no desire to go back.

It is still the middle of the night, and I am still in my night shorts, tank top, and thin robe. My mother, on the other hand, is dressed to walk into a ballroom. She is in light pink tulle skirts and a corset-styled top, looking ever the kind and elegant woman that she is not.

My mother was a barmaid in the mortal world. She has little power, and she makes up for that by using my father's power of office to demand anything and everything she wants. She truly is a remorseless woman. Most people in this world forgot long ago that she is not a full-blooded demon, simply because she fit here perfectly.

I have always believed there is a chance this world could be ruled in a less cruel manner. I even hear rumors of others that feel the same. I have tried countless times to find these rumored people and have failed. It is true that we are demons, and we enjoy falling into our greater sins. However, I never thought to beat the staff for only adding one lump of sugar in my tea instead of two.

Viscountess Mesa Malias stands right inside the doorway in all her elegance with a face so similar to mine and just tsks.

I hold my breath, waiting to hear again how much I disappointed her or how I could try harder. My parents' expectations have always been high, and I am starting to believe they will always be out of my reach.

I'm always just a few inches short of being the person I am expected to be.

"Madis, I do hope you did not go to a meeting dressed like a simple whore. I know you crave attention, dear, but this is not the way to go about getting it," she finally says.

Awesome, I am a disappointing whore tonight.

"Sorry, Mother. I was pulled from my chambers; I did not have the time to find an outfit," I say as respectfully as possible.

"Oh dear, you should feel blessed that the bloody knees are all your father did, then. You deserve worse."

She walks closer to me, shaking her head in such disapproval. Her tulle skirts swish with her hips as she walks.

To the outside world, my parents and I are the closest of families. My parents have fooled everyone into believing their love story. Kaisera even believes, or did believe, that we were the happiest of families, with my parents being this great love match.

Nothing has ever been further from the truth.

I could never tell Kai of the beatings or discipline. I was frightened they would have punished her as they did me if she knew. I preferred to take the hit than to see the one and only friend I have ever had take it.

When my mother reaches my side, I am in such deep thought that it shocks me when she pushes the underside of my chin up to look at her. For the second time tonight, I am looking up to someone.

How is it that the night I become Queen, I am forced to remember my place, that I am still forced to bow to them?

I start to stand. I do not know what is going on in my head, but I am starting to get tired of looking up to people who should be under me now.

My mother only puts her hand to my shoulders and pushes me back down.

"No, daughter. You need to keep off your feet so that the creases in your knees can heal properly," she says, and I obey.

"Now, tell me what you did other than dress in such a dishonorable way to a council meeting." She runs a hand over my chin then picks up a lock of my hair, looking at it in utter disgust. She huffs out a loud sigh. "On second thought, do not speak until I get this horrid rats' nest out of your head."

She snaps her fingers, and a frightened maid runs to her. "Yes, my lady."

My mother does not even turn to look at the poor girl, who is clearly shaking in her powder blue maid's outfit with her head bent.

"Fetch me a brush so I may fix this horses mane that is my daughter's hair." She shakes her head at me.

So, I am a disappointing whore with a horse's mane for hair.

The maid runs off. I do not mean she lightly jogs; she sprints out to fetch the brush.

Untried Origins

As my mother and I wait for the maid to return, she continues to look at me in disgust from over the bridge of her nose.

I start to go back to inspect the damage on my knees.

Not thirty seconds go by before the maid runs back in with an assortment of hairbrushes for my mother to select from.

My mother turns and grabs one, then smacks the maid in the shoulder with it, hard. "That is for taking so long."

The maid flinches with pain. "Sorry, my lady. I will be faster next time."

I want so badly to release the fire and rage in me, but doing so would only show my mother that I care. The things I care about are taken from me, and I would hate to worsen the fate of this maid. I hate seeing my mother abuse the staff. She could hire humans whose souls are here to serve their punishment, those who deserve her punishments. She could choose souls who had done something in their past life, whether it be committing a simple crime of stealing or a major one like murder. They have been deemed rotten and are here to serve their time in whatever way we see fit.

Of course, my mother has no interest in beating the ones who are here to be punished. She likes to beat the demons who are born here, ones who are a part of this realm, of our world. I am starting to believe she likes destroying the innocents of the world.

She walks behind the chair I am sitting in and grabs a handful of my hair roughly, pulling my whole head back with it. "Sit up straight. You were raised to be proper. Act like it." She begins to brush through my hair, ripping half of it out in the process. I am blessed not to be bald after all the damage she has done to it during my lifetime.

After she gets most of the knots out of my white hair by tearing them from my scalp, she speaks. "Madis, you are now to be the Queen of Area Six. Much more will be expected of you. You will have more responsibilities. Your father is already working tirelessly to secure you a match from another Area. Area One has shown great interest. If all goes well, you will be married by the end of the month."

I let my face drop at that. I have no desire to marry the King of Area One. He is the King of Deals. Deals always cost you more than they cost him.

But my only response is, "Yes, Mother."

She yanks the brush through my hair a few more times. "There. Now you do not look as if you are a complete disgrace."

"Thank you, Mother."

She calls for the lady's maid to return. The maid hurries in, taking the brush from her and moving out of the way to stand ready for her next orders, still trembling.

Poor girl, don't you know that only thrills her more?

I would have tried to relay that to her through a look if I could, but the poor petite thing will not even look up from the ground.

My mother starts to walk back out of the room. When she makes it to the door, she turns back to me to speak. "I know it is difficult for you, but please do try to look appropriate for this morning's meeting. A temporary crown will be sent up for you to wear until you have been crowned. Do not make the temporary crown look bad. Do you understand me, Madis?"

"Yes, Mother." This time, a little bit of the fire slips out of me, but not enough for her to truly notice, although a slight shiver does seem to cross over her.

She turns and leaves after that.

I look to my large balcony windows to see that the sun is starting to make its appearance, meaning it is time for me to start getting ready. Time for me to try and not be a massive disappointment to everyone around me.

I spend the next few hours being primped by several lady's maids. They help me scrub down every single part of me. Then, they get to the task of my hair, which thanks to my mother, is thoroughly brushed. Next is picking out a dress acceptable for a queen. Four dresses are brought in, all of which I am informed were hand-selected by my mother. I do not need to be informed of this, though. Every single one of the dresses has my mother written all over them. Each one is tulle with a snug fitting top that fully covers my chest. Each one is also a light, pastel, girly color. I hate each and every one I am shown. I know I have no choice in this matter, not after my punishment from my father. I have no desire to displease them again so soon.

I select the light pink, almost white dress that washes me out, even with my tanned skin. It has a full skirt and corset top that a maid ties tighter than normal. The lady's maid who is tightening up my corset again finally says the first words I have heard since my mother left.

"Your mother requested that your top be tightened a bit more than normal. I am sorry, Your Majesty."

I sigh, because of course they are more scared of her than me, the queen. Even the maids can see right through this charade. I do not wish to be the type of ruler my father wishes me to be, the kind everyone fears.

I do not wish to rule at all.

Deep breath in, count to five, let it out.

The breaths I try and take become more of a struggle with each pull of my corset strings.

The team of lady's maids leave my room, and I am left to myself. I am standing in front of the mirror, staring at my reflection in disgust at what I am letting them make me into. I know this is the way it is until I leave this place to take my seat next to the king my father chooses, I will be forced to bend to his will. I will then bend to the will of that king, and the cycle will continue. I am struggling increasingly each passing day to hold my powers back, to keep myself under control.

The knock on the door startles me, and I jump just a bit as I reach for my dagger that is no longer there.

I miss when I was nothing more than Kaisera's protector.

"Come in," I say lightly.

A guard enters, a guard who is not Tribax, who is usually the only person to escort me. He has ever since the king named me heir.

Where is he?

Ka Lee

The guard speaks, "Your Majesty, I am here to escort you to the throne room."

"Oh, not the councilors' hall?" We never have meetings in the throne room.

"No, Your Majesty. We have a guest in the throne room."

Chapter 25
KAISERA

    I spent the next twenty-four hours saying goodbye to the life I created here. I paid Si from the bakery enough that he would not need a tenant to take my spot for at least a year, or two if he stretched it. I hated that I could not give him more, but let us be honest, I spent too much on partying these last several years. Even though I did well at the shop, I definitely was not breaking any hips with coins sacks attached.

    Elena is coming with me, and if she is forced to stay in Inferis, I will stay with her. She does not seem at all concerned that there is a chance she will be stuck there forever.

    I am not sure what I will do when I return. I should probably get a game plan together, one that does not involve me strangling Madis.

    I decide to go find Elena back at the shop to see if she wants to take a final walk through the streets of our little town. As I make my way through the streets, I spot Alex working on a new blade, a crystal one. He piqued my interest, so I chose to start towards him instead of Elena's shop.

I walk closer to get a look at what he is doing. He looks up, spots me, and a huge grin spreads across his untamed bearded face.

"Glad you at least had the decency to come say bye," he says in his low-toned voice.

"Actually, I am more interested in saying hello to this blade."

It is an exquisitely made blade of white and purple crystals that swirl and shimmer in the light. The handle is black braided iron, with three solitary lavender stones in a straight line up to the base.

Alex lets me admire the sword for a while, and I see his chest puff out a bit with pride.

"I am glad you like it, Princess, because it is yours."

I laugh loudly at this, and I mean a full belly roll, head thrown back, laugh. I can't afford a crystal blade without going into my coffers, which are not even mine anymore.

"I cannot afford that blade." What is he thinking? He has seen my little apartment.

"I do not expect you to pay for it in coins, Princess," he says, crossing his arms with a smirk on his face.

I lunge at him, my fist going straight into his jaw. He collapses to the ground. I may be out of shape and in need of training, but I can still land a painful hit to a human. I could have killed him with one hit, but I did not wish him dead, just injured enough to learn a lesson.

How dare he expect sex in exchange for a sword?

He rolls onto his back, clenching his stomach with laughter.

Okay, now I am confused.

"I should have expected that from you," he says between laughs and grunts.

"No shit. How dare you assume I can be bought with shiny things? And why did you call me Princess?" I say a bit louder than necessary. I stand there with my hands on my hips, looking down at him.

Untried Origins

He lifts his arm up, waiting for me to assist him. I simply raise a brow at him. He huffs a bit trying to get to his feet.

"I should have worded this differently. I expect you to pay for this with the blood of our enemies. The enemies who tried to destroy this town. I saw you take them down the other night without hesitation; I also saw you come to my aid. I am assuming I have you to thank for keeping that thing from causing even more damage to me. Elena and I spoke this morning, and I begged her for answers. No normal Fae or human would know how to take those things the way you did. She told me who you are and that you are going back to prevent this," he waves his arms around the collapsed buildings and rubble that is left of this town, "from happening again."

Of course, Elena told him everything.

"I cannot take this kind of profit from you. This sword must have cost you a year's pay in material alone." I might be a bitch a decent amount of the time, but I do not wish to take from people.

"If you keep me from losing anyone else, it is worth it." He turns his gaze back to the ground.

"Who did you lose?" I say and reach out to put an arm on his bicep.

He lifts his head and looks back at my face. "You were not the only reason I was at the brothel the other night. There was a girl. She has turned down all my advances to take her out of there. I thought her seeing me with you would change her mind and make her want me." He looks genuinely sad.

"Who was she?" I know this is not an appropriate thing to ask. The woman has just been lost to him, but I cannot help my curiosity.

He shakes his head a little at my bluntness. He answers me anyway. "Her name was Lexie; she was the little brunette you got knocked out trying to save. I tried to get to her, too. I could not get to her fast enough. Which is why…" He sighs loudly but seems a bit surer. He walks over to the sword, lifts it, and turns, thrusting the handle of the blade toward me. "This is yours. With a properly weighted sword and maybe a little less drinking, I know in my gut you might just conquer the world."

I am still having a tough time understanding why my one-night stand is willing to give me such an incredible gift, but I am not going to look a gift dragon in the mouth and not take it from him. I reach out and take the crystal sword. It glistens in the dimming light of the afternoon sky.

"It is incredible," I say.

I twirl it around a couple times, then assume a fighting stance with the blade blocking my face. It is well-balanced in my hands and fits my grip perfectly. I stand back upright, playfully twirling the sword in my hand now, loving the feel of it.

"Are you sure?" I ask.

A smile grows on his face. "Go make those fuckers bleed for what they did and what they might try and do again."

My smile grows. "I absolutely fucking will." I nod my head firmly.

I look back down at the blade and then back up at Alex when an idea pops into my head.

"Do you want to come?" I ask.

Alex is already picking up his tools around his workspace. He stops with his welding tools tucked into the crooks of his arms. "What?"

"Do you want to come with us to Inferis?"

For a moment, Alex just stares at me, his expression completely blank.

"You do not have to come, but we have an academy. You could learn to fight Hollows properly. You are a human, so it would cost you your soul, and you could never return to Erathina again, but..." I stop to think about the rest of that sentence, wondering to myself why I am offering to take this man's soul from him.

"Yes," Alex responds.

I grin at him. "So, you want to trade me your soul so you can learn to fight Hollows in the underworld and stand beside me in any and all battles to come until you have no soul left?"

Alex's eyes widen slightly at that. I have never taken a soul to Inferis. I cannot lie and say I am not dying to see this deal through now that I have said the words out loud. This is my nature, to make deals, to bargain with souls. I am not going to give

Alex a shit deal, though. He would live a demon's lifespan in Inferis. He would just have to stand with me in all things as I see fit.

"Yes," Alex responds again, this time dropping all his tools and stepping towards me.

"Then, let's shake on it." I reach my hand out.

Alex grabs my hand without an ounce of hesitation. I feel the power from his soul leak into me at the deal. His eyes widen as a black mist begins to swirl around him.

"See you on the other side," I say with a wide grin.

The look of human innocence on Alex's face fades away into a devilish grin. "Yes, you will."

The mist completely takes hold of Alex, and he fades slowly away as he evaporates into nothing and into his new home, Inferis.

I know he has been transported to Inferis, straight to DWA, where the demons there would sense a deal was made and begin training him.

Alex will train until the heads of the DWA determine he is fit to fight. I may not see him for a century or two, but I know with the deal struck, I will see him again in time.

I turn and quickly make my way the short distance to Elena's shop.

Elena is in her shop, looking around and sliding her hands over the countertops. I stand outside for a bit, just watching her, debating if I should beg her to stay or not. I selfishly want her to come with me, but on the other hand, I will be taking her away from the only realm she has ever known, into quite literally the most dangerous place in existence.

She walks over to the cabinet that Mica and Ellie broke the night before and picks up a piece of glass and smiles. She is probably remembering walking in on them.

I finally decide to walk through the doors.

"Something funny over there?" She jumps a little bit, not expecting my voice.

"Yes, actually." She turns to me with a huge smile on her face.

"Well, spit it out. You know I love a good joke."

She laughs at this. "I am laughing because I believe I am going to love Inferis." She scrunches up her nose.

Giggle, I say, "You know what? I think you might be right."

She walks until she is close enough to put her hands on both of my shoulders and looks down at me. "Do I have to call you 'Your Majesty' down there?" She makes an overly disgusted face at me.

"Do not even think about it." I have always hated titles. Yes, I always wanted to rule. Yes, people should give me the respect I deserved as their queen; however, the titles drove me crazy when they came out of my friends' mouths.

She laughs loudly, shaking her head before turning and looping her arm through mine. "There is a band playing a few blocks away tonight. Let us go have one last party."

I hate this. I hate that I have to go back. I hate that I am dragging her with me. I want to stay here, living our partying, carefree life, but six years has been long enough. If no one answers for the crimes of the Hollows, I will take back my place as heir and convince my father that we must catch whoever is responsible and end them.

Even if no one wants me to have it.

I was hurt when I left Inferis. I was shattered by the betrayal from my most trusted friend, but I will not let that stop me from protecting the innocent and the balance of the worlds.

Maybe my father will even be happy to see me. Not that he came looking for me, though he could have at any time. He could have summoned me back, but he did not. Madis probably talked him into not looking for me.

"I wish we could, Elena, but Ellie and Mica should be here any minute. It's time to go. Especially since I made a deal with Alex to send him to Inferis to train with the demon academy to kill Hollows," I say as quickly as possible, hoping she misses the last part.

"You did what?" Elena screams at me.

"Look. He was sad. He gave me a sword," I try to explain to her.

Elena gives me a deadpan look. "He gave you a gift and in return you what? Damned his soul for all eternity?"

I laugh, but she glares at me. "No. He wants to learn to fight, to help his people. So, I gave him the opportunity to do so."

Mica and Ellie walk into the shop. Ellie looks chipper than ever. "Are you ready to go back to your realm, your…" Ellie starts.

Before she can finish that sentence, I am on her. Clearly, I am in an attack first and ask questions later kind of mood. I have a blade at Ellie's throat before Mica has the time to stop me.

I can feel the tension resonating through the air. I have to do this, though; it's the only way.

"If you call me by a title one more time, I will end you," I grit out.

Of course, I would never actually hurt her. I adore this little ball of sunshine who can brighten anyone's darkest day, even if shadows seem to hold onto her. She is the happiest demon I have ever met.

"Yes, I am sorry." Her eyes are alight, but not with fear. There is excitement in them.

I tighten my grip on the dagger. The look in her eyes is daring me to do more. I'm not even close to breaking her skin. I am being too careful of that.

"Yes, what?" I grit my teeth, acting as pissed as I can without cracking the grin that I want to.

"Yes, Kaisera," she whispers the words.

I back away a bit, then throw my arms around her in a hug. "You are now part of this small group, Ellie. I will never actually hurt you. You must act as if we are friends. You are not below me."

She hugs me back tightly. She whispers in my ear. "I know. I could have unarmed you, anyway."

I leaned back to look into her eyes. Blue and gray ghosts swirl in her eyes as she lets out a little bit of that darkness, I saw years ago in my dressing room.

I smile wickedly at her. "I always knew you were stronger than you let on."

Ellie shakes her head, all evidence of anything dark within her disappearing without a trace, her eyes returning to her normal light brown.

I give her a questioning look. Ellie lifts her finger to her lips in the shhh kind of way.

My eyes scrunch together, but Mica shoves me away from her before I can question her.

He looks pissed. "You may be our future queen, but you will not touch her like that again. After seeing you fight last night, I do not think you have it in you anymore to take me on."

"Ha, that's what you think." Even if he might be right.

I have not trained in six years. I have not even been trying to harness my gifts other than to make simple jewelry. I can bend objects to my will, and yet the most I have done is make pretty things.

Elena walks over to the three of us, throwing her arm over my shoulder and leaning onto me. "So, are we going to go to the realm where devastation surely awaits us or what?"

Everyone but Mica laughs. Gosh, I can't see why Ellie likes him; he is such a grump next to her brightness.

"Yes, let's go see my dear ole' dad and my ex-bestie, and fuck some shit up." I lean my head on Elena's shoulder. At least I will have her.

"Okay, everyone hold on to me," I say. I have only done this once before, and it was just me. Crossing the realm had hurt like a son of a bitch. It is not a fun feeling to have part of your soul pulled from you, only to be shoved back in.

Elena stays with her arm wrapped around my shoulder, Ellie leans over and places her hand on my shoulder next to Elena's, and Mica grabs my wrist, making sure to hold on tight to Ellie. Lilith grabs onto my leg like a child scared that their mother might leave them behind.

I close my eyes and picture my home. I do not know what has happened to my rooms, but I do know the one place that will never change: the throne room. So, I picture that specifically: the two thrones sitting next to each other, mine just a bit shorter than my father's but a throne, nonetheless. I need to show the King of Area Eight where I wish to be placed.

Untried Origins

Then, I call on the King of Area Eight in my mind and drag a dagger over my palm to give him my offering.

Then, I feel myself and everyone touching me being pulled to that one place.

Chapter 26
KAISERA

The first thing I see is a guard coming at me. The first thing I feel is my friends taking a step to the sides of me, everyone seeming to get into a fighting position. My mind is a bit foggy, and my body is a bit tipsy. I shake my head to try to clear it. I can hear murmurs, and I can see that the guards have stopped charging toward us.

The shouts seem to come from everywhere as the voices bounce off the walls and echo through the room. I bend over, placing my hands on my knees to steady myself. My head feels so heavy that I am forced to let it hang down a bit, rather than keep it held as high as I wish.

Shit, that jump was rough.

"Alli, are you ok?" Elena has her hand on my back, leaning down to speak to me.

I wave her off. "Yep, I will be. Just had half my soul ripped out and put back in. No biggie. How are you guys?"

Untried Origins

I am still leaning over my knees, but I turn my head so that I can see Elena. She assesses herself by literally patting herself down. She touches her legs then stomach then grabs her boobs, looking down at them like they might have disappeared in the jump. She moves on from there and checks to make sure her face and hair are still the same.

"I feel perfect. I thought you said it would hurt," she says.

I look over to Ellie and Mica and find that they are perfectly fine too. Maybe because they are not the ones having to use the magic, it did not hurt them?

I know the jump can tear Hollow demons apart, and that you can't make the jump without the right amount of power in your blood, but why did it hurt me so badly when they seem fine?

Well, that's bullshit.

I do not remember it hurting this bad last time. It is taking every bit of strength I have to stand up straight again. I see the people running about. The guards are screaming for someone to retrieve the queen.

Wait, that is not right. Where is the king? My father would not have taken a queen.

Ellie and Mica have stepped away to talk to one of the guards, leaving only Elena to help hold me up. Lilith is circling around my legs, meowing loudly. Her little wings are tucked in close to her black body. She seems fine as well, like the jump did not affect her at all.

I catch sight of a guard standing next to the doors leading into the throne room. He is giving orders to the other guards, so he must be of higher rank. A large red fox sits at his feet, looking directly at me.

The guard's eyes land on mine, and everything stops. Those eyes, freezing my already struggled breaths. He stops talking and stares at me, a wicked smile curving onto his mouth. I start for him. I have to get closer. I have this pull in me, a pull saying I have to get to him. It feels almost like a string is connected to some deep part of me and he has the other end. He starts to tell the other guards standing by him something, never taking his eyes from mine, moving toward me as well.

He takes long strides towards me, and I am moving swiftly to get to him as well, but Elena is still trying to hold me steady, and I do not have the strength to fight her off after that jump.

Elena whispers in my ear, "What are you doing? These people look pissed. Can you try not to piss them off more?"

I do not have the energy to speak back at this moment.

Before he can make it more than a few steps to me, the throne room doors are thrown open, and in walks Madis. The first thing I notice about her is that she is wearing my fucking crown on her head and being escorted by multiple guards. Someone announces: "His Majesty's Heir, Future Queen of Area Six, Madis Malias."

No.

I knew this would happen, but it is still a shock to the senses to actually hear and see it firsthand.

She did it, she took the crown. But if that is the case, where is my father?

She stops right inside the doorway. She is not blinking; she looks shocked. Good. I smile just a bit at having caught her off guard.

Then, she says, "Kai." Her voice is low and soft, and a single tear runs down her cheek.

Oh, no. This crown stealing bitch does not get to act happy to see me.

That tips me over the edge. My anger flares to life, and before I know it, I am charging at Madis. My adrenaline spike gives me strength for the moment.

I make it right in front of her before two guards are pulling at my arms. I bare my teeth and sneer at her, growling a low hiss through my teeth.

"You fucking bitch, where is the king?" I sneer. "I want to see my father!" I yell at her.

Madis looks taken aback. "Kai, it's me. I am your best friend."

"The fuck you are. You are nothing more than a crown-stealing whore." I pull against the guards again. They are not struggling to keep me in place. I'm not getting very far without my full strength.

"Kai." She places her hand over her heart and goes to reach for me, but I flash my teeth at her again.

"You can call me Princess Kaisera. Only my friends and equals may call me anything else," I spit at her.

Her eyes scrunch together in confusion and shock. I do not know what the Inferis she is confused about. I saw her taking the crown for herself the night of the Blood Binding. I saw her taking everything that was mine, and now, I am seeing it firsthand. Everything the crone showed me has come true.

"Where. Is. My. Father, you bitch?" I say again, each word a struggle to push through my teeth. My strength is giving way fast as I continue to struggle against the guards holding me.

Madis clears her throat, straightening her shoulders and standing tall. She looks nothing like I remember, every sign of the once strong warrior gone. She looks like a queen in her light pastel dress and her petite crown atop her head. She is every bit of grace, as if she has been training for it her whole life.

Madis' face shifts to a stern blank stare.

"Princess Kaisera, your father was found murdered near Area Seven, and you will address me by my title: 'Your Majesty.' After the crowning, you will address me as your queen, and queens do not answer to princesses." I feel every slap to the face that those words were meant to send.

Madis turns around and walks away from me, back out the doors she came from. She turns her back on me, a true sign she believes she is now above me.

I try to lunge for her again, but it is pointless. The strength I used to jump from Erathina and the fact I have not been harnessing my powers for the past six years took too much of a toll on me.

The guard I was struggling to get to before Madis' appearance approaches me. "Hand her to me," the man says. No, the Fae? He has slightly pointed ears, but he does not feel Fae. He feels darker. He feels good.

The guards let me go, and I collapse to the ground. All my strength has left my body.

Ka Lee

The guard who asked to have me scoops me up into his arms. The feeling of being there, in his arms, is like nothing I have ever felt before. I am safe here. I do not know why I am, but I am. I know as long as this person's arms are around me, nothing and no one can touch me. I feel a complete sense of rightness, and then I pass out in his arms.

I wake up in a room I do not know.

Elena is lying asleep next to me. I have no idea how I ended up in this bed or how long I have been here. I still have the same clothes on. My head is pounding slightly, but doing much better than it was in the throne room. There is a guard standing by the door. Not the same guard who picked me up off the floor and made me feel so safe; he is a random normal demon guard with a dead stare on his face.

I sit up, and my stirring awakens Elena.

She springs upright. "What's happening?" She throws her arm over me protectively, scoping the room for any possible threat.

"It is fine, Elena. We have guards." I push her arm onto her lap and pat the top of it.

She points to the guard. "Oh, he is not here to protect us. He is here to protect them from you."

Oh, well, that makes more sense.

Chapter 27
MADIS

Seeing Kai at first was so amazing. I thought she came back for me. I thought for a split second that she had come back to help me. I should know better by now to not put hope in anyone ever saving me.

The first thing I noticed was that she did not have her wings. What happened to them?

I nearly started to bawl my eyes out in front of everyone, until I caught my father watching me from the back of the throne room.

Now, I am back in my room, pacing, the bottom of the tulle skirt swishing around me. Nija is pacing alongside me, looking up at me with worry.

"It will be fine, Nija. We will work this out somehow," I say to try to calm him down.

Kai looked so angry; she came after me like she wanted to kill me. No, like she wanted to rip me limb from limb and feed me to that demonic little creature wrapped around her leg.

Something is wrong. Why would she be so mad at me? She is the one who abandoned me. She left me here to manage everything. She looks the exact same as I remember, except she seems weaker somehow.

I should have fought harder to find her; I should have gone to Erathina and found her myself.

I should not have told her that her father is dead that way.

I need to get out of these rooms to talk to her, to fix this somehow. She is back now, so she can have the crown. She can be queen, and I can go back to just being her guard.

I head toward the door to find her and fix this, whatever it takes.

Before I can make it to the door, it slams open. The walls shake with the impact of it hitting the wall. Books fall off the shelves, and things around my room shake.

My father comes barreling into the room straight to me, fire blazing in his eyes. I start to back up from him, but I already know there will be no escaping his wrath. I look to the guards at the door for help, but all they do is close the doors. I was hoping Tribax would be there. I know he never would allow my father to harm me if he saw it happening.

At least, I do not think he would allow it.

My father is always so careful to make sure no one sees the damage he causes me.

Nija growls and starts to grow, but I cannot allow him to be here. "Nija, go."

Nija tries to stand his ground, but as his master, he has no choice but to listen to my commands. Nija is powerful, but I do not wish to see any harm happen to him.

"Now, Nija." This time, he listens and vanishes.

Before I know it, my father's hand is wrapped around my neck, and he is squeezing tight. Out of instinct, my hands go to his hand around my throat, scratching to try and get away.

He only squeezes tighter.

"Be still and listen closely," he says as the fire in his eyes grows stronger. His hand heats up a bit with his power, burning my neck a little. I know he will not let it get hot enough to leave a real mark, but enough that I understand his intent.

Untried Origins

I nod my head up and down the best I can in agreement with his command. I know he would normally want a verbal 'yes, sir,' but I can barely get air into my lungs while he is crushing my vocal cords.

He loosens his grip slightly, and I take in a giant gulp of air before his hand tightens around my neck again.

"You will convince that waste of oxygen princess to go with you to Area Seven. You will find a way to prove that King Reign killed our king, and then you will bring him to justice." He lets go of my neck so I can respond.

"Yes, sir. But why do you want Kaisera there?" I ask while trying to gulp air down.

I receive a sharp slap to the face. It is not hard enough to knock me down, but just hard enough to remind me I am never to question him.

"Because I said to do it. Do you understand me, Madis?" He grabs my face tight enough to pinch my face together and stretch the skin painfully.

"Yes, sir," I try to say, but it comes out mumbled through my pinched cheeks. He releases my face by pushing it down sharply and starts to pace away.

He stops, turns and says, "You will do this by the end of this month, so that you may return and marry King Alibast, ruler of Area One, with a smile on your face. I have struck a deal with him, and he expects compliance out of you. I do not care if that untamed waste of air Kaisera is back. You will remain the heir, as the king declared it so."

My father, done with his demands, swings the doors back open and walks out.

I rub my throat and face.

Why does he want Kaisera to come with me?

What deal did he strike with the King of Deals? No one makes a deal with him without a hefty price. He is up to something.

I have no idea how I will convince Kaisera to even stand in the same room as me, let alone travel to another Area with me.

I cannot allow her to have the crown while my father's wrath is so strong. It would put her in the crossfire.

Ka Lee

There must be a way to fix all of this. I just need to figure out how to stop my father's plans without Kaisera or anyone else getting caught in the middle.

If King Reign did kill King Braxton, it could start a war between our Areas.

So why would my father want to prove he did it so badly? Does he want a war?

If the reports of Hollows attacking are to be believed, then I need to figure out why. Those demons are meant to follow, not lead, so someone has to be controlling them.

I have to talk to Kaisera. Maybe she knows something. She was with Ellie and Mica. They must have told her I am the one who sent them to Erathina to find her.

The best way to handle this is with a letter. I always get my words out better on paper.

I walk over to my work desk, grabbing my writing material, and get to work explaining to Kaisera why she should come with me. I am not bringing her along just because my father told me to, but because I cannot imagine what would happen to her if I left her here with him. I know Kaisera. She will fight back, and that will not end well for her. She doesn't understand the power and sway my father holds here.

I finish my letter, fold, and seal it with wax, and use the black signet ring on my right hand to press my brand into it. The brand a fierce dragon curled protectively around a castle.

I designed it the year I found out I would be heir. It represents all I want: to protect those I care for. And that is what I am going to do for Kaisera. She can hate me all she wants, but I swore to protect her a long time ago and I will, whether she likes it or not.

Chapter 28
KAISERA

Elena and I have been silently pacing around the room they stuck us in when there is a knock on the door. We both stop our pacing and say "come in" at the same time.

The guard from yesterday walks in. My heart rate increases from just his presence.

"Oh, thank the goddess of Valkeria! Please tell me you are here to bring us food." Elena is walking toward him like she has zero cares in the world, with a familiarity.

I catch Elena looking between us curiously before I turn back to stare back at the guard. He has yet to look away from me.

"Mica, can you come in here?" he says, turning his head slightly over his shoulder, keeping me in his sights, like I could disappear at any second.

Mica clearly stepped right back into his guard duties the moment we arrived back in Inferis. *I wonder if Ellie went back to serving that bitch?*

Before anyone moves again, I snap my fingers and blink directly in front of him so that we are inches apart. I expect him to flinch back, like most would if a person magically appeared in front of them, but he does not. I am looking up directly into his eyes. They are dark blue, like the deep ocean waters, with a perfect silver line wrapped around the outer edge of them. He is looking down into me, not at me. It is like he is seeing something behind my eyes.

His scent hits me all at once, and he smells absolutely incredible, like nothing I have ever smelled before. It is like a pine forest with an undertone of rich spices. He smells like outdoors and uncontaminated freedom.

Mica clears his throat. "Yes, Major?"

"Hmm, a Fae Major." I do not mean to say that out loud, it just kind of slipped out.

"Half Fae." His voice is so deep and gruff, nothing but male sexiness. "Mica, please escort Miss…?"

He turns away fully and gestures to Elena with a smirk on his face.

She responds "Elena," looking the Major up and down before putting all her weight to one hip and crossing her arms over her chest, he clearly does not impress her. That makes one of us, because I am becoming more impressed by the second.

"Yes, Mica, please escort Miss Elena to the dining hall and see she is properly fed," the Half Fae Major says.

I feel Lilith, who is curled up on my shoulder, trying to jump down. I do not trust her little wings to help her just yet, so I finally look away from the male standing in front of me to help her get down. It is then that I notice the large red fox standing next to the Major's leg.

I ask, "Your fox isn't going to try and eat her, right?" The fox does not look like he is paying any attention to Lilith, but better safe than sorry. I mean, she might be a demon spawn kitten, but she is still small enough for him to eat.

His simple response is no, then he looks at the fox. "Julian, behave."

Julian finds a pile of blankets that had fallen off the bed and lays down, curling in on himself and tucking his large fluffy tail in front of his face. Lilith follows behind him and curls up next to him.

Julian does not seem thrilled by this but allows it. He gives her a small growl when she tries to snuggle even closer, but after a few minutes, they settle in together.

Elena is still standing there watching this interaction.

"Hey, Erathina to Alli, or Kai. Are you coming? I am starving over here. About to shrivel up and keel over." I roll my eyes at her dramatics.

Before I can respond, the Major in front of me chimes in again. "No, I have a few questions for the lost princess."

Elena makes a move to come to my side, but I put up a hand and stop her. "It is fine, Elena. Go ahead and eat before you keel over. I have questions about this..." I point to the guard.

"Tribax," he says with a smile growing on his face. Not the full smile I saw in the throne room, but a small one. A mischievous one.

I continue, "For this Baxy character as well."

He looks like he is fighting off a wider grin at my nickname for him, which makes me smirk right back.

Elena shrugs and heads out the door with Mica. She knows I can handle myself and that I prefer to. No one handles things as perfectly as you handle them yourself.

As soon as the door closes, Tribax is on me. His hands wrap around both sides of my face. He starts to lean in, and I think he is about to kiss me, and I am so in for it. He is hotter than sin, and after the past two days, I could use the distraction.

He leans in, going straight to my neck. I tilt my head to the side to allow him more access to it. Apparently, I am okay with dying, as long as he takes me first.

He takes a big sniff then pulls away to look back into my eyes. "I thought that smell was lost to me forever." He closes his eyes and inhales a big breath before letting it out slowly. "Lavender and mischief."

I have no clue what the "lost to me forever" comment is about. I do know I want that kiss. I crash my mouth onto his, not allowing him to get another word out. He tastes like my wildest dreams. He tastes like unadulterated sin, with an afterburn of whiskey, my favorite flavor. His smell only makes me become more consumed by him. He feels like a wild animal waiting to be set free fully, but he is holding back. His kiss burns through me, and I want more from this male I only met moments ago. I have a desire to be with him, next to him. Anything he will give me, I will take.

He does not hesitate even for a split second before kissing me back. His hands move from my face into my hair, pulling slightly to tilt my head back further to give him better access to my mouth. His tongue is diving deeper, twisting along with mine in a perfect rhythm.

I claw at his shirt, trying to get closer, but he is an immovable force. I am not going to get anywhere he does not want me. He takes a step closer to me, then he is guiding me back. I let him until I am against a wall. He takes my hair that he has balled into his hand and pulls hard enough to detach my mouth from his.

His stare flickers back and forth between my eyes. I don't know what he is seeing there, but I can tell he enjoys whatever it is. I take in those beautiful eyes of his, enjoying what I see.

I look back down to his mouth, seeing a beautiful smile with two slightly elongated canines showing.

"Princess, I did not know you were so friendly. I hope you do not greet all your guards this way," he says in a light, cocky way.

"Maybe I do." I smirk back at him.

He grips my hair a little harder, forcing his fist full of my hair against the wall. The slight pain causes my core to heat, and

Untried Origins

I have to grip my thighs together to ease a bit of the tension growing there.

He huffs a small laugh. "You like it rough, don't you, little vixen?"

I can only nod my head slowly up and down, curious why that nickname sounded so right for me.

"I think I will make sure to be the only one you ever touch again." He leans down and licks up the column of my neck from the collarbone to the spot right behind my ear.

"Ha, you don't know me at all, or my reputation. After all, I was known as the Party Princess." The way he is making my breath hitch, making a shiver run down my entire body with each touch, make my words not very convincing.

My comment is true, though. I will never settle down. I knew I would be married to another heir from an early age, but I never planned on letting it stop me from finding other men to enjoy my bed.

When you count on one person, you lose.

I counted on Madis and my father and look where that got me. Fatherless, crownless, and the one person I trusted the most took it all from me.

He claims my mouth again. It is not as aggressive as before, but it feels claiming, like he is trying to make his words come to life.

He runs his hand that is not in my hair down my side to my hip, then to my leather-covered thigh, never letting his lips leave mine. Every place this man touches leaves my skin with chills. This could be deadly. I cannot even imagine what his touch would be like if we were undressed. He grips my thigh tightly and throws it around his hip, pinning me even harder against the wall and even closer to him. I can feel his impressive hard length pressing up against my most sensitive areas. I want this man, and I want him now.

I try to claw at him again, to remove his pants this time. He lets go of my hair and leg, but I do not let my leg fall from around him. He brings his hands to clasp around my wrists to still my hands from frantically trying to undo his belt.

He pulls his face away from mine. "Stop trying to undress me. No need to be so eager. We have tons of time." The cockiness of this male is next level, but I am loving it.

I can feel his impressive length trying to break free of his pants, and I can feel how badly he wants me. So, what is the problem?

"Why? You feel just as eager." I roll my hips a bit to put emphasis on my words. I tilt my head a bit and smile sweetly at him, a face I already know looks more devilish than sweet.

"Because I know it will not mean as much to you right now. I know you will enjoy this chase, little vixen," he says, then teasingly pecks a kiss to my nose.

What did he just say? Is he being cute with that nose peck?
I do not do cutesy shit.

My nose scrunches up at the contact, and I look at him with what I hope reads as *have you lost your fucking mind*, because clearly, he has.

"You think I am going to chase after you?" I laugh up at him.

He is still holding both my wrists in his hands, so he raises them up above my head and pins them both to the wall.

I arch my back, causing my center to connect fully with him. We are as close as we can be with our clothes still on.

He grins down at me before leaning in close to my ear, almost resting his head down on my shoulder. A few seconds go by, and I am starting to push harder into him, attempting to ride him so that I can get some friction where I am now aching for it. I am also hoping that it will encourage him to break the restraints he has placed on himself.

He let out a soft grumbling sound, and I think that will be it, but he sucks in one hard breath and breathes words into my ear.

"I do not think anything. I know things that you have yet to figure out, and I know that when it really comes down to it, you will enjoy the chase, and you will love your reward." Those words from him awaken every single part of me.

How can this man I just met already know me so well? Because even though I will not be admitting it, I do believe I will enjoy this particular chase.

There is a knock at the door, and Tribax moves completely away from me, causing me to whimper loudly.

Tribax smiles like it pleases him to know I am not happy about the distance he just put between us.

The door opens quietly, and a young lady's maid walks in, carrying a shiny black plate with a single letter sitting on top of it.

The maid hands me the letter then quickly runs back out the door, leaving me and Tribax to ourselves again. As much as I want to continue our little game, the seal on this letter is from Madis, and I am hoping it has a bit of an explanation in it.

He takes a step closer to me, reaching his hand out, like he wants to take the letter from me.

I push his hand away. "Baxy, back off. The letter is addressed to me."

"How about just Bax?" he says seriously, like he is not enjoying my little nickname.

Hmm, Bax. I like it.

"Fine, *Bax*," I emphasize his new nickname. "Back off." I am only half joking, walking a little bit away so I can have some form of privacy. He might be making me feel all kinds of ways, but I will not be trusting him with my personal matters so easily.

He huffs a little and says, "Fine," but all teasing has gone away. He stands like a strict soldier, watching me closely.

I can feel the way he is watching me so intently, and it makes my nerves spike up a bit. I have to roll my shoulders to relieve some of the tension growing there. I turn away from him, hoping he is taking the opportunity to take in how good my ass looks in these leather, tight-fitted pants. I break the wax seal and read the letter.

> *Princess Kaisera,*
>
> *I do not know what you have been through in the past six years. I sent Ellie and Mica to find you, but it has been so long, and things have changed here. I am taking a team of men to Area Seven to investigate your father's murder, and I would like for you to join me on this mission. Maybe we can get some alone time to discuss the things that have changed us.*
>
> *Please send your response as soon as you can. We are leaving tomorrow at dusk.*
>
> *You still mean so much to me. I hope you can see through your anger so that we may be as we once were.*
>
> *Love,*
> ~~*Heir*~~
> *Your Friend Madis*

I turn around to find Bax is indeed checking out my ass. His eyes jump up quickly in an attempt to hide it, but I do not have time to joke with him about it. Plus, I kind of liked the attention.

I hold the letter up in the air.

"Does your future queen know she is full of utter bullshit? Or has she convinced herself otherwise?" I say, waving the letter around in the air. I walk toward him and when I am close enough, I slam the letter into his chest. It is like slamming it into a brick wall, and I am now consumed with curiosity to see what he looks like with his shirt off.

Bax takes the letter and starts skimming over it.

"I have to go," is all he says. Before he leaves, he stops and looks down at me. "Thank you for sharing this information." His thank you sounds sincere, like he is shocked that I included him.

He clicks his tongue with a strange noise, and his familiar, the fox, hops off the makeshift pallet, causing Lilith to meow in disappointment, then walks quickly out the door, following on Tribax's heels.

He closes the door quickly behind him, leaving me just standing there.

What the fuck just happened?

I am going to need a moment to process the past twenty minutes. I want to know what he is going to do.

I walk to the door to follow him, but when I open the door, there are two guards standing in my way.

"Umm, excuse me, I would like to go get my breakfast." I try to pass them, and they stand like statues blocking my way.

"We cannot let you pass, Princess," the guard on the right says. He is a demon who looks like a demon. He has two short horns protruding from his head and has a red tint to his skin. He also has two lower fangs that slightly show over his top lip.

"And why is that? You let my friend leave." I cross my arms over my chest and hold my head a little higher, giving them my full attitude.

"She did not threaten the future queen," the other guard says, smirking at me in a duh kind of way. He looks more human. He has brown hair and a hint of a five o'clock shadow.

I can try to blink past them, but I will only get a few feet before another guard is on me, and if I blink to any other part of the castle, they will probably take it as a threat to the queen and come at me in full force.

With a very loud groan, I slam the door. I go over to a desk that is in the corner of the room, grab a piece of paper and some writing tools that are laid there, and write the "Queen" a response.

I aggressively fold the paper and walk over to the door, throwing it open. I toss the letter at the two guards standing there. Both hurrying to catch it.

"Take that to your false queen. She is waiting for it," I say, then slam the door shut again.

I do not wait to see if they listen, because I know they will.

I go back to bed, throwing myself on it. I am hungry and sexually frustrated now. Not a great combination. I do not know if I want to take care of the ache from earlier or go to the guards and tell them to bring me food. Finally, I start to undo my pants and slide my hand down them, burning to get the release I am aching for now thanks to Tribax.

The door to my room swings open again, and Elena strolls in with a huge plate of food.

Well, shit. I guess I will just stay frustrated for a while.

She laughs "The guard did not satisfy, huh?" she says jokingly.

"What?" I say, sitting up to button my pants and walking over to help her with the plate of food.

"Oh, do not 'what' me. The sexual tension in this room was so thick, I could have choked on it." She hands over the plate of food and plops down onto the bed, leaning back on her arms.

"Tell me, why are you here trying to get the job done yourself?" I spot something like hope in her eyes, but it is gone in a flash.

I place the plate of food on the desk and take a seat in the chair next to it, letting out a long breath.

"He wants me to chase him." Just thinking of him saying those words into my ear has shivers returning, running across my body again.

Elena sits up quickly, jaw dropping open. "Excuse me? The infamous Allison got shot down. The queen of the pickup game?"

I pick up a grape and throw it at her. She laughs when it harmlessly smacks her in the arm.

"No," I say and shove a grape into my mouth.

"Oh, my Valkeria, you want him, and you want him bad." A huge grin spreads from ear to ear across her face.

I let out a loud groan again. "Yes, okay. I want him so badly that it hurts, but I do not have the time or the energy to chase after Bax right now."

Untried Origins

"Holy shit!" she yells at me, jumping up to her feet.

It makes me jump and look around for what has her yelling and jumping. Even Lilith leaps up and makes a run for me. Lili jumps up onto my lap and hisses loudly, showing all her teeth to Elena.

"What?" I am still looking around for what could have made her so excited.

"Alli, you remembered his fucking name. Holy shit." Her hands fly over her mouth.

"So?" I shrug.

"It took you two months to remember my name! And you remember this random guard's name after two encounters, one of which you were half unconscious?" She is throwing her hands around and pacing back and forth more dramatically than normal.

"In fact, his name is Tribax. But he said Bax was okay too?" I am still confused. So what if his name stuck?

"You actually like this guy." She is now jumping up and down in one spot.

I start laughing. "You are nuts, Elena. Of course, I do not actually like him. I can't like him after two encounters. I do not 'like' guys anyways. He is just extremely attractive, and I think he would be great in bed. I am sure I will forget all about him."

I might have said those words aloud. I might even be trying to convince myself that I could forget about Tribax, but I have a feeling he is here to stay.

"No, Alli. I do not think you will." Her grin is plastered on her face.

Chapter 29
MADIS

Not twenty minutes after sending my letter to Kai, I get a response. The paper itself is a mess: folded raggedly with no seal. I ask the guards if they read it and they both respond no, but I can tell they have by the look on their faces. The letter is short and to the point.

> Dear Queen to Absolutely Fucking No One,
> I will join you. Not to speak to you, but to find my father's killer. I have a feeling I already know who did it, and she is not in Area Seven.
> Make preparations for four to travel. My true friends will be with me on this journey.
> You mean nothing to me.
> Hate,
> ~~Princess~~
> The True Queen, Kaisera Allison Braxton

Untried Origins

Well, this is clearly going to be a lovely outing. I still do not understand what she is so pissed about. Of course, I was chosen as heir after she left. The kingdoms need a merger to make us stronger, so of course the king had named a female heir.

It will be okay because it must be. I sit down at my little table outside on my balcony that overlooks the city of Area Six. I love this place. It is both dry and humid at the same time somehow, but I love the demons who call it home, and the working order of things. We only punish those who need punishment, and we never take souls for pleasure. I believe all the Areas should be this way. I do not know if it is possible now to give Kaisera the crown without putting her in the crossfires of my father.

If I marry a king like King Alibast, that will never happen. I have heard rumors of how horrible his deals can be. Most of the kings are ruthless, but King Alibast is the worst of them. He loves his deals; I have been told by so many that he enjoys watching all forms of creatures from Erathina being stripped of their souls after they break a deal. He enjoys their pain, and he enjoys being the one to cause their pain.

Not that any of the other kings are better. All of them have their own sick and twisted ways. Area Seven has its merciless bloodthirst Vampire King, who has been known to take humans from Erathina before their time and pull them down here to feed from them. Yes, the vampires need the blood to survive, but they can just as easily take it from the punished souls. Rumor has it, the Vampire King prefers to feed from pure souls.

I let out one of my usually heavy sighs.

Tomorrow, we will leave for Area Seven's court to meet this King Reign. I will have to be kind and cordial with him if I want to get information from him about our king's death. Maybe he will have the answers we need about the Hollow attacks. That is, if he is willing to share information with us at all.

I lean my head back against the chair. My lady's maid, who my mother decided I needed after this morning's outfit and hair fiasco, stands off to my right, waiting for me to demand things from her. I hate the feeling of having someone lurking nearby.

Her pretty, golden blonde hair is tied back in a tight bun, and her light brown eyes have a hint of red. The red tint in the eyes is common around the lower ranked Demons. She has a small, round face and long arms and legs.

The lady's maid had shown up shortly after I sent the letter to Kaisera.

I turn to her. "If we are going to be stuck together, I must know your name."

"Whatever you wish it to be, Your Majesty." The girl curtsies.

"I wish it to be your real name."

She looks confused and concerned, like this is some kind of trick. My mother's maids are taught very early on not to be seen or heard unless called upon. I have always hated having them around; I prefer my solitude sometimes, not to mention my privacy, since I have no doubt most maids here will report directly back to one of my parents.

Twiddling her thumbs together, she finally decides to speak up, "My name is Yanci, Your Majesty."

"Okay, Yanci. I do not wish to have a lady's maid." She looks at me ready to protest, but I put my hand to my lips in a shhh. Her mouth is closing and her lips thinning. "But I know you and I both have no choice. So, when people are not around, we shall be friends. Do you think you could do that?"

Goddess above, I would give anything to have one friend I can trust. As sweet as this girl seems, I know it cannot be her. I know she will report back to my mother, but I can at least have someone to speak to on occasions.

Yanci smiles a sweet, sheepish smile, but I can see the wolf that lies beneath.

"Yes, I would like that very much."

"Perfect. Yanci, please fetch us a bottle of wine and two glasses."

She bows then pauses. "What kind would you enjoy?"

"A nice dark red, please." I turn back to look at the city.

Untried Origins

"Your Majesty, I apologize, but your mother instructed us that you are not to have reds, as they may stain your lips and teeth." She looks terrified telling me this.

I just sigh quietly to myself this time.

Of course, she did. Stripping even my choice of drinks away.

"Fine; bring me whatever my mother will find appropriate."

Yanci scurries off to fetch the wine. I wouldn't mind disobeying my mother in this instance, but I am more than sure her wrath wouldn't just fall upon me. It would be the little lady's maid who paid that price.

Yanci returns a few minutes later with two glasses and a bottle of sweet white wine. I would have really enjoyed a harder wine, like the Fae wine that Kaisera and I used to drink, but at least this might help to calm my nerves. Tomorrow will be trying.

Yanci pours our wine and takes a seat next to me. I am a bit shocked at how easy it is to convince her to sit and drink her wine with me as a friend, rather than be my maid.

"Yanci."

"Yep?"

"Yep?" I repeat, with one brow lifted in her direction.

Her back goes board straight. "I mean... I am so sorry... I should not have..."

I laugh a genuine laugh, something I have not done in so long. My voice is almost scratchy from the decibel it is at from lack of use these past few years, as if my vocal cords are also in a bit of shock.

She looks at me with those big round eyes of hers, not sure what to do. She is halfway between sitting back down and standing up.

I wave my hand in the air, signaling for her to sit back down. She sits and stares at me, waiting for me to finally finish laughing.

"It is fine, Yanci. You are not like other lady's maids. Honestly, it is a breath of fresh air. Please stay that way in my company only. Just be careful in the presence of others."

I get profoundly serious on that last part. I already like this girl, and I do not wish to see her harmed.

"Yes, Your Majesty," she replies, sitting back a little more comfortably in her chair.

"You can cut that out too when it is just me and you. It is just Madis."

"Okay, Madis," she says.

Nija appears, and my little dragon makes his way over to Yanci, automatically jumping into her lap. She leans back away from him, keeping her hands from going anywhere near him.

"Umm, Madis."

I giggle a bit. "You can pet him. He should not bite you."

"Shouldn't?"

"Well, he nips sometimes," I tell her, which is not a lie. Nija has been known to get a little snippy.

She does not relax fully, but we both take a sip of our white wine. I grimace a little at the taste; sweet stuff has never really been my thing. I swish it around in my mouth a bit before swallowing it. It has a hint of something I have never tasted before.

Yanci seems to be enjoying it though, and that makes me smile.

Maybe she is not one of my mother's spies. Maybe she wants a friend just as badly as I want one. Or maybe she will abandon me as everyone else has. I try not to hope too hard.

A thought occurs to me.

"Hey, Yanci?"

"Yes, Madis?" She sounds chipper.

"Make sure you have your bags packed by tomorrow afternoon. You will be accompanying me to Area Seven." Maybe, if I get her far enough away, she will trust me more than she fears my mother. Bringing her with me also to ensure she will not be punished by my mother's hand for a while.

My mother and father will not be able to come with us to King Reign's area. They will have to stay here and rule over Area Six in my stead, something I already know they must be thrilled about, and something I am not.

Yanci jumps and turns to me at the same time, causing Nija to fly off her lap. He huffs out a bit of fire, growling at her. She doesn't even seem to notice Nija's disapproval of her actions.

"Really? I have never even left this castle's grounds before. You really want to bring me with you?"

I'm laughing again, which makes me really like this girl. "Yes. You will be accompanying me, but just remember, you must play your role. You must be the lady's maid you are expected to be."

She lets out a high pitch squeal before running around my small balcony table and throwing her arms around me in a tight embrace.

I am taken aback, but pleasantly shocked. No one has touched me in a kind way since Tribax held me in his arms the night of the Blood Binding.

It takes me a few seconds to relax and hug her back. I pat her on the back awkwardly, and then she pulls away and starts jumping up and down again.

"Okay, I am going to leave now. I must go pack and make sure you are packed."

"You do that. I could use a bath and a good night's rest."

She stops jumping up and down and gets serious. "I will run your bath water then. Would you prefer eucalyptus or lavender?"

"You do no…"

She cut me off before I could finish. "I want to. You are taking me out of this castle. I owe you a bigger debt than you can imagine."

I just nod my head. Yanci runs off in a blur to start my bath and returns a few minutes later.

"Your bath is ready. I went with a vanilla scent. I put a small glass of dark red wine by the tub, and a solution of my own making for when you are finished with your wine. It will remove the stains from your teeth and lips." She bows. "Do you need anything else before I start packing our things?" Her excitement has become contagious.

I am starting to think that getting out of here for a while is exactly what I need as well.

"No, that is all." I give Yanci a small smile.

Yanci runs over to me and gives me a quick hug, then runs out the door, hurrying to get all her tasks done before tomorrow.

Ka Lee

What started as a crappy day is at least ending pleasantly enough.

Something about Yanci has caused me to see hope, to trust. It was so instantaneous that I almost do not trust it. Maybe that is foreshadowing of what is to come.

Chapter 30
KAISERA

I wake up yet again with someone else's body thrown over mine. At least this time, it is someone I know. Elena lays with her mouth open, snoring loudly, a little too close to my ear, one arm and one leg wrapped around me like I am her own personal body pillow.

We spent the night eating, drinking, and planning. I told her about the letter I had both received and sent to the queen, and about how the longer I'm here, the more I'm considering fighting to take back my crown.

I found myself longing for Bax to come back. I am having a tough time getting him out of my mind at all.

Before I knew it, Elena and I had forgotten about everything else and ended up drunk off our asses, laughing the night away until we finally passed out. She must have wrapped herself around me in the middle of the night. She has always been a bit of a wild sleeper. There were several occasions throughout the years in Erathina where we would stay up after work drinking until we passed out together.

I shove her off me, and she rolls over, drool hanging out the side of her mouth and a loud growl leaving her lips as she mumbles something inaudible.

I walk to the bathroom to take care of my morning needs. I start to leave the bathing room and catch sight of myself in the mirror.

What are you getting yourself into?

I stand there, staring and wondering about all the things that have happened in the past three days. The Hollow attacks need to be stopped, and I need to find out what happened to my father. I need to get my strength back. The last attack left me weakened too quickly. I have felt this urge to train and to be better after watching the girl from the brothel have her soul sucked out. I have never taken training seriously, but I think it may be time that I do. I feel this tension in the air that things are coming, and I need to be ready.

I grin at myself in the mirror because I think I know the perfect person to train me: a certain major who I am sure has trained hundreds, if not thousands, of soldiers in his years.

I turn and tiptoe back out the bedroom, careful not to wake Elena as I make my way to the door. When I open the door, the two same guards from yesterday are still there, or maybe they are back. I am not sure if the guards I saw at the door last night are the same ones standing in front of me now.

They turn to me. The one with the horns and lower fangs speaks first. "Need something, Princess?"

"Yes. Can you have Major Tribax come to me? That is, unless I can go to him?"

I go to take a step out of the doorway, but my path is blocked yet again. I have been stuck in this room for nearly two full days. I am so glad I will be heading out this afternoon. I cannot take this captivity.

"We will have him retrieved for you," the other guard responds.

"Fine." I slam the door closed. I turn around to find Elena sitting up in bed with her eyebrows wiggling at me.

"What?" I throw my hands up and then slap them back down onto my hips.

"Oh, nothing. Just overhearing that you are already calling for your lover after only being apart for less than twelve hours." She shrugs her shoulders, hopping out of bed and heading for the bathing room.

"He is not my lover."

She turns, bracing her arms on the doorway. "Mmhmm."

There is a knock on the door and my heart rate picks up.

"Oh gosh, Alli, I wonder who ever that could be."

I narrow my eyes at her.

She laughs. "I will be in the bathroom for twenty-ish minutes. Please be fully clothed when I return."

I wish I had something in my hand I could throw at her. Elena smirks an evil little grin at me, turns and closes the door. I can hear her bath water turn on.

I go to the door and swing it open. Bax is standing there with a toothy grin, arms folded, looking down at me. He has a navy, long-sleeved shirt on, with the sleeves rolled halfway up and tucked into brown canvas pants that hug his massive, powerful thighs. The man has muscles on top of muscles.

After I am done enjoying his looks, I drag my gaze back up to his, those blue and steel eyes locking on to mine. I drop my gaze back to his mouth, and the smirk he is wearing tells me he knows just how bad I want him.

"You need me, Princess?" his deep voice vibrates with a growl.

"Yes." It is the only word that comes out of my mouth.

Bax takes a few steps into the room then shuts the door behind him. "What do you need from me?" he says, leaning back against the door, his muscled arms flexing as he crosses them over his large chest again.

Everything

Yep, nope. No, I do not.

I shake my head, as if waking up from some sort of trance. I cough a little then finally speak. "I need you to train me."

"Darlin', I have no doubt you are well trained." He shakes his head, as if trying to forget something.

"What?" I am genuinely confused by that statement.

"Well, you made it very clear to me yesterday that you have a reputation for being a party girl." He shrugs. "I doubt that you need much 'training'."

My mouth falls open. Then, I rear back and punch him in his sternum. It hurts my hand a lot, but it knocks the air out of him, which makes the sting in my knuckles hurt less.

He wheezes out, "What was that for?"

"I was talking about training in combat, you asshole," I spit at him.

"Oh, understood," he says, still trying to catch his breath. He stands back to his full height after he is caught his breath enough, still rubbing his chest where I hit him.

"If that is the case, we can start with the right places to hit someone. Places that will hurt them more than it will hurt you."

My hand does hurts badly from that blow. I try to shake out a little bit of the pain still residing in my knuckles.

"Did you not train with Madis at the DWA?" he asks.

"I did," I say.

He looks at me with a tilt to his head. "Then you are trained?"

"A little. I did not exactly apply myself at the Academy. I never needed to. I had…" I trail off, not wanting to complete that sentence. "But I am ready to learn now."

"I see," Bax responds.

He turns and walks over to the one and only shelf in the room. It doesn't have much on it: a few books with titles that are so worn you can no longer read them and few random trinkets.

I walk up behind him, leaning in close to try to get a look at what has caught his interest.

He turns to me, reaches up, and sweeps all my messy black hair over my shoulder. "I am sorry, my sweet little vixen. I did not mean to offend you."

I pull away, turning to stare at him in confusion. I raise my eyebrow. "One, I am not your anything. Two, I am far from being sweet. Three, what is with this vixen nickname?" I ask, genuinely curious as to where the nickname comes from.

He laughs a deep gruff laugh at me as I cross my arms over my chest. He smiles at me, and that smile does something to my chest that I am not used to. He leans into me. My breath catches. I want him to kiss me again. My eyes fall directly to his mouth, where I see a small smirk sitting on his perfect lips, even with the small scar that sits on his top lip.

He turns back to the shelf and grabs my crystal-bladed sword. "This is a stunning blade. I should have taken it from you when you got here, but it seems to be a part of you somehow. Where did you get it?" Bax asks.

I guess we are just going to ignore all my questions, then.

I bite my bottom lip and stick out my hand for him to give it to me. He reaches for me, and I stay perfectly still as his thumb crosses over my lips. He pulls my bottom lip out from between my teeth. He drops his hand and clears his throat before holding the blade out for me to take.

I am momentarily stunned before I snap out of it and take the blade. I twist the sword around quickly, making it look like the crystal is nothing but a blur of white and purple.

I stop spinning the blade around and look back to him. "It was a gift."

"Quite a gift." His jaw clenches. "Is it from a lover?"

I raise an eyebrow at him again. "I do not have lovers."

That relaxes him a bit. There is no way this male could be jealous already. We have done nothing more than kiss, and this is the first actual conversation we have had. We just met yesterday.

He pulls his bottom lip into his mouth and bites down, mimicking my earlier move. It is a great look on him, and I find I would like to bite those lips myself. Bax steps toward me, not fully into my space, but I can see the intent when I look back up to his eyes.

"If you don't stop looking at me like that, I will be forced to kiss you again," Bax says.

"No one is stopping you," I respond.

"Ahhhammm," Elena coughs, clearing her throat loudly from the direction of the bathroom door. Bax and both turn at the same time to stare at her. She is leaning one shoulder against the doorframe while wearing nothing but a towel.

"I am going to get going. I have to finish getting everyone ready for departure today," Bax says and starts for the door.

"Wait," I call after him. He stops and turns to look at me. "Are you going with us to Area Seven?"

"I am. Someone has to keep an eye on you. I will make sure training equipment is brought so that we can train when we get there."

Elena walks over to me, throwing her arm over my shoulder as she looks at Bax. Then, she reaches out her hand to him. "We have not been properly introduced. I am Elena, Alli's, I mean Princess Kai's, bestie."

He takes her hand but gives her a strange look. He looks back at me. "I am so sorry to hear that."

Elena's eyebrows scrunch together, causing all her tribal markings to move dramatically. "Sorry for what?"

"That you have to be best friends with the little vixen," he responds with a wink.

"Ass," I say to him, giving him a fake death stare.

He lets go of Elena's hand then walks back to the door. "See you ladies in a few hours." Then, he is out the door.

"Oh, you are in so much trouble." Elena releases me, dropping her towel and digging through a pile of clothes that had been brought in last night for us to change into.

"Yea, and why is that?"

"I do not know. You tell me, little vixen." She selects a pair of black pants and a green tank top and changes quickly.

"You will not be calling me that. It is less confusing to everyone if you just call me Kai."

She gives me a blank stare. "But I have always known you as Alli."

"I know, and I love that you got to know Alli, but if we are going to be here in this world—and we need to be in this world—my name is Kai."

She shrugs and says, "Okay, if that is what you prefer."

"It is, thank you. It is just the longer I am here, the more I think it is my time to take the throne. I do not care if Madis thinks she deserves it. If I find out she killed my father, I will have no choice but to end her."

That statement hurts me down to my core. Yes, I am pissed at Madis. Yes, I want to beat the shit out of her for what she has

Untried Origins

taken from me, but she has been such a huge part of my life for so long, I do not want to see any permanent damage done to her.

"Kai, I think you should just talk to her. Maybe things are not as they seem. I mean, that happens, right?" she says.

"Maybe, but you saw her in that throne room with her crown. You saw her call herself the future queen. Everything I saw that night of the Binding has come true."

"Yes, but I do not know her or the situation. Not fully. I just found out three days ago that you are a damn princess. I am just saying, maybe talking to her could possibly do both of you some good."

I swing my sword around a bit, thinking about what she is saying. "I guess it never hurts to talk."

"That is the spirit. Now, let's go find food."

"I cannot get out of this room until they escort me away."

Elena opens the door to find the two guards standing there. She speaks to them in a soft, suggestive voice. "You gentlemen are going to walk away and leave us now. You have better things to do," she says, stroking their arms and letting her gift guide them to her will.

The guards reply in unison, "We have better things to do." They stand up a bit straighter and walk away.

"Looks to me like we can just walk out," Elena says with a bright, innocent smile.

Oh, thank the goddess above.

"Elena, I think you might actually be a demon and not a Fae."

Elena looks pleased with that statement for some reason.

I take off in a sprint, grabbing Elena's hand and pulling her along with me. I hear Lilith jump off the bed and chase after us.

"I know exactly where we are going for breakfast, and then we can go pick our horses for the journey! You are going to love our pristine selection of horses in the Area Six stables."

I am overly thrilled to be out of that room and to get the chance to show Elena just a little bit of the world where I grew up.

Chapter 31
MADIS

    Yanci and I make our way down to the horses, readying to depart to Area Seven. For once, I am letting myself get excited about something. Just the fact that I will not have to face either of my parents for a few days has me thrilled.

    Yanci is walking a bit behind me, wearing the light blue maids' gown, keeping up the appearance that she is just a maid. I have a dress waiting for her in the carriage to change into as soon as we are far enough away from this place.

    She will be coming as my righthand assistant, or advisor. I know it is stupid of me to trust her so quickly, but it is so nice having someone to talk to as a friend again. We had easy conversations this morning, and it all felt natural and simple. Yanci is a luxury I am allowing myself to keep and hold dear for the time being. It is nice to feel like I have a friend again. I am having a hard time figuring out what it is about her that allows me to trust her so easily.

Untried Origins

I am wearing a light pastel-colored dress that my mother selected for me. I do not plan on arriving at Area Seven this way. I do not want to show up in a carriage like a spoiled princess. I want to arrive on my own horse on my own terms. I will be changing as soon as we are far enough away.

We make it out of the castle doors and into the courtyard where our convoy is waiting. The convoy contains six, hand-selected guards, four men and two women, all of whom I trust to keep my parents from knowing anything I do not wish them to know. They, however, are not my friends. They are demon guards I trained in my DWA days who I have earned respect from, but as far as I know, they hold allegiance to my father.

The guards sit on their mounts, ready to ride. A single carriage sits with a footman waiting for me. Making my way to the carriage, I spot Kaisera with her crew. Ellie and Mica ride next to Kaisera and the Fae female she brought back here with her.

Kaisera spots me and gives a single head nod, then goes back to laughing and smiling with her friends. It hurts my heart to see she has replaced me so easily. I am about to step into the carriage when I see a beautiful, dappled gray horse round the corner with Tribax on its back. He is making a beeline for Kaisera's group. I notice Kaisera and him make eye contact, and that stunning smile that I thought was reserved for only me is now directed at Kai.

"Your Majesty, are you ready?" Yanci says.

"Hmmm? Oh, yes. Let's get going." I load into the carriage, sitting back against the bench. Yanci enters right after me and sits across from me.

"Are you ok?" she asks.

"Yes, I will be fine once we are out of this place."

"Would you like for me to tell them we are ready to leave now?"

"Yes." I turn my head, going silent. I hear Yanci yell out the window that the queen is ready to depart. I can only imagine the eye roll or scowl that Kaisera displayed hearing that.

The carriage jumps forward, and Yanci lets out a low, excited squeal as we start on our journey to something new.

Her smile causes a grin to spread across my own face. Yes, this is going to be nice. Maybe it'll even be something life changing. I am one hundred percent okay with my life changing.

It grows into nighttime quickly after we depart, leaving the city of Area Six in a bright glow of lights. The ride is filled with small conversations with Yanci, about her hobbies and personal preferences in life, from what her favorite foods are (cherry pie) to her favorite guard coming with us (Marcus). He has grayish skin and two small horns protruding from his forehead, but he also has sharp facial features and is muscularly built. I guess I can see a little of the appeal. He is also close to my height, which means he towers over Yanci. I wait until the city lights are long gone and we are only in the light of the moon before slamming my fist against the top of the carriage to let the driver know to stop.

I have already changed into riding pants, boots, and a top that fits my curves and hangs low in strips past my hips, flowing out like a dress. It is still too girly for my liking. The footman stops quickly, and I hurry out of the carriage to stretch my legs before I get on my horse.

Kaisera is the first person I see when I step out. She and her friends are all staggered directly behind the carriage on their mounts. "Oh, how exciting. We get to be in the presence of 'real' royalty," Kaisera says sarcastically.

I ignore that. I turn to the footman. "Where is my horse?"

The footman, an extremely slender man with green tinted skin, stands up. "I will have her brought up right away. We had one of the guards riding her." He bows and takes off to fetch her.

I turn back to Kaisera, take a deep breath, and plaster a smile on my face.

"How has the journey been so far? Are you in need of anything?" I ask politely and calmly.

She looks at her friend then back to me. "Who are you?"

"What do you mean?"

Kaisera responds, "Do you even remember how to ride a horse?"

"Of course, I do." I look at her confused.

Untried Origins

She shakes her head. "You know, I always knew you were about honor and duty, but I never thought it would turn you into this." She waves her hand up and down at me.

"Kai, look," I start.

She finishes. "No, not here, not now. We will talk, but it will be on my terms. That does not mean we will be friends after, or ever again."

She takes off at a trot past me to the front of the convoy, where Tribax is talking to some of the other guards.

The Fae Kaisera brought back with her speaks. "Give her time. You hurt her deeper than you know."

"I see, and who are you to give me such wisdom?" I try my best to sound like this interaction is not killing me as much as it is.

"I am Elena. I helped put Kaisera back together."

"She left us; she left me," I say.

"That is true, and what did you do to find her, other than send others? What did you do other than take on her role while she was gone?" the redhead says, throwing her body around animatedly as she speaks.

"I did not have a choice."

"I am not the one you have to convince." With that parting statement, Elena trots off to catch up to Kaisera.

I watch them. Maybe she is right.

"Your Majesty, your horse." The slender footman hands me the reins to Fletch. I named her after the fletching feathers of an arrow. The fletching's purpose is to keep the arrow on the right path.

She is a beautiful horse, I raised her from a colt. She is a palomino with a bright white mane. Fletch has always had a strong, and she has never steered me wrong.

She bumps me with her nose. Nija appears on top of Fletch's head and sprawls out between her ears, tangling himself in her white mane.

They hated each other many years ago, but at some point, they came to an agreement. Nija can ride on Fletch but is not allowed to use any fire or nip. Fletch also seems to hate it when Nija plays around her feet, but he learned that the hard way.

I pet down Fletch's neck, grabbing the reins and mounting her. It feels amazing to be back in the saddle again. My wings fall to drape down either side of Fletch.

The female guard who had been riding her, Jae, pats Fletch on the neck. "She truly is an incredible animal."

"Thank you. You may ride in the carriage with Yanci. Keep her company, please, and keep her safe."

Jae bows and walks off toward the carriage without another word.

"Okay, let's get moving. I would like to be in Area Seven by morning."

This journey would not have been any less dangerous in the daytime, and the sun would have worn the horses down faster, which is why I chose to leave in the evening.

The convoy takes off again. Kaisera, Elena, and Tribax are at the front of the group chatting amongst themselves. I stay close to the carriage, wanting to continue to give Kaisera her space.

We have made it a few hours into our ride and morning is nearing when I sense something or someone.

"Stop," I say softly.

"Stop the convoy on orders of Her Majesty," one of the guards calls out to the rest of the group.

Everyone stops, and a few of the guards come to my side. I can see Tribax, Elena, Ellie, and Kai all at the front, turning in their saddles to see what is happening.

The guard is now to my right and says, "What is it, Your Majesty?"

"Just shhh!" I tell them.

Everyone goes silent. A dark black shape flies inches from my face, embedding in the guard to whom I was just speaking.

It is a large black spear, and it was thrown so hard that it went straight through the guard's throat and into the carriage. Blood drips from the guard's mouth as he coughs on the last few bits of air he has left. The blood from the blow drips down the front of his uniform and onto the ground as his mouth pops open and closed, like a fish gasping to take in water to breathe again, clear shock on his face.

Untried Origins

I spin Fletch around and look to find where it came from. We are in Area Seven and should not be too far from the city.

Is Area Seven attacking us?

They had accepted our request to visit. Had they done it just to kill us too? If so, I have no doubt they had done the same to the king.

I hear the screaming tortured sounds of the Hollows along with the breaking and ripping of branches as they make their way through the thick forest and brush.

"Hollows! Prepare yourselves!" I start shouting out orders. "Jae, stay with Yanci. Marcus, Quincy, go keep watch over the princess and her people. Mica, you stay with them as well." They all take off to my orders without question. I know Mica found a Soulmate in Ellie, and I know he wants to keep close to her.

"Angela, you are with me." I continue to shout orders loudly and precisely. "You all have orders to kill any Hollows that show themselves."

"Yes, your majesty." They all say in unison.

"Go to the carriage, unless I call for you," I say to Nija, who is still sitting on Fletch's head. Nija nods his head before flying off into the open carriage door. As soon as he is safely inside, Yanci seals the door shut.

Nija can shift into a larger dragon, but he is still a young familiar and has a lot to learn. I have never had the opportunity to work with him; my parents would never allow it. I will only use him if I absolutely have to.

Kaisera and her friends do not seem like they are battle ready, but she now has two of my strongest men, along with Mica and Tribax.

I see the Fae girl Elena pull out a bow and crystal arrows, and Kaisera unsheathe a crystal blade.

Maybe they are more battle ready than I thought.

I ready myself after making sure everyone else is ready to fight. I will be taking down as many of these Hollows as possible to keep them away from my people.

I feel a thrill I have not felt in years running through me. I am about to fight, something I have missed for far too long, something that will feel so good, because I can let my frustration and fire run through me.

The first Hollow who breaches the trees is a black demon with cracked skin, four arms, and only one eye. He opens his mouth in a scream, showing off too many rows of razor-sharp teeth to count. I run at him full speed, and a second later I'm shoving my sword through his neck. I pull the blade to the side, snapping off half its head, leaving it dangling off the side of its shoulder. Black and red blood spills from the hole I create in his neck. Spinning, I find five more Hollows breaching the woods surrounding us. The whole convoy is now under attack, and everyone except the footman and Yanci is fighting. The cent of blood and burnt flesh fills the air quickly, and I get to work.

I use my wings to lift into the air and drive my sword down even harder into a two-headed Hollow who looks like he is part tree, with his skinny stick arms and legs and bark skin. His head, however, looks part cow, with a furry elongated face and bone-like horns.

I am slicing upward and downward, cutting through Hollow after Hollow. When I start to feel my strength dwindling just a bit, I take a step back and let my fire come to me. Twisting a large ball of fire into my hand that is not holding a sword, I throw it at the Hollows going for the carriage, alighting them instantly. Yanci and Nija are in there, and I will not let them be harmed.

The Hollows on fire thrash and scream as they are burnt alive. The disturbing smell of their fur and skin will linger in my nose for a while.

The Hollows just kept coming. I see Jae go down, and Angela is struggling to keep her strength up. I still have reserves, but not enough to take on too many more of them alone.

I am swinging helplessly at a Hollow with all my might. This one seems to have some form of outer shell protecting him, and I can see the soft spots I will have to hit to bring him down, but he is fast, and I am struggling. Everyone seems to be tiring quickly, and panic hits me. I have to get us out of here.

The Hollow in front of me freezes. His head tumbles to the ground, and warm blood sprays across my face and white hair.

Untried Origins

The Hollow's body collapses to the ground, revealing the man standing behind him.

Chapter 32
KAISERA

After fighting Hollows for what felt like hours, I am sweaty, tired, and covered in blood. The few guards from Area Seven that had come to our aid took out the rest of the Hollows.

Elena is hopping down from the carriage she climbed on top of during the fight to get the best vantage point with her bow. She is overly good with that thing. She did not miss a single shot during the fight.

How did she get so good?

I trot over to her and hug her with my one free arm, still holding my sword with the other hand. She pushes me back with a rough shove.

"Ew, just ew, Kai. You look like you rolled around in their disgusting blood then in dirt." Scrunching her nose up and looking at me like I have a contagious disease of some sort, she sniffs me. "And you smell like burnt hair and BO."

"Glad you are alive too, Elena."

Untried Origins

"I was watching over you. You were fine. I also noticed how well you and Tribax fought together. Very in sync with each other." She nudges me with her shoulder as we start walking back to retrieve our horses.

"He is a great fighter; I am sure he gets in sync with everyone he fights with." It felt great to fight alongside him. It was like he knew exactly where I needed him to be and when to be there. It had been simple; we had found a rhythm and kept to it. Although Tribax had to pick up a lot of my slack, every time I faltered, he was there without hesitation and without me asking.

Lilith meows for me to pick her up.

"And where exactly did you go during that fight, you little scaredy cat?"

Lilith hisses at me then trots back off and flaps her little wings to try and get back into the saddle of the horse I chose to take from the stables earlier. Tribax sees her little wings struggling, and he helps her back into her spot.

Lilith shows her teeth in a snarl with zero appreciation for his help. Tribax does it right back at her. It is an adorable interaction, and I giggle at it. I shake my head at the little kitten as I watch her get comfortable. "Hey, does she look like she is getting bigger?"

"Who?" Elena responds.

"Lilith. She looks like she has grown a little in the past three days."

"I don't know, maybe." Elena turns me back around to face her. "Who can we thank for this rescue? These men look different. They look like porcelain."

"They are Vampires from Area Seven," I tell her.

"Vampires?"

"Yes, Vampires, or as close to the term as you would know. They drink blood to survive, but they were banned from drinking demon blood centuries ago. They hate the sunlight, though it won't kill them. But these Vampires were born here to bring justice to those vampires who did wrong in Erathina."

"Oh, okay. Cool. Soooo, why can't they drink demon blood?" Elena asks with a curious look on her face.

I forget she knows very little about this world. "It makes them stronger, and it is addictive to them. They will kill the demon if they do not have enough control. Come on. Let's go see who we can thank for bringing these men." I start to look around when I see exactly who I need to thank.

Elena grabs my wrist to keep me from walking any further. "Wait, they are banned from drinking demon blood, but what about mine?"

I shrug. "I am sure you will be fine."

We look around to the Vampires who rescued us and see that quite a few of them are looking in our direction.

"At least, I think you will be," I say.

"Fantastic," Elena replies sarcastically.

Chapter 33
MADIS

    The man standing behind the fallen Hollow smiles brightly at me. He has sharp, dangerous features that are both handsome and terrifying. Everything about the man standing in front of me says to stay away.
    But when he offers out his hand, I take it.
    When I'm back on my feet, I try to dust myself off as best as possible, but all I manage to do is smear around blood and dirt.
    "Are you alright?" the dangerous man standing in front of me asks.
    I look around to see how the rest of the convoy weathered in the fight. I shake my head up and down in relief as I see everyone, but the one lost guard is standing and breathing.
    "Yes, they are fine," I reply.
    He laughs and looks around. "Yes, well, I asked if *you* are alright."
    I lift my brow and decide to ignore his strange comment. "Thank you for taking down that Hollow. I would have handled

them all eventually." I do not want to give this man the impression that I cannot handle things on my own.

"I am sure you would have, but I felt like rescuing you," he says. He smiles at me, and I catch myself staring at his four sharp canines.

Vampire.

Before I get to question him on who he is and where he came from, I hear Kaisera's booming voice coming from behind him. "Reign, what the fuck do you think you are doing here?"

Reign spins around, and I step to the side to see their interaction. Kaisera is charging toward him, looking ready for a fight. I have the urge to step in front of him but hold my ground.

He responds to her with a wicked smile dancing on his lips. "Coming to save the poor little princess, of course." His face goes flat and smooth, a deadly look creeping over his already dangerous features.

"No one asked for a damn thing from the likes of you," Kaisera spits back at him.

"Aw, you hurt me so, Princess. I was sure you would be worshiping me for my heroic acts today." His words sound elegant and graceful. Each one seems to roll off his tongue.

"Praise this, you asshole," Kaisera says before closing the short gape between them.

The other vampires who came to our rescue start to move to protect the man who is clearly about to be attacked by Kaisera. Our guards are doing the same to get to Kaisera. Kaisera throws her arms and legs around him in a tight embrace. She laughs while the man spins her around in circles.

"You have not changed one bit, you crazy kid," the man says.

Kai laughs. "You would never want me to change, and I am no longer a snotty nosed kid."

I know the other kings used to come to Area Six to visit, but I was never allowed to meet them. From this interaction, I guess Kaisera was granted the chance to meet them when she was younger.

He sets her down and brushes a piece of her hair off her face. She smiles a huge smile back up at him.

Untried Origins

"No, I guess you are not," Reign replies.

Tribax steps up to Kaisera's side, his jaw clenched, making him look more than just a little annoyed. He looks like he is downright jealous, but who could he possibly be jealous over? Kaisera, it seems, but he just met her a few days ago. He reaches Kaisera's side, and she looks at him with a frown and takes a bit of a step away from him.

There is something going on between them, I am just not sure what yet. I can see the annoyance radiating from Tribax, and he looks like he is struggling not to move closer to her again.

Tribax looks over to me, and somehow from that look, I already know. He is falling for Kaisera. I do not know how that could have happened so quickly, but Tribax has always been an all-in kind of guy. I nod my head to him in understanding, and he nods back once. I knew after the Binding that Tribax was not meant for me, even if I never truly admitted it to myself.

He turns his attention back to the man in front of him. "Reign, huh? As in King Reign of Area Seven?"

Reign smiles at Tribax, which only seems to annoy him further, if that is even possible at this point. "That would be correct." Reign says.

"Well, King Reign," Tribax says with a bit of sarcasm. "Can you lead us to a safer location? I would hate to mess up your pretty clothes with another Hollows attack."

I can tell Reign is taking Tribax's attitude as a challenge, especially with Kaisera standing in-between them. A jolt of jealousy runs through me. Of course, she would have two men fighting over her. No, I get a jolt of jealousy over the king showing attention toward her.

"Sure thing, you and the lovely Kai." Reign pauses to grab a lock of Kai's hair and spin it around his fingers. The move earns a low growl out of Tribax, but a giggle from Kaisera. "Get back to your horses and I will help…" He looks at me and offers me a friendly smile and a hand.

"Madis," I say, feeling my cheeks heating.

What am I? A starstruck teen? Am I blushing at this man?

Taking his outstretched hand for the second time today, I smile back sweetly at him. I have never trusted anyone in my life, but unexpectedly, here I am trusting two strangers within a twenty-four-hour period. Of course, simply taking his hand does not mean I trust him, but I have the powerful desire to try.

"I will help Madis," he says my name like a wish, "Find her ride and maybe she will be nice enough to lend me a ride back with her. The run here tired me tremendously." Reign says.

Kaisera and Tribax start walking off, and Kai shoves him playfully. I watch them for a second before Reign starts to pull lightly on my hand.

"Do you know which direction your horse went, Madis?" he asks me.

I look over to him. "Yes, of course."

"Which direction did she head? I will go retrieve her." He starts to look around.

I whistle a high-pitched bird call and turn back to look at him. "You know Princess Kaisera well then?" I feel the need to know more.

He laughs softly. It is smooth and honey and seductive. "You could say that."

"What other way is there to say it?"

"Kaisera is like an annoying baby sister I never actually wanted."

Fletch comes trotting up behind me until she is close enough to push the back of my shoulder with her nose. I am still staring at Reign. He has a slender, lean body, all sharp edges, and angles. Those dark hazel eyes look like they hold every answer to everything within the universe.

He has his eyes on me, too, searching for answers I do not have. He has a look of elegance and intelligence. It is in his facial expression and the way he holds himself, not saying any more than what needs to be heard.

He starts to reach out a hand and lean in closer to me, making my heart skip a beat. "What's her name?" Reign asks.

I realize he is not reaching for me, but past me to stroke Fletch's nose. My breath is lodged in my throat. I have had a similar feeling to this one, this feeling that somehow our lives are connected. I felt like this when Tribax pinned me against the wall outside of the cafe. Except this time, it feels different. It feels more personal. It feels like I am more willing to accept this pull to him than I ever was with Tribax.

I realize I have just been standing here not speaking for several seconds now, and I have forgotten the question. "What?"

He shifts slightly so that he is looking directly at me again instead of down at me.

"What is your horse's name?" I can almost feel his breath on me.

"Fletch, like the fletching of an arrow."

"Ah, so she is to guide you," Reign says.

"Yes."

Reign takes a step back, like he had not noticed a thing occurring between us. Maybe because nothing had. It is also possible I am so deprived of human interactions that I do not know how to properly interpret them.

He bows slightly at the waist. "It would be the greatest honor if you would allow me to ride back to my home with you."

I straighten and nod my head but suggest instead, "If you prefer, you could ride in the carriage."

"Actually, I would prefer if you allowed me to ride ahead of the convoy with you to beat the sun and allow some of my guards the privileges of riding in your carriage."

Oh, yeah, the whole sun thing.

"Of course. Let me just get someone for my lady's maid to ride with." I am not going to leave Yanci in a carriage with a bunch of demon vampire men.

"Angela," I call. She turns from the conversation she is having with Quincy and sprints over to me instantly.

Angela is a tall built woman. She has a shaved head with tattoos down the side of her tanned neck. She also has small, short white horns that protrude out of her forehead.

"Yes, Your Majesty?"

"See to it that Yanci, my lady's maid, rides the rest of the way with you, and let the footman know that some of King Reign's guards will be riding in the carriage and to try to keep to the shadows."

We still have an hour or so before the sun fully rises, so we should make it there with a few minutes to spare. Plus, I know sunlight will not kill them, just annoy their skin and eyes a bit.

"Impressive," Reign says. I turn back to him with a look of confusion. "You say the words as a queen would, but you speak to them as if you are a general."

"Well, generals and queens play a similar role. Both lead." I say.

"Of course, but queens are trained to rule with grace. Generals fight to rule with brutality and strength."

"You just met me. How would you know what I have and have not fought for?"

He touches my cheek and brings his bottom lip between his teeth. He bites down on it, displaying the sharp canine fangs. "Touché, but I look forward to finding out."

I pull his hand away softly. "We need to get going."

Reign slides his hands into his pockets and leans back on his heels. "After you then, my darling."

I turn before he can see just how flushed I am getting from that simple pet name. Reign step up right behind me as I go to mount Fletch.

"May I help you up?" Reign asks.

"That is okay, I can do it."

"What if I want to put my hands on you?" His voice and words send heat flaring over my spin. I have to calm myself to make sure I am not going to burn Fletch or anything else.

"Still, I have it this time."

"Maybe next time then," Reign says.

There will never be a next time. You will be bored of me soon enough. I will be carted off to marry King Alibast in a few short weeks.

I mount Fletch and extend my hand to Reign to assist him up. He takes it and hops up behind me, careful not to brush up against too much of my wings, he leans into my back but does not touch me anywhere with his hands. I assume they are resting on Fletch's ass. However, everywhere he is touching me lights my skin on fire. His long muscular legs rest next to mine, and his chest is just slightly resting against me, barely touching the spot where my wings go into my shoulder blades.

"I see you can help others, but you take away my privilege to help you." Reign says.

I think about that then reply. "I do not need the help, others do."

I kick Fletch, and we take off toward Area Seven, toward King Reign's home. Taking off so quickly causes Reign to throw a hand around my waist. He holds on tightly, but he is more respectful than most by keeping his hand near my belly button. I am covered in blood and burnt Hollow flesh. I know I stink, but he does not seem to be bothered by it.

Chapter 34

KAISERA

I cannot figure out what Tribax's problem is, but he looks pissed. He seemed so happy and carefree, even after the Hollows showed up. He bet me that I could not kill three. I had killed two before I started to shake from the weight of swinging the sword. He had been there to take and give the blows as I struggled. He had a shit-eating grin the whole time, too.

But when he stood a bit too close to me when I was speaking with Reign, I took a step back. I am not used to anyone standing over me in such a way. He was being protective, and I am not his property to protect. I can take care of myself.

He huffs out what must be his fifth loud sigh since then, just deep breaths of annoying-as-Inferis sighs leaving his lips.

We are making our way through the city gates of Area Seven, still a good distance from the center of the Area where King Reign's castle sits. Everything in this Area looks dangerous and dark. The buildings are all made of dark gray and black stones. Reign is the one heir I always enjoyed seeing. He was already an adult when we met, and I was nothing but a scrawny little kid, but he always treated me how a cool uncle would treat his niece. He helped me terrorize the kitchen staff until they would find me treats that my father would have never allowed me to have before mealtimes. He would even feign defeat against me in training exercises.

As I grew up, he became like a big brother, teasing me and picking on my height and short temper every chance he got. We have not seen each other in a very long time.

Tribax huffs again, messing with my train of thought. I have had it with him.

"What?" I half scream at him.

"Nothing," he says, but he is looking straight ahead and shrugging his shoulders.

"No, spit it out. Something is clearly bothering you."

He grinds his teeth. "I just forgot you were the princess for a minute."

"And?"

"And I think if you are going to go after another royal bloodline, you can do better than fangs."

"You mean KING Reign?" I make sure the word king really stands out, just to annoy him further.

"Ha, yeah, sure, the 'king'." He air quotes the last word with his fingers. I am learning he likes his air quotes.

"He is the king, and who I go after is not of concern to you."

What is with this guy? Yes, we have been having moments. I know I have felt a strange draw to Tribax, but that has too just be sexual. *Right?*

I start to think of how it felt for him to kiss me, how badly I wanted him to do more after that kiss. I adjust myself in my saddle to try and wiggle those thoughts away, trying to convince myself that he is just some guy I met, and that the draw to him is nothing more than sex appeal.

Bax moves so quickly, I hardly notice him move at all. He grabs my reins from me and jumps from his horse onto the back of mine. He kicks the stallion hard in the side and gives a loud verbal "Yaaa!"

I hear Elena shout. "K, I am just going to stick with the group."

We charge between buildings and then out through a wooded area until we are far enough from the group that I do not think anyone can hear us. Bax slows the horse down to a steady walk.

"What the shit, Bax?" I try to turn around to see his face, but he pulls me back tighter into him. My smaller frame is consumed by his massive one, his arms on the reins caging me.

"I am making it my business," he says.

"Making what your business?"

"Who you go after. Now, stay still. You do not move unless I say so."

I must admit, I am intrigued, but am I willing to let him boss me around like this? I ponder for a moment before I decide I want to see what he is planning. "Fine."

"You can tell me to stop at any time, but those are only words I want to hear from you until I say otherwise." He switches the reins over to one hand and moves all my long black hair over to one side. I know it is tangled and coated in blood, but Bax does not seem to care.

Now that my hair is out of his way, he gently runs his fingers up and down the exposed side of my throat. It is nothing more than a caress, but it sends shivers down every inch of me.

"Can you agree to that?"

I shake my head yes, only because his hand feels too good with every passing stroke of his fingers on my neck.

"No, I need to hear you say it," he whispers, so close to my ear that I can feel the moisture from his breaths and his mouth softly grazing the shell of my ear.

"Yes, I can agree to that." I squirm my butt a little closer into his thighs in the hopes that will get him to do more, to touch more, but he seems unaffected by my efforts.

He reaches down with his free hand, wrapping it all the way around my hip, forcing me to be still before it moves on to my stomach. His hands are so large, they cover the vast majority of my stomach, and his pinky finger is centimeters from my waistline.

Untried Origins

"I said do not move unless you're told." His hand wanders from my stomach down to the hem of my shirt, then under my shirt so there is no longer a barrier of clothing between his hand and my skin. Bax slowly starts to glide his calloused fingers over me, toying with the skin just above my belt line.

I want him to move that hand lower, so I push my hips up to force his hand down to where I want it. All I get is a soft chuckle before his hand retreats to my hip to steady me. He pulls the horse to a stop and stays very still before leaning back into my ear.

"You want my hand to slide into you, don't you, little vixen?"

A breathy whimper is my only response.

"I thought so. If you want that, you are going to have to listen to someone for a change and be still. I know following the rules is not your strong suit."

He stays silent, waiting for my response. I want to tell him to fuck off, that I do not listen to anyone. If I want to be pleased that badly, I can find someone willing without this bullshit. I am not going to do that, though, because I want this man. For reasons I do not know, his body is the only one I can see wanting right now.

Alright, let's play your game, Baxy.

"Okay," I finally say.

He taps the horse to start moving again. The hand resting on my hip takes the same path it took the last time, playing with the waistline of my pants. I can tell he is evaluating me now to see if I am going to move, but I am not going to this time. I want what he is offering, and if that means playing by his rules for the moment, fine.

I swear I can feel the smile on his face when he says, "Good girl. I am going to give you some orders, and you are going to follow those orders exactly."

I roll my eyes but comply.

"Unbutton your pants."

I quickly move my hands to do as I am told. I unbutton the three buttons holding my pants up then put my hands back on the saddle, waiting for my next order.

"So eager."

He has no idea, but I do not want him to know that.

"Do not push it, Baxy."

He laughs "Ok, sorry." I can feel his smile when he leans down to my ear.

"Now, lean your head back onto my shoulder and close your eyes."

I do exactly as he instructs. I rest my head back on his chest, turning as much as I can to inhale his pine tree and spice scent.

"That's right. Relax for me," Bax says in a seductive-as-shit voice that causes my already-heated core to want to combust.

I try to do as he says. I let all the tension leave my body with a few deep inhales and exhales.

"Now, the only thing I want you to focus on is this." He starts to move his hand in small, soft sweeps across my stomach, drawing little pictures with his callused fingers.

I nod my head yes.

"The only thing you know right now, Kaisera, is the feel of my hand on you."

He starts his descent, going all the way to the center of me before dragging his finger all the way back up to my clit. The movement causes my whole body to jolt up. That one pull of his finger is so insane, I am already having a harder time breathing.

"Kaisera, you have to stay still." He starts to pull his hand away.

I make my body turn into a statue, not wanting him to pull away again. My full name has never been my favorite, but on his lips, it sounds like I am being called away to my greatest desires. "I... I am sorry. I am trying."

I tilt my head upward to him, and he leans down and captures my lips with his. He returns to my bundle of nerves at my apex, moving his middle finger around in circles, increasing pressure as he goes.

I moan into his mouth. This man is stealing my soul with his touch, and I am loving every second of it. He pulls his hand out of my pants, causing me to whimper into his mouth. He breaks the kiss as he brings his glistening fingers to his lips and sucks them into his perfect mouth. His deep-sea blue eyes with that perfect ring of silver are dilated fully when he pulls his fingers out of his mouth to speak. "Oh, goddess above, you are going to be my damnation and salvation, aren't you?"

I am starting to think the same of you, Baxy.

"You taste of my dreams, like fresh summer fruits." He dives his hand back down my unbuttoned pants, sliding his rough hands down my whole core until he comes to my center again. He waits a minute, giving me a chance to object, an objection I already am realizing I may never give him.

After a second of waiting, he plunges his thick, long finger into me hard and fast. I stay as still as I can while his finger drives into me at a maddening pace.

He starts to pump roughly in and out of me with that single finger. My breath starts to catch, moans and soft noises escaping me. Bax moves his head down to my neck and starts nibbling and kissing every inch of my exposed skin that he has access to. I wish he had access to all of me.

I am starting to reach my peak of pleasure, my breaths and moans coming harder and faster. My core is tightening and wrapping around his finger. Bax presses down on my clit with his rough palm, causing the pressure to grow even more.

"That's it, little vixen, come all over my fingers. I want your scent on me." His deep voice has a hint of an animalistic growl to it. It vibrates all the way through me. Between the vibration, the words themselves, his relentless pace, and just the feel of his hand on me, I tip over the edge.

I moan loudly and arch my chest and back up. Bax continues to kiss up the column of my neck through the whole orgasm. For a moment, all I can feel are his lips on my neck and the pleasure that just ripped through me.

He slowly removes his hand. Even with how soft he is now; my whole body seems so tender. I am still trying to catch my breath.

He turns my head up and over to kiss my mouth, and I dive my tongue in. I want to feel so much more of him. If just his fingers feel that good, I have to know what the rest of him feels like, what he will feel like. I try to turn around in the saddle, but Bax is not having it.

"Relax," he speaks against my lips with a soft smile dancing on his face.

"No." I try to turn again.

He locks his arms around me. I throw my head back into his shoulder in frustration.

Bax laughs softly behind me. "You are so stubborn, and I enjoy that about you. We are here, so unless you want a lot of witnesses, you will have to wait to have me."

I pick my head up off his shoulder and look. He is right. We are walking out of the edges of the forest to the front gates of King Reign's castle, leaving everything we just did in the woods behind us. "I still will not chase you," I say, barely loud enough for him to hear.

Bax laughs, leaning down to whisper to me. "Oh, I do not think you will chase me. I think you will get down on your hands and knees and beg for me to take you in all the darkest ways that only I can. I think when you finally do break and beg for me, I will make you come so hard, you will never wish for another man to be between those beautiful thighs of yours ever again. I think after that, you will continue to beg for more."

I am the one grinding my teeth now, because after what we just did in those woods. I know he might be right.

Chapter 35

MADIS

Reign and I made our way into the castle first. The ride back was silent with little conversation other than the occasional direction given by Reign. He did ask about Nija and how long I have had him. Nija seemed weary of him. He never approached him during the ride and stayed put in Fletch's mane toward the top of her head.

As soon as we arrive at the castle, Reign hops off gracefully, extending his hands to help me off. I allow him to grab both sides of my hips, and I place my hands on his forearms. I turn, and he slowly and gently slides me down. I am close enough to smell him, even over the disgusting smell of the Hollows blood and gore caked on me. He smells like a rainstorm and aged bourbon.

"Thank you for the lift," He reaches out and pinches a blood-soaked lock of my hair between his fingers.

"How about you let me repay you with a bath?" His hazel eyes darken just a bit.

My mouth falls open. As stunning as this male is, I am already promised to the King of Area One. My parents will kill me if they find me doing anything with this man, or any man, for that matter.

I pull his hand away from my hair softly. "I will not be bathing with you," I say firmly.

A wide grin grows on his face. "Well, that is an enticing idea. I had not meant I would be joining you, though."

My cheeks heat in embarrassment. I am positive my olive skin is turning a dark shade of burgundy right now. "Oh, well then, yes. A bath would be nice," I say.

He turns to walk away but stops and looks down to my hands fixed together in front of me. He grabs one and starts to walk up the castle steps.

What is with this man wanting to hold my hand?

I do not mind it. It feels nice to have my hand held, but I am wondering why he feels the need to grab it every chance he gets.

The castle is stunning. It is all sharp edges and points, a lot like the king of this realm. The castle doors are made of dark, intricately carved wood, and swing open on our approach.

Perfectly placed stained glass windows hang high above, bringing in very little light. The light that does come through shows beautiful colors of all ranges throughout the grand entrance room. Two large staircases wrap upward to the right and left. Ivy and vibrantly dark flowers grow up the walls in some places, making the room look wild and untamed. For a moment, I wish to be one of those vines, to grow in my own way without repercussions.

A man hurries over to us.

"Miles, fantastic. Can you see to it that Madis is taken to the queen's suites and given everything she will require to get cleaned up. Also, have some fresh fruit brought to her rooms," Reign demands of Miles, who must be the butler here, then turns to me.

"Dinner tonight? After you have rested? We have much to discuss."

Untried Origins

I start to release Reign's hand to walk away, but he grips a bit more firmly. I look down to our joined hands and then back up to him.

Reigns lifts my hand to his mouth and places a kiss to the back of it before releasing me.

I curtsy then move forward to let Miles know I am ready to go. I am not sure why I curtsied. I am covered in blood guts and smell of death, I am sure.

"Tonight, then," I respond.

"I will have your lady's maid and clothes sent to your suite when they arrive," Reign adds.

Miles chimes in. "Right this way, Queen Madis."

Miles is an older looking Vampire, older than I thought they could get. He has graying hair and wrinkles in the corners of his eyes. He is still an attractive man in some ways. He is a few inches shorter than I am and seems fit.

I follow him through the dark hallways covered in beautiful works of art. Red carpets line the staircases and hallways along the way. There is no one walking about. It is silent here, peaceful even.

"Where is everyone?" I ask Miles after passing through another hallway and seeing no one.

"This is the time for rest. The castle will be spilling over with people tonight."

"I see."

Of course, they are all sleeping. It is early morning, and vampires prefer the darker hours.

We approach massive wooden doors. Carved into the doors is a picture of two faceless people, probably vampires, sitting on their thrones and holding hands. When the doors open, their hands are torn apart.

When the doors are fully open, I walk into one of the grandest rooms I have ever seen. Plush couches circle around a massive fireplace that is already burning. Exotic rugs in deep reds and blues lay across the majority of the floors. A massive four poster bed with silk draped down the large, elegantly carved wooden posts sits against the back wall. Even with all the elegance in this room, it still has a cozy warm feeling. I start to walk toward one of the large couches to take a seat, but then remember I am covered in gore.

Miles is still standing by the door. "If you need anything at all, just pull this string here." He gestures to a large golden string with tassels hanging by the main entrance.

I nod my head in understanding. I turn back to take in the rest of the room and notice I do not see any other doors.

"Miles?" I call after him before he exits the room.

"Yes, miss?" Miles says kindly.

"Where are the bathing rooms?"

"This way." He walks to the far right and pushes on part of the wall that seems to just be a wall, but it swings open at his touch.

"I believe you will find everything you need here. I will have your things brought up shortly. The convoy has just arrived."

"How do you know they just arrived?"

Miles touches his ear with two fingers. "Vampire hearing is a wondrous thing."

"Ahh. I am sure that does come in handy. Thank you."

Miles bows at the waist and leaves, closing the large double doors behind him.

I hurry off to the shower, wanting to get clean as quickly as possible.

The bathing room is just as glorious as the main room. It is done with all rough-cut stone, and the cabinets are in a dark rich wood with delicate carvings. There is a large, gray stone tub off by itself a dark corner, with hundreds of candles wrapped around it waiting to be used.

I hope I get to use you at least once.

No time for soaking and relaxing today, though. I turn the water for the shower on.

The shower I am using is made of dark stone as well, curving around like a maze before it opens into a large stone room with multiple shower heads. I strip and jump into the burning water as quickly as I can. I bathe quickly, wanting to be clean and in need of a nap before tonight. As soon as I step out of the shower, I hear Yanci coming in.

"I am in here." I call out to her.

Yanci hurries in a few brief moments later, looking excited.

She says, "So how was it?"

I respond to her in confusion "How was what?" *Is she wondering if my shower is nice?* That would be odd.

"Your ride with the sexiest king in all of the realms?" She is bouncing on the balls of her feet.

I roll my eyes. "It was just a ride. I am to be married at the end of this month to the King of Area One."

"I know, but a lot can happen in a month. Heck, a lot can happen in a day. Yesterday, I was worried I would get fired and beaten by your mother. Today, I am standing in a beautiful room with you and not wearing that hideously blue maid's gown anymore."

She had changed on the road before the attack. Yanci is wearing black pants, a red top, and a black jacket. She has even managed to get some dark kohl around her eyes. I have no clue how she managed that in a shaky carriage, but she looks pretty. Her blond hair is down and out of its bun, waving almost to her hips.

"I cannot disobey my parents. If they believe this is the best choice for Area Six, then I will see it through."

She crosses her arms and smirks at me. "Your parents are not here, and neither is the king of Area One. I say you live it up for the week we are here."

How did this rebellious girl make it in my mother's services without being killed? "It really does not matter. The king is more interested in Kaisera than me."

I turn to look at myself in the dark, wood-trimmed mirror as I wrap a towel around me and leave the shower. I convince myself that I am making sure all the blood and gore is out of my white hair. In reality, I am looking to try and see myself, something I do not think I have ever truly seen. When I look at my own reflection, I only see the person I was trained to become.

"Well, Kaisera is more interested in Tribax."

I stare at her blankly, wondering how she figured that out so quickly, then turn back to the mirror, picking up a brush to start detangling my hair.

"What would make you think that?"

"Earlier today, he jumped onto her horse, leaving his own behind, and they just took off together. I still have not seen them come back," Yanci says. "I do not think the king is interested in Kaisera, seeing as he put you in the room that is connected to his."

I pause my brushing. "And how do you know this?"

Yanci is like a little spy, absorbing everything like a sponge. I am beginning to wonder if she is a little too good of a spy to have ended up in my room yesterday.

"This is the queen's suites; they are always connected to the king's."

Of course. I should have known that, but we have never had a queen. Kaisera's mother died giving birth to her. I am not even sure if I was alive while the queen was. Most of my youth was spent with my father, in the room he kept me in for punishments and lessons.

I finish brushing my hair and walk past Yanci back into the bedroom, trying to quickly vanish any thoughts of that room and time spent with my father.

"I will be attending a dinner with the king tonight and will need something to wear. Can you pull out my dresses? Then, you can return to your rooms. I need rest."

She nods and takes off out of the room.

I wake up in a daze. Yanci is moving about, setting things out for me.

"What time is it?" I yawn out. I do not feel rested at all.

"Nearly evening. Your dinner is two hours from now."

I hop out of bed and wander over to the dresses. "Yanci, what is this? I thought you were going to bring dresses that were not of my mother's style?"

Untried Origins

All of them are light pinks, purples, and blues with tight, thick corsets. They scream my mother.

"I did. The luggage must have been switched before we left." Leave it to my mother to take even my clothing choice away from me. "I can go into town and see if I can find you something different, but I do not believe I will be back by your dinner with the king."

"No, it is fine. I will wear the purple one."

She puts the rest of the dresses back into the crate as I head into the bathing room to start the process of braiding my hair up into a neat bun. When I'm done, I quickly dress with Yanci's help. We are finishing up when there is a knock at the door.

"Come in," I say softly.

The door swings open to show King Reign standing in the doorway, holding a beautiful bouquet of black lilies and dark red roses.

"For you." He holds the flowers out, and I walk the few short steps over to him before reaching out and taking them.

I smirk and smell the flowers. "They are beautiful, thank you. You did not have to do this." I gesture to the flowers.

"I know, but just because I do not have to, does not mean I shouldn't," he responds.

I hand the flowers to Yanci. "Please have these put into water."

I turn to Nija, who is sprawled out across my bed on his back with his feet in the air, trying to nip at his tail. "You will be good here for tonight?" Nija jumps up to sit on his feet and tilts his head to the side. I walk over and pet him. "Behave and I will bring you some steak." He huffs out a ball of fire in excitement, and I catch it before it can light anything on fire. I extinguish the flame and narrow my eyes at him. "That is not behaving." Nija walks to the pile of pillows and curls in on himself before huffing out a bit of smoke.

I shake my head at him, then turn back to the king.

The king gestures to the door with his hand and offers up his elbow. With a half smirk on his face, he asks, "Shall we?"

I nod my head and take his elbow. We start our walk out of my room and down the long dark hallways.

"Can I be frank with you?"

I have to smile a little at how proper he is. His words sound more elegant than necessary. "Yes."

"That dress doesn't suit you."

I stop walking and turn to look at him, releasing his arm. I agree with him.

But how can he know what suits me?

"I mean no offense. It is just, you are too fierce for these girly colors and fabrics."

I am speechless and stare blankly at him. He grabs my hand again, placing it back into the crock of his elbow. We walk in silence all the way to his dining hall.

When the doors are opened, I admire all the craftsmanship around me. There are black chandeliers covered in diamonds in the shape of teardrops, giving off the impression that it is raining. The massive table in the middle of the room looks to be of solid steel, with twisted metal carvings up the legs. To the right of the table are several huge windows that look out over mountain peaks, with a city twinkling with night lights below.

The table is only set for two at the far end, lit by several candles. Reign lets go of my arm and pulls out the chair at the head of the table that is normally designated for the king. I look at him confused.

"It is just a chair, and it is just a spot to sit. People choose to give power to it."

I smile softly at that. No one else in all of Inferis would agree with him on that. I take my seat. I stick out so much in this purple tulle dress, I look like a ripe flower in the middle of a dying field. I hate it. "Do you have a seamstress here or stores close by?"

Reign sits down softly and leans his elbow on the table, resting his hands on them. "As much as it would thrill me for you to change your appearance on my behalf, I would not want you to do such a thing."

"I...I would not be doing it for you."

"Then why?"

I sigh. "If you must know, this clothing was selected for me, and while I am here, I would like to select my own clothing."

Untried Origins

"If that is the case, I can send my seamstress to you after dinner. I look forward to seeing you as you wish to be."

Yeah, I would like to see her as well.

The servants enter moments later with plates for me, different foods of all kinds. There is salad, bread, pork, chicken, and sides, even various side dishes delicious-looking desserts that I know my mother would not approve of me eating.

"Sorry for the overload. I was not sure what you wished to eat. We keep food stocked for the human servants, of course, and the cooks are human as well, so the food should taste good."

"It smells amazing," I tell him because it does. My mouth is starting to water from the smell alone. I put a bit of salad on my plate and a piece of chicken.

"Would you mind if I have my dinner as well?"

"Not at all."

Reign waves to the servant standing by the door. I assumed he would have the servants bring him a glass of blood.

We sit silently as an incredibly attractive woman walks in. She has on a tight red dress that shows off all of her. She has dirty blonde hair, deep brown, seductive eyes, and pink, full lips.

She has a small smirk on those pink lips as soon as she sees me staring. I catch out of the corner of my eyes that Reign is not watching the woman who has entered the room, but he is watching me watch her with a curious look on his face.

I am sure the large gulp I take is audible from a mile away, so I am one hundred percent positive that Reign hears it. Being from Inferis, I have grown up around blood and gore, so I am not sure why this is intimidating me so much.

The woman bows at Reign then asks, "How would you prefer it tonight, my King?"

The way she says "my" sounds very possessive, like she is asking how he would prefer it in the bedroom, not how he would prefer his meal.

"The arm will be fine," Reign replies. The woman hands her arm over to him. Reign takes it and licks her across the wrist, all while looking at me from under his eyelashes. We are both ignoring the woman so completely, I am having a tough time remembering she is even in the room with us.

He opens his mouth, and his fangs grow just the slightest before he sinks them into the blonde woman so swiftly and smoothly, he could have been biting into butter.

The woman instantly starts to moan, and I should look away. I should be respectful of this moment and him. However, the only thing going through my mind is that I want to know why it is making her moan like that.

Vampires are not allowed to bite demons, not unless the demon allows it. Demon blood is more potent to vampires, so once they get a taste, they do not want to stop. Most demons in their right minds would never allow it.

After several long moments of the woman writhing and moaning, Reign releases her from his mouth. He moves the woman's wrist over to a goblet on the table and lets it fill halfway with the blonde woman's blood.

"You may go," he says as he licks the last droplets of blood from his mouth slowly.

"But Your Majesty..." the blonde woman responds.

Reign moves his gaze to her, the look in his eyes promising pain and punishment. The woman whines but bows and retreats from the room.

"She cannot be one of your pure souls from Erathina," I say without thinking.

Reign looks at me in question, "Why would she be a pure soul?"

I gulp again, not sure if I should answer that, but I do anyways. "Because you enjoy capturing pure souls from the mortal realm to torture and drink from."

He laughs loudly. "No, I do not," he says with one eyebrow raised and a small smirk left on his face. Reign grabs his wine glass that he filled with her blood, still shaking his head, and takes a sip. "Now that we are full, we have much to discuss."

The way that Reign is looking at me makes my heart skip beats and my hands begin to sweat. I clear my throat that seems half swollen shut. "Yes, we do. Did you murder King Braxton, and did you attempt to murder us with the Hollows attack?"

He chuckles and leans back into his large metal chair, then leans up to speak. "Ah, so I save your life and you accuse me of murder? Princess, if I had wanted you dead, you would be dead, and I would not have sent Hollows to do a job I enjoy."

Reign leans back lazily in his chair, crossing a foot over his knee, sipping his blood wine as if the accusation of him murdering someone and enjoying it means absolutely nothing.

"You did not save my life, and I am not a princess," I say, trying to hold my chin high, even if it feels a bit too heavy.

"That's right, my dear, you do not need help."

I would love help, but it is not a luxury I am allowed.

"Did you have the king murdered?" I try again.

He sits back up, placing his wine glass down and leaning his elbows on the table, crossing his fingers together and setting his chin on top of them. "No."

"No?"

He is leaning in close; I swear I can smell the fresh blood on his breath. It is intoxicating. I almost want to try some. He sits back in his seat again, seeming to find everything in the room more interesting than me all of a sudden.

He sighs. "No, I did not kill your king. I tried to aid him the same way I aided you and your people, but in his case, I was too late. No, I did not try to have you and yours killed. I would not have been planning a welcome ball just to have the guest of honor murdered beforehand. That would spoil all the fun."

I perk up a bit. "A ball?"

"Ah, something will crack that mask of yours."

I know people think I am emotionless, and I am okay with that. It keeps people from knowing that I am always three seconds from breaking down. My father taught me long ago in that damn room to keep my emotions on lockdown. Emotions show your weakness; they show the enemy what they need to break you. Reign, as far as I am aware, is an enemy.

"I have never been to a ball." That's what I choose to go with, just a simple fact.

"You are the future queen, are you not?" His eyebrows scrunch together a bit, those hazel eyes looking into my blue ones. He seems so invested in my answers for some reason. My guess is he wants to use every bit of information he can find out about me against me and my people.

"I am. After I am married, of course." I tilt my chin up a bit higher and take a sip of my wine. It is Fae wine, the good stuff. I will need to be careful if I care to keep my wits about me.

"Right," he says.

He taps the small black ring with his crest seal against the metal chair he is sitting in. The noise echoes throughout the empty room loudly. He seems to have finally come to a conclusion of some sort. "I will be your escort to the ball."

I should not be seen with another man, especially another king, when I am promised to a entirely different king in just a few short weeks. I nearly choke on the wine I started to sip again.

Reign stands and pushes my chair back so that he can stand between me and the table. He leans over, placing a hand on each of the arms of my chair. He has me boxed in, and out of instinct, I start to weigh all my options of escape. I take a deep breath in and a deep breath out. I do not want to offend this king, and I find I do not wish to escape from him just yet. His sharp eyes are drawing me in and soaking into me slowly, like they are trying to embed themselves into my memory forever.

"I want to see the real you, Madis. I want to see what that body of yours looks like in something of your choosing. I want to see if there is more to you than what someone else has made. I want you to choose to share that woman with me." He is looking at me and seeing more of me than anyone ever has. My eyes dip from his face to his still-bloodstained lips.

He cannot know what those words mean to me; to be able to choose anything for myself would mean everything. I want that, but I squash that option quickly. That option cannot happen. My parents will never allow it.

"How do you know I was made?" I say it more as a dare than an actual question. It was the other part of his sentence that had given me pause. He cannot know of my past; no one does.

Reign smiles widely showing his white teeth. "Because no one from Inferis is this refined." He shrugs his shoulders lightly, barely even a movement. His smile fades just a bit.

I suck in a sharp breath, placing a hand on his chest as I stand, pushing him back as I go.

Untried Origins

"What if this is all I am?" I am not even sure that I know the answer to that. I don't even know if I am asking myself that question or him.

He gives me that toothy, sharp-edged grin of his, the one that looks more terrifying than welcoming. "I think we may just find that answer together, Madis."

Giving him a short curtsy, I start to head off to my rooms. I am finished with my food, and I have gotten my answers. He did not kill or try to kill anyone.

Reign steps in my way before I make it far. "I will pick you up at your room tomorrow night for the ball."

"You can send Miles for me."

"No." he says quickly and firmly.

I nod. "Ok, I will be ready."

Reign gives me a low, mocking bow then steps out of my way.

I walk swiftly back to my room, not expecting what is there waiting for me. When I enter the room, there is a team of seamstresses with every color and style of fabric imaginable.

Chapter 36
KAISERA

A sword is coming right at my face. I try and snap my fingers to will the sword into my hand and out of Bax's. He is too fast for me, though; it comes at me again and again. His speed and accuracy are like nothing I have ever gone up against. The only thing I can do is block his attacks over and over.

We have been in the training yard for hours now. I went to my room after our trip here, hoping to get a bit of rest, but I had barely changed after a shower before Bax was banging on my door, yelling about how it was time to start training.

So far, we have done a stretching warm up, a regular warm up, cardio training, strength training, and now we are working on combat skills. This has not been work for Bax; he has not even broken a sweat yet.

The flirtatious man who had his hand down my pants hours ago is gone. This is Major Xanadriel, ball busting asshole who does not give a flying shit how hard I hit the ground.

Untried Origins

"You do not have time to snap those pretty little fingers in a true combat situation, Kai. Try something else," he barks at me.

I try to blink away behind him, another one of my tricks, but I still have to snap my fingers. He grabs my arm before I can jump. He can anticipate my every move. I am getting angrier by the minute.

I am tired and getting weaker with each swing of my sword. I tighten my grip on the training sword with both hands and slam it in a downward motion toward Bax's right shoulder. He is there, ready for the attack again.

He starts to back me up toward a wall in the courtyard where we have been training. The sun is starting to set, and Vampires have started to peek out from the shadows, though none of them seem overly concerned about us.

I reach up to snap my fingers again, but Bax grabs a hold of my hand and grips it tightly. In seconds, he spins me around, plastering my entire body to the stone wall. He reaches down with his free hand and rips the sword out of my other hand before pulling both my hands above my head and using his whole body to hold me firmly to the wall. I have no escape. He has his fingers laced between mine, so there is no way I can snap my fingers.

I let out a loud frustrated scream.

Tribax chuckles at that. "I want to see you get out of this, little vixen."

I buck and try to push my hips off the wall and into him.

"Easy there. All that is doing is turning me on."

"Ugh, this is pointless." There is no way I can move. He overpowers me in size and strength.

"Yes, you can. Blink away from me." He leans in close to my ear, breathing into it softly. "Blink away from me and grab your discarded weapon."

"I can't; you have my hands. I can't do it without the snap." I have never been able to move more than a few feet, and I have always used the snap to channel that energy.

"Close your eyes and focus. Think of your magic, feel it, own it. It is your magic to wield as you want," Bax says.

"Bax, it doesn't..." He shoves his hips into me again, causing me to grunt with the impact of my hipbones against the wall and cutting off my words.

"You are telling me the great and stubborn Kaisera, the same Kaisera who would tell a mountain to go around her, is allowing her own powers to decide what she can and cannot do?"

Fuck! He has a point.

"Fine. I will try," I say through gritted teeth. I roll my neck and feel for my powers.

"Concentrate."

"Stop talking and I will."

Bax laughs but stays quiet after that. I close my eyes and focus. I only need to jump to the left about two feet to where he flung my sword, and then I can pick it up. I focus on where that spot is, my fingers itching to snap, to release the power. I try to channel that to the rest of my body, try and feel where else it can be released from. Maybe I can literally blink my eyes; I had called it blinking after all. I open my eyes and then slam them back shut. Nothing happens.

I buck back against Bax again in frustration, ready to surrender.

Fuck that, I cannot let this asshole win.

"Focus, my little vixen," Bax says into my ear.

I take a long, slow breath. Maybe I do not need an actual snap or trigger. Maybe I can imagine myself snapping my fingers and it work.

I close my eyes and visualize the snap. I feel the move the second it happens, and I am there, kneeling to pick up the sword. Bax falls toward the wall but catches himself and leans against it with the most shit-eating grin I have ever seen.

"I instantly regret doing that," I say.

"Oh yeah? You regret learning something new? Because, if that is the case, you are going to regret a lot in the future. You have so much more to learn," he says, and I get the feeling he isn't talking about the combat training we have been working on.

"I regret pleasing you so much, but I do think the only things you could teach me are things involving a sword. Others have already taught me the rest." I spin the practice sword around

Untried Origins

as I start to walk away from him, knowing that will get a rise out of him.

He has me by the waist and pinned to him before I make it more than two steps, then he is spinning me around to face him. He grabs a chunk of my hair with his fist. He isn't hurting me; at least, not in a bad way. I can tell he just wants to show me he is there. He is mixing the perfect amount of pleasure with pain, and I am here for it. I enjoy his dominance.

"You will only be taught by me from now on. Did I not make that clear on our ride here?"

I give the same glare he is directing at me right back to him. "You do not own me, Bax."

"Do not lie to yourself. You know you want to be owned by me, and in the end, you will be begging for just that: for me to own you in every way possible." He pulls my head back a little further, giving himself full access to all my neck and to my lips. At first, I think he wants to go for my neck like a vampire, and it thrills me just a bit. But then, he focuses back on my eyes. He is searching for something. I don't know what that something is, but whatever it is, I want to help him find it.

His grip loosens from my hair, and I do not want this moment to end. I jump into his arms the second his grip is loose enough. He catches me with grace, as if I weigh less than a small sack of flour. I look into his eyes, waiting for him to make the next move. His strong arms hold me tight, and then he is pinning me back into the wall.

The sheer force of how hard he shoves me causes a small growl to crawl out of me. I love how rough he is with me, like he knows exactly how much I can handle before I break.

Oh Baxy, maybe I want you to break me.

He finds something in my stare he approves of, because he gives me a smirk before his mouth is against mine. He kisses me aggressively for a few moments before pulling away. Even though I have my legs wrapped around his waist, he is so much bigger than me that I am forced to crane my head up to him.

"What makes you so sure I will be the one begging?"

His laugh rumbles all the way through me. "Because I can tell how much I am turning you on." He brushes a lock of my sweaty hair that had fallen out during training behind my ear before he leans in and whispers, "And the only thing my lips have touched so far are yours."

I want to deny it, but he is right. Instead, I just scowl at him when he pulls back to look down at me again.

The day has turned into night, and more people have started to make their way out to the courtyard. Bax slides me back down to the ground.

"I will pick you and Elena up from your room tomorrow at nightfall. Get some rest," Bax says.

I am confused. "Pick us up for what?"

I hope he does not want to train again. I am not sure if I will be able to walk for a week after today's training.

"For the king's ball, unless you have someone else in mind to escort you?" The way he says this sounds more like a dare than an actual question, and I want to challenge him on it. I enjoy a good dare.

"Hmm." I pace around him. "I might."

He narrows his eyes in response.

"Maybe I need to see what one of these vampire's teeth feel like."

"Do not test me, Kaisera. You may not like the end result." He turns to walk away.

I grab his arm this time, stopping him. He turns his head downward to look at my small hand gripping only part of his large arm and cocks a brow at me.

"Something else to say?" he asks.

I bite my lip. I do want him to escort me, but he does not need to know that.

"Elena and I will meet you there," I say quickly.

He huffs a small, fake laugh. "Have it your way, Kai." He leans in close to my face again. "You can be as stubborn as you like. I have all the time in Inferis, and I will wait."

With that, he walks away from me. The little red fox, Julian, stands from where he had been sprawled in the grass during our training to follow after Bax, leaving me to contemplate if that was the right call, leaving the air just a little stuck in my lungs.

Untried Origins

I make my way back to the room. The gothic-styled halls and architecture here are so beautiful. A tad gloomy for my taste, but still beautiful. I like the color black, but only because it brings out brighter colors in our world.

I reach my doors and the room with the large carved wood doors holding a scene of a beautiful woman tending a rose garden that the butler showed me earlier. I open them, noting the large as fuck bed is only half made. Elena is passed out on the unmade half. I want to plop onto it and pass out next to her, but I stink yet again and need my second bath in twenty-four hours.

As I head toward the shower, Elena turns over and peeks an eye open. "You have been gone a long time."

I had not seen her when Tribax and I had made it to the castle, so this is the first time I am talking to her since the ride here after the battle.

"Yeah, Bax and I were in the training yard."

"Do you trust him?" Elena says.

"I don't know," I reply. That is the truth. Elena is the one person I know I can always be honest with.

She does not say anything in response, so I head for the showers. I bathe and wash my hair before towel drying off as quickly as I can. My body is hurting down to the bones; I swear, even my teeth are worn out.

I walk out of the bathing rooms and make my way over to the made side of the bed, throwing the covers back and hopping in.

Elena rolls over and throws her arms open to invite me in. I roll over to her and place my head in the crook of her neck as she tucks me in tight.

"You think you might be in over your head with this Tribax guy?" she asks.

"I know." I have been starting to realize the same thing. He is crawling under my skin.

She runs her hand up and down my arm in a soothing way. "Maybe that is a good thing, Alli," she replies.

I tilt my head up to look up at her. She giggles. "Sorry, *Kai*. It will take some adjusting."

It was not that she called me Alli that caught my attention; it was that she thinks Bax is a good thing. "It is fine. Why do you think he could be a good thing?"

It has been just me and her against the world for three years now. We have been each other's rocks, holding each other up when the other starts to fall. We both had wounds from our pasts, but we have healed each other enough that all that is left now are scars.

"Do not look at me like that, Kai. We can have other people in our lives." She brings her hand up and tucks a lock of my wet hair behind my ear.

Elena and I have always had this kind of connection, a friendship closer than a blood relative. I lean over and place a soft kiss on her cheek and lay my head back down on her shoulder.

"Let's get some rest. We have a ball tomorrow night."

Elena does not reply. We just snuggle up and fall into deep sleep.

Chapter 37

ELLIE

I am awoken by a pleasant feeling between my legs. It is Mica's way of sweetly waking me up. I enjoy those moments when it is just me and my mate, doing nothing else but being in each other's space. In these moments, I forget about what is coming and what must be done.

A moan crosses my lips, and his large, wet tongue slides up my center in a slow, torturous way. I roll my hips to show him how I want it.

I have not had a day apart from this male since the first time we went on a date to the caves of Warrantless all those years ago. We have had this connection in all the right ways from the moment our lips met. We just fit instantly. He always seems to know exactly what my needs are before I even know I need them.

Mica slides a finger into my core, and I clench around him. He is rubbing that one finger on just the right spot, in just the right rhythm, knowing my body so well after six years of practice.

I moan loudly and roll my hips against his mouth and finger. He is urging me on, licking and rubbing me everywhere all at once.

My orgasm builds, and I start to breathe harder and harder until I am falling, yelling out my approval of Mica's efforts. When I finally come down from the high of my orgasm, Mica makes his way back up to me from under the sheets, kissing every inch of me on his way. His lips are glistening, and a huge smile is on his face. He leans in and kisses me.

"Good morning, beautiful."

"It is a very good morning." It is not morning. It is closer to midnight. We had gotten to our rooms after the convoy, showered, and have not left this bed since.

Mica and I have been away from our realm for so long, looking for the princess, and have not had the luxury to just be. The mortal world was nice, but here in Inferis is where we belong. I want to soak up this time with Mica. I have this feeling in the pit of my belly that this will not last forever.

I cannot believe this beautiful man is my mate.

I love his boyish features and his muscular build. They almost do not go together, but somehow, perfectly match. I love that even though he is not the most powerful male in the realms, he is the most caring and loving. He would stand between me and all the Hollows in Inferis to keep me safe. I know that fact down to my very being, which is why I have to get the girls together. They must do what has never been done.

If Madis and Kaisera cannot come together and solve the problem growing in Inferis, I fear this world, this realm, will not make it through it. Something rooted deep inside of me says they will be our saving graces, but only if they learn to come together.

"What is it?" Mica frowns down at me. My face must be showing all my thoughts.

"The girls are going to have to come together," I say.

"Have you seen them? They cannot even be in the same space for longer than five minutes before they are at each other's throats." Mica plops onto the pillow right next to me, putting one of his muscular arms behind his head, looking up at the ceiling.

Untried Origins

"They are untried in this world Mica. Besides, this is only the beginning of their story, their origins. They just need a push," I say.

"I would hate to be the person who pushes either of them," Mica says.

"We are going to be those people. If they cannot work together, Mica, I just know the world will not survive it."

Mica is the only one who knows my secret. He does not question me. "Then we will get them to work together," Mica responds.

"I think it is time we bring them in on the Ruthless."

The Ruthless are a group of rebels who have been forming for a few generations. They are a mixture of all the creatures of Inferis, and they believe it is time the prophecy of our ancestors came true.

Mica sits up quickly. "You cannot be serious? Kaisera is a snobby brat who listens to no one, and Madis is an emotionless robot. You really think those two can be trusted?"

I sigh, knowing those are accurate descriptions of the girls. "Maybe it will help them see what is really going on."

Mica shakes his head but replies, "I trust you."

I lean up and place a gentle kiss on his shoulder. "Good. Now, come show me what else you can do to me before we leave for the ball tonight."

Mica gives me his big, boyish grin before he attacks.

Chapter 38
MADIS

    I spin around and around in front of my mirror, twirling in my new dress. I have never felt so beautiful. The seamstresses Reign sent to my room had worked all night and day to get this together for me.

    My shiny black heels click across the ground as I spin and look myself over. Above my shiny black heels, I have black lace stockings. The dress itself is long and a deep dark red color, with slits all the way up to my hipbones, a fitted top hugging my slight curves and cut low in the back, with long, tight lace sleeves. It is dangerous and practical while also being beautiful and elegant. It is the most outrageous thing I have ever worn.

    Reign also sent a team to help me get ready; he sent everything from perfumes to different colored kohl eyeliners. He had thought of everything. The women who had helped get me ready were all vampires, and they worked quickly and quietly, only speaking to ask my preference on things.

Untried Origins

I kept my makeup simple: just a dash here and there to bring out my blue eyes, and a darker shade of red lip liner that my mother would have killed me for if she saw. She would do more than pull out my hair if she saw me at all right now. My father would tell me I was dressed more like a whore than a princess or queen, even though I was never meant to be either. Not that being a princess ever stopped Kaisera from wearing whatever she pleased, but I guess her father knew that would have been a losing battle.

I also had the team Reign sent help Yanci get ready, and I had commissioned a dress for her as well. It is a silk gown in a royal blue that hugs her hourglass figure, with a small train that trails like a pool of water behind her.

"What did you get into today?" I ask Yanci. I am curious.

"Just went into town to see all the sights." She shrugs and goes back to inspecting her own gown, smiling widely in the mirror next to me. The mirror has three sides and is decorated in what looks to be handcrafted thorny vines wrapping around the outer edges.

I am not sure I believe her, but I am also not going to question her. She is a new friend, and I do not want to scare her off by second guessing everything she does.

She gives me a twirl. "What do you think? I think it makes me look damn good."

Every time Yanci speaks, I wonder how she did not get murdered in Area Six with such a spitfire attitude, an attitude my mother would have snuffed out the first chance she got. It also makes me wonder why she was selected to be my lady's maid.

I laugh a little. "You do look beautiful."

"Hmm, maybe I will catch the eye of a handsome vampire and see if that bite feels as good as it looks." She wiggles her eyebrows.

My jaw drops. "You will do no such thing; you know our blood is overwhelming for them."

"Maybe I want a little danger."

"Yanci! One of them could kill you," I whisper to her, even though the vampire women who had been helping us stepped out moments before.

Yanci rolls her eyes. "Oh, come on, Your Majesty. You know you want to feel the King's fangs sink into you." She pauses before giving me a devilish look. "Maybe you even want more than his fangs in you."

"Yanci! That is enough." I say, perhaps a little too aggressively. I know I should not let my temper get the best of me, but I cannot have her speaking like this. If someone overheard this conversation and it got back to my parents, they would lose it.

Yanci tucks her hands behind her back and is instantly transformed back into the timid little maid I saw in my room three days ago. It is amazing how quickly she jumps out of one role and into another. It is almost unnatural.

There is a knock on the door, and Miles the butler speaks from the other side. "I am here to escort you to the ball whenever you are ready, Your Majesty."

It seems the King of Vampires lies.

"Just a minute," I say back. I turn around to look Yanci over with a questioning look. "Are you ready?" I ask Yanci.

She curtsies and heads for the door. When she reaches it, she waits for me with her head bowed down.

"Yanci, I didn't mean to—" I pause, because I am not even sure what it is I am sorry for.

"It is fine, Your Majesty. I should apologize to you. I forgot my place for a moment."

I huff out a long sigh. "Let's just try and have a little fun tonight, shall we?"

"Yes, let's." A little bit of glimmer shines through her eyes, a little less hurt puppy.

Miles leads us down through hallways, turn after turn, until we reach where we first entered the castle. He then leads us down the staircase. Past the spiraling staircase, near the entrance to the castle, are two large iron doors. I had been too focused on the direction Miles was taking me that first day to have noticed them. A mistake on my part. It seems that when attractive men are in my presence, I lose myself just a bit.

As we approach, two guards on either side of the large door reach for the handles and usher us into the ballroom. We are greeted with a ball in full swing. There are people of all types

Untried Origins

dancing, drinking, and eating in every square inch of this place. The ballroom is made of glass, everything shiny and dark, made of sharp edges, like the man who owns this castle.

There are reflections of everyone everywhere, in an almost dizzying way. The music is wonderful, and there is a female on a lifted stage singing a dark and glum song. She is singing in a language I do not understand, so I am not sure of the meaning, but I know I would like the song just by the melody. I have never been in a room that has so much of everything at one time.

Yanci squeals and starts to take off toward the tables full of food lining the walls, but she thinks twice and looks back at me for approval.

"Go, have fun."

She lets out another squeak, turns, and runs full speed, halfway knocking over people in the process.

Nija pops up on top of my shoulder, and he lets out a little growl at so many people around us. I reach up and pet the top of his head. "Easy, boy." He rumbles again. "Why don't you go back to my room and relax? I will not be long."

He licks my face with his sandpaper tongue and looks at me with a tilted head.

"Yes, Nija. I am sure. I will be fine." With that, he pops away to wherever it is Nija wanders off to. I am starting to think that the familiars have a world of their own somewhere.

I walk further into the ballroom and start looking around. I am not sure who or what I am looking for. I spot Tribax spinning Kaisera around and around. She looks stunning. She is in an emerald dress that matches her eyes beautifully. It fits every bit of her perfectly. The material is thin and glimmers in the light, like it is lined with jewels. Kaisera always knew how to dress for an event. I might not have been privileged to attend balls, but for Kaisera, this had been her life for years.

Kai throws her head back, laughing at something that Tribax said. He grips her tightly and pulls her close, neither of them taking their eyes from the other.

I notice someone standing close beside me, and I tense.

"Is that the one who hurt you so?" King Reign's voice is teasing, but he does not know how close he is.

Bax might not have been the right man for me, and I might have been the one to break things off, but knowing they have something I will never have the privilege to know or have hurts.

I stay silent but turn to look at him.

"Dance with me." He did not ask it as a question, but as more of a demand. A demand I want to follow.

"Should I dance with a man who lies?" I am only half serious when I ask.

His eyes scrunch together, and I can tell he is trying to think of my meaning. He holds his finger up in the air like a grand idea had occurred to him. "Ah, you are upset I did not personally escort you?"

"Upset is not the correct word."

"Aw, come now, I did not do it to offend you. I was otherwise occupied for a moment."

I roll my eyes at him. "I see. Was it a pretty blonde? Or do you not get occupied with the same women you feed from?"

Reign's smile grows into something wicked and delightful. "Is that a hint of jealousy? If so, I could feed and occupy my time with you, if you prefer."

My eyes widen, and the thought has my blood pounding through me.

Reign takes a step forward, placing a single hand onto my hip. Smiling down at me, he says, "Let me make it up to you by not leaving your side again tonight."

I am not even sure what the correct response would be, but I go with, "Okay."

He takes my hand right as a new number turns over. It is a little more upbeat than the last song, and suddenly, I feel silly for accepting his offer. I am a terrible dancer, even though my father had given me many teachers over the years. I had never truly learned the art of it. The teachers would always tell my father I had no soul in it, which made him try to beat a soul into me.

I can hear my father's voice in my head: "Royals should be able to dance. Your lack of skill gives away the fact that you are simply nothing and nobody. Try harder. You are worthless to me if you can't do a simple task like dance." I shake my head to get rid of his voice and take a calming breath to bring myself out of my dark thoughts.

"You alright?" Reign looks down at me with what might be concern.

I swallow down the spit that is starting to fill my mouth. "Umm, yes. I feel I should warn you. I am a terrible dancer."

Reign does not laugh or make a cruel joke as most would. He nods his head in understanding. "Relax," Reign says, leaning close to whisper into my ear then leaning back to look into my eyes. Then, we are moving, gliding softly across the dance floor. "Do not think of it as a dance. Think of it as a battle, a fight. Each step is a stance against your enemies."

I do relax. I stay focused on his hand on my lower back and his other hand holding mine. I finally start to move with him to match his footing, like I would in a hand-to-hand combat. The hand holding mine is so firm and stable, more stable than anything with which I am familiar.

"This dress seems more like you; it is absolutely stunning. You are absolutely stunning," Reign says.

I respond with a genuine smile. Thank you."

"It has this edge about it, an edge I think you hide. Why is that?"

"I am not hiding anything."

He smirks. "Oh, but you are, princess. I know there is more to you than what everyone is seeing."

"And how would you know that?"

Reign smiles largely. I think he likes making sure people see his sharp canines, as if to remind everyone that he is not just a pretty face, that he is, in fact, dangerous.

"Because before I entered that field to 'not' save you, I saw you fight. I have never seen anyone more beautifully covered in so much blood. You were in your element. You were not that prim and proper doll I saw at dinner last night. You were dark and dangerous."

"I am dangerous. I have been trained to fight all of my life."

"You are dangerous for more reasons than just your fighting skills."

What does he mean? *Fighting is the only kind of dangerous that matters.* I cannot for a second believe he saw all that in one fight.

"I liked it," Reign responds.

The way he is looking at me says he wants to eat me alive. I cannot tell if that is figuratively or literally, but I am not sure I would mind either option. It does not matter if I think he is the hottest male in Inferis or that I find him charming. *I cannot do this.*

I stop dancing, something I forgot we were doing. "It does not matter what you like."

I begin to walk away, but Reign is in front of me in an instant, his vampire speed allowing him to move so fast, I didn't even notice him move. "Do you not enjoy my company?" he says with a slight tilt of his head, his cocky smile no longer on his face.

"It does not matter what I enjoy." *What is this man not getting?*

"I believe it does," he says.

"I can see how much you truly know now, King." People are getting close to bumping into us because we are in the middle of a dance floor in full swing. Every time someone gets too close to touching me, Reign blocks them with an arm or leg, never letting anyone get too close. It takes me a minute to realize he is keeping everyone from touching me, allowing others to bump into him instead.

"I know I want you to keep touching me," he finally says.

I look at him with my eyebrows scrunched together, because now I am the confused one.

He gestures down with his head to guide my eyes. When I look to where he gestures, I notice I have placed my hands on his chest. I had not meant to do it, but here I am, touching this man, and he does not want me to stop. I guess the whole touching thing isn't just on him.

I drop my hands. "I can't."

"I think you can, and I am willing to wait around to see the day you do. After all, all we have is time on our hands."

I turn and walk away, for real this time. He has no idea the things I will never have, the things I will never enjoy. I feel myself breaking down.

Untried Origins

Count to five. I need to get back to my room before I lose it in front of everyone.

I am not paying attention to where exactly I am walking, and I bump directly into someone.

"Hey!" Kaisera says as she stumbles forward a bit. She turns when she catches her balance and looks to find me.

"I am sorry. I didn't mean to."

"Sure, you didn't. Do you ever mean to do anything, Madis?" Kai crosses her arms. She is joined by Elena, who is wearing a dark blue gown of a similar style to Kai's. They look like a perfect pair. I look behind them to see if I can spot Tribax.

I do not want to do this here, and I know he will not allow Kaisera to get too close to me and cause a scene. That is his job, and if Tribax and I only have one thing in common, it is that we believe in the honor of our duties. With my poor luck, however, there is no sign of him.

"Kai, none of this has to be this way," I finally say.

"You mean the way where you plotted against your best friend to take everything from her? Or the way you just stepped right into her shoes without a second thought? Or what about the fact that you sent demons to find me, two demons who could not return without me? One of which was your friend!"

"That is not what happened. If you would let me explain…" I try.

"I do not want to hear your excuses. You practically begged me to do the Blood Binding. I bet it was your idea from the start." Kaisera looks at me with nothing but dismissal.

Something in me snaps a little. If she will not listen to what truly happened, then I will not force her to listen any longer. "Why are you such a brat?"

Kaisera's jaw pops open just a bit, then closes back quickly. Vampires, Demons, and mortal souls alike are all looking in our direction and starting to form a circle around us, probably hoping to see someone draw blood.

"Excuse me?" Kaisera says.

I cross my arms over my chest and hold my head a little higher. "You heard me. You left, Kaisera. What did you expect would happen? That this realm would fall to pieces without you?"

Kaisera snorts and shakes her head. She takes a step forward to get in my face, but of course, all that does is make it so I'm looking down at her, seeing as I'm a good half a foot taller than her.

"A whole lot of good you have been doing here, Madis. I will not stand here and justify my actions. I am not the one who should answer for my crimes."

I have no clue what she is talking about. I never committed a crime. I feel a hand on my back, and I can smell the storm blowing in that is Reign. His scent is already starting to calm my nerves. I tilt my head to see him standing there.

Moments later, Tribax breaks through the crowd and is at Kaisera's side. He looks between the two of us. I am assuming he is deciding whose side he will take. He reaches for Kaisera's arm and pulls her out of my face.

At this point, we are having a stare down. My anxiety is rooting deep inside of me. I do not know how to fight this way. I do not know how to talk back to her, and she knows it.

She smirks an evil little smirk. "You cannot even stand up for yourself, 'Queen.' How do you expect to stand up for your Area and Realm?"

My chin dips a bit. She is right. I know that. I am just a puppet, after all. My father or husband will rule, not me. I will fight when needed, but other than that, I will sit prettily as I was raised and trained to do.

Tribax pulls her arm a little harder. "You had your fun, Kai. That's enough."

Kai turns and glares as Tribax. "Let. Go. Of. Me." Kai is half growling the command at him.

Tribax grins down at her. "Make me."

Before I can pay attention to any more of their encounter, I am heading for the door, over this party, over this life. I just need to get somewhere I can breathe again.

I search for Yanci for a brief second, catching sight of her leaning into a guy's chest, laughing. I will not cause her to have a bad evening along with me.

Untried Origins

I am through the doors and back to my room in moments. I close the door and slide to the floor, reminding myself over and over to breathe. Deep breath in…count to five. Let it out.

Tears start to fall. I hate everyone right now: my father for his punishments, my mother for her cruel remarks, Kaisera for the lack of faith she has in me, Tribax for not seeing me. I hate it, and I feel so alone in a fight that I truly do not want.

I hate that I am becoming easier and easier to break, like the pieces of me are never quite set back right so that I may stay whole.

Deep breaths. Count to five. Let it out. Find my ground.

The fear of never saying the right thing or being the right person at the right time has always consumed me, no matter the front or walls I build up. I know everyone sees a determined woman staring them down. I stay thankful my mask hasn't slipped out of place. If others see me as a strong confident woman born to rule, why can't I? What will it take for me to feel that?

Deep breath. Count to five. Let it out.

That is, everyone except Kaisera. She knew. She knew within seconds that she was breaking me, and she kept pushing anyways, with a smirk on her face.

There is a slight *tap, tap, tap* on the bedroom door that I am leaning against.

Shit. Please, please, please be a member of the staff who isn't allowed to speak of things seen or heard within these walls.

Tap, tap, tap. "Madis, do you have a moment?"

Oh no, not him. I slap my head back against the door.

That's Reign's voice, the absolute last person I want to see me so broken.

I respond. "Um, I'm already indecent. Can we speak in the morning?"

"I'm sure we have both seen many indecent things. What makes tonight different?" I can hear the joke in his voice. I can already picture that toothy grin.

I don't have a response for that.

Reign loudly sighs through the door. "Look… I just wanted to say you looked spectacular tonight. Can I please tell you that face to face and not through what seems to be the thickest door ever made? Really, I may have it burned and rebuilt with thinner material, something more near a sheet."

I do have to smile a little at his attempt at joking. *Another deep breath. Count to ten this time.* I'm pretty sure I'm turning purple. "Fine, but I warned you."

I hear a soft deep laugh through the door, and everything in me is as stiff as the red clay my Area is built with. I open the door, and his eyes grow a darker green than his normal hazel. A look of pure displeasure is in his eyes.

I turn to walk away. I'm sure it is my weak appearance he's displeased with. "I know. I am a mess. My apologies."

He grabs my wrist and spins me around so fast my world tilts a bit. I am now facing him, and both of his hands are on my face.

Our eyes lock so intently that I want to look away. I want to find my escape. Why does he look at me like this? He looks concerned.

"I am not one you can escape, Madis," Reign says.

I gulp, wondering how he knows I want to escape.

Rushed words leave him. "What happened? Did someone touch you on your way back here? What's going on? Was it that idiotic oversized guard?"

He goes to continue these questions, but I place a single finger on his lips. "Stop. I'll be fine." I say. Because It's me. I will be. I must be. Plus… nothing happened other than me not being enough or being the person, I'm expected to be.

A hand leaves my face, and he removes my finger from his lips. "You are lying, Madis. I can hear it in your heart rate." As he says this, he wipes the lines of kohl from under my eyes. "I will end whoever made you shed these, if you desire."

My eyes go as wide as they can.

No one has ever cared like that. Not for me. The look on his face grows even more concerned, which has my breathing evening out and me thinking a little more clearly. Both his hands return to gripping my face. We are standing so close. This. This feels different. It feels good, as if someone is truly here for my benefit and not their own, but I can't feel this. I can't feel what I feel with him right now. I have to be focused on what's best for Inferis. My father has already sealed my fate.

I go to pull away, but Reign isn't having it. "Stop. Why do you do that?"

"Do what?"

"Do not play with me. I notice how you pull away from my touch and how you look away when you feel our connection take hold. Why?"

Connection? Does he feel the weird tug and spike of awareness too? It doesn't matter even if he does. "We can't."

"Why? Tell me one good reason why I should not slam you up against that overly thick door and taste every last drop that you see fit to give me."

I want that. Please. Yes. I can almost see myself begging for that.

I feel Reign's hand slide from my jaw to under my chin and stroke all the edges of my face softly. He is looking at every inch of my face, searching for the answer.

I have to stop this. "Look, I just can't be worried about what I want. I have to be focused on Inferis. There is a war coming if I do not play my part, and it will end badly for everyone."

Reign's eyes are still roaming. I'm not even sure what he sees. "All that says to me is that we should be enjoying this time we have. Although, I do not think once I have you that I will ever give you up. My darling, there is a war coming no matter what."

With that, he gently leans in and places the briefest of kisses on one corner of my mouth, then the other. I'm holding my breath again, not moving, scared of what acting or not acting will do. All thoughts of his final words blur in my brain.

Reign pulls back and takes in my expression and stiff body. My hands are pushed against his chest in the small space between us.

"Tell me to leave," Reign says. The look on his face is almost sad.

When I do not speak, he gives me a timid smile that I have not seen from him before. "Then tell me to stay."

Another tear slides from my eye, and I watch as Reign tracks its movement over my chin and down my neck. When he leans in this time, I tilt my head to the side to give him full access. I do not know what I am expecting or wanting. I just know I want to see what will happen.

Reign licks that single teardrop all the way up, from the top swell of my breast all the way back up to under my eye. My breathing is rigid, and I know if I do not stop this now, I never will. "You should leave."

"I should do a lot of things. I don't think that is one of them." Reign takes a step back, his eyebrows scrunching together at my lack of response. He drops his hands from my face down to his sides then slides both into his pockets. He tilts his head down, then nods it a few times.

"What if we just sit and talk? I will keep my hands exactly where they are," Reign says.

"What would we have to talk about?"

"We are both rulers. We both have been trained in battle. I am sure we can find some common ground."

I consider that. *What harm could talking do?*

I shake my head and intertwine my fingers, fidgeting a bit. "Alright, let me freshen up then."

Reign removes his hand from his pocket and gestures to the bathing room.

"You said those would stay in your pockets," I say in an attempt to lighten the mood before walking to the bathing room. I go to clean up my face and hair and get out of this dress.

Reign shoves his hands back into his pockets quickly. "My apologies. It will not happen again."

Chapter 39

KAISERA

My night started so wonderfully. Elena and I had made our way down to the ball and were quickly met by Bax. He swooped me into a dance before I could even try to deny him. We were drinking, laughing, joking, and having a wonderful time.

How in the crap did we end up like this?

I am staring Bax down. He had the nerve to pull me away from my confrontation with Madis, the one I was winning. It was time everyone saw her for the cowering traitor she really is.

"If you do not release my arm, you will regret it," I say through gritted bared teeth.

Tribax only leans closer. "I am doing you a favor. Trust me." Then, he is half dragging me out the doors onto an open balcony. The few people who are out enjoying the night air quickly move back inside when they see us. Elena watches the whole interaction, taking a swig of her wine then heading further back into the party.

"Who the fuck do you think you are? Just because I let you get me off does not mean you have any say in my affairs." I am fuming at him.

Bax is on me in an instant, his hand around my throat, applying just a bit of pressure. I continue to stare him down. I have never bent to anyone, and I am not starting now.

The silver lining in Bax's eyes grows a bit and seems to hone in on something inside me, like a wild animal ready to devour his prey. It should terrify me, and it does just a little, but I also welcome it. *Show me what you really got, Bax.*

"First, you enjoyed every moment of my fingers deep inside of you. Second, I think you should be saying thank you, not being a brat."

What the actual shit? That is the second time a person called me a brat tonight.

I bare my teeth at him and jerk my head deeper into his grip around my throat. "Thank you for what?" I grit out.

Bax lets out a deep, angry growl matching and then doubling my own. "Madis is a trained killer. You would not beat her in a physical fight."

I burst out in laughter. Bax looks so confused, it only makes me laugh louder.

"I do not see the humor in this, Kaisera."

"Do you even know Madis?"

"I would like to think I know her better than most." Bax releases me and takes a step back, going back to his full height and crossing his big arms over his big chest.

He is not in his usual black suit of thick leather armor or his guard's metal armor; he is in a dark navy blue dress coat and pants with a black button-up undershirt. The dark blue makes his ashy blonde hair and blue eyes really pop.

"Clearly not. Madis would never lay a hand on me. She would prefer to play dirty and let someone else do it for her."

"She is the heir now. You may not want to piss her off."

"She will not be the heir for long. I will prove she had my father killed, and then she will be off to the pits."

"You really are a brat."

Untried Origins

I rear back to strike Tribax in the face, but he is too quick and catches my arm. He tilts his head, lips thinning, and looks at me angrily. "You are only proving my point here, Kaisera."

I rip my arm back from his grasp. "Then you tell me, oh great wise one, what should I do? Just let her keep my crown after she betrayed me and killed my father? She could be the one letting the Hollows out, for all we know. We cannot just let her get away with all of it."

"We, huh?" Bax says with a cheesy grin.

"That's all you got out of that?" He gives me a soft laugh as I cross my arms and tap my foot in a very Elena way.

"No." Bax sighs and runs his hand through his hair. "Look, Madis has been looking for you for years now, since the day you vanished, against your fathers' orders. I do not think she would bring you back if she planned to keep the crown."

I pinch my lips together. Ellie and Mica had said the same, that they were sent to find me, that Madis had been looking for me for a long while. *But none of them were there that night.* "That does not make sense."

"Why? You are the one who left." Tribax unfolds his arms and slaps them to his sides.

"I left because of her, because of what I saw."

"Then tell me Kai, what did you see?"

Elena walks on to the balcony to join us, followed by Mica and Ellie. "I would like to know what it was to make you so angry with that woman. Really, Kai, she looks broken already. I do not see why you are beating her down further," Elena says.

"What are you talking about? Madis is far from broken," I say.

Tribax chimes in, "Are you sure you were ever really her friend?"

"Oh, she has you all fooled. Madis is nothing but a traitor. She took my crown from me."

"No, she did not. You left," Bax says.

"You do not know anything! Neither of you! You weren't there!" They look at each other, then back to me. "You know what, go fuck yourselves. Actually, better yet, go fuck each other." I catch a look of disgust from them both at my statement.

Ellie chimes in next. "There is no need for all this anger Kaisera."

I cut daggers from my eyes in her direction. I cannot believe this. Elena is teaming up with Tribax? How could she take his side over mine? I try to push past them, and they each grab one of my shoulders.

"Oh no, you don't," Elena says as she pushes me back.

"What is it with you two tonight?" I say.

Bax responds instead. "We think it is time you talk to Madis. This feud looks bad on all of us. If we stand a chance against the other Areas and the Hollows, you two are going to have to work this out."

I look between them confused. "What are you talking about? Why would we need to stand against the other Areas?"

"Look, Kai, the Hollow outbreak you saw in Erathina was not the first one," Elena says.

What does she mean it was not the first? I had been in Erathina for six years and never saw a Hollow. Not a single one, and I know what to look for. How would she have known what they were?

"Why wouldn't you tell me that? How would you even know?" I ask. I thought we were closer than this. I trust her. I know she has a past she doesn't talk about, but could that past involve Hollows?

"I did not know you were a damn Demon Princess for starters!" Elena is pacing back and forth and talking with her hands. "How was I supposed to know I had befriended someone who might actually be able to do something to stop this outbreak?"

Maybe that is true, but now, I have even more questions. Where were these attacks, and why was Elena looking for a way to stop them, and how did I know nothing about this?

By asking one motherfucking question at a time, that's how. I turn my gaze back to Tribax. "What about this war with the Areas?"

"That is why I believe Madis is being promised to Area One. They have the best army. War is coming. The Areas want to expand and grow, and they are sick of being sectioned away. They

Untried Origins

each think that they know what is best for Inferis. Some even believe we should claim parts of Erathina as well," Bax says.

I think this all through. Why am I just learning this? Why hasn't Madis done anything to stop it?

Elena grabs both my shoulders and rests her hands on them. "Someone has to take control, Kai."

Bax nods in agreement with Elena. "There are people ready to fight with Madis, but she seems to be listening to the wrong people. Someone is guiding her in the wrong direction. I do not think the Hollow attack on the way here was by accident. I think someone wants you both out of the way."

This is a lot to take in. *Fuck.* The Hollows spreading through the veil, a war between areas, Madis being controlled? I am still not sold on that last part, but maybe they are right, and I need to help, even if I still am not ready to forgive her for the Blood Binding.

Ellie speaks again. "They are right, Kaisera. Madis needs you if she stands a chance in facing what is to come," Ellie says.

"Does everyone know what's going on but me?" I ask.

Elena says, "I do not think Madis knows everything. I think she knows less than you." Elena shrugs in an *if-that-helps* kind of way.

It doesn't.

"All of you decided it was best to keep the two people who stand a chance to actually rule Area Six out of the loop?" I look around between all of them and.

In unison they all say, "yes."

I roll my eyes at them all.

Ellie speaks. "Madis cannot rule alone, Kaisera. She will not survive what is to come alone, and if she marries King Alibast of Area One, he will destroy any chance you may have of ruling Area Six."

"I will try and talk to Madis in the morning," I say.

"You can try but be careful with your words. Madis is hiding something, and I do not trust her father. He is as slimy as they come." Tribax pauses before continuing. "I have been her guard for six years, and she keeps too close to herself. I do not know if we can trust her to keep things from her father, which is why I have never tried to bring her in on things happening."

This is a lot to process and think over, and I cannot think with everyone staring at me, waiting for a response. This time, when I walk past them, they all let me through. Moments later, however, Bax is at my side.

"Can I help you?"

"Why, yes you can," Bax responds.

"Oh, and what else might I be able to help with besides saving the world?"

We are walking through the crowd of people at the ball. Vampires have paired off, either feeding off each other or their human servants. There is the smell of sex and sweat mixed with champagne and chocolate, making me smile just a bit.

Damn, I missed this place.

I am so distracted by the party goers that when Bax leans over to whisper in my ear, I jumped a little.

"I think I would like to taste you again."

I love this man's dirty talk. "I will not be chasing you tonight."

"Ha." Bax smirks down at me as we make our way back to my rooms. Before we get there, though, he opens a door a couple before my own.

"Goodnight, then," I say, ready to go on my merry way.

"Oh no, you don't." Bax swoops me up and throws me over his shoulder.

"Put me down!" I slam my hand playfully into his shoulder. He grunts a little at the impact. Maybe it was a little harder than playful.

He kicks the door shut and walks straight to his bed, where he tosses me down. I hit the bed with a small thud. I throw my head back and look up at the ceiling.

"This was such a pretty dress."

I scrunch my eyes together. "Was?"

I look down at my emerald gown with all the tiny crystal beading. Without any further warning, I hear a loud ripping sound. I look to where Bax is now kneeling, tearing the fabric of my dress, making a large slit up the left side.

"Bax! I like this dress!" I yell at him.

I only had time to grab a few of my old gowns from a storage bin I had found in Madis' old rooms. I figured they moved it over when they put her in my room.

"I am sure Ellie can fix it later." Then, he tears the tight material all the way to my hips.

My eyes widen at him. "She better be able to."

"Hey, Kaisera?" Bax stops and looks up at me.

"Yes, Bax?" He shivers a bit when I say his name, and I enjoy the way I get to him.

"Shut up." Then, he grabs my knees, slides my ass all the way to the edge of the bed, and throws my legs over his shoulders. I am spread wide open for him.

He starts nipping up my leg. I throw my head back on the bed. Even his light bites to the inside of my leg have me melting, and my core is tightening in anticipation.

"Goddess above, little vixen, you are already ready for me, aren't you?" I respond with a little moan. "Keep making those little moans for me."

His touch is so electric, it leaves my skin shivering in every spot it touches. I continue to make soft moans for him as I enjoy the feel of his lips on my skin.

"Tell me you want this." He starts kissing up toward my center. Bax stops everything. I whimper. He crawls up toward me, catching my dress and making it bunch up all around me. Bax places both of his hands on either side of my face and stares down at me. His delicious smell envelops me. "Say you want this out loud. Say, 'Tribax, I want you to make me see stars.'" He has a shit-eating grin across his face that says I will not get anything from him if I do not comply.

"Yes, I want this," I say breathlessly, realizing I just gave in way too easily.

"Is that what I told you to say?"

Bax leans down and starts to nibble on my ear and down my neck. When he reaches the top of my chest, there is another rip. He sucks the very tender peak of my breast into his mouth. I gasp at the pleasure of his mouth on me again. I start to wiggle and rock into him. In return, he puts what must be his full weight down on me to keep me from moving any more.

I whimper again.

"You are still being a brat, Kai, and you will not just get your way with me. You will have to learn to listen."

Did I really want this man so badly that I was about to give in? *Yep.* I cave. "Tribax, I want you to make me see stars."

That earns me an even bigger grin. I am happy I caused it; I enjoy being the one to make this big, scary man smile.

Bax leans over to one side, then rips what's left of my dress down the middle, exposing all of me except the parts still covered by my sheer blue underwear.

Bax stays off to the side of me, leaning in to suck on my breast again, rubbing my other nipple between his fingers. He moves his hand down my belly to play with the skin just above my underwear.

"I like this color on you," he says between nibbles and kisses.

I was thinking of Bax's dark blue eyes when I picked them out, so it is humorous that he likes them.

He gently slides his hand into my underwear and pulls them down my legs, careful not to rip them.

Yeah, rip the expensive dress. Save the cheap underwear.

"You are going to come for me. You are going to rock and move however you wish to make this the most pleasurable for you. I want to hear you scream, little vixen. I want to hear my name coming out of your bratty mouth so loud that it rattles the walls."

All I can do is shake my head. He leans in and inhales me. I think my scent does the same to him as his does to me. I can feel how hard he is through his slacks. His mouth crushes against mine. Bax explores my mouth with his tongue like he is trying to draw a road map. He is so all consuming with his kisses. I grip onto every part of him that I can, needing him closer, wanting him all over me. Bax breaks the kiss and begins his path down me, nibbling, kissing, and licking every inch of me, over the swells of my breasts, down the plane of my stomach, and to my very center.

Untried Origins

He gets back on his knees and pulls my right leg over his shoulder. He slowly licks straight up my folds until he lands on that little bundle of nerves, and I let out a moan. I can feel his smile of approval on my clit. Then, he is sucking hard on it. I buck my hips off the bed harder into his mouth. He holds onto my hips as he sucks and fucks me with his mouth and tongue.

His tongue makes swirls around my clit then dives into me, like a starving man looking for his last meal. He growls, and it vibrates all the way through me. I start to roll my hips up and down against his face, rocking slowly. I want to enjoy this. I have never felt something so intoxicatingly good before.

Bax removes his mouth from me and quickly replaces it with his hand, sliding his finger up and down my center, then sliding a thick, calloused finger deep inside me, rubbing around until he gets a gasp from me. Once he finds that spot that has me clenching tightly around his finger, his mouth is back on me, nibbling me in just the right spot. He figured me out so perfectly so quickly, unlike any other male. He is watching my reactions to see what pleases me the most.

I am riding his finger and face faster and faster. I am gasping and moaning loudly, not holding back a damn thing. I do not care that we are in a house full of Vampires with insanely good hearing; let them hear how this man makes me scream.

"Bax!" I gasp loudly. I am on the edge. I am trying to hold back, but at the sound of his name, Bax growls loudly, causing the vibrations of it to ripple through me again, and I crash over that edge. I squeeze my eyes shut, gasping for the air that is leaving me too quickly.

Bax keeps pumping in and out of me while sucking harder on my clit until the very end, until I am nothing but a lump of flesh gasping for air on his bed.

"That was the most beautiful thing I have ever seen," Bax says.

Bax is crawling back up to me, being careful of my now overly sensitive body, before his mouth is on mine again, and I want so much more. I can taste myself all over his lips, and I fucking love it. I wrap my legs around him quickly, and I start to try to remove his shirt. I want to feel all of him on me, and I want to feel it now.

I will chase or even beg if I must.

I thought maybe him getting me off again would ease the ache and draw I have to him, but it is even stronger now. I only want more of him.

He is still kissing me, and I have to turn my head to get away for a minute so that I can breathe again. He pulls away, untangling my arms and legs until he's free to walk away.

He grabs a piece of cloth from the bathroom and sweetly and softly cleans me up. He is taking such gentle care of me, and it is a side I have not seen from him, a sweet, kind side.

Bax crawls back up to me, careful not to put too much pressure on me still, and crashes his lips onto mine again.

I hope he is craving me the same way I am craving him.

I pull back a little. Bax takes that as a sign that I want him to back off and he does. I grab at his shirt to try to take it off again. He grabs my hand and holds it against his chest.

"Why are you stopping this?" I ask. The rejections from him are starting to get to me.

Bax smiles at me. "Because you are not ready."

"Of course, I am ready."

Bax laughs a deep chuckle. "No, my little vixen, you aren't. When I have you, and I will, you will never be able to walk away from me again."

"You think very highly of yourself, don't you?" I ask with a brow cocked up.

"Possibly."

"Mmff" is my great comeback, because honestly, with the way I am feeling right now, he might be right. I might not want to walk away. I am enjoying the challenges of him.

"How about we play cards?"

I sit up naked with the scraps of my dress all around me. "Cards?"

"Yes, cards."

"Fine." I snap my fingers, and I am back in my rooms a few doors down, grabbing the comfy clothes I had laid out for myself earlier that day. I snap again, and I am back in Bax's room.

Untried Origins

I quickly get dressed and start to head back over to Bax's bed until he stops me. He reaches for me, and I stop him.

"Do not rip these. I like this shirt." It is a loose-fitted top with holes in it from how often I wear it. It was the top I had worn to Warrantless so many years ago, before the Binding.

Bax sniffs the air, then growls at me.

"Take that shirt off. Now." He looks pissed. There is a shift in his eyes, then his fox is at his side, checking for what has caused Tribax such distress.

"What is your problem?" I am overly confused.

"You were with another male in that shirt. I can smell him on it. Take it off before I take it off for you," Bax replies. Bax looks downright terrifying. There is this animal aspect to him, like he could become a beast at any moment. I swear, even his canines are slightly longer than before.

Well damn. I rip the shirt off and toss it over to a chair, now naked from the waist up.

Bax gets up and walks over to where the shirt landed, picks it up, walks it over to a lit candle, sets the shirt on fire, and drops it out of his open window.

"Hey, fucker. That was my favorite shirt."

Bax shakes his head, and his features soften just a bit, but he still looks pissed. "I am sorry." It's all he says before he walks over to a trunk lying on the ground. He picks up a deck of cards and an article of clothing, a black T-shirt.

"Here, you can have this one." He holds the shirt out to me.

I snatch it out of his hand and hold it up in front of me to examine it. "This is going to be a dress on me."

"You can manipulate objects. Make it yours," Bax says.

"You just want me to smell like you," I say jokingly.

"Fucking right I do," Bax says not jokingly.

I roll my eyes at his drive to claim me, but I am also starting to enjoy it. I would normally fight that or tell the guy to get lost. However, the way Bax says and does it makes me want to play along.

I study the shirt still in my hand, looking at how I want to change the fabric. Once I decide, I hold up my hand to snap, but Bax grabs it.

"No snapping."

I let out a little huff. Not snapping requires a lot more concentration. Snapping has always come easily to me.

I close my eyes and focus on my magic, focus on where I want it to go, how I want it to change things. I open my eyes. The fabric begins to shift, and I concentrate on how I want the material to look. The bottom half of the shirt falls off, and the sleeves tear halfway from the top of the shoulder, shrinking to fit my much smaller biceps.

I grin up at Bax, who is standing over me as I sit topless on his bed.

I pull the shirt over my head. It's still a bit oversized, but not so much that it looks like a dress. The black material is soft and worn. It does smell just like Bax: pine trees and delicate spices. I pull the front of the shirt up over my nose and sniff. It smells amazing. When I open my eyes again after inhaling as much of Bax as I can, I find Bax grinning wildly at me.

"What was that about?" I ask.

"What was what about?" He looks at me confused, then takes a seat next to me.

"When you got angry, I swear I saw a bit of a wild animal in your eyes." I can't put it fully into words. It was overly strange.

"Sorry about that. I should be more careful with my temper around you, although you do have a knack for getting under my skin." He grins and picks up a lock of my curly black hair laying against my chest. He looks fascinated with that lock of hair, swirling it around his finger.

"Okay, but what was that?" I ask again.

"It was my fox," he says, dropping the lock of hair and looking back at me.

My eyebrows bunch together in confusion. "Your fox?"

"Yes. I am a shifter."

"You are a Fae shifter, who is a Major for a demon army?"

Untried Origins

"I am half Fae shifter, half demon." He shrugs it off like it isn't a big deal at all, but I have never even heard of such a combination.

I know there are Fae shifters, though I've never met one. They are pretty rare. To be part demon? Being with different species isn't against any rules or anything; it's simply rare. Good Fae do not end up in Inferis. Well, except Tribax and Elena, obviously. Oh, and that Alex who gave me my sword.

Wondering how he is holding up at the DWA. I will have to remember to have someone check on his progress soon.

So maybe there are some exceptions. Nonetheless, it is still pretty rare to have a half Fae, half Demon running around, let alone one who's a major in a Demon Army, who seemingly showed up out of nowhere.

He reaches over and grabs the deck of cards he tossed on the bed, before handing me his shirt. "Do you know how to play Crossroads?" Bax asks.

I laugh, letting my questions and thoughts about Bax be for now. "I am a demon princess. What do you think?"

Crossroads is a Demon card game where there can never be a tie; someone must always lose. Each player gets six chances to get three correct guesses of the other player's hand, and each player only has nine random cards from a full deck. Losers usually give up a part of their soul, but I do not think that is what we will be playing for tonight.

"What are we playing for?"

Tribax leans back onto his hand and taps the other hand against his chin, in the universal I am thinking pose. "If I win, you run with me in the morning." I narrow my eyes; morning is in like three hours. There is no way in Inferis I want to do that.

"And if I win?"

"You tell me. What do you want, little vixen?" He says it in such a seductive way, my brain short circuits for a few moments. Then I lean back on my arm and tap my hand against my chin, mocking his earlier move.

"Tell me your darkest secret."

See, the bets in Crossroads cannot be broken. If he agrees to the terms, he cannot lie, and although I am liking this male more and more each day, I think he might be hiding something.

Bax seems to pale a little, and for a second, I don't think he is going to take the bet.

"Deal," Bax says and holds his hand out, awaiting mine.

"Are you sure, Baxy Waxy? You can counter my offer," I say teasingly, knowing he will not back down from me.

He narrows his blue and silver eyes at me. "Are you going to shake my hand?"

I take his hand and the deal is sealed. I feel the faint magic flow between our hands, sending a quick shiver down my spine. Bax shuffles the cards then throws them into the air. They float around before nine cards come down into my hand, then nine cards into his.

I have three sevens, a king, a ten, a four, an eight and two threes. Not too many of the same number, but more than I would like. Bax frowns at his cards, and I know then that I've got him. I grin widely.

Bax shakes his head at me. "You go."

"You have two queens," I say.

Bax face shows nothing, and then he says, "Strike one of three."

My grin falls away, because I know I am about to go for a run.

Chapter 40

MADIS

Reign and I stayed up until the sun rose talking of politics, war, books we liked, and books we wish we had the time to read. It truly was an amazing night. He never tried to make any more advances on me. He was just simply there. He could not have known that was exactly what I needed, but it was. Just someone to be there for no other reason than good company.

I plop myself down on my bed and roll over onto my stomach, throwing a pillow under my chin and grinning like a young schoolgirl. At least, what I picture one to be like. I had missed out on those years. I will not think of those times now. I want to live in this moment of peace for just a bit longer.

I notice Yanci never returned to the room. I was sure she would have at least stopped by at some point last night. After all, she is technically still my lady's maid, if only for appearances.

I jump up from the bed and head for the door. I changed out of my gown and into a less formal gown earlier. Yet another one of my mother's surprises is that she made sure I only had my gowns packed. I have no pants, other than the ones I had worn here that the servants are still trying to get the Hollow blood and guts out of. I grab my boots that I had thankfully hidden in the carriage, slipping them on as I walk toward the door.

    I walk down a couple doors to where Yanci is staying. I knock on the door a few times with no answer. I open the door and walk in. It is obvious no one has stayed in the perfectly made bed. I decide to go check for her out in the courtyard. Maybe she is taking in the sunrise. To be perfectly honest, I do not know her well enough to say what she prefers to do in her free time.

    I walk down all the dark hallways and down the spiraling stairs to the doors on the left that lead out to the courtyard. There's not a soul to be seen anywhere, making my self-defense instincts kick in. Something isn't right. I reach for my daggers at my hip, only to remember again that I stopped carrying them the day the king named me heir.

    I hear a woman scream off in the distance. I take off after the sound. I cross the courtyard filled with beautifully grown flowers, vines, and plush grass into an area with thick bushes packed with thousands of tiny thorns.

    The woman screams again, and I recognize the scream. I take off at an even faster pace, branches and thorns slicing into my skin. I do not have time to run around them; through the thorns are my fastest route.

    When I finally break through the bushes, it is a sight of horror.

    Kaisera is being dragged away, kicking and screaming, by a group of haggard-looking old witches, while Tribax is on the ground with blood leaking from his nose and the back of his head. His sword is a few feet away from him, and I break off into a sprint toward it. I bend down to grab the sword, but before my hand grasps the handle, something hits the back of the head.

    The first thing I smell is death. It is a vile smell of rot and decay. The first thing I feel is a sharp pain in my wrist. The first thing I hear is Kaisera saying my name over and over. I try to open my eyes, but they seem swollen and heavy, not wanting to obey what I am telling them to do.

"Kai?"

"Yes, it's me. Madis, open your eyes."

I struggle, but finally get them to open. Everything is a bit off kilter. My vision is blurry, and I try to right myself, but before I can, I am throwing up. I try to swish spit around in my mouth and then spit a few times trying to get the taste of it from my mouth.

I hear Kai still, but my vision is too blurry to make out more than just her shape. "Madis, we have to get out of here. I am going to need you to pull some of your ninja shit and get us out."

She starts to come more clearly into view. Her hands are tied above her head the same as mine, and she looks pretty beat up. She has a broken nose with blood leaking from the side of it, a black eye, and a swollen bottom lip. She is kneeling on the ground. She has to sit all the way up to keep the pressure off her shoulders. She could probably stand, but standing for too long could be just as damaging.

I assume she got all the damage to her face from fighting off her kidnappers earlier. If that is the case, we have not been here long. She is of royal blood and a very powerful demon, so she would heal quickly.

"How long have we been here?" I rasp out, my voice breaking before I go into a violent coughing fit.

When I quiet down Kai tells me, "I am not one hundred percent sure, but at least a day."

A day?

"Did they come back to cause that damage to your face?"

"No, I have not seen them since they tied us up here," she whispers.

"What about Tribax? Did you see what they did with him?"

Kaisera shakes her head. "No, I think they left him there. It seems they were only after us."

Two figures walk past the tent we are in. The walls are not very thick, and we can see the silhouettes as the figures pass by.

As the light from their candles pass along with them, I get a good look at what this tent is made from: skin and bones. From the smell and texture of it, it seems to be *human* skin and bones.

"I think the ropes have some kind of crystals laced in them," Kai informs me.

Crystals can nullify demons' powers or, if used to puncture a heart or the brain, it could easily kill us. Lucky for us, mortal injuries like a broken neck will not kill us, only keep us down for a bit.

"I am guessing that is why you haven't snapped your fingers and gotten us out of here?" I ask, almost hopeful that she hasn't tried it yet.

"I cannot manipulate crystals," she responds.

Leave it to the world to give me one perfect night then take it away with this crap. Okay, no time to sulk. I need to figure this mess out, and I need to figure it out quick.

"Do you know what they want?" I ask.

"I mean, they haven't come to tell me their evil plan, if that is what you are asking." How she manages to stay sarcastic in the worst of situations is beyond me.

I try to light the ropes on fire, or at least get a bit of my fire going, but no such luck. Whatever the witches used on these ropes is dampening everything, even Kaisera's healing capabilities, it seems. I hear movement outside of the tent, then a voice.

"I'll get them to talk. We will know all the Area's secrets by morning. We will find her."

Secrets? Her? What are they talking about?

The tent flap opens, and in walks a younger-looking witch. Not young—she still is covered in wrinkles and warts—just younger than the crone we met during the Blood Binding.

She is carrying a long stick in her boney, sharp-nailed hand. Her wand, I am assuming. The witch is dressed in old scraps of clothing. They look and smell years old and unwashed. I cannot stop myself from gagging from the smell of it all, but I stop myself from vomiting again.

"Who will we start with? The wannabe princess or the real one?" the witch says, her voice high-pitched and nasally. She starts to stalk over to Kaisera.

"Start with me," I say quickly.

"Ah, perfect. Thank you for volunteering to watch."

What? No.

The witch walks straight up to Kaisera and stabs her through the left shoulder with the wand, which now seems to be surprisingly sharp. It goes all the way through Kaisera's arm like it is nothing.

Kai screams out in agony. She looks to the witch, "You bitch!"

"Stop!" I scream out. "She does not know anything."

The witch turns to me. "Oh, I know that. This is to make you talk." The witch turns back and stabs Kai back through the same hole she already created, then spins the stick around in circles. She is tearing the wound wider. Kai screams again, tears streaking down her dirt and blood-crusted face.

"What do you want to know?" I try.

"What is the King of Area Six up to?" The witch turns back to me.

"He is dead." I am confused. They must know that. News travels fast in Inferis, even in these far-off backwoods Areas.

"Wrong answer," the witch says.

Then, she drags her long sharp nail into the side of Kai's bicep, carving a deep line all the way through the muscle. I can hear the skin ripping.

Kai's screams are ringing in my ears now. I jerk and pull on my restraints, to try and rip them from the ceiling to get to Kai.

"My father is dead," Kai says through gasping breaths and cries.

"Oh, sweet child. I know your father is dead." The witch is running her hands sweetly down the side of Kai's cheeks. Then, she slaps her hard across Kai's face.

Kai's face jerks to the side, blood spurting from her mouth. Her head dangles a bit. Then, she looks up and spits blood into the witch's face.

"Kai!" I yell at her. She is only going to make things worse for herself. Doesn't she know that?

"Madis, do not tell this bitch a thing," Kai says, staring the witch down.

Ka Lee

The witch screeches out a terrible, high-pitched noise. It is a mixture of a laugh and a scream. I try to cover my ears the best I can by pressing my raised shoulders into my ears. I feel a warm liquid leaking from my ears and into my eardrums from the vibrations of the noise.

I can see Kai's ears are bleeding too. The witch grabs Kai's slightly hanging chin and pinches her cheeks in her hand. "One of you will tell me what the King has planned with our crone, or you will both die. Slowly."

"What king?" I scream. I do not want to watch this witch tear Kai apart, and I know she will. We serve no benefit to them other than the information they are looking for.

The witch walks over to me and backhands me across the cheek. "Your father, you stupid, naive girl."

The sting on my cheek is nothing more than I am used to, so I recover quickly. "My father is not the king."

The witch throws her head back in a cackling laugh. "Oh, but he is, girl. If you believe otherwise, you really are naive."

My father? What has he done?

"I will leave you here to stew on these questions for a bit. When I return, I expect answers." The witch makes one more pass by Kai, running her finger into the gash running down her bicep again. Kai lets out a low whimper, and it breaks me. The witch takes her blood-soaked fingers and sticks them into her mouth.

"You are not as you seem, are you, girly?" the witch says rhetorically before walking out of the door.

When the witch is far enough away, I get off my knees and stand. We have to get the pressure off of our shoulders before it causes permanent damage, especially with the weight of my wings pulling downward.

"Kai?"

"What, Madis?" She sounds pissed.

"You have to stand up."

"Fuck you," is her response.

"Seriously, Kaisera. Stand up. You have to take some of the pressure off your shoulders."

Kai grunts, but she must see that I am right, because she starts to get a foot underneath her. She cries out short whimpers of pain. When your arms have grown used to the pain in one position, it tends to hurt more when you finally give them relief. It feels like tiny little needles hit every single one of the joints and nerves in your body all at once. Kaisera gets one foot firmly under her then the next.

"There you go, Kai. Now, stand up straight."

"Have I told you that I fucking hate you?"

I huff a small humorous laugh. "As a matter of fact, you have. On multiple occasions as of late."

"Well, now I truly mean it."

"Good to know," I say. "How does your arm feel?" I need to keep her talking. I am hoping if she feels strong, maybe her body will heal itself a little bit. With the loss of blood, I do not want her passing out.

"It feels like a witch shoved a dull stick through it," Kai says.

"It actually looked pretty sharp to me."

Kai looks up from the ground to me with a sharp glare. "So why is it that she only wanted to make me bleed and all you got was a slap to the face?" Kai says accusingly.

"I think they know this is worse for me."

"I would beg to differ. I would much rather watch you get stabbed than be stabbed," Kai says.

"I think that is the point, Kaisera."

She shakes her head. "Whatever. What is the plan?"

"What plan?"

"The plan to get out of this shithole, Madis." Kai tries to move her hands around, but all it does is earn a wince out of her.

"You really should try and keep still. You have lost a lot of blood." Kai huffs in frustration. "And you should try and keep your heart rate down." I add.

Kai glares at me. "What are you, some fucking expert on torture?"

If she only knew. "Kind of," is all I give her.

"Fine, I will calm down and I will try to keep still. Now, tell me how we are going to get out of here, Madis."

"Why do you assume I have a plan?"

She scoffs. "Because you are you."

"I do not even know what that means."

"Madis, you always got us out of trouble. You were the problem solver."

"No, Kai. I got *you* out of trouble. I would end up taking the punishment."

"What are you talking about?"

This really is not the place or time. Before I have a chance to even start explaining, a witch comes in. This is a different one, still just as ugly as the last. This one looks as if she has some kind of scales growing up the side of her face. She makes a beeline for Kai.

"Hey, you lizard." I try to give my voice as much mockery as possible.

The witch whips around in my direction and starts to stalk toward me. *Good. Come and get me. I can take it.*

The witch slaps me so hard with the back of her hand across the face that I instantly taste coppery blood filling my mouth. She might have knocked a tooth or two loose with that blow.

I turn my head back to await something else, but she is already stalking toward Kaisera.

Kaisera screams, pleading with this witch. "No! No, no no! Get away from me."

I try again, jerking violently against my bound hands. "Hey, you scaly bitch, is that all you got?" It does not even sound halfway like I mean it. It's not the strong, confident way Kaisera seems to make things sound.

The witch turns and looks at me but stays right by Kaisera's side. She watches me as she cuts the top of the rope holding Kai. I watch as Kai falls to the ground in a heap and lands with a loud grunt as all the air is punched out of her.

The witch leans down, grabbing a handful of Kai's hair and ripping it upward. I can hear the hairs being ripped from the roots of Kai's head. Kai screams again. "Stop! We will tell you."

The witch laughs "I do not think you know anything, little princess. I do think your little friend over there knows exactly what her daddy did with our crone, though."

Untried Origins

The witch drags her long, skinny nails down Kai's back and cuts shallow grooves into her back. Kia's screams are growing softer. They are becoming more like moans of pain.

"Kai! Look at me." I must help her in some way, and if I cannot stop the witch, then I can at least help her control the pain. Kai cries again softly.

"Kaisera Allison Braxton. Look at me."

Upon hearing her full name, Kai turns her head in the dirt to look up at me. Her face is covered in a mixture of blood, tears, and dirt.

"Breathe, Kai. Breathe a deep breath in and hold it."

The witch drags her claws back down Kai's back, ripping through her tank top and skin, causing the shirt to fall to the sides. I see a light black tattoo: Kai's wings. The witch is tearing small holes into them. I do not know if it will affect her actual wings, or if them being hidden in her skin will protect them.

Kai lets out a loud scream again as the witch starts to draw symbols into Kai's back, right over the wings.

"I think this little bird needs her pretty little wings clipped."

"No! Get away from her, you evil twisted freak."

"Careful, little girl, or I will take yours next."

"Fine! Come and take them!" *Just stop touching her.*

The witch stops drawing and looks my way. "Yours would look pretty hanging in my cabin. They would sit beautifully over the fireplace."

"Yes, they even sparkle in the right lighting."

I look back to Kai. She has curled in on herself. Her shirt is half hanging on her, and she is covered in her own blood. If I do not get those ropes off her and get her out of here soon, she will not survive.

The witch stands and starts toward me. She stops close to me and takes out a long sharp wicked-looking knife made of crystal.

"This is going to hurt, little heir. I think it is better if you keep your wings but are not able to fly." I fully believe her. This is going to hurt, and in more than just the physical sense. I love my wings.

Ka Lee

The witch tears my shirt from my back and begins carving into my shoulder blades.

Chapter 41

ELLIE

I quickly spring upright in the bed. "Something isn't right," I say.

Mica is at my side within seconds, hugging me tightly. "What is it, my love?"

"Madis and Kai. Something is wrong." I am up and throwing on one of my simple dresses and walking shoes as quickly as I can. Mica is up with me, throwing on his training leathers and strapping his two swords to his hips.

"Where are we going?" Mica asks.

"To the courtyard," I respond.

Seconds later, we are out the door, running for the courtyard. I cannot for sure say what exactly I am running off to, but I know exactly where I am going.

We get through a few feet of thick brush and thorny bushes to a clearing just before the woods. I can tell a fight took place here, and I can smell blood. I look around for a bit before I spot the source: a large male is bleeding from his head and nose.

Mica notices too. "Tribax!" Mica is off running for him.

I sprint after him. Mica is at Tribax's side first, turning him over. Tribax grunts but slowly starts to wake. When his eyes open, they're bright silver, all the blue gone, and his pupils are massively dilated. He bares his teeth and shoots upright, but as soon as he is on his feet, he stumbles a bit. He reaches for the back of his head and touches what I am sure is a tender spot, then moans softly.

"You should probably sit down," I tell him.

He growls. "No."

Mica goes to Tribax's side and places a hand on his shoulder. "What happened here?"

Tribax looks a little confused, like he is trying to sort it out himself. Then, he speaks. "Kai had lost a bet and we were out for a morning run." Then, he goes pale white, and his eyes turn into saucers. He starts frantically searching around.

"Where is Kai?" Tribax looks from Mica to me and then back. He looks terrified. Gone is the growling angry man, and in his place is a man facing pure terror. "Where. Is. Kaisera?"

"We haven't seen her," Mica says.

Tribax starts to pace, holding his hand under his chin then running his hands over his face. He drops into a squat with his elbows on his knees. He looks at me. "They took her, didn't they?"

I nod my head yes. Mica looks between us. "Who took who? Someone took Kaisera?"

I walk over and tuck myself into Mica's side. "Tribax, who took Kaisera?" I ask softly.

He looks up from his squared position. "The Witches."

I knew in my bones that something was wrong, but the witches is past wrong: it is terrible. The witches are vile, evil creatures. They make a sport of watching people bleed.

Mica leaves my side and walks to Tribax. "We will gather our people here and talk to Madis and King Reign. They will help us get her back."

Tribax stands. "Thank you, brother."

Tribax and Mica have not always seen eye to eye. In fact, when they first met, they got into a fight at a cafe that ended when

Untried Origins

Madis stepped in with a throwing knife, leaving Mica with a nasty scar I healed the night we first hung out. Still, they are brothers in arms and will stand together on serious matters.

I start to walk back toward the castle when I notice a long strand of white hair hanging from a torn bush. "Hey guys, I do not think Madis will be assisting us on this one."

Tribax walks over, taking the hair from me and sniffing it.

"It is Madis'." He starts to pace with his hands in his hair, pulling at it. "Shit."

Mica says, "So the witches have both potential heirs to Area Six's throne."

"No, love. The witches have the only two who can save us all from a Great War and absolute destruction of the world as we know it," I respond.

Tribax stops pace and drops his hands to his sides. "Oh, is that all?"

Mica walks over and grabs my hand. "Then we must get them back."

"We will get them back. Kai is..." Tribax starts but pauses before he continues. "I will not lose her to those scheming witches."

"Let's go find King Reign. The evening is coming soon; he should be waking," I say.

The men nod, and Mica leads the way back through the thick bushes and then back through the courtyard. We find King Reign in the dining hall eating breakfast. He is draining blood from a servant's arm into a large metal wine glass.

"Good evening to you all," Reign says very happily. When he spots all our faces and the bloodstained Tribax, he stands from the table and makes his way over to us at vampire speed, all calmness gone. "What has happened?" he says to Tribax, knowing he is head of our security.

"The witches have taken the heirs," Tribax says with his head hanging low in what looks to be shame.

Reign is in front of Tribax within a half second, grabbing him by his shirt tightly. Tribax is just a bit taller than Reign so it would look comical, except the look in Reign's eyes says murder.

"Is it not your job to prevent things like this from happening?" Reign says through gritted teeth, his canines fully exposed.

"Back the fuck up. I do not answer to you." Tribax swings his arms down on Reign's arms, causing Reign to lose the grip on Tribax's shirt. Reign hisses at him, and Tribax growls deeply right back at him.

"This isn't helping," I chime in. Mica goes to get between them. I put a hand on his chest to stop him. I love my strong, protective mate, but he will not survive getting between these two.

Reign stands up tall and wipes his hands down his suit, smoothing out imaginary wrinkles, and then runs his hand through his jet-black hair. "When were they taken?" Reign asks while he straightens out his shirt sleeves.

"Early this morning," Tribax says. He is standing as if waiting for an attack.

"This morning! Why am I just now being notified?" Reign asks.

Tribax seems to steady himself. "I was knocked out and just recently came to."

Reign huffs an unamused laugh. "Some guard you are. Cannot even protect your own."

Tribax starts to shift, his blue eyes turning to solid glowing silver. His canines elongate, and his skin starts to grow gray and black fur. His clothes rip and his nose grows into a boney snout. The shift happens so fast, I barely believe the wolf-sized gray fox with a skulled face standing in front of us is Tribax.

"Ha! Is that supposed to intimidate me, boy?" Reign hisses out.

Tribax lunges at Reign, who dodges too fast for Tribax to land a blow of any kind. Tribax lets out a nasty snarl, and Reign hisses back at him, showing all his teeth. Tribax lunges for Reign again, knocking Reign back onto the dining room table this time. The heavy metal legs scratch harshly across the floor; glass, metal, and candles all go crashing. Reign has Tribax by the throat, but Tribax has Reign pinned down to the table by the weight and sheer size of him. Both men are snarling and hissing at each other.

"Stop this!" I scream. Mica is holding me back from getting to them. "Stop this now!" I try again. Reign and Tribax stop their growling long enough to look at me. I continue once their attention is fully on me. "While you alpha idiots are fighting each other, the witches are more than likely tearing Kaisera and Madis apart bit by bit."

Tribax growls one more time at Reign before shoving off him aggressively and walking away. He paces by the large windows off to the side while he cools down. After a few moments, he shifts back into his Fae form. He is completely naked now, all his clothing shredded to pieces with his shift. Mica leaves my side, taking off his jacket and handing it over to Tribax.

"Thank you." Tribax says, wrapping the coat around his waist enough to cover him up a little bit.

Reign straightens himself and looks at me. "Any suggestions on how to get them back?"

Tribax turns to Reign. "Why do you even care? Aren't they your competition? Come to think about it, maybe you are the one who set this up?"

Reign tugs his coat down to adjust and straighten it back to its perfection. "Why I care is none of your concern, and I would appreciate it if everyone would stop accusing me of things like murder and kidnapping," Reign responds.

Elena comes running in screaming. "I found a little dragon and a red fox tied up with some kind of rope in Kai's room. I have not seen her since last night!"

Tribax is jogging out to meet Elena. "Where are Julian and Nija?"

Elena scrunching her eyes together, causing her face to twist up. "Why are you naked?"

Tribax shakes his head and gives Elena a death stare. "The animal familiars you found tied up, where are they?"

We have all made our way over to Elena, standing by, waiting for her answer.

"They are in mine and Allie's room. I'm not sure why they were tied up." Elena is looking amongst all of us.

"Who is Allie?" Reign says.

I'll take this one. "It is Kaisera's middle name, the name she went by in the mortal world of Erathina."

Everyone leaves the room then, Tribax leading the way and sprinting up the curved staircase and down the hallways. He bursts through the door and sprints over to the little animals tied tightly together. He falls to his knees and starts trying to tear at the rope, but he rips his hand away. When he pulls his hands back, they are covered in small little cuts.

Elena speaks up. "Yeah, that's why I didn't untie them."

Reign is through the door last, and he goes straight to Tribax, handing him a knife from his dress coat. Tribax takes it with a nod in appreciation, then gets to cutting the ropes.

Nija is twisting around, seemingly terrified of everyone in the room. I go to him and pat his little head. "It is okay, little one. We are going to get you out of this."

The little blue and black dragon whimpers. Whatever these ropes are, they are keeping him from using any of his powers. I touch the rope and it tingles against my skin. I jerk my hand away.

"What is it, Ellie?" Mica asks me.

"The ropes are laced with crystal bits."

Reign chimes in, "That must be how they are keeping Madis and Kaisera."

Reign is right. Both girls are fighters in their own way; they would fight back if they could.

"Hold up. Who is keeping Madis and Allie, I mean, Kaisera?" Elena asks. She is standing, arms crossed and tapping her foot. We turn around and look at her. She throws her arms into the air and starts looking between us. "Is someone going to tell me what is going on?"

There is a muffled sound coming from the other side of the room. Everyone turns to look at each other.

"What the hell was that noise?" Elena says.

Everyone turns to look at me. I shrug, then go to the other side of the room to investigate. A young girl with dirty blonde hair, wearing a blue ball gown, is tied up and gagged next to the bed.

"Tribax, we are going to need that knife over here when you are done," I say.

Elena walks over to me first "Who the hell is that?"

I shrug at her. Tribax finally gets the last of the ropes off his fox. Julian is purring and rubbing up against his owner. He pats the fox on the head and stands. Nija pops onto my shoulder and snuggles into my hair, as if to hide from everyone else in the room. He looks up to my face as if he is waiting on answers as well.

Tribax hands the knife back to Reign. Reign walks over to us and starts cutting the ropes off the young girl. "Her name is Yanci. She is Madis lady's maid. How do none of you know anything about your future queen?"

Elena answers for everyone. "That is yet to be determined."

Elena looks as if she is going to cry. "Bax, tell me what is going on."

"The witches took the heirs," Reign says.

Tribax turns and glares at him, then snaps back around to Elena, who now has a tear falling from one of her eyes. "That cannot be true. Bax, is it?"

"What he says is true," Tribax responds.

Elena grabs hold of Tribax and throws herself into his shoulder, sobbing loudly. "Shhh, it is ok, Elena. I will get her back for us." Tribax runs his hand over short, strawberry blonde hair, trying to calm her.

Yanci, the blonde girl on the floor, sits up, gasping for air as Reign cuts the final rope off her.

"Are you okay?" Reign asks her.

Yanci shakes her head up and down. "Yeah, I have had worse," she says with a sad smile.

Reign stands and starts to survey the room. I walk to Reign, who stares down at me in confusion. I reach up to my shoulder and let Nija walk into my hands. I hand him over to Reign, who takes the little dragon in his huge hands.

"I think you should hold on to him," I tell Reign.

Nija crawls up Reigns arm and makes himself right at home on Reign's shoulder.

Ka Lee

Reign looks to me softly. "We will get them back. They are both strong women."

Chapter 42
KAISERA

The witch who had tried to carve out my wings had gone to Madis and started to carve into her back, but I could not understand what exactly she had been doing until Madis' left wing disappeared. The witch left the left side of Madis' back and began on the right, until that wing was gone too.

Madis did not scream or move. She stood perfectly still with a locked jaw, and only a single tear had fallen from her eye. I do not think that tear was from the pain; I believe it was for the loss of her wings. After that witch finished with Madis, she stood back, looked at her work, laughed a cruel laugh, and left the tent.

I am still on the ground, covered in cuts, a hole all the way through my left shoulder. The witch had at least cut the ropes from the ceiling, leaving each wrist individually wrapped in these blasted ropes. The sharp pieces of the crystal sink into my wrists every time my heart beats.

Everything hurts. I can feel each cut in my back and the deep gash still leaking blood down my left arm. I felt sticky and dirty all over. I try to pull my uninjured arm up to wipe some of the dirt and blood from my crusty face, but it pulls the muscles in my back, and I scream out for what feels like the one-hundredth time in frustration.

"Kai, it is going to be ok. I will figure this out. Just breathe for me," Madis says.

"I will breathe for myself, not for you," I grit out. I should not be talking at all. It hurts to push air through my lungs, and my throat is growing scratchy from the screaming.

"I do not care who you breathe for, Kai. Just keep breathing."

I did not respond this time. I want to close my eyes and rest. My head is so dizzy, I do not know if I can take any more damage to my body. *Fuck these witches and fuck this place.*

I try to push my arms back underneath me. My left arm is useless. The damned witch cut all the way through the tendons, leaving me with nothing but a limp arm. She must be skilled with a blade, though, because she somehow managed to miss every major spot, which would have made me bleed out by now.

"Remember the time you kicked the guard?"

I know what she is doing, and I am going to join in, because I do need this distraction. "You mean the one who called me shorty?" There was a guard who would pick on me daily, thought I was 'cute as a button.'

Madis laughs a small chuckle. "Yeah, that one."

"Yeah, I remember him. He learned that day that I could in fact reach his face with my foot."

Madis chuckles again. "I also remember you talking him into lusting over a female guard twice his size, who proceeded to kick his ass further."

I laugh a little. It hurts to do so, but it hurts a little less with the memory. "Yes, your father threw a fit and made me run eight miles that afternoon," I say to Madis.

I have finally gotten into a seated position. I am leaning against one of the support beams for this tent. I am not sure I could stand, even if I wanted to.

Madis' eyes drop. "Yes, my father." She shakes her head.

"Madis?" I ask.

"Yes, Kai?"

"We aren't going to get out of this one, are we?"

She looks up to me. "I will get you out of here."

"What about you?" I ask.

"I will get us both out," Madis says, but she sounds so defeated. "I promise you the night of the Binding that I would always be your rock." Madis pauses and takes a determined breath. "I will keep that promise to you Kaisera."

I remember how much I felt that promise in my soul that night, how much I believed it then, and I want to believe it now.

The first witch with the sharp stick comes back into the room. I try to back away from her, but there is nowhere to go, and every move I make hurts a little more.

"You are starting to look like one of us," the witch says as she makes her way over to me. Madis is pulling at her binding, blood dripping down from her wrists into her white hair and down her long, tanned arms.

"Stay away from her." She tries over and over again to get free. It is of no use. The witch has her eyes set back on me.

"Please," I try.

"Aw, is the little princess going to give in? All out of spunk, huh?" the witch says in a mocking tone.

That comment lights a spark back in me. "Go screw yourself. I know no one else will."

The witch lunges, grabbing me by my ankle and dragging me to her. Her long, pointed nails dig deep into the flesh of my ankle. She pulls me so fast, it causes my back to slam across the ground, and I cry out as my back and badly damaged shoulder are dragged across the rocky dirt floor.

The witch turns and looks to Madis and pulls out a small, burgundy pouch.

"Don't," is all Madis says. Her eyes are wide and staring directly at the little burgundy pouch.

What is in the little bag?

The witch dumps the bag over, and small, sharp looking rocks and crystals fall into a neat tight stack. I look between the witch and Madis confused.

The witch rips my arms together then ties them with more of the crystal rope. I scream in agony. My voice is finally going out, though, and it comes out more of a rasp as the tiny shards of crystal burrow deep into my arms.

The witch drags me over the pile and points. "Kneel."

"Fuck you."

The witch stabs the wand back through my shoulder wound for the third time. "If I stab you just one more inch to the right, this wand will go straight through the center of your wings. You will never fly again."

I am gritting my teeth to keep the sobs from pouring over. I try not to give her the satisfaction. I cannot help the tears sliding down my face, though.

The witch gets right in my face this time and screams, "Kneel," pushing hard on my shoulders. I am forced to my knees. I cannot fight her off in the state I am in.

The rocks go directly into my skin, and I throw my head back in pain. I try to collapse to the side, but the witch has her hands on both of my shoulders, holding me in place.

"This is where you demons have always belonged: on your knees, worshiping us, the true holders of magic and power," she says with her cackling voice.

I try to wiggle to give my knees some relief, but it doesn't help. The only thing I can do is let the tears fall and try not to break any further.

"Tell me what the king has planned for our crone," the witch tries again, looking at Madis.

"All I know of his plan is that he wishes to marry me to Area One's king, King Alibast," Madis breathes then continues. "I truly do not know anything more. Please, let her go. We have not seen the crone since the Blood Binding years ago."

The witch laughs again. "Stupid girl. That was no Binding."

The sharp rocks are digging deep into the skin of my knees, but her words have my attention. "What do you mean? We performed the Blood Binding with your ugly crone."

The witch presses her weight down on my shoulder, causing the rocks to cut deep enough to touch bone. I try to hold back my cries. "Our crone performed an Unbinding, you insolent little demons. She showed you what would tear you apart, and you both so easily let it happen."

The witch lets go of my shoulders and pushes me to the side. I collapse over to my left, landing on my already injured arm. This time, the pain is too much to hold back my hoarse screams.

The witch comes after me again. Madis lets out a whimpered, "Please," as if this really is tearing her apart. The witch throws me up against the post, and the pain of my shoulder ramming into it causes everything to go black.

Chapter 43

ELLIE

Everyone is standing over a map in a large office, with bookshelves from floor to ceiling and from wall to wall all the way around the room.

Books I am casually scoping out for answers to questions I have been seeking.

Reign, Tribax, Elena, and Mica have been going back and forth on the right way to enter the witches' Area with as few men as possible so that we do not start a war.

"The west side will be their weak side," Reign says.

"Yes, but it is covered in swamps. I will not be able to pick up their scents as strongly as I can if we enter from the south." Tribax points to a spot on the map.

Neither man has slept in the four days since Kaisera and Madis were taken. Both have beards starting to show and dark circles under their eyes.

Elena is seated somewhere off to the side, listening while stroking Kaisera's little black kitten we had found hiding under the bed in their room, trembling under her small wings.

Untried Origins

Mica and I had searched for the servant girl, Yanci, for two days after we released her from her bindings. We had zero luck finding her. She was Madis' supposed lady's maid, but she vanished. No one knows where she went.

Nija has stayed close to Reign ever since I handed him over. The little dragon is pacing the floor right now alongside Tribax's red fox.

Everyone is on edge. We do not know if the heirs are still alive, or if they have been killed by now. No one other than witches survive very long in the Witch Area. The witches thrive on the pain and suffering of innocents. Even in the mortal world, there are very few good witches to be found. The nasty ones enjoyed killing the good witches more so than anything else, so the good witches keep to themselves if they can.

I find a book titled *Book of Bindings*. I add it to a small stack I have growing on a desk off to the side. The others in the stack are *Witch Deals*, *Cracking the Veil*, and *Rulers of Queens*. I don't know if I will find what I am looking for in any of these, but it never hurts to read.

"It is settled, then," Reign says as he stands up straight from where he was leaning on the table. "I will go in as a distraction, and Tribax, Elena, and Mica will get the girls out."

"What about me?" I ask. I am small, and most people believe since I am a seamstress and lady's maid to the princess that I am useless, but of course, only Mica and I know the truth.

Reign turns to Mica, looking for guidance on what to say. Mica, being my perfect match, raises his hands up and steps away. "Hey, she makes her choices." Mica turns and winks at me.

I smile sweetly at him. He will get rewarded for that later. "I will go with you, King Reign, as a sort of counsel. We will tell them that we are there to negotiate the girls' releases, while the others get them out."

Reign crosses his long arms over his chest and takes a wider stance. "What if we are captured?"

I smile at him. "We will not be."

Tribax claps his hands together. "Then it is settled. When do we leave?"

Reign steps forward a bit. "Everyone, get your rest now. We will leave when the sun is fully set." He looks out the window at the sun. "Which gives us about four hours of rest."

Everyone stands and makes their way out the door to their rooms to rest for what is sure to be a very long night ahead.

I grab my little stack of books on the table and Reign lifts a brow at me. "Doing a little light reading?"

I smile shyly at him, seeing as I never really asked if I could take the books. "Is that okay? I will return them in the same condition."

Reign smirks at me. "Read whatever you like; my library is at your disposal. Are you sure you are up for this? The witches can get nasty," Reign says.

I look around the room to see that everyone but myself, Mica, and Reign have left. "I am sure, but I need you to swear to never tell anyone what you see while we are there."

Reign's eyebrows scrunch together as he looks at me. "Will it help save Madis?"

'Yes."

"Then do whatever it is you have to do; I will never speak a word of it." Reign bows slightly at the waist, turns and leaves the room. Mica and I follow behind him and make it quickly down the dark hallways back to our rooms.

Mica scoops me up into his arms as soon as our room door closes behind us, stack of books and all. He leads me over to the nightstand and asks, "Think you could put those down for me?"

I do as he asks. He hurls me onto the bed as soon as the books are out of my hands. He crawls directly on top of me, playfully kissing me all over my face except on my lips. I try to wiggle away.

"Oh no you do not, " Mica says.

Then, he is tickling me. I am laughing and squirming. "Mica, stop it."

"Okay, okay." Mica stops and leans in to give me a soft kiss. He pulls away to look into my eyes, seeing deeper than any other ever could. "You know I love you, right?"

"I do." I scrunch my eyebrows together at him. "Where is this coming from?"

"Just if something happens later tonight, I want, no, I need you to know you are my whole life and soul and reason for being," Mica says as he drops to an elbow and starts to play with my loose light brown locks.

His shaggy blonde hair is falling into his adorable face. "Everything will be fine."

"Do you know that for sure?" he asks.

"No, I do not, but I have faith we will be fine." I stroke my hand over his face. He kisses my nose then rolls over, dragging me to my side so that he is behind me and wrapped fully around me.

"Then let's get some rest."

Chapter 44
MADIS

    We have been in this tent I think for close to four days now. It is hard to keep time in a place cast in a constant shadow. Even when the sun is at its highest, the trees here are too thick to see it. The witches have force fed us a few pieces of stale bread and almost drowned us by forcing us to drink the dirty water they brought for us in rusted cans. "Ungrateful, spoiled brats" is what they called us when we tried to refuse the dirty water.

    Kaisera has been in and out for the past two days. She hardly speaks, unless it is to fight back with her words, her body too weak to do much else. The witches have made it a game of who can make her scream louder for them.

    My only saving grace, other than the witch who carved into my back, forcing my wings to retreat, is that I have had no other damage done to me. At least, not physically. Kaisera's screams will haunt my dreams for the rest of my life. I can feel the deep gashes in my back, and I can feel that they are starting to get infected. Smelling the infection is probably a better way of

Untried Origins

describing it. I can smell my own decaying skin around the wound. If I do not get it cleaned and tended to soon, I know it will cause permanent damage to my back, and I will have no hope of reversing whatever that witch did to my wings.

I hear the witches stirring outside of the cabin, like they are all running toward something. If they are all gathering away from the tent, this is our chance to get away. Anticipation and adrenaline start to course through my veins.

"Kai!" I try to get her attention, causing her to stir a little. She is in a fetal position on the ground, where she has been for several hours now. I have been monitoring her breathing, and it has been steady enough.

"Kai!" I try again, a little louder this time.

She whimpers then says, "What?" She does not move or open her eyes, but that is okay. She is listening.

"Kai, they all just ran away from the tent in the same direction. If we're ever going to have a chance to get out, it is now." Kai opens her eyes just a bit, her eyelashes stuck together from the dirt mixing with her tears and causing it to turn muddy and crust over her eyes. "One of the witches left a short knife over on the table by the tent's opening. Do you think you could crawl to it and cut those ropes off yourself?"

If she could start to heal, we would have a better chance of getting free of this place.

Kai tries to lift herself up, but both of her arms are injured now from the countless brutal cuts the witches took turns making. Kai only makes it a few inches off the ground before she plops back down.

Think, Madis. Think. I scold myself.

"Your wings, Kai. Can you stretch them out?"

She grunts. I think she is trying, then she says. "I need magic to get them free."

I have to think of something. There are screams and movements all around us. Everything around the tent seems to darken further. I hear footsteps outside of the tent, and then I smell something other than decay for the first time, just a slight scent. Pine and spices. *Tribax*

"Tribax?" I scream, praying to all the goddesses of Valkeria that the witches are too distracted with whatever else is going on. "If you can hear me, we are here!"

Moments go by, then a redheaded woman with tribal tattoos across her face and a bow strapped to her back enters the tent.

"Elena?" I say.

Her head whips over to me, and then she screams, "Tribax, I found Madis." She runs to me, whipping out a knife and starts hacking away at the ropes around my wrist.

"No, go to Kai. She needs you more!"

Elena looks me in the eyes. Tribax bursts through the tent moments later. He does not even glance my way; his full attention is already on Kaisera, as if he could sense she is in the room.

He looks helpless and shattered as he bends down to her half-lifeless body covered in blood and cuts, completely naked from the hips up. Tribax has his shirt off a second later, covering her up then scooping her into his arms.

I hear him whisper to her, "What have they done to you, my little vixen?"

"You have to get those ropes off her." I take the knife Elena used to cut my ropes off me and walk as quickly as I can to where Tribax is holding Kai. She looks much smaller in his huge arms.

Tribax bares his teeth and growls at me in warning. Elena is grabbing his arm and shushing him. I hold my hands up. "Tribax, those ropes are keeping her from healing. Please let me get them off her."

He loosens his grip on her just a bit so I can have better access to her wrists. I work quickly cutting them off. Elena is at the door checking to see if any of the witches have returned.

"What is going on out there?" I ask as I try to cut the ropes as quickly and as gently as I can.

"Reign and Ellie are causing a distraction," Elena says.

"Ellie?" I ask a bit loudly.

"It does not matter. Let's get out of here," Bax says the second the rope pops off Kai's wrists.

Untried Origins

My entire body is sore from being in the same position for so long, but I suck it up quickly. I need to help get Kaisera out of here.

Elena calls from the door, "Bax, we have to get moving."

He quickly pushes past me and makes for the door. Once he and Elena are out the door, I follow behind.

"So, what is the plan?" I ask quietly. Elena turns to me with a who the Inferis knows shrug. I narrow my eyes in her direction. "Great plan."

Bax turns to us. "Shut up. We are going to make a run to the north. Reign and Ellie have lost the witches' interest by now." Bax whistles a weird note. Mica appears from behind the trees, holding onto four horses, one of them being Fletch.

We start off toward them, mounting as quickly as we can.

We make it through a thick cluster of trees and are forced to cross through a deep, swampy patch. The horses slosh around loudly, and I pray to the goddesses above that the witches are not interested in what is making all the commotion.

We make it out of the thick woods and swamp to flatter, smooth riding. A few minutes later, Reign and Ellie ride up from our left on the same horse. Reign gets as close to Fletch as he can before leaping from his horse onto Fletch right behind me. I wince as he hits my tender shoulder blades.

"Let me take over," Reign says.

I nod and we switch places so that Reign is in front of me, now guiding Fletch. I place my hands down by my sides, but Reign reaches down and places them around his waist. It feels comfortable; it feels good. I know I shouldn't, so I place my hands back down by my sides.

When my hands fall away, Reign kicks Fletch in the sides hard enough to jerk her forward. I grip onto Reign tightly to keep from flying off. I smile at his persistence.

"I have you," Reign says over his shoulder.

For once in my life, I do not fight for control or argue. I hand over the control, lean my head into Reign, and let him carry all my weight. I do not care if everyone else came to save both of us, or just to save Kai. I know deep in my heart that Reign came for me.

I doze in and out as we make the long ride back to Reign's castle in Area Seven. Reign never complains about my weight leaning on him or how terrible I smell.

I wake fully to the morning sky starting to rise. "Are you going to be okay?" I ask.

"You have been in a torture tent in the Witches Area for almost five whole days. You do not get to worry about me," Reign states.

I smile and lean my head forward again into Reign's back. I can see the castle's shape taking form anyways. We will be there sooner rather than later. I look over to Tribax's dapple gray horse trotting alongside us. Tribax has one hand on the reins and the other supporting Kai's way too still head. He has not taken his eyes off her, other than to glance up at the road occasionally. Elena has stayed as close to Tribax and Kaisera as her horse will allow.

I turn my head a bit toward Reign, and he looks over his shoulder at me. "What is it?" he asks.

"Has anything with Kaisera changed?" I ask him.

"No, she hasn't moved this whole time, but Bax says she is still breathing," Reign responds. Bax? I did not know Reign and Tribax had gotten so close that they were using nicknames.

We make it to the castle a short while later. Servants and guards rush around under the covered horse stalls, awaiting our arrival. Bax jumps off his horse and sprints quickly to a doctor and nurse waiting just inside the castle doors.

I go to jump off Fletch and head after Tribax and Kaisera, but Reign grips me tighter. "Oh, no you don't. Your shoulder must be looked at, Madis," Reign says.

"I am fine. Kaisera needs me," I say.

"No, she needs doctors, fluids, and rest, and that is what she is getting. It is the same thing you are going to get right now."

"Fine. I will get my back fixed up, but then I am going to Kaisera."

"Madis, I think you need to stay away from her and Tribax for a while."

"What? Why?" What is he talking about? I have to make sure she is okay. I was there watching her get all those horrid things done to her, and I want to be there as she heals.

"Madis, why aren't you more beat up? I mean, do not take that wrong. I am personally grateful you are so healthy right now."

Less beat up? I am missing my damned wings. "What?" I am overly confused.

"Look, Kaisera is barely alive, and you are walking around. The others are going to question what kept the witches away from you."

I just stand there dumbfounded. "My pain was watching her in pain," is what I say, but I already know with our history, no one is going to believe me. Reign is right. This looks bad. Really bad.

Reign walks over to me and grabs my face with both his hands gently, but I still flinch from the touch. Reign notices and starts to pull his hands away, but I reach up and hold them in place with my own. I want to feel the kindness of his touch right now.

"Thank you." I am looking at him fully for the first time since the rescue. He has a black beard coming in and dark purple circles around his eyes.

"Madis, I know we only met a week ago, but I feel I will always come to find you." Reign leans in slowly, glancing between my eyes and my lips.

I tug away, and Reign drops his hands to his side. "Right." He lets out a slow sigh then tucks his hands into his pockets.

It is not that I did not want to kiss him. I did, I do. I just can't let that happen, no matter what else happened the past four or five days. I still will be marrying King Alibast.

"Let's go get you cleaned up. Again."

When we walk into the castle, we are greeted by Miles. He bows at the waist. "Madis, in need of another bath, I see."

I look down at my filthy clothes and then back to him. "You would be correct, Miles."

I go to follow Miles back up the stairs to where my bath will be waiting. Reign stops me by grabbing hold of my hand gently. "Wait. There is someone here to see you."

Nija appears on Reign's shoulder, and when he spots me, he flings himself into my arms, purring and clinging to me as hard as he possibly can.

"Nija! Oh baby, I missed you too!"

Reign reaches over and takes Nija from me. My little dragon crawls his way up onto Reign's shoulder like he's done it a million times now. Reign reaches up and strokes the little dragon under the chin, receiving a cute soft purr. The image of them makes me smile. "How about I keep an eye on him until you are cleaned up?" Reign says.

I nod my head in approval. "Thank you again, Reign." I grab ahold of his waist and pull him into a tight hug, resting my head on the shoulder Nija is not occupying.

"Anytime," Reign says as he rests his cheek against the top of my head.

I step away, smiling at Nija and Reign one last time before I make my way up to my room to wash off the smell and grime of the past five days, knowing I will be stuck with the events that occurred in that tent for a very long time.

Chapter 45

KAISERA

The next few days—at least, I think it's days– are nothing but blurry people and noises, none of which I can make out. Except one. One voice breaks through it all. One voice allows me to feel safe. There is one voice that makes me know in my heart that nothing else can happen to me now. *Tribax.*

I can feel him sitting next to me, holding my less-injured right hand. I try to open my eyes a few times to talk with him, to tell him I will be okay, but they would not open.

People came and went throughout the days. I can feel people lightly touching my skin and poking me with sharp objects. A few times, I hear Bax's low growl when he thinks something might be hurting me.

Today is different. Today, I feel stronger. I can feel my body healing, and I squeeze the hand next to me.

Bax jumps up. "Kaisera?"

I slowly open my eyes, and Bax comes into view. I take in his rough appearance. "You look terrible," I say.

Bax is unshaven and looks like he hasn't slept in weeks. Bax chuckles. "I do not think you can talk about looks right now."

I try to sit up, and Bax is there quickly to help me to do so. I wince and struggle as I get to an upright position. I look down when the bedsheet covering my torso slides down. I have bandages wrapped all the way around my torso and both arms.

"How long have I been out?" I ask Bax.

He sits down on the bed, careful not to bump into me. "A week."

I lean my head back, bumping the large wooden bedframe with it. There is a large thud, and I wince again.

"Easy."

"Where is Madis?" I ask.

"No clue," Bax replies stiffly. He is grinding his teeth.

"You did get her out too, right?" I am a little concerned that he might have left her there.

"Yes, although we should have left her."

My head snaps up and my eyes go wide. "How could you say that, Bax? You are her sworn guard, are you not?"

"Yes, but after seeing the witches had barely touched her, I wonder if she set the whole thing up. I am confident she left practically untouched," Bax responds.

"She did not set it up," I tell him, grabbing his hand tighter and squeezing, remembering Madis' words of being my rock. Those words have stuck with me. We now know that the crone did something else to us, that she caused this tear.

That is a later conversation. "How did you find us?"

"Did you doubt I would find you?"

"Honestly, I did not know if you were dead or if you would come for a random girl you have only known for three weeks." I honestly had not even given it much thought while I was there. My only concern was not dying.

"You are not some random girl, Kaisera, and you know it." I might be blushing a little bit. "Are you blushing?" Bax says taken aback.

He would call me out on that shit.

"No, I think I have a fever. Call a nurse," I try, but I can feel the burn of the blush going down my neck now.

Untried Origins

"Little vixen, do you like that I came to your rescue?" A toothy bright grin spreads across Bax's face.

"I should have figured you would come. You are kind of a stalker."

"A stalker? How so?" he laughs.

"You just seem to always be around, lurking in the corner."

Bax's eyebrows scrunch together. "I do not lurk."

I lean up as far as I can, reaching my hand out to his face. Bax does not move. I run my fingers over the scrunched area between his eyebrows to smooth it out. "You are going to get wrinkles if you do not stop that." Bax laughs his deep laugh. "How did you find us?" I ask again.

Bax leans in close. "I followed that sweet intoxicating scent of yours straight to you."

"Oh yeah?" My body starts to warm and shiver all at the same time, as it always does when this male gets too close to me.

"Yes, and now I am going to kiss you. Do you think you are up for it?" Bax says as he continues to inch closer to me. His eyes move slowly from my eyes to my lips.

"Always." I reach up and cup his face with my hand.

"I like the sound of that word coming from your lips," Bax says before he places a soft kiss on my lips. He is so gentle with me, unlike the demanding alpha I have seen in the past. This is slow, and I am melting right into it. He slides his tongue along the bottom of my lip, and I gasp out. I am enjoying every second of this slow pace he is taking with his kiss.

There were times in that tent that I did not know if I would get to feel his touch again, and that thought almost broke me more than the claws of the witches.

A loud boom sounds, and Bax is off me with a sword in his hand within a nanosecond. As soon as he realizes who it is, he slowly sits back down on the bed, and then I see Elena. She gives a high pitched squeal before taking off to a sprint to my bed.

"Easy," Bax says toward Elena.

"Oh, hush," I say and lightly slap him on the arm. The hit costs me. My arm has shooting pains going up it, and I whimper out a small cry.

"That goes for you too," Bax says.

Elena calmly and softly sits on the bed and runs her hand over my hair. A single tear runs down her face. "I thought we lost you." She looks to Bax and reaches over to grab his hand.

I can see that these two have formed some kind of bond while I was gone, and that thought warms my little black heart. "You cannot lose me that easily."

Elena smiles wickedly at me. "Good to know."

"I think I am going to keep you two around for a bit," I say.

Bax and Elena are looking at me, and I am looking at them. Elena with her charm and crazy facial and body expressions. Bax with his sternness and caring nature. These two are mine. I may be hurt and healing, but I am so happy in this moment, having them both at my sides. I try to ease back down, but a small gasp leaves my throat as tiny, needle-like pains hit me all over my body.

"What hurts?" Bax asks.

I laugh a little. "I think it would be easier to ask what doesn't hurt."

Elena being Elena, she perks up. "Okay, what doesn't hurt?" Bax rolls his eyes at her, and I just laugh a bit.

"Well, they did not do much to my legs, other than my knees. I think my wings are still intact," I say.

Bax and Elena look at each other, then back to me. Both go very still and seem to be having a silent conversation without me.

"Goddess above. What?"

Elena tilts her head to the side and nods a couple times in my direction at Bax. Bax looks at her with a death stare, then sighs and turns to me.

"It might not be permanent..." Bax starts.

I look between the two of them, terrified of the next words to come out of his mouth.

"The witches carved a symbol into your left wing. They did not finish the symbol on the right one. We do not know if your wings will function, and the doctor has advised that you not try to use them until your back fully heals," Bax informs me.

Elena and Bax look at me cautiously, waiting for my reaction. If I had to guess, he is waiting for me to lose my shit, but I don't have that in me right now.

"Okay," I say.

Elena leans toward me and places a hand on my shoulder. "Did you hear what Bax just said, Kai?" Elena says.

I scrunch my eyebrows together. "Yes, Elena. I heard him."

"Kai, I think what Elena is trying to get at is, we expected a bit more of a freak out."

Why would they assume I would freak out? Do I love my wings? Yes, but I have gotten used to them being hidden over the years, and I do not think they are gone for good.

"No, what Elena is trying to say is you should be freaking the fuck out," Elena says.

Bax cuts a sharp look at her. "Maybe Elena should keep her mouth shut."

"No, Elena is concerned she," she nods her head in my direction, "is not grasping what is happening."

"Um, can Elena stop talking about herself like that?" I finally chime in. "Not that I do not enjoy this new banter you guys have taken on. It is just that I do not see a need to freak out just yet. We will know when I have healed," I finish.

Bax looks at me and smiles and gives me a cute little wink.

"Where is this new Kaisera coming from? I am used to the girl who jumps and looks where she is going after she starts to fall," Elena says.

I pull her hand off my shoulder then pull her toward me. We are now sitting side by side. Elena slowly drops her head down to my shoulder softly, careful of all my injuries.

"I don't know. Maybe someone finally knocked some sense into her," I say.

"That is not even remotely funny," Bax says.

I pat the spot on my other side. Bax crawls up next to me and gently tucks me and Elena into his side. "It is okay, Baxy. I have you two at my side now."

"I hate that name," Bax says.

"I know. Now shhh, I need some rest."

Bax slides us down so that I can lean completely on him while Elena is curled up to my other side. I have never felt more complete and safer than I do in this very second. I close my eyes, and even with my injuries and aches all over, I fall into a deep, comfortable sleep.

Chapter 46
KAISERA

I wake up in utter bliss. I am warm and safe, something I haven't felt in so long. No nightmares plagued me. I can smell Bax's scent all around me. We are lying in bed still, and I am using him as my personal body pillow. He is wearing nothing but a pair of loose-fitted pants, his bare muscular chest on full display. I am only wearing thin light pink silk shorts and a matching silk tank top. I feel completely at home, laying here listening to his steady rhythmic breathing and heartbeat.

I admire the curves of his pecks with their light patches of ashy blonde hair. I tilt my head back so I can peek at him. He looks so peaceful sleeping. I place my hand under my chin and watch him just breathe and be.

I am feeling stronger than I have been, my body almost completely healed. The doctor removed all my bandages late last night. All that is left of my bloody wounds are welted red skin that will soon become nothing more than faint scars.

Elena had said she wanted to go help Ellie with something earlier this morning, so it is just me and Bax. He moved all his things into this room in the previous days and has not left my side since I returned. He has been allowing me to use him as my own personal body pillow every night.

"If you keep looking at me like that, I may forget you are injured." Bax peeks a single eye open at me.

I bite down on my lip. "I am not that injured anymore."

"Is that so?" Bax says, both of his eyes on me. He tightens his already firm grip on me a little more.

I stretch my neck up so that I can place tiny kisses on the column of his neck. A deep muffled noise from his throat automatically melts me to my core. I need to hear more of those noises from him. I kick my leg further over him so that I can fully straddle him.

I continue to kiss him up his neck then back down his chest, making sure not to miss a single place. Bax has his hands firmly on my hips, digging his fingers in softly. I can tell he is holding back, and that is not what I want.

I roll my hips over his, and I am rewarded with another deep moan from him. I sit up and place my hands down on his large chest. I feel small even sitting on top of him.

Bax's eyes open, and he pins me with his dark blue and silver stare. "Do you really want this?" he says with just a hint of plea in his voice. I can tell his walls are cracking down, along with my own.

I look down at him with a sheepish grin on my face. This feels like agreeing to so much more than sex. I start to shake my head yes, but I know Bax is going to want and need to hear it. "Yes, Tribax. I want this. I want you."

He needs nothing more. He sits up and wraps his large, callused hands behind my head and into my hair. With the other hand gently on my cheek, he looks into my eyes.

"You are everything I'll ever want." He leans in slowly, and then he devours every bit of me with his kiss. His mouth on mine has always been amazing and felt even better, but this one is all consuming and claiming.

Untried Origins

I want him to claim me. Something in that tent made me snap, and I realize I want to feel what it feels like to be wanted so fully by someone and to want them back. His touch, his passion, and that smile that only I get out of him were the things I missed the most while suffering in that tent. I didn't want to admit it, because that would mean admitting he has captured me so wholly.

Bax tilts my head to the side and starts to trail kisses down it, then over my collarbone where my little dagger tattoo sits, then down to the top of my thin nightshirt.

He slides his hands from my face down to the hem of my silk nightshirt before sliding it up and over my head gently and slowly, taking all the time in the world. The pain in my left shoulder is only brief. As soon as my shirt is off, Tribax leans back a little and takes me in, his eyes wandering over every visible inch of me. He runs his figures over the scar where the witch shoved her wand through my shoulder.

"I will take great joy in ending the witch who did this to you." His tone says he is not bluffing.

I smile at him. "Don't pay attention to my scars; they will fade."

He smirks at me. "Your scars are beautiful. They show you are a survivor. They show you are strong. But scars leave more than just physical damage, and for that, I will give that witch the same treatment she gave you."

I lean in and kiss Bax again, knowing his words are true.

Bax's hands start to roam, and everywhere his calloused hands touch me, my skin pebbles and turns to ice. He removes his mouth from mine, trailing kisses down my neck and to the swells of my breasts before slowly licking my peaks. I throw my head back, basking in the feeling, my hands on his shoulders to hold myself steady.

Bax gently grabs ahold of my waist with one hand and flips us both over so that my back is against the bed, and he is settled perfectly between my legs. He stands for a brief moment to remove my shorts, followed by his own.

His body is like nothing I have ever seen muscles curve and dip in all the right places, and the sexy V leads to an impressive velvet length I already know is going to take time to adjust to. He crawls back between my legs and takes greedy kisses from my lips. Bax moves his hand down to my center and slides his fingers up and down it.

"Always so ready for me." He smiles down at me before thrusting two large fingers into me. I throw my head back, and an embarrassingly loud noise leaves my throat. "That's it, my good girl. Are you ready for me?"

I give him a breathy, "Yes."

Bax slides his fingers out of me and lines himself up with my entrance before slowly sliding in. "Goddesses above, Kai, you feel like sin itself." Bax continues to slowly slide into me, careful not to hurt me. He fills me beautifully. I can feel every inch he is giving me in all the right ways.

Once he is deep in me, he stops and kisses me softly.

I am clawing and grabbing at him, wanting him to move. He doesn't immediately start moving, so I start to rock my hips up and down to get friction. My core is tight and wanting.

Bax laughs softly. "My vixen is always so eager."

The way he just said 'my vixen' sends my body into overdrive. I need him moving and giving me all of him.

Bax pulls out slowly before thrusting fully back in, then again slowly pulls out before a quick thrust in. The feel of him sliding back and forth is like nothing else. Bax starts to move fast and gets into the perfect rhythm, and I am rolling my hips to match his pace.

Bax is all over me in every way, pulling at my nipple with one hand and nibbling on the other before he is back to kissing my neck, jaw, and mouth.

My breath starts to come quicker, and more moans leave my mouth. Bax's eyes start to turn more silver than blue, and his canines lengthen.

"Fuck, you ready to come for me?" Bax says breathily.

I scream out a yes as Bax licks his thumb then brings it down to my clit and starts to make small circles. It sends me over the edge.

He moves his mouth to my shoulder and bites down; not hard enough to break the skin, but I can tell how much he is still

Untried Origins

holding back with me. The mixture of pain and pleasure intensifies everything, and I scream out Bax's name. He releases his mouth from my shoulder and captures my moans and my release with his mouth. Bax's thrusts become wilder, and a deep rumble comes from his chest before one more thrust sends him over the edge to bathe in bliss with me.

Chapter 47

MADIS

    I spent the last week with Reign. I have even completely switched to his sleeping schedule. The healing process has not been easy, but the nightmares have been even worse. I have woken up every day in a fit of terror, with Kaisera's screams leaving my own throat. Reign ran through the shared door of the king and queen's suites to be by my side the first time it happened, and he chose to stay with me after that night. I fought him at first, but his company calmed me, and I eventually gave into my own selfish wants. We never touch or kiss; we just stay in each other's company.

    Reign and I have taken to reading in his library most nights, or taking quiet strolls through his gardens. I was due to visit King Alibast two days ago. I expect my father to send word any day now, demanding I return.

    Today, Reign is sitting in a plush chair with a book in his hand about a wild Fae king who stole the hearts of hundreds of women. I find it an odd read for a man in his position, but when I ask him why he enjoyed fictional books, he said, "It is best to escape reality at times." After he said that, I asked him to give me his best recommendation.

I am stretched out on the couch directly across from him reading that very book. It is about a secret pirate and his love for a princess who had once been his but was now promised to another. I find the irony in it to be a bit much, but the book has had my attention since page one.

The office doors slam open, and in walks my father. I jump up from the couch in a complete panic. I am wearing riding pants and a loose-fitting shirt that Reign lent me when I mentioned I would like more comfortable clothing.

"What is this?" my father demands. He is walking straight for me, and I automatically ready myself for the hit that is to come.

Reign has different plans and steps in front of my father.

Miles runs into the room. "I am sorry, Your Majesty. He burst his way through the castle."

Reign lifts a single eyebrow at my father, not the least bit amused. "Did he now?"

My father, Commander Pike straightens out his dress coat angrily. "Your imbecilic staff were not moving at my requested pace."

Reign adjusts the sleeves on his long sleeve shirt before he looks at my father like he is less than the trash he would find on the bottom of his shoes.

My father huffs and tries to stand a little taller. I got my height from my father, but he is still not tall enough to be eye to eye with Reign. It gives Reign a bit of an upper hand to literally stare down at my father.

"You burn your way through my home, insult my staff, and then burst into my private suite."

I can see the fire burning in my father's eyes. He is pissed, but he knows any strike against this king would cause problems for our Area and for himself.

"I am here for my daughter. I will take her with me and be out of your way," my father says before attempting to step around Reign. Reign steps in his way again.

"No," Reign responds to my father.

My father takes a step back and glares up at him. "No?"

Reign crosses his arms and glares right back. I walk forward and touch Reign's arm and look at him. He looks back at me, his expression easing as he looks into my eyes.

"It is fine. I will go with him," I say.

My father smiles at Reign like he has won. *Which he has.*

Reign softly pushes me behind him. "She is staying."

My eyes might have bugged out of my head. If I do not go with my father now, the consequences would only be greater later.

"Reign," I say. He turns around and leans over so we are eye to eye.

"Tell me you want to go with him," Reign says.

"I… I must go." He does not get it. I do not have a choice.

"I am giving you the choice right now, Madis. You can stay and he can go."

My dad clears his throat angrily. "Come here now, Madis."

I peer over Reign's shoulder to see my father's anger growing. *What if I did stay?* I look back to Reign. He sees something in my expression that makes a smile form before he turns back to my father.

"Madis will be staying. She will be my queen, and our Areas will merge," Reign says.

"What?" The words are out before I can think better of them.

My father sneers, "No. She is promised to King Alibast."

"I will talk with the King of Area One. We will come to an agreement that will benefit us all," Reign says.

"You cannot give me what I want, boy. King Alibast can." My father spits the words out.

Reign laughs loudly. "Get out of my castle before I prove to you who the boy in this room is."

My father does not have a choice. He has to leave. You cannot stay in a King's area without their permission. My father trudges out of the room, pausing at the door and turning around to face me.

Untried Origins

"Madis, this is your final chance. If you come with me now, the consequences will be lesser." I gulp and start to move toward the door. Reign throws out his arm to block me.

He bares his long canines and hisses loudly. "If you even set a finger on her, I will end you. Personally."

For the first time in my life, I think a flash of fear crosses my father's face. Then, he is out the door in a blink. I hear his fireballs hitting walls all the way out of the castle.

I shocked. "What just happened?" Reign turns to me with a grin on his face. I look at him confused. "What. Just. Happened?"

"You are free," Reign says, and the smile leaves his face when he sees my expression.

"Free?" I ask him with a sarcastic laugh. "Free is getting a choice. You just took that from me, just like every other man in this world has done to me."

"Wait, you are mad at me? I thought you would be thrilled." Reign puts his hands in his pockets, and now he looks like the confused one.

"Why? Because now I get to be forced into a marriage with you instead of Alibast?"

"Well, yeah," Reign says with a shrug. "Do you not enjoy our time together?"

"Yes, but that is not the point," I say.

"Look, Madis." He approaches and takes his hands out of his pockets to reach for me. His touch is always so comforting that I let it happen. He grabs both my arms and rubs his thumb in circles. "I would never force anything upon you." He is looking between my eyes. "You would not have been able to say the same about Alibast."

Reign might be right on that point, but I am right about the fact that he is just another male taking my choice from me.

"I think I need time to think," I say and start to move away. Reign lets his hands drop and watches me walk away.

Reign is back on me seconds later. He moves so fast, I don't notice he has moved us back into the closed door. My back is against the door, and his is pressed against my front. He has his thigh tightly tucked between both of mine, and my whole body starts to burn. Reign must see the fire in my eyes, because he is looking at them and smiling his huge, sharp, toothy grin.

"You know, I like the fire I see in you, Madis," Reign says.

I gulp down a few mouthfuls of saliva. The gulps are clearly audible. "Maybe you do. That does not change the fact that you decided my future without me," I say.

Reign leans his forehead against mine softly before banging his fist against the door a few times. I do not flinch away from him. I am frightened down to my very core, but it is not a fear of physical pain that has my body trembling.

Reign picks his head up off mine. "What if I promise never to make a decision for you again?"

"What would you get out of such a deal?" I say.

"You." He is glancing down at my lips again, and his throat bobs a few times. He catches me watching the movement. "Are you thinking of biting me for a change? Because it is one of the many things I have thought about doing with you," Reign teases.

"Possibly," I respond with very shaky vocal cords. I should be mad at him. I shove him to get off me, but I can't.

That's the thing, isn't it? I do not want him to get off me. I do not want to escape him.

I look back up at Reign's eyes, the green and yellow shining brightly, the candlelight on the wall next to the door shining into them. I imagine it is a similar fire as Reign sees in my eyes.

I gently push Reign off me. The sadness that shows in his eyes makes me smile just a bit, just knowing I am wanted. Reign steps away, and I push lightly against his chest as he sticks his hands back into his pockets. He has always let me be the one to make my choices.

"No," I say so softly, I am not even sure if he can hear the word.

"No?" He looks up at me with a slight tilt to his head.

"Yes. No." I kick off the wall and stand a little straighter, even though I have no idea what I am doing.

"Is it a yes or a no here? I am a bit confused." Reign's eyes crease in the middle. He crosses his arms and widens his stance.

"No, I will not let you choose my future."

"But you will let your father."

"Yes. I mean no. I don't know. That's different." For once, I would like for no one to make my choice, but I do not know how to make that dream a reality. However, I do know I cannot allow Reign to choose for me, either.

"So, you will choose King Alibast?" The hazel in Reign's eyes seem to darken into a hunter green, and his jaw starts to clench tighter.

"I do not know." A small smile forms on my lips at how annoyed that statement seems to be making him.

"Then what are you saying…"

I start to pace a little. I do not know how to explain this to him, but Reign stands there quietly, waiting for me to figure it out. I can feel his eyes watching me pace the library floors. I think he realizes I need these moments to figure things out on my own.

After a few moments, I finally speak.

"I am saying I will choose what my future has to offer. I am choosing to take the path I have never been able to before. I am choosing to take the difficult path. I need to know what it feels like to choose. Even if it's the wrong choice, it will be mine."

I have no clue if I truly mean that statement, but it feels right, and feeling right after feeling wrong for so long is eye opening. Reign sighs but shakes his head in understanding.

"We will still need to go to Area One. Your father will be notifying King Alibast of my proposition, and he will want answers and compensation for the loss of you if you "choose" not to stay with him."

The way he says the word 'choose' sounds strangled in his throat. I can tell he is fighting to hold something back.

"I know," I say, bowing my head a little. "When do we leave?"

Reign walks over to me and ever so lightly puts two of his fingers under my chin, tilting it back up. I try to keep my eyes turned downward. I am not sure I can keep from kissing him if those eyes meet mine again.

"We will leave tomorrow at nightfall," he says, but then pauses for a few seconds before he continues. "Since you will not marry me, will you do me one simple favor?"

I finally turn my eyes to his. The look in his eyes…I cannot fully place it. It looks almost sad but also alight with lust and pride.

I do not speak; I just nod my head slightly in answer.

"Do not ever let your head fall again. Hold it high. Bow and bend to no one ever again. Be the queen and warrior you are."

My throat is dry and scratchy, but I manage to get out, "That is a high favor to ask."

Reign smirks; not his toothy grin, but a slight pull of his lips. "No higher of a favor than telling me I cannot have you and not fighting you on it."

His eyes have gone from a light hazel green to an almost black green in the span of this conversation. They are drawing me in fully. Reign isn't even blinking. He is just staring back at me as hard as I know I am staring at him. He takes a step closer, leaving only a few centimeters between our bodies, so close to being flush together.

Reign leans in, and I remain perfectly still, not even breathing. He moves so slowly, as though he's afraid that if he moves too fast, I might run. He's not wrong; I might just do that very thing.

Reign's lips brush over mine in the ghost of a kiss. Our eyes stay locked on each other. Reign waits for me to pull away, but when my eyes shut and I relax, his hands are gently grabbing my face before his soft sweet lips encase my own. My breath is stripped from me, my heart pounding frantically. Reign's lips on mine are like nothing else this world has to offer. Reign pulls away, leaning his forehead on mine while he just breathes for a moment before pulling away from me completely. He take two small steps backward.

"I had to do that at least once," Reign says before he moves so quickly, I barely blink before he is gone. The sound of the door closing echoes through the room.

Untried Origins

I stand there shocked at how much my body is reacting to that one kiss. Our bodies barely touched. *Am I being stupid by not accepting his proposal?*

I mean it really wasn't a proposal, if I am honest with myself. It was a demand.

Yes, I made the right choice for myself. At the very least, it feels like a step toward the right direction. Now, it is time for the next right choice.

Chapter 48
KAISERA

I'm getting out of the shower, turning to take in my back in the large, fogged up mirror.

The bloody wounds on my back have been replaced with raised scars in the shape of the symbols the witch had carved. The top one is a circle with a triangle on top, with a line through the middle of both. The second one is a zigzag with a line drawn through it from top to the bottom. The third symbol is the unfinished one. It has the shape of two Ls overlapping each other, one upside down and the other upright. All of these sit on top of my left wing.

I catch sight of movement in the mirror. I look up from my back to see Bax leaning against the doorframe, arms crossed and one foot over the other. I pull the towel back over my exposed back. I smile at him. I am not embarrassed of my scars. I just feel they show a little too much of my soul.

"They are looking better," Bax says.

Untried Origins

"I still think the witch who did it needs to have a matching set." I want my revenge on those bitches. I cannot let them get away with what they did to me.

"One day, they will pay. I will hand deliver their heads to you if you wish. I would really enjoy it if you allowed me to get in a few blows of my own," Bax says, a gleam in his eyes saying he would take pleasure in it.

"No, my hands will be the ones to deliver those blows." I grin back at him.

I grab my clothes for the day and twirl my fingers for him to turn around. I get he has seen me naked, but that does not mean I want him blankly staring at me as I get dressed.

He rolls his eyes but pushes off the door to turn around before leaning back on the doorframe, facing the opposite direction.

"We are going to train today, right?" I ask. I have been bringing this up for two days now. I am getting my strength back, and it is time. I will never be taken like that again. I will never again be as helpless as I was with those witches in that nightmare tent.

Bax lets out a loud sigh. "We have time."

"No, Bax, we do not. I need this." I hate that I sound a little whiny, but it is true. I need to get out of this room and start getting to where I can feel strong again.

Elena walks into the bathing room as I am pulling my tank top over my head. Rubbing on Bax's arm as she passes, she says, "Bax, sweetie," while batting her red eyelashes and giving him a sweet puppy dog face.

Bax smiles down at her. "Yes, sweetheart?"

"Let her fucking train," Elena says before reaching up and patting Bax possibly a little too hard on the cheek.

He growls at her. Elena only deadpan stares at him, not the least bit intimidated by what most people would run for the hills from. "Oh hush, you overgrown kitten."

"I am not a cat," Bax says.

"Hmm? You sure? I remember a big fluffy tail and pointed fluffy ears." Elena turns to me with her hand on her chin, tapping a finger against her cheek. "Kai, wouldn't you say that description sounds like a cat?"

"Why yes. Now that I have heard that description, Elena, I have to say that does sound a lot like Lili, who is indeed a cat."

Bax turns and stares me down with narrowed eyes, a growl building in his throat.

"He seems to be angrier now. We better watch it before he scratches us," I say.

Elena walks over to me and leans a hip so that we are shoulder to shoulder facing Bax. Elena acts as she is thinking hard on something. "Ah hah! I know, we must have forgotten to clean his litterbox!"

I laugh loudly, and Elena joins. Bax growls as we are rolling over on ourselves. Bax charges both of us. He grabs me first around the waist before I have the chance to even think of an escape. I continue to laugh and playfully kick out to try and get away. Elena tries to avoid him by jumping on the tub's ledge before attempting to make a run for the door, but when she goes to jump from the tub, Bax catches her midair, folding her over her shoulder.

She laughs but yells out, "Put me down before I get fleas."

Bax carries us out of the bathroom straight toward the bed. Elena and I are squirming and trying to escape his grasp. We never stood a chance, though. Bax is double the size of both of us.

"Oh, you are worried about fleas, huh?" Bax says playfully. He chucks Elena down on the bed and leans over her to rub his head and hair all over her face playfully.

"Get off of me, you furball!" Elena yells, but she laughs and is no longer trying to get away.

I am still being held in Bax's other arm, laughing and enjoying the three of us having fun. Bax turns on me next, rubbing his head over me like a kitten trying to rub his scent on something he has claimed as his. Now that I am thinking about it, that is probably exactly what Bax is doing, and I do not mind one bit.

Bax throws me lightly next to Elena on the bed, still being cautious of my injuries. He leans over us. He places one arm on each side of us, boxing us in with his massive arms.

He looks between the two of us, smiling, before he leans down to my face. First, I expect him to kiss me, but he sticks his long tongue out and licks up the side of my face.

We both squeal. "Ew!" And "Yuck!"

Before we can try to escape Bax again, he says, "Neither of you are going anywhere." Bax pulls us back together, Elena and I breathing hard with all the laughter and playful fighting.

"Yeah, and why is that?" I ask Bax.

"Because you both are mine now," Bax says, leaning down again to nuzzle into both our necks and playfully nip at me while simultaneously tickling Elena.

Elena and I lean into each other and giggle a little devilishly. As we all start to quiet our laughter, Elena and Bax share a look that I do not like.

I sigh, because these looks between them have been going on since I returned from the witches' Area. I lean up onto my elbow, while Bax and Elena sit up onto the bed. "Tell me," I say. Elena and Bax look at each other again.

"What the fuck, guys? Enough with the glances. You two are keeping something from me. Now, spill it," I say a little too loudly, because they really are starting to scare me with this shit.

"Look, we wanted to tell you," Elena starts, but she stops to fidget with her hands in her lap.

Bax continues for her. "But then you were taken, then you were injured, then things were nice for a while." Bax stops, and I can hear an audible swallow.

Elena and Bax look at each other again then hang their heads low. There is a knock on the door.

Bax yells first. "Not now!"

There's another louder knock on the door, and we all scream, "Not now."

There's another knock on the door followed by, "This is Madis, and I have to talk to Kaisera. Now."

Well, she sounds like she might have finally grown a pair. I go to get up. "When I am done speaking with her, you two will tell me everything."

Bax nods his head, but I can see he is growing restless. When I turn to look at Elena, she sucks in a deep breath before nodding her head as well.

I have no idea what they are keeping from me, but their actions are giving me reason to suspect it will not be a good.

There is another knock on the door. Bax gets up and makes it to the door before I do, throwing it open and greeting Madis. "What the fuck do you want?"

"Tribax?" I hear Madis say. She sounds surprised by his tone.

"I will ask Your Majesty again. What do you want?" Bax says 'majesty' as more of an insult than an important title.

"Tribax, there is no need for this hostility toward me. I wish no one any harm," Madis tries.

"Tell that to the scars now covering her body." Bax is visibly shaking at the door. I can tell he is holding his temper back with all his might.

"I got this, Bax," I say softly. I know he is only being protective of me, as he has always been. Bax looks down at me at his side. He huffs a loud breath but shakes his head and walks away.

"Hey, Madis. What's up?" Madis is dressed in such casual attire, it almost shocks me. She is in a large, oversized, men's shirt and stretchy looking pants. I have never seen her look so relaxed.

"I came to check on you."

"That's rich," Bax comments.

I turn to him fully. "Bax, calm down. Now."

He shows his teeth for a brief second, like he is going to protest or growl at me, but he snatches a jacket off the chair by the desk before he storms out the door. He nearly takes Madis out, but she jumps out of his way.

"Men," I say to Madis in a joking way.

She isn't paying me any attention. She is watching Bax storm down the hall. I clear my throat and Madis turns around. I step out of the doorway so that she can walk into the room. She looks back toward Bax one more time before walking into my room.

Untried Origins

Elena gets off the bed and walks to me. "Do you want me to stay?" she asks.

"Nah, go make sure Tribax doesn't do anything stupid," I tell her. She nods her head, grabbing a jacket hanging on the wall by the door.

"Full room, huh?" Madis says in an attempt at a joke, I think.

I laugh because it is true. "Yeah, we like to stay close."

When it is just me and Madis in the room, I gesture to the little sitting area around a lit fireplace. It is cozy, and this might be a conversation I need to be seated for.

Madis sits upright as I slouch into the chair and throw my leg over the side. I was raised as a princess, but as the princess of the underworld, my father had always taught me to take and do as I please, which is why I cannot understand Madis' perfect little girl act.

Neither of us talks for what feels like several minutes but is probably only a few seconds. The silence is killing me, though, so I finally decide to break the ice.

"I do not blame you," I say.

"For which part?" Madis asks. She is looking down at her hands, fiddling with them in her lap.

"The witches. I still blame you for scheming to take my crown," I say, even if I am not one hundred precent sure it happened any more.

Chapter 49
MADIS

"Kai, I do not know what you saw the night of the Binding, but I did not scheme to take your crown. We now know that was not a Binding after all. I do not know what the crone did to us, but whatever it was, it tore us apart rather than Bind us together." I figure that's a good enough place to start.

"Regardless of what was done to us that night, how can I believe you? You have been prancing around as if you are the goddess damn…well, queen," Kai replies, and I can see that fiery part of her coming to the surface quickly.

"I did not have a choice, Kai. Things are different for me than for you, and you were gone." I try not to let my anger at that flare.

"I saw what was going to happen. It was best that I left."

I huff a frustrated breath. "Best for who, Kaisera?"

Her eyes snap to mine, and this time, I hold her stare. I cannot keep backing down. She does not respond to that.

"It was best for you, because that's all that ever mattered. What happened to our vow to only leave each other in death? What happened to 'Till Our Ends Meet?' I trusted you to be there, and then you were gone." My fury is burning brighter. I've never said this out loud, but I am pissed Kai abandoned me that night, as if I never meant anything.

Kai does falter a bit at that and looks at me with a bit of surprise. Maybe I have crossed a line. I do not want to hurt her further.

"You have no clue what I went through that night," Kai says between gritted teeth.

I stand up quickly, my anger and frustration building. After the week I have had, I do not have the strength to tamper it down right now, and I'm not sure I want to anymore. She is right; I don't know what happened to her. It has never been my fault that I did not know, though. She has refused to talk to me, to tell me what happened to her.

"That is because you will not tell me. Have you told anyone, Kai? You cannot keep using that excuse if you are not willing to explain it to anyone." I throw my hands up in the air, then let them slap against my sides.

Kai stands up then, getting face to face with me. I can see her fists balling at her sides and see her fury match my own. "You." She pokes me in the sternum. "Were. There."

"I was where?"

"You were with me in those dark corners. You were there fighting those dark shadow creatures, until you weren't. You were there until you were offered more. Until you were offered to take my place on the throne. Then, you weren't there. Then, you were laughing as you took everything that was supposed to be mine." She inches closer to me with every word until we are toe to toe. Even though I am a good foot taller than Kai, the fury burning in her green eyes is enough to make me want to back up.

I have no clue what she is talking about. I did not see her in that Blood Binding. I saw no one. I was alone and lost until I awoke and then the one person I thought would always be there left me. I start to explain that to her when Area Seven guards start running past the door, yelling for people to get back to their rooms.

Kai and I both turn and make our way to the door as more guards run toward the main entrance of the castle. I take off toward the front of the castle after them, not sure if Kai is following. I round the top of the stairs and come to a screeching halt at the scene before me.

Bloody body parts and chunks of vampire and demon remains lay around the entranceway to the castle. A large, handsome man with long, shoulder-length blonde hair is standing in the middle of all the gore with his arm elbow deep in a man's chest. He rips his hand out, pulling with it a long white strand of something. My eyes widen when I realize it is the man's spine, and that now spineless dead man was Miles.

I move my eyes from the spine dangling in his hand to his face, and he notices my movement. He stretches his arms wide, as if he is waiting for someone to run into his arms for an embrace. "My bride," he says cheerfully.

Reign appears next to me. "Not anymore."

"Oh, come now, Reign. I made a deal for her. I expect the terms to be met," the large man says.

I am frozen in shock as that information clicks into place. This must be King Alibast. I look at Reign and he gives me a nod with a reassuring smile. Kai comes barreling around the corner with Elena and Tribax at her side.

"You have two princesses here, Reign. You will give one of them to me. It is only fair," Alibast says as he takes in Kaisera.

Tribax growls, "Over my fucking dead body."

Alibast laughs, his huge shoulders bouncing up and down. "That can easily be arranged, little shifter."

I know Tribax is strong, and I have seen him fight, but something about this man's demeanor tells me that Tribax might not stand a chance against him.

Tribax lets out a growl and steps a little in front of Kaisera but makes no move to go after Alibast. Alibast chuckles again as he steps around all the fallen body parts.

"I want the girl I was promised, little shifter."

Untried Origins

How does he know Tribax is a shifter? I had not known until Ellie told me of the fight between him and Reign in the dining room.

I hear a voice in my head. It is so calming and relaxing. "Come here." My feet start to walk of their own accord as I feel the need to go to Alibast.

"That's right, little starlet, come to me," the voice says, and I am mesmerized by it. I want to go to the voice.

I am ripped from my trance when Reign grabs my arm, spinning me around and slamming me to his chest.

"Cut the shit, Alibast. You aren't getting her." I look up at Reign and he looks down at me. "I won't let him take you. I know I said I would let you choose, but I can't." He looks desperate.

I nod, not sure what else to say, knowing that if a deal was made with the King of Deals, we may not have a choice in this matter. Deals with him are sworn in blood and cannot be broken.

Alibast overhears our conversation. "You are not a part of this, Reign."

I turn around. "But I am. What was the deal?"

Alibast chuckles, "So you do speak." His bright white teeth barely show, and his smile is not really a smile, more of a dark smirk.

I finally get my nerves about me and try to walk to him, but Reign still has a hand on my shoulder. I turn to him. "Let me go," I mouth to him.

He grinds his teeth together but gives a curt nod and lets me go.

"I do, and I speak for myself. So, what was the deal?"

Alibast, still with a look of amusement on his face, crosses his bloodied arms over his chest and speaks. "I gave your father the information he needed, and in return, I get you, along with the merging of Areas One and Six."

"What information did you give my father, and why would you want Area Six when Area One is thriving?" I ask.

He laughs a small laugh. "Me explaining myself to a little princess was not part of the deal. I already had to go out of my way to retrieve you when you should have been delivered to me a week ago."

His eyes leave me and over and up to Reign and the others still standing on the staircase behind me. I turn to glance back at them. Reign is gripping the banister like it is his lifeline, and his jaw is locked so tightly, I am surprised it has not shattered any teeth. He tries to take a step toward me, but I shake my head. I know he wants to help, and I wish he could, but in this, I fear that he will only make things worse.

Kai is standing slightly behind Tribax, with Elena standing at her back with a hand on her shoulder. I turn back to Alibast. He is looking at me with one eyebrow raised high on his blood-spattered face. He still has not tried to remove the blood from any part of his body, as if it does not faze him in the slightest.

"What will happen if I refuse you?" I have to try to get out of this, or weigh my options at the very least.

"You won't," he responds.

"Why is that?"

Alibast sighs then leans down so that we are eye level, not in the way Reign does so that we are equals. No, this is more like a parent getting eye level with a child to make sure they understand their coming punishment. I should have paid attention to the look in those eyes. That is not what I am doing though. No, instead, I am noticing the light and dark red lines in them and how intense they seem; they're maybe even a little sad underneath. I must be wrong, though, because from the looks of this man, nothing can make him look sad.

"Because, Princess, if you do not come with me, I will kill every single person in this place, and then I will go to Area Six and destroy it until it is mine anyway." Something in his eyes tells me this is no bluff, and something also says he is desperate.

He stands up straight. "Plus, I can always just make you." A voice rings in my head. "That would be the most fun way."

My eyes widen. I thought King Braxton was the only telepath left. They are so rare. He presses his pointer finger over his lips and gives me a wicked kind of "Shhhh" before he winks at me. He is taking pleasure in doing this.

Sick, twisted bastard.

"Aw, that is not a nice thing to say about your future husband." The voice comes into my head again. It is deeper and

Untried Origins

more seductive than the voice I hear coming from his actual throat.

"So, you see, everyone, I will be taking the Princess now."

"I have a name."

"Ah, so you agree that you are coming with me, then?" Alibast says happily.

"I do not have a choice."

Reign charges down the stairs and jumps in front of me. "She is not going."

I peer around him. The smile on Alibast's face is both beautiful and terrifying. Reign looks about ready to rip his throat out. A loud bang and then blood-curdling screams come from outside the castle walls.

"Fuck, now what?" Tribax yells from the staircase.

I hear him say something like "Stay here" to Kai and maybe Elena. Reign, Tribax, and Alibast run out the door, walking quickly toward the main gates to see what all the commotion was. I reach down and pick up one of the swords from one of Reign's fallen guards. Kai and Elena do the same.

"I think it is going to be one of those days," Elena says to Kai before throwing down the sword she picked up and running for a bow with a quiver of arrows next to it.

Kai responds, "And it started out so nicely." They give each other wicked grins while Kai spins her newly acquired sword around to get used to its weight.

The three of us take off after the gate. Another loud bang with screams that I know only come from Hollows echo through the large stone gates. Demons, Vampires, and mortal souls scream in terror, and I run faster.

I reach the gate right as Reign is having the guards open them, and we are met with people of all categories running past us to seek shelter behind the wall. The Hollows are openly attacking the city. Everyone who rushes through the gates is covered in sweat, blood, and debris. A horrifying screech rips from a Hollow as it chases down a woman carrying a small child, and I take off after it. The others rush into the street to help whoever they can. I spot King Alibast slamming his sword into a

Hollow with multiple heads. Surprised he is willing to help defend an Area other than his own.

I reach the one going after the woman and her child and slam my sword down on its back, catching it by surprise. Unfortunately, the Hollow is coated by a protective shield and my sword barely makes a dent. The Hollow turns around to face me, blood dripping from its open, gaping mouth. He has no lips and rows upon rows of sharp-edged teeth. He has no nose, only two holes where a nose should be. His large red eyes bores down at me before he lets out a loud scream directly into my face. Then, he attacks. I fight back, hard and fast, cutting off one of his arms when he reaches me. He throws his head back in frustration, letting out another scream, and I take the opportunity to shove my sword directly through his chest. The Hollow crumbles into a pile of black melting blood and ash.

I turn to take on the next one. It is a tall, skinny thing with four arms and legs, and when it spots me, it goes down on its arms to charge at me the way a bear would charge its prey.

Nija appears on my shoulder, and I smirk. I inhale a large breath of air into my lungs before blowing it out in a gust of fire. The Hollow screams as it burns and melts down to nothing.

I set Nija down on the ground and say, "Shift." Seconds later, he grew triple his size. He is now towering over me in a much more aggressive version of his black and blue dragon self.

"Burn them down, but stay high enough that they can't reach you." Nija nods to me and starts attacking the Hollows wreaking havoc down on the city of Area Seven.

I spot Reign surrounded by three of the Hollows and see he is moving at his vampire speed to try to take them down, but they are quick too. I rush over to him, chopping off the head of a distracted Hollow that has horns growing out of every angle of his skull. His horned head lolls to the side before the whole thing drops off its shoulders onto the ground.

Reign grunts out "Thanks," before we press our blades in unison into the other two Hollows.

I turn and smile at him. He smiles back "There it is."

"There what is?"

Untried Origins

"That fire, and the happiness I saw that first day. You enjoy this," Reign softly chuckles.

I look at him confused. "I do not enjoy it."

"Mmhmm," Reign hums. "Duck," he says, and I do not hesitate. Hesitation costs lives.

Reign swings his sword over my head, and I feel the blood from the Hollow drip down onto my back, alerting me to just how close they had been to me.

I stand and try to turn to assess what is going on behind me. I start to stumble, my feet getting stuck on the remains of the Hollow Reign just killed, and, without the familiar balance of my wings, I start to fall. Strong hands wrap around my arms and pull me close, keeping me from faceplanting into Hollow guts. The smell of lemon and sunshine mixed with the metallic smell of fresh blood enters my nose. I look up into the ruggedly handsome, barely-smiling face of King Alibast.

"Easy there, Princess. I know it's tempting, but I cannot take you in front of all these people, plus the whole Hollows attacking thing." He smiles at me, then continues. "I do promise to let you ride me when we get back to my castle, though."

I push out of his arms. "Your modesty is truly a wonder, King Alibast."

"Come on now. We are to be wed. You can just call me 'king'," Alibast states.

Reign steps to my side. I look up to him, and he is baring his teeth at Alibast. "She should be calling you what you are: trash."

I roll my eyes. I hear a loud scream and take off in the direction of it. Elena is on the ground, and Kai and Bax are standing back-to-back, surrounded by Hollows.

Reign is at my heels, but soon, he speeds past me. I hold out my hand to throw flames at the Hollows when I'm close enough and scorch two of the Hollows trying to get to Kai and Bax. Reign slams into the group of Hollows, throwing them off-kilter and tumbling away from Kai and Tribax.

"Thanks," Tribax yells to Reign over the Hollows' screams.

"You can pay me back later," Reign replies.

Ka Lee

I reach the group and stab my sword upward, straight into the skull of the Hollow closest to Kai as she slices her sword across the throat of another.

The last Hollow falls, and I turn to Kaisera, looking her over. She pushes me to the side and sprints to Elena, who is lying completely still on the ground, soaked in blood.

Chapter 50
KAISERA

    I push past Madis and run as quickly as my body will allow me to towards Elena.

    "Elena!" I scream. "Elena, wake up!"

    Elena had been struck in the back of the head by a Hollow early in the fight. I kept trying to get to her, but they just kept coming. The Hollow who hit her had been reaching over her, sucking at her soul, but I thought I had gotten to her in time to stop it before being pulled back into the fight.

    "Elena, please!" I cry as tears run down my face. I cannot lose her. I just can't.

    I feel Bax come to my side. "Let me see her," he says softly.

    "No." I don't want anyone else touching her.

    "Kai, I cannot help her if you do not let me," Bax says.

    I know he is right. I slowly ease Elena's body back to the ground, but I do not back away. Bax stands and walks to the other side of Elena and starts looking her over.

    "She has a concussion," Bax says.

Ka Lee

A loud book and crack fill the skies. I look up, but no rain or clouds seem to be over us.

Great. Just what we need right now, a storm. This really has turned into a shit day.

"So, she is going to be, ok?"

A female voice rings out across the field. "She will be fine."

I turn and see a tall, beautiful woman. When I spot what is attached to her back, my mouth falls open in shock.

"Who the fuck are you?" I ask.

The woman's eyes snap to me with a terrible glare. "You have not earned the right to speak to me, child."

I laugh a little. "Oh yeah? Says who?"

The woman barely flicks her wrist, like a gnat is bothering her, and I am slammed backward into Bax, so hard that the wind is knocked out of me, and from the sound of Bax's grunts, he can no longer breathe either.

The woman snaps her fingers, and Elena's body disappears from where it had been laying and appears in front of her.

I try to suck in a breath, but nothing happens. I look around to try and seek help, but Madis is being held behind Reign and Alibast, both seemingly protecting her.

I turn to see if Bax has recovered from the blow. He looks from the tall woman and then back to me, but I cannot read the expression on his face. He looks frightened of something, and it's not the woman standing in front of us.

"Thank you for this, Tribax," the woman says, and I turn around in time to see her blowing a kiss his way.

I look to Bax in question, but he turns his head away from me. Before I can question him on what the woman means, the fiercest battle cry cuts through the city.

I turn to find Ellie running straight at the woman with all her might.

"No, Ellie!" I try to catch my breath to get up to run, but I feel like I have been knocked down by a whole building.

I look back to Madis to find Reign and Alibast holding her back, and it seems both are struggling to keep her from stopping

Ellie. She is screaming at Ellie to stop and screaming at the men to let her go.

The tall woman waves her hand like she had with me, but it does nothing to falter Ellie. Ellie reaches where the woman is standing in a few more strides. She attempts to bring her sword down on top of the woman's neck, but before the sword makes purchase, the woman wraps her arms around Ellie's neck. There is a sickening crack, and then a thud when Ellie's limp, lifeless body hits the ground.

The tall woman looks back at me with a smirk on her face. She snaps her fingers, and seconds later, the tall woman with white hair and black feathered wings is gone.

To Be Continued...

Printed in the USA
CPSIA information can be obtained
at www.ICGtesting.com
LVHW051353310823
756844LV00033B/131